A Botanist's Guide to Tradition and Treachery

ALSO AVAILABLE BY KATE KHAVARI

Saffron Everleigh Mystery

A Botanist's Guide to Rituals and Revenge

A Botanist's Guide to Society and Secrets

A Botanist's Guide to Flowers and Fatality

A Botanist's Guide to Parties and Poisons

A Botanist's Guide to Tradition and Treachery

A Saffron Everleigh Mystery

Kate Khavari

NEW YORK

Published in the United States by Crooked Lane Books, an imprint of The Quick Brown Fox & Company LLC.

Crooked Lane Books and its logo are trademarks of The Quick Brown Fox & Company LLC.

Library of Congress Catalog-in-Publication data available upon request.

ISBN (hardcover): 979-8-89242-439-4
ISBN (ebook): 979-8-89242-440-0

Cover design by Meghan Deist

Printed in the United States.

www.crookedlanebooks.com

Crooked Lane Books
34 West 27th St., 10th Floor
New York, NY 10001

First Edition: June 2026

The authorized representative in the EU for product safety and compliance is eucomply OÜPärnu mnt 139b-14, 11317 Tallinn, Estonia, hello@eucompliancepartner.com, +33757690241

10 9 8 7 6 5 4 3 2 1

For all the women who've supported me,
loudly and quietly

Chapter 1

October, 1924

The glowing orb of a sinking sun lit the horizon. Dark waves gently rolled beneath a sky smudged orange, red, and indigo. Saffron Everleigh took in the vista with great satisfaction. If someone would have told her a year ago that instead of digging through piles of botany textbooks she would be on her way to dig through ancient ruins, she'd have firmly grasped their arm and insist they sit down, as surely they would be out of their senses.

The darkening horizon meant it was nearly time for dinner, however. It was the worst part of the day, when she was forced to leave her secluded excitement and face the sneers of the expedition crew.

"Lost in thought?"

Saffron turned to the approaching figure with a smile.

Black hair, heavy black brows, and eyes so dark they often appeared black, together with his height and a firm line of a mouth, conspired to make Alexander Ashton an intimidating man. Saffron had once seen him as such, but now those features were dear to her, from the curl of his sable hair to the way his mouth softened with smiles and plied her with kisses.

Her fiancé came to a stop before her. He was already dressed in a close-fitting dinner jacket that made him look rather dangerously handsome. "Are you ready to go to dinner?" he asked.

The sunset had dwindled to a bruise of dull purple. She turned away from it. "If we must."

Although Saffron was more than capable, in her opinion, of handling a few treks across rocky hills and taking samples from ancient storehouses, the rest of the expedition crew was not convinced. Her application to join the expedition team had caused a stir. Her selection had raised eyebrows and elicited whispered comments, and her official acceptance had brought the kind of outright prejudice she hadn't experienced in years. Her colleagues in the botany department at University College London had more or less accepted her presence, or ignored it, but apparently this had lured her into a false sense of security. Many of the men who formed the expedition crew had balked at her inclusion, and even now, a week into their voyage to Turkey, continued to make their disapproval known.

Alexander leaned on the metal rail. "At least in Smyrna you'll work mostly with our team and not the whole group."

Saffron huffed. "I doubt the team will be any better. Clark is absolutely determined."

"It would seem so." He drew closer, draping his arm along the rail behind her. "You're cold."

"Perhaps you can accompany me to my room to retrieve a wrap?" Saffron asked with what she hoped was an innocent look.

"I'm sensing a change in temperature," Alexander said dryly. "Besides, I thought we agreed we should stay out of each other's rooms."

It was astonishing, really—almost worthy of scientific study—how quickly one might go from caring deeply how one is perceived by others to not giving a fig. But when on a stressful journey far from home, with privacy only a short hall and a locked door away, Saffron found it was very tempting to corner her fiancé. Not to mention it was good fun to see him squirm—or Alexander's restrained version of squirming—at the suggestion of going behind closed doors together.

She rolled her eyes. "I'll see you in the dining room."

The interior of the boat was close but tastefully done up in shades of blue and well-lit with sconces in the shape of seashells, easing the foreboding Saffron felt each time she went below deck. She'd long disliked going below ground, but the prospect of cave-like spaces now outright alarmed her after rescuing her mother from an underground room. Months later, her skin crawled and her heart pounded when she contemplated the stairs she'd descended that day. Getting to her cabin through the narrow hall wasn't quite the same, but it was uncomfortable.

"Something wrong, Miss Everleigh?"

Resisting the temptation to keep walking and ignore Mr. Clark, she forced a pleasant expression on her face. Joseph Clark leaned against his open cabin door behind her, dinner jacket slung over an arm. He was a tall man of early middle age with dishwater-blond hair, light blue eyes, and a large wedge of a nose. He had ruddy, tanned skin of one who spent a great deal of time outdoors. He smiled unpleasantly at her.

"Nothing is wrong, Mr. Clark," Saffron said. "I just forgot something in my room."

"Hardly surprising," he said with a smirk. "Shall I wait for you, lest you get lost?"

Biting her tongue on a rude retort, she maintained her pleasant expression. "No, thank you." She continued down the hall, determined not to turn to see if he was watching her.

A few moments later, she had retrieved the wrap that matched her blue evening gown and made her way back up to the dining room. She was glad to see a good number of people were still making their way through the elegant room to their seats. Saffron wove through the tables to her empty place at one of six tables claimed by the expedition party. Alexander helped her into her seat and she smiled awkwardly at the men who half-rose from their chairs. Their interrupted conversation resumed as the meal began.

"I don't see why we've got to dance to their tune," Dr. Balthazar complained. His gravelly voice matched his humorless, granite face. "It'll only slow us down."

Dr. Henry, looking smothered in his dinner jacket, huffed impatiently at the archaeology team leader. "We'd be daft not to agree to their demands! We've got to get in their good graces and stay there. The rest of the world is going to realize what a treasure trove the place is soon enough. With their war at an end and that fire destroying half the bloody city—"

A few pairs of eyes darted to the ladies at the table. Saffron barely took note of Dr. Henry's curse—she'd far heard worse from the historian, not to mention her own flatmate—but Mrs. Demirel, across the table, looked scandalized. Her watery blue eyes went round, and color rose on her care-worn cheeks.

Mrs. Henry appeared unperturbed by her husband's language, simply continuing to listen politely. Saffron very much admired the way Cynthia Henry never seemed the least concerned with any attention she received. Then again, she was used to it. Not only was she beautiful, with stylishly short black hair framing dark eyes and an angular face perfectly made up, but she was frightfully poised. Mrs. Henry always had some perfect remark or barb waiting on her tongue.

Saffron had first met Mrs. Henry at a dinner party moments before watching her fall to the ground after she'd been poisoned. It had been Saffron and Alexander who'd proved it was not her philandering husband who'd tried to kill her, but rather her supposed lover. Mrs. Henry was no stranger to scandal, and accompanying her now-faithful husband to Turkey was the least of her eyebrow-raising feats.

"—other academics will come crawling out of the woodwork looking to get a foot in the door," Dr. Henry continued. A burly arm rose, as if he had to the urge to pound on the table to emphasize his point, but a glance in his wife's direction seemed to dampen the impulse. "We've got one foot in. Agreeing to their plans to escort us about won't slow us down."

Watching Dr. Henry's impassioned speech, Saffron wondered if he'd repeated these same points to the others on his crew when he and Mrs. Henry had dined with them on the other nights of the voyage. She couldn't imagine him getting so worked up every time he explained that the crew was expected to work with the Turkish officials' men and follow their government's protocols.

"It would hardly make the right impression if we didn't accept their assistance," Alexander put in.

"More like their spies," Balthazar muttered.

Clark regarded his wineglass without interest. "Even if the local guides are spying, what will they have to report? That we're doing our work, and nothing else. Not one of our *men* would make trouble."

Saffron could tell from Alexander's narrowed eyes that he, like her, understood this last comment was a jab at her. "It's more likely they want to ensure we're not trampling over their ruins," he said. "It would be unfortunate to revisit the plundering of the Parthenon on the agora."

Dr. Henry looked affronted. "Elgin was an idiot."

"Still, it's reasonable the Turks would be concerned," Saffron said. If her homeland was drawing the sort of attention Greece and Egypt had, she certainly would want to monitor visiting scholars, too. "I believe I read something from Gertrude Bell"—here, several of the gentlemen scowled upon hearing the name of the British explorer—"about her shock at an ancient castle being gifted to the Kaiser. One day it was there, and the next they knew, it had been turned to rubble. And that was under the Ottoman regime, which had strict rules against—"

"We've agreed to abstain from the universally accepted tradition of partage," Balthazar interrupted. "What have they to fear? We do the digging, they get the artifacts, and we—"

"Get to publish," Alexander said.

"Damn right," Dr. Henry grunted. "Don't you worry, Balthazar, your name will be the one in the newspapers. You'll get the credit, all right."

"One might have hoped to have one's name in a museum, beneath the artifact," Clark said in a light tone Saffron didn't believe, "in a country where one might expect anyone with the correct level of appreciation to be reasonably able to visit."

Saffron couldn't help but frown at him. "The Turks who visit their own museums will certainly appreciate any artifacts we uncover. After all, it is their history."

"Quite so," Mrs. Demirel agreed. When eyes around the table turned to her, she looked like she regretted speaking. "That is, anyone might appreciate their own history being uncovered. Don't you think, my dear?" she asked her husband hopefully.

Mr. Demirel was serving as the group's cultural liaison, more or less, as he was a Turk himself and had spent many years in the Ottoman Empire as a diplomat before it was dissolved into its individual countries. Sea travel did not agree with him, it seemed, and he had taken not one bite of his meal. He looked unwilling to open his mouth to answer his wife. He merely nodded, then pressed his handkerchief to his lips.

The subject soon turned to the faults of French academia. Saffron could have contributed, as she'd attended a conference in Paris less than a year ago, but held her tongue.

The meal ended with Saffron tallying Clark's thinly veiled comments and pointed looks at three, one less than the night before. Saffron had specifically spoken less this evening and saw the result.

Alexander offered her his arm and they went to walk about the deck. The breeze was wonderfully refreshing, crisp and salted with sea spray.

"I believe that is the first time I've ever spoken more than you during a meal," Alexander said. "Are you feeling well?"

"I'm conducting an experiment. I'm trying to narrow down the precise number of words I'm required to speak to earn one of Clark's eye rolls."

"I don't think you have to say anything. I suppose I can understand him being uncomfortable being your partner for your study, with you being—"

"A woman," said Saffron acidly.

"I was going to say inexperienced in the field. Clark likely expected to be paired with someone who's been out more, or perhaps he expected to choose his partner. But they'll all see before long that you're a credit to our team, Clark included."

Saffron smiled at him as they rounded the corner and found themselves in a particularly poorly lit and lonely stretch of deck.

"Those are nice words," Saffron said, her eyes falling to his mouth. His lips curved into a smile and soon they were on hers.

But not for long. An embarrassed throat was cleared and Saffron peered around Alexander to see a young man looking somewhat awestruck at them.

"Neill," Alexander said, turning. His voice was smooth and even, as if they'd been in the midst of discussing some of his bacterial research rather than a heady kiss.

"Excuse me," Martin Neill stammered, shifting on his feet. His dark hair gleamed in the light from the strings of lights strung over the deck. "I was told to remind you, er, Mr. Ashton, that the game begins at ten thirty in Dr. Johnson's room."

Alexander nodded and thanked Neill, who hurried back down the deck and out of sight.

"I don't know why you need a reminder," Saffron grumbled. "It's the same every night. I do hope you're winning pools of money in all the hours you've spent pent up with your mates."

"'Pools' would be an exaggeration. As would be referring to them as my mates."

Saffron raised a skeptical eyebrow. "These lads must be gluttons for punishment if I'm to believe the gossip I overhear."

Alexander shook his head, the little smile that so often caused her heart to beat a little faster making an appearance on his shadowed face. "You're not to believe gossip, especially among this lot."

"Very well, off you go, then," she said with a sniff, adjusting her wrap. "I'll just return to my cabin, *alone*, and read over my notes again. Or maybe I'll examine the book Banks lent me. I ought to brush up on my Turkish." She peered at him from beneath her lashes. "Though I'd much rather improve my Greek."

To her utter delight, a hint of color rose in Alexander's face as he cleared his throat and glanced back the way Neill had gone. Then his arms were around her again, proving she and Alexander together required no improvement at all.

Chapter 2

The suite was dim and so full of smoke it was hard to make out anything more than the shapes of a dozen men sitting at tables and milling about. It was like this each time Alexander had joined the other crew members for cards in the evenings. Johnson, one of the archaeologists, hosted the game each night, and each night several hundred pounds were lost and won. It was a closed game, offered only to members of the crew, so the losers had until the end of the expedition to win back whatever they lost instead of settling when they reached their destination. Alexander didn't mind; he was content to wait to fill his pockets.

He was immediately offered a seat at the nearest poker table and dealt in. Geoffrey Kent and Ellis Wakefield sat at the table, too, along with Martin Neill. It was not the first time Alexander had seen Neill, the assistant his team had been assigned, in the makeshift casino, but usually he played with a less aggressive group. Today, he'd joined men known to play deep, and he looked like he was barely keeping his head above water. His brow shone with perspiration, his tie undone.

In an attempt to put him at ease, Alexander asked, "How do you like the journey so far, Neill?"

Neill seemed startled to be addressed by Alexander. "Oh, very much, Mr. Ashton. I've never been on a ship like this before."

This elicited smirks from several of the others. Wakefield barked, "Just don't dangle over the side of the boat when you're letting go of your lunch. It'd be a pity if you slipped off."

They played a few hands, Alexander coming up the better of the others at the table, and he relinquished his seat to speak to a few of his fellows. He was gratified no one tried to force a drink onto him; perhaps this time they would believe him when he said he had no interest in alcohol.

Martin Neill, however, was plied with whatever was being passed around. Alexander was no stranger to the tactics of some of the more ruthless of the crew; they often chose an inexperienced man to prey on and it appeared this time it was Neill. It didn't escape Alexander's notice that of all the newcomers, it was a relative outsider with no academic connections and a slight lilt in his voice suggesting otherness who was selected as their target.

After a few more hands he looked both exhausted and ready to, as Wakefield put it, lose his lunch. As Neill was assigned to his team, Alexander felt he had some responsibility for what condition he was in when he arrived in Smyrna, and so when Neill once again suffered a bad beat, he clapped him on the shoulder. "Let's get some air."

He shuffled the young man out of the room and up a floor to the deck, where a curt breeze swept away some of the smoke clinging to their clothing.

Neill gulped down the fresh air and blinked away some of his haze. He couldn't be more than twenty-one, with just a semester left before graduating in the spring.

"Might I make a suggestion?" Alexander said. "If you plan to continue taking a seat at the table, hold off on the liquor. No one plays well when they're drunk."

Neill nodded, then rushed to the edge of the deck and vomited.

"What's this, now!" crowed Wakefield, approaching with Clark at his side. Wakefield was a contrast to Clark, a compact, energetic man with dark hair cut very short. "We can't have lightweights bogging down our crew."

Clark smirked around his cigarette. "We have quite enough extra baggage already."

"Unless you're going to be useful, perhaps you should return to the game," Alexander said. "Last I checked, Clark, you were rather behind."

Clark released a stream of smoke that quickly disappeared into the night. He held Alexander's gaze. "I appreciate the concern, Ashton. However, I'm not the one with a bride-to-be hanging about like a millstone. You should worry more about stacking up enough chips to provide for your happy life together."

"If you continue playing as you have been, I needn't stay at the table long."

Clark flicked his cigarette over the rail. "I look forward to plundering your honeymoon fund." He and Wakefield stalked away.

Neill hung his head. "I'm awfully sorry, Mr. Ashton. I think I'd better go back to my room."

He watched Neill stumbling to the stairs as the ship rolled slightly, and contemplated his next move. It was tempting to follow Neill's lead and turn in early. He could maybe fall asleep before his roommate started snoring like an old motorcar engine. He might find some of their party still in the dining room, where music and dancing went on until the early morning hours. Saffron had already returned to her room, Alexander knew, having escorted her there after dinner. His lips curved, recalling her latest attempt to coerce him inside.

But Clark's comments, as harmless as they were, soured his mood. He'd like to tell Clark to lay off Saffron, but he knew better than to attempt to fight Saffron's battles for her. She'd known what she was getting into. She would have to manage him herself, however much Alexander hated to leave her to his poor attitude.

But, Alexander thought as he turned his steps back toward the smoke-filled suite, that didn't mean he couldn't do his bit to put Clark in his place, even if it was just by beating him at cards.

"You did what!"

Alexander gave her a quelling look, and Saffron realized she'd come very close to shrieking in the middle of the sunny breakfast room. "Sorry," she whispered. "But you couldn't have expected a quiet reaction to you nearly bankrupting Clark last night."

"It's bad form to bankrupt a man. I put a dent in his solvency, that's all." The smug tilt of his mouth naysaid his statement.

Perhaps it was petty to be pleased Alexander had done something to aggravate Clark, but Clark had been particularly nasty the previous day, outright ignoring her when she'd approached him to begin working on their study and spending dinner scoffing at her. "Well, one can only hope it encourages him to take our work seriously."

"This is not an auspicious beginning," Alexander said. "Clark is refusing to work with you, and our assistant is quickly becoming entrenched with the worst of the bunch."

"Martin? Surely not."

Alexander sent her a wry look over his cup of coffee. "Martin? A little informal, don't you think?"

The man in question walked into the breakfast room a moment later. Martin Neill winced at the bright light streaming in the windows, stumbling as an older couple cut across his path from the buffet.

Saffron bit her lip on a smile. "It feels too formal to refer to anyone that hopeless as 'mister.' Martin Neill is the equivalent of a baby duck. A lost, motherless baby duck."

Christopher Banks paused before the chair he'd pulled out next to Saffron. "If you're discussing waterfowl, I might as well just go off to sit with Ames and Donnelley. I don't care what they say, there is simply nothing interesting about livestock farming techniques of the fourth century BC."

Banks was a linguist and, like Alexander, was the young, strapping sort who seemed to be designed for exploring, with reddish-brown hair and striking eyes only a few shades bluer than white. He and Alexander had become fast friends. Saffron enjoyed learning about the paper he planned to write exploring the layered linguistic history of the agora of Smyrna. With the land having passed hands between several eras of Romans, Greeks, and the Ottomans, Smyrna offered him much to study.

"Agreed," Saffron and Alexander said simultaneously. Saffron added, "We're not discussing ducks. I simply said Martin Neill reminded me of a duckling."

Thus reassured, Banks sat next to her. "Who?"

Saffron nodded to Martin, who was now walking very slowly, both hands full of breakfast dishes, as he surreptitiously peered around the room in search of a seat. Taking pity on him, she called and waved him over.

"Good morning," he said as he approached, still walking painfully slowly.

Everyone returned the greeting, and when Martin was settled opposite Saffron, Alexander and Banks rose to retrieve their own breakfast. Saffron, having been the first to arrive, had only crumbs left on her plate.

"Is there anything I can help you with today, Miss Everleigh?" Martin asked before he took an enormous bite of eggs.

A tense sort of irritation crept over her shoulders at the innocent question. It wasn't Martin's fault that Clark was being the worst study partner in the history of the university. She forced a smile. "That's very kind of you to ask, but no. I'm sure once we reach Smyrna and get a look at the agora, there will be many tasks to assist with." He nodded eagerly, cheeks bulging with food. "Mr. Ashton mentioned you're to graduate soon. Do you plan to stay at the university to pursue a master's?"

A panicked look came over him, and his jaws worked to finish chewing quickly. After an awkward gulp, he said, "I graduate soon, yes. In the spring. Of course, when else?" He laughed uncomfortably. "I haven't decided about a graduate program. I do plan to do one."

He took another bite, and rather than send him into a panic again by asking another question, she took a moment to really look at him. They'd met in passing a handful of times as preparations ramped up at the U, but she'd been in such a tizzy that she'd rather ignored him. For all that he and Alexander shared similar coloring, dark hair and eyes, their similarities stopped there. Martin was a small man, almost delicate. If she had to guess, Saffron would have pinned him as an artisan, someone who specialized in small, detailed work from his hunched shoulders and elegant, long-fingered hands. His eyes were large and expressive, his nose narrow and aquiline, and his lips distinctly bowed and vividly colored. Elizabeth, Saffron's flatmate and best friend, would have envied the naturally rosy color.

"What is your degree in?" Saffron asked him when he'd set down his fork to pat his mouth with his napkin.

"Biology," he replied. "Just biology. General, you know. There are so many things one can do with a biology degree. Zoology, botany, microbiology, even medicine. That's why I chose it, so I would be set up to choose just whatever I wanted when I was finished, but now I've nearly finished and I haven't a clue."

Alexander and Banks returned, setting down plates piled even higher than Martin's. Where they put all the food, Saffron couldn't fathom. Neither man had an ounce of fat on him.

"That's why I was so happy to be selected to join the team," Martin said, eyes darting to Alexander eagerly. "So happy. I'll be able to observe so many different disciplines in action. I'm hoping it'll help me settle on what I want. Academically."

These last words were more directed toward Alexander than Saffron, but she didn't mind. Watching Martin's admiration of Alexander was endearing. He was rather like a puppy.

She clearly had animals on the brain. Perhaps she ought to seek out Ames and Donnelley after all. It would likely go better than seeking out Clark, but she really didn't have a choice. Their ship would arrive in Turkey the next day, and they had absolutely nothing planned. Saffron had her own study proposal, and she assumed Clark had one of his own, and they were meant to merge them into some cohesive plan to study ancient botanical specimens and their preservation and storage. Dr. Henry wasn't likely to give

Clark the go-ahead to open the jars found in the agora otherwise. They had less than two months at the site to get all the specimens, data, and observations they would need to write their paper, and any delay could mean the difference between success and failure.

She'd managed to finish two papers in the year she'd been a researcher in her department, but one she'd relinquished her claim on after learning the study had been funded by the government, something she had a moral objection to, and the other had been decent, but hadn't gained any traction with publication. Her own master's studies were on hold since she'd be abroad most of the semester. She needed this paper to be solid, a cornerstone of the rest of her career.

And for that to happen, she needed to find Clark and get him working. She briefly squeezed Alexander's shoulder before departing in search of her wayward study partner.

Chapter 3

It took four hours, several cups of coffee, and an ironclad constitution for Saffron to get Clark through three pages of notes. Saffron was so exhausted by his willful ignorance and selective deafness that when she retreated to her room to dress for dinner, she fell asleep instead.

She woke to hesitant tap-tapping on her door. Groggily, she got to her feet and opened it a crack.

Mrs. Demirel's anxious face greeted her. "Miss Everleigh? Are you feeling well?"

"Oh, hello, Mrs. Demirel," Saffron said awkwardly, opening the door more fully. "I am quite well, thank you. I merely laid down for a nap and clearly overslept."

"I see, I see," the older woman replied. "Mrs. Henry said as much at dinner, but I felt it best to check. There can be nothing more important than maintaining one's good health. Especially on the high seas!"

Saffron could only agree before excusing herself to dress. She was surprised to find, when she emerged five minutes later in a mauve gown beaded with silver, that Mrs. Demirel had waited for her. She hovered just outside, wringing her hands. Her worried eyes brightened when Saffron stepped outside and locked her door.

"But you look marvelous, Miss Everleigh! What an exquisite color," she said, and walked side by side with Saffron as they went down the hall. "And how clever your shawl matches so well. I'm afraid my own style is very dull indeed." She looked down at her gown of uninspiring beige satin, a poor choice with her fair hair and skin. "I've little need to cultivate a fashionable wardrobe in Silchester. I'm usually tromping around after my boys."

They mounted the stairs leading to the deck, and Saffron found no hint of sunlight on the horizon but a vast array of stars overhead. Sounds of the band drifted from the deck's dance floor, and Mrs. Demirel led her in that direction.

"You've missed supper, but I'm sure a waiter will oblige you should you wish for something to eat," she said. "Going about the ship on an empty stomach is an awful idea. I'll summon something for you, shall I? Blancmange, perhaps?"

"Er, no, thank you," Saffron said. "Thank you for checking in on me, Mrs. Demirel. I see Mr. Ashton there."

He sat with the linguist Banks, the archaeologist Balthazar, and the Henrys at a table near the dance floor. To Saffron's surprise, Mr. Demirel was cutting a path through the dancers with a handsome older woman on his arm, nearly twirling her into Martin Neill and his own dance partner. Saffron was pleased to see Martin socializing with someone other than the rougher members of the expedition crew. From the stars in Martin's eyes as he gazed down at the girl he carefully waltzed with, he was rather taken with her. She was pretty, with reddish-gold hair bound up in a glittering pin and a floating gown of seafoam green.

Mrs. Demirel went stiff at Saffron's side. Her eyes were fixed on the dancers, color slowly draining from her face.

"Mrs. Demirel, are you all right?" Saffron asked her, worried the woman would swoon.

She turned a tense smile on Saffron. "Just so shocked to see my husband up and dancing. He'll make himself sick, moving like that." Her hands fluttered at her sides before she clasped them together. "I-I believe I might be feeling a bit off myself. Yes, I think I will go below deck. Goodnight, Miss Everleigh."

Deep pity echoed in Saffron's empty stomach as she watched Mrs. Demirel hurry away. Was it concern for her husband that had shaken her so, or shock at seeing him dancing and smiling at another woman?

Her stomach rumbled, clearly uncaring about matters of the heart. She made her way to Alexander, who greeted her with a warm smile. He and the other gentlemen around the table rose to greet her.

"Everything all right?" Alexander murmured to her as he helped her into a chair.

"I fell asleep," Saffron said sheepishly. "Nothing to worry about."

Conversation flowed freely, as did the champagne the Henrys had ordered for the table. With the impending restriction on alcohol that entering Turkey would bring about, many among the crew were imbibing with enthusiasm.

Saffron was given a glass of champagne, then another. She danced with Alexander, who danced divinely, and then with Dr. Balthazar, who did not. After a foxtrot that was more of a fox-limp, she made her way back to the table.

Alexander remained on the dance floor with Mrs. Henry, gracefully whirling across the floor. Dr. Henry was at the table, and by the time Saffron had made out who stood with him, it was too late to find somewhere else to be. Clark, Wakefield, and two others crowded around one side of the table, sipping what looked to be whiskey from stout, sweating glasses. Saffron skirted the dance floor so she might creep up on the table to retrieve her handbag.

Naturally, the moment her hand touched the beaded purse, Wakefield caught sight of her. "Why, it's the future Mrs. Ashton."

For weeks, they'd referring to her as if she were already married. She wasn't sure why they thought it made for a good taunt. "Good evening," she said politely.

"Good evening," the others chorused, save for Dr. Henry. His face had gone rather red, and he nodded stiffly at her.

"We were just discussing the entertainments available in our downtime in the city," Clark said, eyes glittering.

"How . . . nice," she ventured. She knew there were markets and tea houses, of course. Dr. Henry and Clark, at least, were quite experienced travelers and likely knew where to find the more interesting areas. And for once, Clark wasn't regarding her as if she were a slug on a prized hosta. "What sort of entertainments do you think Smyrna is likely to have?"

"Do you have much interest in entertainments, Miss Everleigh?" asked Wakefield, twirling the liquid in his glass.

"Of course," she replied, wishing a moment later she hadn't sounded quite so eager. She likely sounded as green as Martin Neill. She added, "When I visited Paris, I took in quite a bit of what the city had to offer."

"Oh, France is renowned for its entertainments, in my experience," Clark said, nodding sagely. "Matchless, wouldn't you say, Henry? In fact, if memory serves, Marseilles was a particularly *entertaining* city, was it not? The conference there a few years ago provided us many opportunities to take in the sights and pleasures."

Had Clark's exaggerated tone not told Saffron that they were no longer discussing things like theaters and museums, the way Dr. Henry determinedly looked away from the group now sharing knowing smiles would have been more than enough to clue her in.

Annoyance bubbled up in her chest, and not even for her own sake. She was used to off-color barbs being leveled against her, but to poke at Dr. Henry when he was clearly uncomfortable with whatever ribald reminiscence Clark alluded to was simply not very nice. "That's enough, Mr. Clark."

"Oh, you're still here," he cooed at her.

"If your eyesight is faulty, you might want to see a doctor before we rely on your perception on the expedition."

"I see things *very* clearly, I assure you."

A clever retort was very nearly on the tip of her tongue when Martin Neill hurried up to her.

"Miss Everleigh," he breathed, smiling broadly. "I want—that is to say, would you be kind enough—"

"Spit it out, Neill," groaned one of Clark's younger cronies.

Martin's dark eyes darted to him, his cheeks flushing. "Oh, quite right. Miss Everleigh, may I, er, borrow you for a moment? There's a young lady, Miss Moore, who I've just been dancing with, when I told her I was to assist a female scientist in the field—"

A chorus of snorts and smothered laughs interrupted him.

"—she, er," Martin stammered, trying very hard not to look at Wakefield as he apparently choked on his drink, "she mentioned she'd be very pleased to make your acquaintance."

Saffron determinately ignored Clark, who hooted with laughter as he thumped Wakefield on the back. "I would be happy to meet her."

"Looks like Neill is getting a head start on his share of the entertainments," Wakefield managed between coughs.

One of the younger men cackled. "Who knew he had it in him?"

"Would it be possible," Saffron said, rounding on them, "for you lot to at least pretend to have some maturity?"

The younger men gaped, as surprised by her snapping at them as Saffron was herself. It was like she'd opened her mouth and Elizabeth had spoken through her. It felt rather good, actually. Good enough that she added, "I could swear I'm in a crowd of undergraduates with the childish rubbish I hear you all spouting."

"Oh dear," Clark said with a chuckle. "If you think the subject of our jokes 'childish rubbish,' then I have terrible news for you about what happens after you take your vows."

This elicited uproarious laughter. Saffron's face burned. The Elizabeth in her head, so witty moments before, only sputtered with outrage.

Martin took an uncertain step forward. "I s-say," he stammered, "there's no call f-for being offensive, Mr. Clark."

All the amusement drained from Wakefield's face. He straightened up and took a threatening step toward Martin, who blanched.

"Neill, go back to your wooing," Clark said, slapping a hand on Wakefield's chest. The other man stopped, but glowered at

Martin. "You might at least learn something from *that* girl." He let out a laugh. "Maybe even some biology."

Color flooded Martin's face, dark and blotchy.

It was then that Saffron, searching for a good put-down or, in the absence of it, something with which she could rescue Martin, realized Dr. Henry was no longer standing among them. He hadn't been any help to begin with, but surely he would have spoken up by now. It was on her, then, to put a stopper in Clark and his friends' drivel. "For someone who claims to be a connoisseur of *entertainments*, you spend your time in a curious manner."

The lazy sneer on Clark's face remained in place, but his eyes sharpened on her. "What do you know of my preferences for entertainment, Mrs. Ashton?" he asked silkily.

Saffron crossed her arms. "I'm simply surprised that someone who's supposedly so worldly lowers himself to harassing a boy and beating him at cards every night."

At her side, Martin made a weak noise of protest.

"Bold words," Clark said, "considering you'd sooner send the fellow you've got by the short hairs to do your dirty work. Where is Ashton, by the way? Lurking in the shadows, awaiting your bidding, is he?"

"I don't need him or anyone else to do whatever dirty work you refer to."

"Is that so?"

"Yes."

"So it'll be you at the card table, putting me in my place?"

Before she knew what she was saying, she announced, "Yes."

A slimy smile formed on Clark's lips. He leaned forward so his boozy breath clouded in her face. "I'll see you at the card table, then."

After being told by what felt like every single member of the expedition that his fiancée had challenged Clark to a game of poker,

Alexander felt he had no choice but to spend the evening in the card room, if only to put the rumors to rest. Saffron clearly hadn't felt well—she'd slept most of the afternoon and vanished from the dance floor before he could bid her good night—and so Clark and the others decided it would be clever to use her absence to fuel a silly rumor. His presence was generally a good deterrent against their juvenile mischief, and thus there he was, sitting a smoky room, listening to drunken guffawing and off-color jokes.

He tossed a winning hand onto the table, concluding the desultory round of cards he'd been roped into and eliciting groans from his companions. It was barely past midnight, still plenty of time for the more idiotic of the bunch to make trouble, but late enough that the anticipatory looks directed at the door had dwindled. Now no one expected Saffron to show up, he could probably slip out.

A great hush filled the room with such suddenness that it was almost like the immediate aftereffect of an explosion: muffled and tense, then unraveling into noise and chaos. Men stood from their tables in an abrupt shuffle.

Alexander rose to his feet to see what the emergency was.

Urgency drained from him, leaving his insides hollow. Standing in the doorway, eyes darting around the room and hands balled into fists at her side, was Saffron.

He was at her side before she could take two steps. "Good evening," he said evenly, offering his arm.

Warily, she took it and allowed him to draw her to the side. The scent of coffee and her usual perfume clung to her. "Good evening," she replied.

"I do hope you are here," he murmured, angling himself before her to block the gawkers, "to dispel a ridiculous rumor floating around that you told Clark you'd thrash him at cards."

Her blue eyes did not meet his, instead roaming what little she could see of the room from behind him. "Don't be silly, Alexander. Of course I didn't say I would thrash him."

"What did you say, then?"

"I said I wouldn't let *him* thrash *me*. Or Martin Neill, for that matter."

He raised a questioning brow.

Saffron sighed, bravado slipping. "Clark was taunting Martin horribly, right in front of these fellows. It was really quite cruel. I could hardly say nothing, could I?"

"And your recourse was to challenge Clark to a poker game?" He wasn't sure if he should feel frustrated or amused. "I didn't know you played poker."

"Oh, well." A flush crept up her neck and flooded her cheeks. "It's a rather recent pastime of mine."

"How recent?"

"What time is it?"

"Twelve fifteen."

She gave him a trepidatious smile. "I've been playing poker for all of three hours. Practically a master."

Alexander withheld a groan. "These games are played for money, Saffron. Real money. Not just a few pennies."

Her sheepish look soured, and she frowned at him. "I know that, thank you. I have money."

"Happy to hear it." Clark had sidled over to them, and his loud drawl had drawn the attention of most of the room.

"If the lady is ready for our game," he said, sweeping a hand toward the nearest table.

The desire to put himself between Clark and Saffron was strong, but her hand tightening on his arm told Alexander it was not the right thing to do. Saffron felt she had to prove something to Clark, and the rest of the crew. In truth, she did.

And even if it was the last thing he wanted to do, Alexander stepped out of her way.

Chapter 4

Along with the rest of the ship's passengers, Saffron and Alexander stood at the rails on deck to watch the approach into the city of Smyrna. Saffron shaded her eyes against the sun, so hot and bright it overwhelmed the shelter of her hat's brim, and so weary were her eyes.

Three hours of Martin Neill feverishly coaching her on the rules and strategy of poker had not been enough to teach her all she needed to know to beat anyone, let alone Clark with half the crew looking on eagerly. She'd played for nearly three hours and lost so much money that whenever she thought of her IOU in Clark's pocket, her stomach went sour.

It had been dreadful, but she had stood up to Clark, and that made it worth it.

The shadows on the horizon steadily resolved into shapes, and then shapes into buildings. The glaring sun carved the shoreline into sharp relief. She had familiarized herself with the story of the Smyrna Catastrophe that decimated the city two years previous, but she hadn't been prepared for the reality of the destruction. It drove from her mind any lingering ghosts from the previous night.

The city must have looked idyllic before the fire. Sweeping arcs of dusty green-and-gold mountains served as a backdrop for a brilliant blue bay lapping against a seafront street. Skeletal remains lined the coast, strangely solemn in the bright sun. Two years of rain might have washed away much of the soot and smoke, but heaps of rubble and broken buildings remained. In places great piles had been assembled, in others the buildings remained as they must have fallen. All but a few seemed significantly damaged if not destroyed.

Next to her, Alexander's mouth was set in a grim line and his eyes were soft, almost wistful.

"I didn't realize . . ." She trailed away.

"Me neither."

She drew closer, so their shoulders pressed together. "Was . . . was any of your family here?" She knew it was a foolish question; surely if any of his family been present when the fires ravaged the city in 1922 or when Greeks were exiled from Turkey in the aftermath of the Turkish-Greek conflict, he would have said so before.

"No," he said, eyes on the line of destroyed buildings. "None of my family were here. My uncles were outraged when it happened, of course. You know they weren't fans of Venizelos, and it was his government that decided to claim this bit of the Ottoman Empire for Greece. The war and the exodus of Greeks from Turkey wasn't popular, even though Greece exiled their Turks in return. But I needn't have had family involved in the conflict to be upset by such violence and destruction."

Saffron turned back to the approaching shoreline, eyes catching on shells of buildings. "To have the city burn so soon after two wars . . . I can't imagine what it must have been like for the people here."

"I suppose that's why we are here," he said. "Smyrna was once a great port city. Hundreds of thousands of pounds worth of goods passed through this place every year. The government is keen to bring the city back to life with business and tourism. We were invited, in part, to demonstrate that Turkey is a stable place, suitable for foreigners to travel to and work within."

Something about the way he said it, so carefully neutral despite the privacy of their conversation, signaled to her that Alexander was worried this would not be the case. The wreckage seemed less sad and much more ominous.

She shook away her feeling of unease. She was on an *expedition.* She would be exploring ruins and taking samples from vessels not opened since antiquity. And best of all, she was here with her fiancé. The trip would be a success. She was determined to make it so.

Disembarkation and customs took up a good part of the afternoon, even with a bevy of men from the Turkish government assisting their party, and Saffron was starving by the time they were invited into a small cavalcade of motorcars. She was pressed into the side of one of the topless cars next to Alexander, who was squashed next to Banks and one of the assistants. Saffron was keen to get her first glimpses of the streets of Smyrna and found the area immediately surrounding the quay was really quite European. Pale, angular buildings with trim and wrought iron fences lined the street. The pedestrians were almost entirely dressed in the style of Europe, too, with only a few men and women in billowing garments.

She might have been driving through a slightly out-of-the-way town in France or England. How silly to have expected something so very different! It would have been easy to blame Elizabeth and her insistence on romantic visions of jasmine-perfumed gardens populated by women in gauzy veils, but it was Saffron who'd allowed herself to expect stepping off the ship would mean stepping into an exotic world entirely different from her own.

The motorcar's driver, a round fellow with a jaunty red cap—some expectations were fulfilled, after all—gestured to the right, and Saffron followed his pointing finger to a short tower just next to the street. The bone-white stone was tessellated with intricate patterns that were unmistakably Eastern in their design. It was topped with a copper dome, and Saffron only realized it was a clock tower when she glimpsed the small white face as they sped past.

The hotel they were to stay was in the Bornova district, to the northeast of the city proper. After a few minutes of driving, Saffron realized they were going in quite the wrong direction. The driver took them to the south through narrow, crooked streets.

Saffron was saved from being thrown forward into the driver's seat by Alexander's arm, thrown out across her chest; only her head snapped forward as the driver slammed on the brakes.

He gestured to the left and spoke animatedly. Though she understood not a word, Saffron could see what he was so keen to show.

A field lay to the left, bordered by scruffy red-topped buildings and hemmed in by a fence built of fresh timber. A trio of white pyramids just visible over the fence indicated tents had been erected within.

"This is the agora," Banks said excitedly. Saffron glanced over her shoulder to see her three companions were peering around each other to get a look at the field. Alexander caught her eye and grinned.

She turned back to get a better look, but the driver zipped away, throwing her head back once again.

There were more rough stops and starts, not unlike when London traffic was at its worst and Saffron had found herself passenger to an impatient driver. At times, buildings and people flashed by, nothing more than fleeting impressions. At others, she found herself staring at a scene while the street was occupied by a slow-moving cart, giving her the chance to absorb the facades of dull white buildings with colorful awnings and clotheslines stretched over the heads of people milling about at a neighborhood market, picking out produce from merchants' neat stacks.

The cramped city streets gradually broadened as they pressed further and further away from what Saffron presumed was the city center. They zipped past a long stone building with dozens of windows and a peaked red roof, which Banks translated from their driver's shouts was a train station, and then they were passing by what Saffron knew to be a mosque, an elegant building with a domed top and a delicate tower next to it. She had to quash her frustration at not getting a more thorough look at the building before they'd passed by it. She would be in the city for six whole weeks, she reminded herself. She would get the chance to see that mosque and any other fascinating site.

Soon they wound their way up a hillock rippling with short golden grass. At the top stood a massive house, and they pulled to a stop in front of it alongside the rest of the party's vehicles.

The sheer size of the building relative to the others they'd driven past was shocking. It was only slightly smaller than Ellington Manor, her grandfather's estate where she'd grown up. The house itself was rusty red, brightened by a lacy white pediment shading the elaborate doorway. Spires of lavender gamboling in the shadows of deep green cypress trees promised a garden on one side of the house.

"Welcome!" called a portly man who came striding out of the hotel. He raised both hands, a huge smile on his round, mustachioed face. "Welcome to Turkey, and welcome to the Bornova Hotel. I am the proprietor and your humble servant, Namik Koray. Please, come inside and take some refreshment."

Aromatic tea served in small glasses alongside tiny sweets awaited them in a large parlor. Saffron perched on a divan alongside Alexander and sampled a walnut covered in a tacky sweetness that perfectly complemented the strong black tea.

When the enjoyment of the refreshments had dampened conversation, Mr. Koray stepped to the center of the room, where he looked from one side of the parlor to the other. The space was painted light green, and the sun from the numerous windows reflected off it to make everyone's face a slightly sickly hue. The furniture was a little older, again like something she might find in the lesser-used rooms of Ellington Manor.

"Dear friends," Mr. Koray began with a smile that lifted the curled ends of his waxed mustache, "I am very pleased to welcome you again. You are among our first guests to stay in this magnificent home in its new purpose of hotel. The Bornova Hotel was once called Barudi House. It is a home of much history and importance in our community."

"That's one way to describe it," muttered Banks from his seat in the chair next to her.

He and Alexander exchanged a look, and Saffron nudged Alexander with her elbow for an explanation.

"This place was likely seized when the family who lived in it was sent away," he whispered. "The government made it into a hotel for foreigners like ourselves. It's far from the quarters destroyed in the fires, and, being up in the hills, has a much more pleasant view than we would have gotten closer to the agora."

"Anything you need, I ask that you make it known to me or any of the staff," Mr. Koray continued. "And now, if you will allow, Yasin Hayrettin *efendi* of the Foreign Affairs Ministry."

The proprietor shuffled backward somewhat awkwardly as a tall, thin man stepped into his place. His skin was bronzed and heavily lined, though his hair, cut severely, was perfectly black. With a long nose and slumberous eyes that looked steadily around the group, he gave the impression of utter competence. Something in Saffron relaxed at that; this fellow looked like a man who'd brook no mischief from two dozen foreigners.

He welcomed the group with a slow, intentional speech that suggested to Saffron that he was not as comfortable speaking in English as the hotel's proprietor. After speaking for a few minutes about cooperation between Turkey and England, he introduced another official.

Mr. Assam spoke through an interpreter, and the young man could barely keep up with Mr. Assam's enthusiastic commentary on the wonderful ancient history of Smyrna. Delight shone through his large, dark eyes, deepening the creases of his weathered face. By the end, so wrapped in his visions of unearthing treasures the world would laud as extraordinary, Saffron was ready to pull on her boots and set off for the dig site right then and there.

Mr. Hayrettin smiled tightly at his colleague's speech, and gently concluded it on his behalf by placing a hand on Mr. Assam's shoulder. "And now we would like to speak to the leaders of this expedition. Dr. Henry, if you please?"

Dr. Henry got to his feet from where he sat next to his wife and the Demirels. Mr. Demirel stood also, and the two Turkish officials drifted toward them, hands outstretched in greeting to their former countryman.

"Ashton! Templeton! Hazelwood! Balthazar!" Dr. Henry barked over the heads of the Turks, who stood at least a head shorter than him, even Mr. Hayrettin. They flinched as one. "Meeting, now!"

Alexander set his empty tea glass on the coffee table and stood, giving Saffron a beleaguered smile before joining the gentlemen on the other side of the room.

Disappointment and envy coiled in Saffron's belly. She was glad to be distracted from such unworthy feelings when Mr. Koray called to the rest of the crew that keys for their rooms awaited them at the desk.

Saffron was the last to leave, not wanting to run into Clark or his friends in the lobby. This had been a good day so far, an auspicious beginning to the true expedition. She wanted nothing to ruin it.

Saffron's vague irritation at not being invited to meet the Turkish guides returned when she stepped into the parlor before dinner to find Alexander standing in the center of a group of guides and expedition leaders, looking quite at ease.

All around, talk revolved around the coming days. Dr. Henry had declared that they would waste no time in getting their feet wet—dusty, rather—at the excavation site on their first full day, tomorrow. It seemed the old hands, people like Clark and Wakefield and a number of fellows Saffron knew to have traveled with Dr. Henry before, disparaged the decision not to give the men a day or two to get adjusted to their new setting. The number of times she caught mutters about "tiresome wives" was disheartening, as if

Mrs. Henry was to blame for Dr. Henry's determination not to waste time. The younger members of the crew were eager to get to the ruins. It was with these younger men she was drawn into conversation.

"Is it true that Mr. Ashton is going to be hiring a research assistant next semester?" one assistant asked, a slender man whose spotty face made him look too young to have been accepted to university, let alone graduated.

"Yes, he is," Saffron replied. A few of the other young men shot each other excited looks. To the one who'd asked, she added, "Are you interested in the position?"

He cleared his throat, suddenly chagrined. "Oh, well, yes," he said in a conspicuously casual way. "Mr. Ashton's got quite the reputation. Published a dozen times, multiple disciplines."

Martin Neill jumped in, saying, "He revised Cunningham's latest study"—his voice dropped—"and *found errors in the data.* And Cunningham wasn't even angry with him!"

Saffron bit her lip on a laugh at their worshipful air. She admired her fiancé's scientific prowess, but these young men apparently saw him as rather godlike.

"I heard," said one dark-haired man with the air of disclosing a great secret, "he's in talks to jump ship to Dr. Henry's new anthropology department."

"Is that true, Miss Everleigh?" the spotty one asked eagerly.

The four assistants swung around to her, eyes alight with curiosity.

Many saw Dr. Henry's new department as a foregone conclusion, but Saffron knew the anthropology department Dr. Henry had been working to form was not quite yet confirmed.

She gave the assistants a polite smile. "Mr. Ashton is quite committed to Biology, I believe."

They dissolved into a comparison of Alexander's credentials versus Geoffrey Kent's, one of the biologists on their team, and Saffron was soon forgotten. She stood at the periphery of their conversation, that same out-of-place feeling swelling inside her. Though she, too, had been a research assistant just eighteen months ago, she couldn't remember ever being half so enchanted by her position. But a lack of camaraderie would do that.

Women in the sciences were not so uncommon as her unfortunate experiences in the biology department at University College London might suggest, and she certainly could make friends with some of the men she worked with. It was just that it never seemed to work. Scholarly discussions often led to being given more clerical work, and humor was usually seen as an invitation for flirtation. The taint of rumors would pollute her working relationships before a friendship even had a chance to germinate. Lee, a medical doctor with whom she'd worked on a study—and several murder investigations—was the only lasting friend she'd managed to make at the U and he hadn't worked there for nearly a year.

Saffron's eyes strayed across the room to Mrs. Henry, who stood at her husband's side. Dressed to the nines in aubergine silk, she looked formidable and lovely, and Saffron wasn't likely to be the only one intimidated by her. The Turkish guides and officials looked to be very deferential toward her in their conversation. Next to her, Mrs. Demirel looked like a chastened schoolgirl, barely raising her eyes from the ground.

Dinner was a very casual affair for the majority of the crew, a buffet offered in the dining room, while the Henrys, Demirels, officials, and team leaders would dine formally in a private room. When the doors to the dining room were opened and the crew made a slow shift in that direction, Saffron hung back, anxiety reducing her appetite nearly to nothing. She'd probably have no one to talk to and would end up a sad wallflower.

Rather than waste her evening being ignored, or worse, teased, she would simply collect some food and take herself up to her room to go to bed early. The motorcars would arrive before dawn the next morning so they might start work before the heat of the day set in. Retiring early would be wise.

Plan settled, she made her way to the tables set along the center of the room, stacked high with platters of roasted mutton, herb-laden salads, and aromatic rice dishes. She took a bit of everything until her plate was full, and looked regretfully at the foods she didn't have the opportunity to sample before heading to the door.

She'd made it halfway up the stairs without notice before Alexander's voice interrupted her.

"There you are," he said, smiling up the stairs at her. His eyes touched on the plate before returning to hers. "I thought you knew you're meant to dine with the officials."

"Am I?" she asked. "But I'm not a team leader."

A pair of footmen chattering in Turkish strode through the lobby, pausing to bow at the pair of them before they disappeared down a corridor.

"Mr. Hayrettin and Mr. Assam have been telling us about the agora and the progress made thus far on the excavation. And Sir Randolph, the British consul general of the city, just arrived. He'll be dining with us," Alexander said.

That did strike her as exciting, but gloom settled over her as she remembered all the Clark-shaped reasons she couldn't say yes. "But . . . this will look like preferential treatment. None of the other regular crew have been invited."

"It isn't preferential treatment," Alexander countered easily, almost as if he'd expected her to say it.

"But it will *look* like it," she said, "and that's almost more important. If I wasn't your fiancée, I wouldn't be included." Not that she was actually being included. She was a tagalong, and that was nearly as disappointing as not going at all.

"I understand your concerns," he said quietly, "but you need to understand we are holding up dinner from being served. If the Turks are anything like the Greeks, meals are important."

Saffron hesitated, trying to recall what her guidebook had said about the societal expectations surrounding dining. Insulting their hosts—on the first day!—would be a terrible mistake.

"Mrs. Henry pointed out that you ought to be at the table, and she did so loudly and in front of everyone. At this point, it will be uncomfortable for everyone if you decline to join us."

She was being ridiculous, and she knew it. Unfortunately, the patient look on Alexander's face told her that he knew it, too. She blew out a breath and summoned a gracious smile. "Very well. Of course I will come to dinner."

Chapter 5

Dinner with the officials was as educational as Alexander had suggested, but not in the way he'd anticipated. It was less an opportunity for him and his fellow team leaders to get to know the agora, the city, and the policies the Turks had put in place and more a lesson in what to expect of their hosts.

Politeness. Rigid, never-ending politeness that was gratifying, if one took the attitude of Mr. Demirel, or aggravating, if one identified with Dr. Henry. Demirel preened at the attention his countrymen offered him, apparent even in the snatches of conversation in their shared language. Henry's attempts to turn the conversation to the business at hand was rebuffed again and again with such delicacy that Alexander wasn't sure Henry had realized what was happening until halfway through the meal. When the topic was gently diverted away from timetables and directed toward the glorious past and promising future of Turkey yet again, Dr. Henry's tenuous hold on his impatience was slipping.

It was then that Mrs. Henry had stepped in. Mr. Tawfik, Mr. Assam's young interpreter, missed the entirety of the third course after Mrs. Henry asked why Assam's office, the Office of Turkish Antiquities, was a part of the Ministry of Education rather than belonging to some other ministry. Tawfik had watched his untouched dish disappear from the table with resignation, while

Assam seemed to forget he was meant to be eating in the onslaught of his enthusiasm.

Sir Randolph Waverly, the consul general, was a plain man of late middle age, with the complexion of a Brit who lingered too close to the equator for too long. He was bald and comfortably rounded and took little interest in the conversations around him save for when Mr. Assam paid obeisance to him in his long-winded comments.

Saffron had finally relaxed into enjoying the meal and the byplay of the officials. They'd exchanged more than one amused glance across the table as Assam waxed on about the weighty responsibilities he was honored to shoulder to protect and promote the history of his culture. Mr. Hayrettin's eyes grew more and more remote until, when the last of their roast mutton was cleared away, he started so violently in surprise that he nearly knocked the footman with his plate over. Alexander had had to fake a cough to cover Saffron's laugh.

When the meal was completed and the ladies rose in the tradition of Western dining to adjourn to a sitting room, Alexander was relieved his fiancée seemed to be at ease. He hoped Saffron wouldn't note Mrs. Demirel had cried off. He was sure to hear her opinion on why she was forced to attend the dinner if the wife of their liaison hadn't, though he thought any comment in that regard was likely to be half-hearted. "Forcing" her to this dinner gave her access to more information and Saffron was nothing if not a philonoist.

Conversation around the table took a forceful turn when Dr. Henry said, "Now, Hayrettin, I want to know more about the security your people have put in place at the dig site. You said men would be stationed there, but how many? And who are they? What is their pay?"

Mr. Hayrettin slowly lowered his glass of tea to the table, untouched. Mr. Assam glanced between Henry and his colleague uneasily as Tawfik murmured in his ear.

"Dr. Henry," Hayrettin said, drawing out each syllable, "you must understand the security of the agora and its treasure is most important to the republic."

"Yes, but in practical terms—"

"I hope you will trust we have taken all considerations to ensure our site is carefully guarded." Hayrettin seemed to think this was a sufficient answer.

Dr. Henry did not. His chest inflated, threatening the buttons of his shirt, and his face, already flushed, went red. "Do you know what happens to sites that are 'carefully guarded' if the men are commoners off the street, given a few pennies a day? Artifacts are stolen and pawned for slightly more pennies," he growled. "You pay trained men good money and arm them. That's what they do at any dig site worth its salt. Better yet, we'll do what my friend Ingholt does. He's planning a big dig in Palmyra. He says he'll pay his locals for what treasures they find. The bigger find, the more coin they get. That way nothing wanders off in the middle of the night."

Clearing his throat, Hayrettin lifted a bold brow. "And who will make such payments, Dr. Henry?"

"You will!" Dr. Henry barked. "Your ministries"—he flicked a hand between Hayrettin and Assam—"want to keep the goods here, don't you? Cough up, or you'll find yourself with empty museums."

On one end of the table, Tawfik and Assam put their heads together as if trying to decide how exactly to respond to such brash talk. Hayrettin, meanwhile, was stony-faced. He didn't look likely to respond.

Dr. Henry turned to the team leaders, oblivious of their equally uncertain expressions. "Templeton, what did we pay the fellows who worked on that site off Rio Jari?"

"You mean the place you thought might have been an ancient village site?" Templeton asked.

Dr. Henry scowled at him. "I mean the place I was told by the Brazilian officials was the location of a settlement of stilt houses dating back nearly a millennium!"

Templeton winced. "I believe it was something like twenty *milréis* for the week."

Henry harrumphed. "Good money! And not a thing was stolen out from under us."

Templeton could have said Dr. Henry had found nothing worth stealing on that ill-conceived, weeklong dig at a supposedly "known site," but he looked no more likely to point that out than Alexander was.

Dr. Henry swung back around to the officials. "See, that's what you've got to do. You all have trained soldiers in the city, don't you? Too many wars fought around here not to. Find a few old hands, arm them, and station them about the site. Our fellows won't mind; most saw action themselves and will be glad for a few fellows on our side of things!" He reached for the enameled box of cigarettes sitting on the table and lit himself one. In a puff of smoke, he asked, "Did you bring the diagrams of the site in its current state? The last I have are six weeks old and I want to know what progress has been made."

Hayrettin's already sour look pinched. "You will see it tomorrow, Henry *efendi*."

"I want to know just where we'll be putting our boots." He tapped ash into the glass dish next to the cigarette box. "Templeton, make a note. We'll put two teams on each market stall. Two archaeologists and one historian, and whatever assistants are assigned to them. We'll make quick work of them."

"Henry *efendi*," Hayrettin said, "if I may—"

Mr. Assam was frowning at his translator's murmurs, and then he questioned Hayrettin in a low voice.

Hayrettin looked grim as he raised his voice to interrupt Dr. Henry's continued instructions to Templeton. "The market stalls are not yet prepared for your men."

Dr. Henry barked, "What? What do you mean, they are not prepared?"

"The first is, yes," Hayrettin said smoothly, not quite looking Dr. Henry in the eye. "But the second is not yet opened."

The other team leaders stirred at this. Hazelwood looked confused, Balthazar's heavy brows were lowered over his dark eyes, and Templeton looked nervously at Dr. Henry.

"Opened?" repeated Henry incredulously. "It hasn't been breached at all? What the devil have you lot been doing for the past month?" He glared at Sir Randolph, who watched the exchange with mild interest, but Henry seemed to understand the man wouldn't be much help. "We were brought here with the understanding that both market stalls were unearthed and prepared for work." He jabbed his finger onto the table. "This sets us back weeks! And you don't have security in place? What sort of ship are you running here, Hayrettin?"

The rest of the group was spared the awkward silence that fell by a footman inconspicuously opening the door the ladies had left through. Hayrettin got to his feet immediately, and with a look that suggested he'd rather eat his shoes than continue the conversation, he gestured for the company to follow him through the door.

Saffron and Mrs. Henry had only a few minutes of quiet conversation before the thunderous sounds of Dr. Henry's displeasure began leaking through the door. They'd sipped their coffee while listening to the one-sided argument about the dig.

The setback would be significant to the entire expedition, but Saffron couldn't help but wonder what it meant for her, specifically. The details provided to the applicants of the crew had promised ruins, not underground rooms. If one of the two storerooms in which she might find botanical matter was still underground, did that mean she would have to go underground to retrieve it? Her hand grew damp around the small cup of coffee in her hands, and not because of its heat. And if she found she could not venture underground to attend to her duties, what would become of her study?

The gentlemen joined them a moment later. Mrs. Henry declared it best if the rest of the crew were given the opportunity to mingle with the Turkish officials, and broke up their party to join them. Saffron thought this a clever way to disperse the tension and give Dr. Henry a chance to cool his temper.

There were nowhere near enough ladies present in the party for the usual after-dinner entertainment of dancing, and so conversation and cards occupied the crew. Several sets of French doors in the parlor and connected dining room were thrown wide to the night.

Alexander was almost immediately drawn away into conversation with a flustered Templeton, so Saffron wandered to an urn of hot tea. A footman in a Western uniform—the hotel seemed to have embraced the Western tradition of servants' black and white—served her a glass of dark, fragrant tea. She took the small sweet offered along with the glass and went to sit near an open window. Warm air scented with lavender and grass drifted over her. It would have been soothing, if not for the loud laughter and conversation coming in through the window, too.

Dr. Henry had made his way outside, and she could hear him grumbling. It seemed he'd reached his limits of tactful amiability, for he was saying things she prayed the Turkish officials did not overhear.

She managed to tune him out, instead watching the interplay of the crew and officials inside. There was much muddled Turkish and handshakes and bows and all manner of entertaining behavior, especially from the younger members of the crew who'd likely had limited experience traveling abroad.

Though, now she looked about, there were fewer young assistants about than usual. Martin Neill came to mind, and Saffron wondered if he would do better than his peers, though she rather doubted it, with his tendency to stammer and ramble. She looked for him amid the crew but didn't find him.

A loud curse erupted from the open door leading to the hotel's front foyer. She leaned over, only to see Dr. Ames bearing down on a fellow she recognized as one of the historians. Considering Dr. Ames was barely above her own height, it was impressive he managed to menace the younger man so effectively. "What do you mean, they're gone?" Dr. Ames demanded

"They've gone down into the city," the other historian said. He didn't seem affected by Ames's poor temper.

"They went into the city? What city?" spat Ames. "Half the damn city is still burnt to a crisp!"

The historian shrugged. "They said something about finding a bit of fun before work got underway."

"Work is underway!" Ames cried, pointing to the stairs. "They were meant to be preparing the papers for drafting the maps tomorrow!" Nostrils flaring, he marched away, calling, "Henry!"

Through the window, Saffron could hear Ames as he exited the foyer and rounded the house to the garden that Dr. Henry occupied.

"What is it, Ames?" he replied. Saffron could see he'd calmed down and was now smoking a cigar with a few other people. Alexander had joined the group, dark eyes watchful as the drama unfolded.

"The assistants are gone," Ames said, coming to stop before Henry. He was nearly two feet shorter but made up for it in pure vitriol. "They took off to the city."

Dr. Henry chuckled. "Can't blame them for wanting a bit of fun, can you?"

"I don't blame them," Ames cried, jabbing a finger at Henry, "I blame you! You told me this expedition would be different! No nonsense. No alcohol. No disappearing into brothels for days at a time! It's not even the first day and the assistants you selected can't even grid a piece of paper before haring off to dip their wicks—"

"Now, Ames, see here—"

"You see here! I only agreed to come on this expedition—to give you my endorsement for this new department of yours—because you promised me research worthy of publication." Ames drew closer, looking almost like he might try to poke Henry in the chest out of agitation. "Thus far, I have no one to do the very basics—"

Dr. Henry waved dismissively. "All right, all right, keep your shirt on. You'll have your grid papers. I'll get the damn assistants back."

It was not a particularly diplomatic response, but Saffron was rather shocked he'd replied without shouting. She hadn't seen much of the infamous Lawrence Henry temper, and even the exchange after dinner was mild compared to the tales she'd heard of him shouting birds out of the trees during the Amazonian expedition. Dare she hope it a good omen of his leadership on this expedition?

"Ashton! Banks!"

"Yes?" Saffron could hear the resignation in Alexander's voice.

"You'll go round up our wayward youths," Henry declared.

Saffron sighed. So much for a good omen.

"I can't go—Cynthia would kill me." His joking smirk seemed to mask real disappointment. "But you can track them down, I have no doubt."

Alexander and Banks left the group. Saffron rose from the window seat to meet them in the foyer.

It was slightly cooler in the tiled foyer, with the doors open and a delicate breeze circulating.

Alexander came to a stop before her with an apologetic smile. "I take it you heard that?"

"I would be surprised if the errant assistants didn't hear it all the way down in Smyrna. Do you think you can find them?"

Banks cleared his throat meaningfully, exchanging a look with Alexander. "There are only so many places a group of rowdy young men would go, Miss Everleigh, if you'll pardon the allusion. I doubt it'll take us more than a few hours." He must have noted how her face fell, for he added, "But have no fear, we'll be dragging the lot in by their ears before long." He flashed a grin at her and clapped Alexander on the shoulder. "Meet you here in five minutes. Can't go out like this, can we?"

Two foreigners out in the city at night in dinner jackets would likely draw quite a lot of attention.

Alexander waited until Banks had disappeared up the stairs to take Saffron's hands, lifting one to press a kiss to the back. "And I'll see you tomorrow morning."

"Be careful," she said softly, squeezing his hands back.

After she bade Alexander and Banks goodbye, she idled in the foyer, wondering if it was time for her to retire. The Turkish officials and the consul general had made their departures moments before, and now the gathering felt even less appealing.

"Miss Everleigh, join me, won't you?"

Fighting the way her muscles tensed, she turned to see Clark, who leaned against the door to the parlor. For once, he seemed to be alone.

"I think I'll be heading to my room now," she said. "Good night."

"Oh, come now, don't be unsociable."

She'd rather eat dirt than socialize with Clark. But if there was a chance they could actually speak about their work—which began tomorrow—then she had to take it.

He offered her one of the full glasses he held. "Champagne?"

She eyed the bubbling golden liquid in a plain water glass. "Where did you get champagne?"

Tipping one of the glasses to the light, he smirked. "With our esteemed hosts gone for the evening, a bottle mysteriously appeared on the sideboard. I suppose someone's luggage was not very carefully examined at customs. Or perhaps one of their customs officers finds their prohibition laws as tiresome as the Americans do." He shrugged and held out the glass of champagne again. "A peace offering. I put you through the wringer on the voyage. It's all a part of the expedition, you know. We've a tradition of giving the new blood a hard time. But now we're here, it's time to move on." He tilted the glass toward her again. "Colleagues?"

She saw nothing in his gaze to suggest this was genuine, but neither did she see his usual contempt, so she took the glass.

He smiled and lifted his own. "To our success."

Warily, she clinked her glass against his. "To our success."

He gulped down his champagne, and a look of mild disapproval crossed his face when he saw she'd only taken a small sip. Unwilling to be the first one to undermine their new truce, she dutifully finished the glass, wincing a little at the sharp brightness of the bubbles.

"Excellent," he said, plucking the glass from her hand. "Enjoy the rest of your evening, Miss Everleigh. I'll see you bright and early."

Chapter 6

"I will take you to *Kemeraltı Çarşısı*," the driver said as soon as Alexander and Banks explained their task. Alexander knew from his brief study of his guidebook that a *kemeraltı* was a marketplace. The driver added something in Turkish, which Banks quickly translated as, "It is where I took the others."

The motorcar was forced to stop when the streets grew too close to pass through. The driver and Banks held a brief conversation, and Alexander took in their surroundings. The streets were not as busy as they had been hours earlier on the way to the hotel, but there were plenty of people out despite the fact that it was nearing ten in the evening. Men sat in clusters, tobacco smoke drifting up to the swooping awnings stretched between buildings, the various colors glowing from the lanterns set on tables or hung beside doors. Men and women walked in and out of deep shadow, some in Western dress, others draped in flowing robes. Vendors of fruit and vegetables had taken away their carts for the night, but down the street was someone curled under a covered stand, looking to be guarding their wares.

Homesickness swept through him in an unexpected, confusing wave. The uneven stones under his feet, the murmur of conversations mixed with the quiet sounds of family life in the homes above the market stalls, and the battling scents of smoke, food, and humanity—this place was so similar to his grandfather's town of

Kyllini. He'd spent weeks there as a boy, caught between feeling like he'd found his home and being an outsider with a funny name. Here, he was just as much a stranger, even if it felt very right to be standing on this street.

He had no further time to dwell on the odd, displaced feeling. Banks was waving at the driver as he carefully backed the motorcar out of the street.

Before Alexander could ask, Banks said, "He's going to park somewhere less conspicuous and then take a rest in that *han*"—he nodded to a red awning a few stalls down, where a group of men sat talking as one might at a pub—"until we find him."

"Did he have any ideas where they might be?" Alexander asked.

"There are many *hanut* in this part of town," Banks said, nodding to indicate they should start moving. "He suggested we check each one. Some places are livelier than others." Banks cast him a speaking look.

Lively could mean anything from a pub to a brothel. Alexander had no idea what to expect of a place where the former was illegal and the latter was not. He heaved a sigh. "Lead on."

They walked the length of one street, peering into several tavern-like spaces. Turks drank tea or smoked within, usually spilling out onto the crooked pavement in the front. They spotted the occasional Westerner, usually in pairs or groups of three. They did find one place Alexander was quite sure *was* a brothel, with red fabric draped over the doorway and two men standing idly outside, but he and Banks had found no trace of their colleagues there or anywhere else. By the time they reached a crossroads in the sprawling market, they were both a few coins lighter and none the wiser about where the assistants had gone.

A breeze laced with tangy seawater pushed momentarily away the scents of smoke and cooking. A string of magenta blossoms fell over a cracked wall where they paused, stepping into the shadow of a darkened two-story building. Banks leaned against the wall and smoked as they watched the passersby.

"Maybe we should head back, Ashton," Banks said at long last. "I'm not willing to risk missing going to the agora tomorrow because we've exhausted ourselves."

What would become of four naïve men of twenty looking for a thrill if they left them to their own devices? He considered the street again, avoiding giving attention to a pair of women across the street who'd stopped and, despite their dark coverings, were showing interest in them. Alexander shook his head. "You go. Send the driver back for me. I'll give it another hour and then return. Hopefully they've already made their way back."

Banks flicked his cigarette butt to the ground. "Very noble, but a little sideways. You can't walk about alone around here, even if you could speak the language."

"Let's try one more place then," said Alexander. "A few Westerners have walked down that way."

The two women, floating like ghosts cloaked in their dark robes, shadowed them. The hairs on the back of Alexander's neck stood up. Women they might be, but he knew better than to underestimate a motivated woman.

It wasn't long after Alexander was called away that Saffron began to feel quite tired. She'd allowed Clark's show of goodwill to encourage her to socialize a bit longer, but each passing minute added weight to her eyelids, she decided to call it a night.

The richly carpeted stairs felt inordinately long, and Saffron mused she'd have to toughen up quite a bit if she was to make it through a more than a month of research in the agora. It was on flat land, and in the middle of the city, but she would be doing much more physical work than her occupation at the university entailed. She could practically hear Clark teasing her about being too weak to do so simple as climbing a staircase.

The first floor appeared before her eyes hazy and twinkling with its electric sconces covered in colorful mosaics. Saffron blinked hard. Perhaps the smoke from the constant stream of cigarettes and cigars throughout the evening was irritating her eyes, as Martin Neill had complained. She rubbed her eyes and blinked again, but the hall before her was still blurry. Saffron took another step up the stairs toward the second floor, her mind conjuring the cloying scent of incense, and shook her head slowly. It was like her brain had melted to slush. But a nagging thought kept surfacing.

Saffron gripped the stair rail and lowered herself to the bottom step. Sudden lethargy, blurred vision, and the feeling of moving as if she were under water . . . Someone had slipped her a sleeping drug. Again.

That realization sobered her up by half. Her heart began to pound very loudly in her ears and she tried to concentrate. Someone had given her something to incapacitate her. She was in a hotel full of strangers in a foreign land. Alexander wasn't here. Was that purposeful?

Her head reeled with panic and sudden nausea. She fought down the urge to vomit.

Wait! She stood up too fast and stumbled, barely catching the rail before falling. She concentrated on the feel of the cool wood under her hands. If studying poisons had taught her anything, it was that the body's inclination to vomit was very apt. She surely hadn't been injected with anything, nor was it the smoke she'd inhaled as none of the others were stumbling around. Getting up her stomach contents would likely be helpful, though not appropriate for the hallway.

Concentrating all her might on not falling over, Saffron took slow steps up the stairs. The climb seemed to take forever and she wasn't sure she'd make it to her room before collapsing into sleep. It was tempting to call for help, but she didn't know who would answer her. Possibly whoever had done this to her to begin with.

Fighting against a riptide of exhaustion, she dragged herself to the white paneled door of her room.

Sweat beaded on her forehead. Even breathing seemed to challenge her, but she made it to her hotel room's door. Her beaded purse slipped from her lax hand and she sank to the carpeted ground to retrieve it. Though her body longed to recline there, head leaning against the door jamb, legs sprawled beneath her, that would not do. With an almighty effort, the thousand-ton key was brought to the lock and turned.

Saffron stared at the door. Now it was unlocked, she had to go inside. With a groan of effort, she clung to the curved door handle and pulled herself back up. A deep breath and a step forward brought her inside the dim room. The bell pull was endlessly far away, the blurry outline of the corded rope taunting her.

She refused to allow herself to sit during the long minutes she waited for the maid. If she allowed her eyes to close or her body to rest, she'd fall into the abyss and who knows what would happen. Imagining dreadful uses for a drugged woman proved a good way to stay alert.

She tore a piece of paper from her notebook and began scrawling a note to Alexander, getting only a few words down before she stopped. Even in her hazy mental state, she could see his alarmed expression, wide eyes hardening into determination as he realized who was the likely culprit. He'd probably confront Clark and that would lead to even more resentment. She put the pen back down. She'd deal with this on her own.

A quiet knock on the door came at long last and Saffron told the very confused-looking girl who stood at the door she needed water, salt, and if they had it, ground mustard seeds. The maid stared at her, large brown eyes in a round face shocked at such a request from such a strangely behaving guest. Pale, sweating, and slurring her words was not how Saffron wanted to present herself to anyone.

The maid returned a few minutes later with Saffron's requested items and agreed to remind the reception desk to have a girl come to wake her in the morning. Saffron took the tray to the small table in front of the opened window, dumped the contents of the dishes into a glass with water, then, with a mumbled curse, drank it down.

The emetic was effective before long. Heart pounding and mouth sour, she pushed herself away from the basin and onto the bed.

Chapter 7

The two spectral figures mirrored Alexander and Banks's movements down several streets. The dim glow of lamps in doorways threw harsh shadows, obscuring the unlit and contorting what the light touched. They'd strayed from the main thoroughfare of the market and now walked on a narrow street that was more an alley covered with tattered awnings. Fewer *hanut* made their home there, but a dozen tanned faces turned to them as they passed, and dark eyes roved over them with interest.

Banks gave Alexander a sidelong glance and jerked his head toward a closed stall, and they stopped within its shallow cover. Banks tapped a cigarette against his case and lit it. Alexander glanced about the street casually, his eyes searching for the two women who'd followed them. He spotted them huddled in the corner of a haphazardly arranged set of chairs in front of an elderly man with an urn, perhaps a makeshift tea stand. They were speaking to a young man in a rumpled shirt that might have once been white. His overlong hair was pushed back from a slim face raptly focused on the smaller of the two women. A moment later, his eyes met Alexander's.

An enormous smile spread across his face. He detached himself from his companions and made toward Alexander and Banks.

"Hello, my friends," he said, but this appeared to be the extent of his English. He continued tentatively in Turkish, eagerly looking between the two of them to see their reaction.

Banks translated for Alexander. "He said welcome to his neighborhood, and asked if we were looking for hospitality." He jerked his head at the two women lingering across the street.

"Ask if he's seen them," Alexander instructed, extracting a few coins from his pocket.

The young man accepted the money without hesitation as Banks asked his question. He must have given some signal to the women, for they drifted away into the darkness.

As the conversation between them progressed, Banks became more aggravated and the boy more reticent. The dark eyes of the boy lost their sheen of excitement and Alexander was quite sure whatever use this boy might have been would soon be lost.

"Behlul—that's his name—says he might have seen some Westerners, three or four young men. He's asking for more money," Banks said, looking at the boy with distaste.

Behlul's eyes darted between them again, smiling nervously, and he inched away as though he might run.

"Wait," Alexander said.

Behlul paused with a hopeful grin. His teeth gleamed like his eyes, bright despite the darkness of the alley.

Alexander smiled at him and then at Banks as he said easily, "Tell him we also want to go where they went. Make it seem like we want to have a good time, not that we're retrieving them. He probably works for someone around here and will get in trouble for losing business if we burst through the doors demanding their customers."

Banks all but gaped at him. "We're not actually going to follow this boy into some dark house where we'll be robbed!"

"Tell him we want to find a place to come during our lengthy stay in Smyrna and I'm paying double tonight if I'm pleased. Returning customers have to be worth more."

Banks pinched the bridge of his nose. "'Whenever a man does a thoroughly stupid thing, it is always from the noblest motives.' Very well. Let's be stupidly noble."

Behlul's wide grin grew as he nodded several times to Banks's words. He said something that sounded agreeable and beckoned them to follow him down another alley. Alexander and Banks followed, Banks looking frequently over his shoulder as they went.

Through a flurry of shadowed alleys, they followed the boy until they came to a house whose lit windows were glaringly bright after the sleeping market. It stood apart from the rows of buildings, a house by itself rather than a flat. From it emanated the sounds of conversation and music.

Behlul knocked on the door and they were admitted by a handsome older woman, her tanned face set with lines. She nodded at Behlul with approval and beckoned them inside. They followed Behlul through a hallway and a large sitting room arranged with a dozen low tables populated with men, dressed traditionally in robes or suits and fezzes, better attired than the men in the alleyway. Through a doorway, Alexander could see a cluster of women in similarly mixed dress sitting together at a table with tea glasses, chatting. The place was modestly but tastefully decorated. Several wooden tables held large contraptions with glass bottoms bubbling with aromatic steam. Alexander watched as one guest serenely puffed on a long mouthpiece connected to it.

"That's a *nargile*, a water pipe," Banks said, following Alexander's gaze. "But surely the assistants haven't come all this way just for a water pipe."

Alexander had heard of such a thing from Geoffrey Kent, who'd researched in Syria. He'd also heard that tobacco was not the only thing that could be smoked using a water pipe. A bad feeling crept over him as Behlul beckoned them from another doorway.

The next room was curtained with patterned cloth and more dimly lit. Within, reposed on embroidered cushions with a bubbling *nargile* on a table between them, lay three young men in dinner jackets, smiling stupidly. They started upon seeing Alexander and Banks glaring at them but broke into snorts and laughter a moment later.

Banks snatched one of them up by the jacket front and said, "You think it's funny, do you? Being stashed away in some hash house with no one knowing where you are?"

He thrust the blinking man back into his cushion and glowered at the three of them. They were far gone; clearly, they'd not had just tobacco in their pipe.

"Banks, ask what this lot owe and let's get out of there," Alexander said. The sweet-scented lingering smoke was making him lightheaded.

Banks did so, but Behlul shook his head with a frown. He was insisting as he spoke, gesturing to the intoxicated assistants and Alexander. Banks translated, "He's angry we want to leave since you said we'd be good customers. He says he doesn't want to get his boss, we'll all be in trouble if he does."

Alexander cocked an eyebrow. "He's made a threat? That's rather bold." Banks shrugged. "Let's speak to his boss then. I'm sure he doesn't want five guests of the government to go missing in his place of business."

Alexander's cool attitude toward meeting Behlul's boss didn't reflect the real anxiety simmering within him. There was no way of knowing if this boss would respect their status as guests of the government. It was a new government that no doubt had its detractors.

At the end of the hall, Behlul knocked and opened the door for them.

Alexander and Banks stepped into a well-lit room, blinking at the colorfully chaotic interior. It was made up like a study, something between an old-fashioned European library and a Turkish sitting room, with art plastering the walls and lamps on every surface. The furniture, far too much for the small room, was also mixed, some of it clearly high quality, but most of it inexpertly repaired such that even Alexander could see the uneven rendering of the legs and imperfect staining of the wood.

He was so lost in the decor, he barely noticed a wizen man among the cluttered tables and bookshelves, sitting on one of a series of cushions making up a sort of low couch on the floor. His face was a maze of wrinkles, and he wore a well-tailored Western suit with a burgundy fez on his head. He squinted up at them and took on a cross look as he spoke sharply to Behlul. His main feature was a generous mouth, which in its current state of displeasure was puckered into something like a pout.

The two Turks spoke for some time, Banks interjecting at one point with irritation. Alexander let his eyes stray from the interaction to a document on the table before the old man. On a table layered with papers of Arabic characters—for written Turkish used that language's characters—it immediately caught his eye. It was a shipping manifest, but one written in Greek.

The man must have seen him looking, for he surprised Alexander with the sudden change to the same language. "You are Greek, boy?"

Expression as neutral as possible, Alexander replied in kind. "I studied it."

The old man frowned, his wrinkles deepening and his mouth growing more trout-like. "You insult me, boy. Am I not descended from your same ancestor? Here, we are all from the same family."

Alexander smiled slightly at this statement, and the man's accent. He might speak Greek, but he was certainly not from there. He would have been cast out, if he had. "There are few in this city who would agree with you."

The old man huffed. "The city has turned itself anew. Half the population has been killed, exiled, or fled. Who is left? Turks, now poor and beaten down. I would have kept the Greeks. They have better merchandise."

"Indeed," Alexander said shortly. "I asked to speak with you regarding our friends who partook of your hospitality. I wish to settle whatever they owe."

The old man shifted slightly in his seat. "We do not do business in a rush. We are civil, for our behavior determines what treatment we receive in return, eh?"

Considering the man had immediately set to arguing with his young employee rather than introduce himself to the newcomers or offer a seat, Alexander took that to mean that, despite his statement of civility, he and Banks were on thin ice.

"*Havadan sudan konuşmak,*" the old man said, then in English, "We sit, we drink tea, and we discuss the weather and the crops in the way of our grandfathers." The older man spoke the Turkish word for tea to Behlul, who scampered away, closing the door behind him. He gestured to the table before him.

Alexander resisted the urge to immediately sit, as he would have done if one of his uncles had waved a hand at him like that. Taking care to look regretful, he said, "I must ask your forgiveness and insist we be allowed to pay our friends' debts and collect them. We are scholars invited to study the agora. Our work begins tomorrow."

The old man scrutinized him for a long moment, then shrugged. "Tell me your residence, and my man will drive you there."

Banks's lips parted, perhaps to refuse, but Alexander said quickly, "You are most generous, but our driver awaits us in the *kemeraltı.*"

"You will return here to my tea house," the old man said, lumbering to his feet. He was short and wide, prosperous-looking in his elegant suit. He offered his hand. "*Inşallah*, it will be so. You tell your man to bring you back to the *han* of Ali Fethi Bey."

CHAPTER 8

Morning came far too quickly for Alexander. He prepared for the day, trying not to think about how difficult it would be to manage his team, and how much more so when he'd slept only four hours. He wanted to accompany Saffron while she scouted out the dig site because she was stuck with Clark. He didn't like to think how Clark would treat her if he wasn't within earshot, especially in a place like the agora, which was spread out and full of niches. But doing so would only feed into whatever negative views the others held of her. Perhaps he could send Neill along with them. Neill might be inexperienced and impressionable, but he didn't seem like the sort to turn a blind eye to improper behavior toward a woman.

Alexander's descent down the stairs to the breakfast room was interrupted by Saffron. Rather, her attire interrupted his descent down the stairs.

He didn't recognize her at first, with her short brunette curls obscured by a wide-brimmed hat and her figure camouflaged beneath a long, tan dust jacket. He realized it was her when she turned at the sounds of his footsteps on the stairs behind her. Her blue eyes were wide with something like alarm at first, then her face broke into an embarrassed smile.

He could see why she might feel sheepish; he was sure she'd never worn jodhpurs before, nor boots laced up to nearly her knees.

The effect, in Alexander's opinion, was charming. The khaki jodhpurs were tucked into shining leather boots and flared at her thighs before being tightly tied at her waist with a sturdy leather belt. It threw into relief her figure, which he took a moment to appreciate before she swatted him on the arm, cheeks pink.

"Stop that," she whispered. "Or we'll be late."

He grinned. "I might be willing to be late."

She bit her lip, but unsure if it was in invitation, he forced himself to look away. They were about to be surrounded by a lot of grumpy men on their way to being covered in dust and sweat. He wouldn't mind getting one last enjoyable moment together, but he couldn't show up to the first day late, and neither could Saffron.

On a sigh, he said, "Let's go down to breakfast."

"I take it you found the assistants, considering Dr. Henry isn't shouting the place down," she said as they descended the winding stairs.

"They were three sheets to the wind by the time we got to them." It was possible the trio of idiots still were, it being only a few hours since he and Banks had plucked them from the *han*.

Alexander described the search as they crossed the foyer to the dining room, busy with eating crew members. He was glad to distract her with the tale, as her clothing was drawing more than a few eyes. They piled their plates high with fruit, eggs, cheese, and bread, and Alexander finished relating the strange interaction at Bey's *han*.

Saffron nearly choked on her coffee. "He wants you to go back? What on earth for?"

Alexander shrugged. "He likely wants our business. Banks imagined he might be involved with the drug trade, considering the state of the assistants. From how he spoke, I think he must have dealt with the Greeks before the war. He didn't seem particularly nefarious."

They said no more about it as the breakfast room filled with their colleagues. Plates were stacked with food and coffee was guzzled, despite the strength of the hotel's brew being double that of what they were used to. Just as they finished breakfast, Dr. Henry announced the cars and drivers were outside. Saffron excused herself and said she would be outside. That was fine with Alexander; he wanted to speak to Clark before they drove to the agora. As much as he wanted to tell himself this was solely because he wanted their team to work together seamlessly, the truth was that he wanted nothing to spoil Saffron's first expedition.

As Clark entered the room, he went to join him at the buffet table.

"Good morning, Ashton," Clark said, his unpleasant grin spreading across his face. "I heard you and Banks were successful finding the assistants. What sort of place did they end up in? I daresay they must have had some fun; they look nearly as bad as you do."

"I want to remind you of why we're here," Alexander said. "We're here to work. The sooner you finish your work with the biology team, the sooner you can join your team."

An eyebrow cocked and a smirk about his thin lips, Clark said, "I'm sure I'm not the one you need to worry about. I'm here, am I not?" He brushed past him. "I'll be present and prepared at the agora. I do hope everyone else will be, too."

The drive to the agora of Smyrna was, in a word, bumpy. The streets of Bornova were replaced by tremulous unpaved roads that skirted the mountains and took them in a wide arc over Smyrna. They saw a brief taste of the untouched fields and rocky valleys cloaked in the blue prelude to dawn before the road skirted a river and made their way back down to the houses and shops of Smyrna.

After what felt like an hour of jostling around in the cramped motorcar, Saffron gratefully decamped to the cobblestones of the street. A headache threatened behind her eyes, brought on perhaps by the sedative she'd been given, or perhaps the overly bumpy ride, but the air was fresh and cool, and a day of exploration awaited her. She eagerly looked about the place they'd come to.

With the pale gold light of emerging dawn casting deep shadows of the surrounding buildings and the fence protecting the site, it was not easy to make out much. Through the planks of the fence she saw only grass, dirt, and hunks of stone.

The *kemeraltı* sprawled just beyond the close-knit buildings looking down on the agora, the sounds and smells of which permeated the crisp morning air. It added a definite urban feeling to the site. She'd always imagined researching abroad to involve jungles and rivers rather than cities with busy markets, but it would be a fun place to take her breaks. From what Alexander had told her of the market, it was layered with all sorts of goods to explore.

Excited noise swelled behind her as the rest of the crew assembled. Several members drew near to the fence to get a better look, including Clark and Wakefield. Clark was pointing to something, looking like he was, for once, concerned with work. But a moment later his eyes strayed to the group.

A most satisfactory look of shock clouded his face when he spotted her. Saffron grinned and waved. He glared and turned away.

What a pleasant way to begin the day, and her suspicion was confirmed by his surprise she was present at the agora.

Dr. Henry shouted for the crew to follow him into the site before offering his arm to Mrs. Henry. The older woman had mentioned she would be joining the crew sporadically, and so Saffron was not surprised to see her in elegant white walking daintily over the uneven ground.

They passed through a gate manned by a Turk wearing something that looked a good deal like a military or police uniform, though he wore no weapon that Saffron could see, and then they were inside the agora.

It was, in fact, a stretch of land that was mostly field, undistinguishable from those they'd passed on the way down from Bornova. The agora was, first and foremost, largely still underground, but part of the field had been transformed into an archaeological dig the likes of which she'd seen in newspapers and journals. Three large tents sheltered tables laden with all manner of equipment and what looked to be rocks. A handful of cracked columns, some broken to resemble oversized stubs of candlesticks and others taller than Alexander, lay in a loose row beside a long pit.

Dr. Henry marched to the nearest of the tents and waved the crew to follow. He went to join the three men who stepped out of the tent: Mr. Hayrettin, Mr. Assam, and his translator. They shook hands, and Mr. Assam, through Mr. Tawfik, waxed on for some time about the excitement of the government, as well as the honor it was for representatives of University College London to discover what amazing things awaited in the agora. Saffron lost interest early in the largely familiar speech, and her gaze wandered to the excavated area.

Stone arches, like the ribs of a whale partially buried on a beach, arced over the pit some twelve feet across. These would be the remains of the west stoa. Alexander had said something about the locals fitting together the stones they'd found in the earliest excavations, proving what the structure had been before it was buried and built over. She guessed she would spend some time in that area if the archaeologists had discovered any wares left behind in the market stalls that had once occupied it. She couldn't wait to see what they had discovered down there.

Mr. Assam's speech came to an end, his proclamation of great successes to come from the partnership met with lukewarm applause from those who had been listening. Just when Saffron thought they would be moving on to the actual work, he added, "This is the excavation crew." He lifted his hand, drawing the crew's attention to the twenty or so men standing a dozen yards away.

Saffron wondered if these were the men who had already been working in the agora. Many wore vests over dusty tunics with loose-fitting trousers, and all were weather-worn bronze and tough-looking. The easy way they stood together in their informal clothing made Saffron suddenly feel ridiculous, trussed up in her pristine cotton and canvas sport togs. Her boots didn't even have dust on them. And they were, in fact, rather uncomfortable despite her efforts to break in the leather before the journey.

She shifted from foot to foot, trying to concentrate on what Mr. Assam was saying about the schedule for working hours.

"The local men work from one hour after sunrise until sunset, with breaks for the *namaz* and lunch at noon. Water is available at the tent, and today we will be providing light refreshment," Mr. Assam's translator managed to relay his cheerful tone. He clapped his hands. "*Kolay gelsin!*"

The crew applauded stutteringly, as if unsure they were meant to.

Dr. Henry nodded to the officials. To the crew, he called, "Form up into departments to go over your assignments. We've got work to do."

CHAPTER 9

Saffron went to join Alexander where he stood a few yards away in the field and they were soon joined by Geoffrey Kent, Martin Neill, and Harvey Dunmore. Kent, tall and somber, was a colleague of Alexander's, there to discover what he could about the quality of the water that used to flow through the agora. Dunmore, short, round, and fussy, was a herpetologist, specializing in lizards. He would be doing preliminary research into the coloring of the reptiles dwelling in the city versus the countryside. Not that he himself had told Saffron anything about it. Martin Neill was the assistant for their department, and he'd shown Saffron some of the materials Dunmore had demanded he memorize on the voyage, including some hundred-fifty species of lizards, snakes, and toads.

"We'll be touring the land here in a moment," Alexander told them, "to get a feel for the scope of the property. The local fellow assigned to assist us will show us around." He looked over his shoulder at the cluster of locals speaking with the officials and the Henrys. None of them looked likely to be moving in their direction any time soon.

"Oh!" Dunmore craned his neck in the direction of the nearest hunk of stone. Saffron thought for a moment he was intrigued by the designs carved into the stone—it was clearly a relic of the agora—but he darted forward and went to his knees just before the stone. "Neill! Bring me my measuring tools, quickly!" he hissed. "This is a prime specimen of agamid!"

Martin darted a look at Alexander, whose lips had thinned. He nodded, grudgingly, and Martin trotted off, extracting a flexible ruler from his satchel.

"I'll just go collect our guide," Alexander muttered, and strode off in that direction.

Saffron glanced about the field for Clark, who should have been with them. He was no doubt off pretending she—and their work—didn't exist.

Alexander soon returned to their group with a short man in a fez. Mr. Apak, as he introduced himself, admitted to not knowing much about the history of the agora other than the information he'd been provided, as he was no scholar but a tariffs clerk that had been asked by the officials to act as a guide due to his mastery of English.

"But that's all right," Saffron said, charmed by the man's pleasant manner. It felt more like a private conversation rather than a group introduction, since Dunmore and Neill were still examining the lizard and Kent contributed about as much as the rock on which the lizard sat. "Most of us are here for the things living in the agora now, rather than what used to live here. And we do have someone meant to help us with the history, anyway."

Mr. Apak inclined his head to her. He was middle-aged, with a little paunch and a big smile of excellent teeth. "You are too kind." To Alexander, he said, "I have only a few things to discuss with you before we begin the tour, Mr. Ashton, if I may have a moment?"

Alexander agreed, adding apologetically to Saffron, "Do you mind going to find Clark?" It looked like the last thing he wanted to request, but Kent had wandered off toward Neill and Dunmore, who now looked to be attempting to lift the stone on its side, ostensibly so Dunmore could see what was underneath it.

She found Clark standing at the mouth of the pit with a handful of the archaeology staff. "Mr. Clark, Mr. Ashton says—"

She was rather hoping to catch him off guard, still surprised she'd managed to beat his little scheme with the sleeping draught, but without missing a beat, Clark took one look at her and stifled a laugh. Saffron would have loved to head off whatever comment was no doubt forthcoming, but she didn't know which aspect of her presence he was preparing to insult.

Clark cleared his throat in a futile attempt to rid the laughter from his voice. "Beg pardon, Miss Everleigh, I'm afraid I've never seen a woman attempting so vainly to take on the appearance of her male superiors."

Saffron cocked an eyebrow. She was sure that was meant to be an insult, but she rather liked the idea that her masculine clothing didn't entirely suppress her femininity. She and Elizabeth hadn't spent hours figuring out what she would wear for nothing. Still, she didn't enjoy being laughed at in front of their colleagues. "If you're ready to get to work?"

"Of course," he said easily, planting his red-banded straw fedora on his head. "Best I come with you. Left to your own devices, you'll be careless and damage something priceless."

"We are walking with a local guide. I can't imagine anyone would do anything to harm the site."

Clark looked down his large nose at her. "And who will be responsible for you when you inevitably walk onto something valuable?"

Saffron felt heat rising in her face. "I will be responsible for myself."

He laughed. "I'll let the responsibility slide to poor Ashton. Lord knows he'd better get used to picking up after you." He walked off, leaving Saffron stewing.

Clark had joined the others by the time Saffron returned to their bit of field. Mr. Apak set off at a spritely pace toward the southern end of the field where they had entered. "Here," he called, "is where the agora begins. *Agora* means 'market,' but in ancient times, it also means meeting place. Farmers selling crops, artisans selling goods, and any who wished to hear the news of the day, they came here. And the basilica is believed to be there"—he pointed to the far end of the field—"where the government did its work. This was the heart of Smyrna."

"New Smyrna," Clark said from the back of the group. Everyone turned to him, and he shrugged, a little smile on his lips. "It was New Smyrna, here. Hellenistic period."

Mr. Apak nodded. "Yes. This one belongs to the *Roma*, the Romans. And records of this place tells us—"

"Not just the Romans, but the Greeks, too," Clark drawled. He shot a nasty look at Alexander. "Alexander the Great, in fact, had a hand in rebuilding this place some three hundred years after the pillaging of Alyattes, did he not?"

Mr. Apak nodded again, but his bright enthusiasm had faded somewhat. "He did, sir, and when they reconstructed the city center here, rather than—"

"Atop the peak there," Clark interrupted again, turning around and pointing to the south, where a modest hump of a mountain stood. "The acropolis still stands there, along with a few other bits of old rock. There was a theater, I believe, and cisterns. Are there cisterns here, too?" He addressed the question to Mr. Apak, who looked startled Clark was asking him.

"Ah, the cisterns."

"The cisterns," Clark repeated with obnoxious emphasis. "You know, for holding water?"

Mr. Apak's expression flickered before brightening. "Ah, yes, the cisterns. Please, excuse me, but my knowledge of the language is mostly from reading, rather than speaking, and all too often the words sound differently than they are spelled." He chuckled, and Saffron liked him all the more for being able to laugh off Clark's rudeness. "If you will come with me, over here . . ."

Saffron and the others hurried after him as he strode toward the pit. Clark, of course, did not hurry, though Mr. Apak was sure to wait for him until he spoke. A handful of the local workers were already down in the pit, extracting rock and dirt in buckets, while others carefully tapped at more rock with digging instruments.

"Historical records tell us the cisterns are here, beneath several layers," Mr. Apak said proudly, gesturing down at the workers. "The lowest floor was made into cisterns in the time of the *Roma*. We will find them before long, I am sure."

Anticipating another snarky show of knowledge, Saffron looked at Clark, but his eyes were on the workers. It was as if he was interested in what they were doing, rather than preoccupied with being as annoying as possible.

He remained surprisingly quiet as they continued their tour, forgoing any commentary on the pit where the workers were digging, the overgrown field pockmarked with exploratory holes and large chunks of rock clearly belonging to the ruins, and even when Mr. Apak shared theories of what the surrounding buildings had been built on top of. If Mr. Apak was correct, this entire area could become one massive dig site. If the Turkish government intended to unearth the rest of New Smyrna, the houses and businesses immediately surrounding the field would be demolished and the ground beneath them dug up. Ancient Smyrna held a great deal of importance, he said proudly, and the leaders of not only Turkey but academic institutions around the world would watch the progress of their work with interest.

Throughout Mr. Apak's speech, Dunmore had rushed off no fewer than six times to catch and measure snakes and lizards, even going so far as to demand Neill race back and forth to the tent for small specimen cages. He seemed to be oblivious that his interruptions were distracting. Saffron half expected Alexander to say something, for he looked just as annoyed as she felt, but he kept silent. Perhaps he planned to speak to Dunmore privately.

At the conclusion of his talk, Mr. Apak bowed graciously in response to their thanks and said, "Mr. Clark is your historian and will guide your work, I understand." He looked between Alexander and Clark for confirmation before continuing. "I will introduce him to the men excavating. Come, come."

When Mr. Apak left with Clark to meet the locals, Alexander suggested they pause in the mess tent for a water break. By now, the sun had risen high above, bright and hot in the clear sky. The men had damp patches on their white shirts, and Saffron was no better under her duster.

She slipped off the jacket and placed it on one of the carpets covering the uneven ground of the mess tent, then blotted her brow with a handkerchief while the others accepted glasses of water from the young man manning the table laden with urns of water and tea.

Alexander mopped his own brow, and not looking at her, said, "Take Neill with you when you join Clark later."

"I doubt Dunmore will let him out of his sight. How many lizards do you think he managed to measure in the hour we spent touring the site?"

His smile was brief. "Too many, and not enough. I've already told Neill he'll be working with you and Clark."

"We don't need an assistant yet. If they haven't even begun to excavate the other market stall, I don't know if they've dug up anything more for me to see, apart from the wares from the first stall." Those wares were what allowed her to come on the expedition. The excavation team had opened one jar, saw there were botanicals preserved inside, and had immediately set the rest aside for more careful study. She and Clark would be opening and examining the clay vessels later today, when the expert from Istanbul University joined the team.

Alexander looked away, squinting out over the field. His silence said plenty.

Saffron frowned at him. "Why do you want me to take Neill?"

"There are several reasons. First is you will be kind to him. The other fellows had been giving him a hard time, including Clark, as you well know. Second, I want Dunmore to get used to hauling his own gear. He'll be going off soon on a trek through the hills to find his control species for his study." He shot her a humorous glance. "He's not exactly a sportsman. I don't want to get a report he's keeled over somewhere between here and Mount Sipylos."

Dunmore did rather resemble a contented little mole, complete with large, round spectacles. She wasn't willing to be distracted, however. "I don't need a nanny, Alexander."

To her surprise, Alexander let out a laugh. "Martin Neill isn't your nanny. You are his. Now, here come Clark and Apak." His eyes twinkled as his hand rested on her shoulder for a half second. "Go, enjoy. Be brilliant. And try to stay out of trouble."

Chapter 10

When the lunch hour came, and all the local workers rose up from the pit to perform their prayers and eat their meal, Saffron took advantage of the temporarily empty site to take a more leisurely look at the ruins. She was not alone in this idea, for several of the archaeology contingent joined her. Not to mention Martin Neill was still trailing her like a lost puppy.

It was perhaps not accurate to call it a pit, as all the crew did, she thought as she stepped carefully over discarded picks and brushes. It was more like a very rough bowl comprised of twenty-foot walls which showed the striations of its history. Dirt revealing the white roots of the faded grass sat atop a layer of irregular rocks, which preceded stones placed by human hands. Those stones formed walls, which were interrupted every five feet or so by pillars jutting out from the uniform surface. It was from these pillars that the first three arches grew, the ones rebuilt by the locals to demonstrate what the stoa would have looked like. Mr. Apak said this stoa extended all the way to the far side of the field, connecting to the basilica. Saffron could see it in her mind: dozens of these arches creating a passageway, the glaring sun striping the ground with their shadows.

The trench—but that word wouldn't do either—extended some forty yards to the north, and several areas branched off of it. The first market stall, where her wares had been discovered, was found just next to the rough stairs constructed to allow entry into the pit. Halfway down the length of the pit, they'd uncovered something the archaeologists decided was a stair, suggesting the location of one of the cisterns Clark and Apak had mentioned. From the talk about her, that was of some interest. But she moved on from it, as she didn't particularly want to spend her lunch hour peering down at a single rectangular piece of stone in the midst of hard-packed dirt.

She left the cluster of archaeologists—which luckily did not include Clark—and wandered to the far end of the pit, where the most work was happening to dig out the second market stall. Martin dawdled near the archaeologists' mysterious step, and when she glanced at him, he looked away quickly as if embarrassed. He'd done that most of the morning, looking anxious to be helpful yet equally anxious whenever she spoke to him.

Sighing, she idly examined the tools laid down randomly in the dirt and the section of wall they'd been digging into. At the bottom, a stone was lodged in the compacted earth, surely one of the stones that made up a fallen arch, given the perfection of its angled edge.

After a while, she gave up on trying to make out anything from the dirt. The others must have decided it was time to down a quick meal before work resumed, for the pit was now silent and empty save for her and Martin. They ought to go eat, too.

"Don't touch the wall," she murmured when Martin pressed himself up against the wall to let her pass.

"Oh!" He leaped away into the wall nearly into her and caused her to knock against a toolbox, which clanged loudly as a pick fell from where it rested on the edge into the metal basin.

Grimacing, she planted a hand on the wall to keep from falling.

"Don't touch that," snapped a voice.

Martin's rounded eyes met hers. "Oh no, I am sorry—"

"It's fine," Saffron muttered, straightening up to see Clark watching her from the entrance to the first stall. "I wasn't touching the wall intentionally, Mr. Clark."

"Intentionally or not," he said loudly, "you might destroy something important, just as I feared." He stepped away from the stall toward the steps. "I hesitate to tell you, since you plainly don't know how to handle yourself at an archaeological site, but I've found something that you might find interesting in one of the little nooks carved into the walls inside there."

Despite herself, Saffron perked up. "What is it? Will you show me?"

"Oh no, not now. I've worked up quite an appetite," he drawled, already walking up the steps. "Some of us have actually done work today, you know."

She ground her teeth together to prevent herself from retorting. She *had* done work this morning. She'd made preliminary sketches of the stall, the pit, and the vessels they were to open that afternoon, which he would have known, had he not wandered off an hour after they'd settled into work. She'd seen him hanging around in the shade of a tent when she'd been standing in the sun to make her sketches.

Clark had disappeared. She looked longingly into the stall. Though the mostly underground state made her skin crawl, she was eager to see what it was Clark had found.

A loud grumble interrupted her thoughts. She turned to Martin, who looked like he wished he could sink right down into the dirt.

"I-I beg your pardon," he stammered, pressing a hand to his stomach.

"It's all right," she said quickly, "I'm hungry, too. Let's go to the tent to eat."

"But . . ." He looked at the stall guiltily. "Shouldn't we see what Mr. Clark found?"

Would it be better or worse to look at it now? If she did, Clark would likely say she'd damaged whatever it was. This might be a ploy to get her to inadvertently break some artifact. But what good would that do Clark? He'd benefit far more from intact pieces, not broken ones, even if it would damage her reputation.

On the other hand, Clark would probably proclaim her a coward, or say by not looking at whatever he'd found without him meant she didn't believe in her own abilities.

She didn't know what would be worse. But between herself and Martin, she was sure she could manage not to ruin it.

She grinned at Martin. "Let's take a quick look. Light that lamp?"

Martin snatched up the lamp sitting on the last stair, fumbled for matches from his pocket, and lit it. She allowed him to go into the stall first, and certainly not because stepping into the dim space gave her the shivers. She refused to be frightened. They were not even properly underground, she told herself.

Within sat several large carved stones, set aside and numbered with chalk, likely for later reconstruction. The walls were packed dirt, the ceiling reinforced with wood beams. This room had been the first they'd uncovered, and so many feet had passed through, the floor was quite even.

It was that reason that, as Saffron looked around at the walls, she realized Clark couldn't have actually discovered anything new within. Dozens of people had already examined this room.

"We might as well go up to the tent," she said sullenly.

"Oh, but look," Martin said, pointing to the wall.

There were a number of nooks, almost like shelves of stone built into the walls. Some were smooth, while others had looser stones. Martin was pointing to one that looked especially loose.

Saffron stepped forward and tugged on it. It gave, sliding out. Excitedly, she grinned at Martin. "Do you think this is it?"

"I don't know," he said, peering at the stone. "It looks ordinary, doesn't it?"

"Lift the lamp," Saffron said. "Maybe Clark meant it was behind the stone?"

Martin did, and she leaned closer to the hole the stone had left behind.

Something gleamed gold in the lamp's light. Saffron's breath caught. Carefully, she put her hand into the hole to take the treasure out. Her fingers touched something cool and textured.

She jerked her hand away with a strangled yelp.

It was not a treasure. It was a snake. And it was *not* pleased to be disturbed.

"Mr. Ashton!"

Alexander looked around for the source of his name and saw only the crew digging into the simple but delicious fare Mr. Assam had promised the crew for lunch. The rice, fish, and roasted vegetables could not have been more welcome after the morning on-site, though he heard a number of grumbles about eating sitting on rugs spread over the ground.

A ripple of interest went through the assembly as Martin Neill came dashing into the shade of the mess tent, looking a little wild.

"Neill?" Alexander hailed him, and the boy scrambled over to him, nearly tripping over Kent to get to him.

"Mr. Ashton, where is Mr. Dunmore?" Martin asked, dark eyes shifting over the crew. "I need him to come down to the first stall right away."

Alexander swallowed a sigh. "You don't have to report every reptile you spot to him."

"It's not that—it's a viper!"

That got the attention of the dozen or so crew members sitting on the ground around them.

"What? A viper?"

"Where?"

"Someone grab a shovel—"

Annoyed the assistant had stirred up a building uproar, Alexander put a hand on Neill's shoulder and pushed him from the tent. "What's going on?"

"It's a viper, sir," he panted. Sweat trickled from his brow. "It's down in the stall. Miss Everleigh sent me for Mr. Dunmore—"

"What?" Alexander snapped.

Neill flinched at his harsh tone. His voice dwindled as he spoke. "S-she sent me for Mr. Dunmore, because he'd know how to catch it . . ."

Struggling for patience, he asked, "And where is Miss Everleigh?"

"In the stall," Neill whispered.

"Find Dunmore." And then he was jogging to the pit and down the steps.

He found her in the stall, lit by a lamp she held up and away from her body at an odd angle.

Her look of expectation fell to dismay when he entered. "Martin couldn't find Dunmore?"

"He said there's a viper down here," Alexander said, coming to a stop as he remembered if there was a viper, he ought to pay attention to where he was walking.

"Well, yes," she said, "that's why we need Dunmore. Anyone else would likely just kill the snake. But Dunmore should see to it, to make sure no one gets hurt. Including the snake."

"If there is a viper," he ground out, "why are you still in this room?"

"Someone had to make sure it didn't slither away and hide in some crack, only to bite someone later." She said it like it was obvious.

"Where is it?"

She wiggled the lamp, which she was now supporting with two hands. "It's in an alcove behind the lamp. Martin suggested we could use it to block it from getting away."

Alexander decided not to say something like *Why isn't Martin Neill holding the lamp, then?* and instead came forward to take the lamp from her, not moving it from where it hung in the air.

Saffron sighed with relief as her arms dropped to her sides. "Thank you."

Footsteps thundered down the steps of the pit, and a moment later, Dunmore rushed into the room followed by two locals armed with shovels and a bucket.

Dunmore came forward, his round face bright with excitement and his hands clutching a metal rod with a hook at the end. "What have we here, then? Neill said we've got a viper! I didn't expect to find one here in the agora!"

The assistant chose that moment to careen into the room with a specimen cage.

"Ah, good!" Dunmore waved the hook at Alexander. "Step aside, then, Ashton, and let's see this little beauty!"

The Turks set down the bucket and raised their shovels. Dunmore glared at them. "None of that, now. Put those down."

The Turks looked at each other. Dunmore looked at Alexander. "Tell them to put the shovels down. I don't want them harming my specimen."

"It isn't a bad idea to be prepared in case—"

Dunmore's mouth fell open. "No one is going to be hitting any of my specimens with a shovel!"

Neill looked between Alexander and Dunmore before saying brightly, "I'll get Mr. Banks." He dashed back out of the room.

Dunmore turned back to the Turks. Loudly, he said, "Put the shovels down!"

Next to Alexander, Saffron sighed. "I really didn't mean for this to turn into a circus."

But the sound of more feet coming down the steps told Alexander the real circus was about to begin. Neill had apparently summoned not only Banks to translate, but also Dr. Henry and Mr. Hayrettin. They packed into the tiny stall, pressing Saffron into his side.

"What's all this about?" asked Dr. Henry.

"There's a snake," Alexander said.

"A viper!" Martin added.

"Tell these men they will not be harming the snake," Dunmore told Banks.

Banks, who looked on the verge of laughter despite the fact he was tucked up against the wall, his head nearly brushing the ceiling, spoke to the Turks.

This led to an argument that lasted all of one minute, involving the two locals, Banks, and Hayrettin, who tried to gesticulate but couldn't, being pressed between the locals and Banks. Martin Neill was saying something to Saffron, and Dunmore was trying to speak over everyone about the potential importance of an urban specimen of viper. Meanwhile, Alexander's arm was starting to burn from holding the lamp up.

The last straw was when Clark appeared in the door, and with a barely concealed grin, asked, "May I be of some assistance?"

"Everyone out," Alexander called, silencing the argument. "Except Dunmore. Neill, give me that specimen cage."

To his relief, everyone filed out of the stall. Saffron gave him a sympathetic look from the open door, where she crowded around with the rest of the group.

Eagerly, Dunmore came forward, hook at the ready. Alexander slowly removed the lamp from before the gap in the wall, and Dunmore stepped forward to fish the snake out.

Alexander held his breath as the creature was extracted. It was small, but a small viper could still hurt someone badly.

But something was strange about the twisting body of the snake. It looked as if the bottom two-thirds of its body had been dipped in paint.

Dunmore scowled, swinging around to the door. "You said this was a viper!"

Saffron blinked. "I—"

"This is *Platyceps najadum.*" He lifted his hook where the snake writhed. "A whip snake!"

"Is it dangerous?" Alexander asked, wary of how insecure the animal looked, dangling from the hook.

"They do produce venom, but this species never developed fangs—" Dunmore squinted at the snake. "This—this is the same bloody one I caught earlier today! Neill! What the devil have you been doing with my specimens!"

Alexander couldn't see past the group to Martin Neill, but he imagined the boy looked aghast. The rest of the group grumbled as they dispersed, apparently dissatisfied there wasn't actually any dangerous animal at hand.

"Put it in here," Alexander told Dunmore, and once the creature was settled into the cage, Alexander was able to get a better look at it. Its head and the first few inches of its body were light brown, with darker spots on its sides. The rest of the body was a ruddy tan, uninterrupted by pattern. For anyone glancing into a dark cranny in the stone wall, it would appear to be a different kind of snake.

Dunmore took the specimen cage and muttered about wasting his time and mishandling his specimens. Just outside the stall, Clark was speaking to Martin Neill, who was looking at the ground, clearly crestfallen. Saffron stood several feet away, looking thoughtfully at them.

"Chin up, lad," Clark was saying to Neill. "Not your fault the girl doesn't know a viper from a harmless little worm."

"But I—"

"He's right," Saffron interrupted. "I didn't realize the snake wasn't a viper. I'm happy to be wrong, in this case."

Clark betrayed surprise for a half second before giving her a condescending smile. "Don't worry, Miss Everleigh. You'll soon learn very little we will encounter on this expedition will be cause for putting up such a fuss. You don't want to be interrupting the entire crew every time a little snake crosses your path. People will think you're not up for field work."

"Of course," Saffron said. "I do wish you would have warned us about the snake before you sent me into the stall. You were coming out of it just before we went inside. You must have seen it, since you recommended we examine the walls' alcoves." She tapped a finger to her chin. "But perhaps you'd forgotten that was where you'd seen the snake, considering I saw you standing outside the tent with Dunmore's specimens earlier."

Alexander glared at Clark.

"That sounds like you're trying to make an accusation," Clark said with the hint of a smile.

"I'm not *trying* to make an accusation—"

"You have no sense of humor." He shook his head. "I can't help it if you lost your head over a harmless little snake. You even had Neill with you."

Saffron's mouth hung open. "It is venomous—"

"It doesn't have fangs," Clark said, enunciating each word. "Surely you heard Dunmore say that just now."

"That doesn't mean someone couldn't be harmed by it."

Clark waved a hand lazily. "No one *was* harmed. It's a bit of fun."

Alexander cut in before either of them could provoke the other more. "Clark, you shouldn't have taken one of Dunmore's specimens, even a nonlethal one, especially not for a joke. We are here to do work."

Clark glanced meaningfully between Alexander and Saffron. "Right. *Work*." He laughed softly as he strode past them to the stairs. "I'll be sure to remind you both of that, should you forget."

He disappeared over the top, still chuckling.

Saffron's face was red, and not just from the heat of midday. Fists clenched, she stomped up the steps after Clark. Was she angry at just Clark, or Alexander, too, for how poorly he'd handled that?

He pushed his hair back, frustration churning in his chest. The only way it could have gone worse was if the snake actually had been a viper.

Chapter 11

The rest of the day passed with far less excitement. That would have been a good thing, but for the fact Saffron had gotten a look inside the vessels from the market stall.

Rather than the excitement she'd anticipated, she felt very little when she looked down at the preserved botanicals from the vessel that Clark carefully set down on the tray before her. He'd been very nearly a perfect gentleman the entire time they had worked together alongside the fellow from Istanbul University. Banks and Mr. Apak had both sat with them in the tent, anticipating a language barrier that proved not to be too significant. The one time Clark had made a snide comment about her abilities, Banks had interrupted him, asking him to speak up so he could translate for the others. Clark had shrugged it off, and Saffron had sent Banks an appreciative smile.

"Good work today," Banks told her when they were finished, and the Turkish scholar had departed the dig site.

"And you," she told him with genuine appreciation. "I'm terribly impressed you know the words for all those herbs. I can't imagine cloves and coriander come up often in the historical texts you study."

"They don't, but they do come up often in cooking," he said, ducking his head so he didn't hit it on the tent's flaps as they exited. "And I'm nothing if not serious about food."

Saffron ended the day with a strange mixture of relief, disappointment, and the sort of pleasant exhaustion one experienced at the end of a long day of physical activity.

The evening, too, was unremarkable, apart from the crew's seemingly collective decision to tease her about the snake. Not one, but three of the men pointed at the floor at her feet to warn her of a viper as she circulated the parlor after dinner that evening.

The jest continued into the morning, where one of the historians, a crony of Clark's, had stopped her lifting the lid off the tray of eggs.

"Watch out!" he cautioned before pulling the lid away slowly. He let out a gusty sigh of relief and revealed the eggs to her. "Oh, I thought there might have been a snake under there!" He guffawed as he walked away, along with the others at the breakfast buffet.

It was a relief, then, to spend the day in the tent, organizing the materials from the urns. She and Martin sorted the bits of preserved plants with tweezers until she had a neatly organized selection of leaves, flowers, stems, seeds, and even roots for seven different plants. Even with Martin's restless company, it was pleasant to sink into the sort of meditative menial work she was used to. The day passed quickly, and the next, and she was almost disappointed when she came to the end of it the next morning. She'd enjoyed keeping largely away from the rest of her team, except Alexander, of course. They'd barely spoken, apart from greetings, farewells, and check-ins in his capacity as her team leader. He was busy in the evenings, speaking to Dr. Henry about the day's progress and difficulties, or being pressed for his company by the other men. She didn't want to hold him back from socializing, and her presence always seemed to put a damper on their conversations.

She understood. These men were used to being off on their own, outside the usual expectations. Free, in a sense.

She envied them their freedom. They walked about in their shirtsleeves, sweat on their brows and beards on their chins, uncaring of their appearances. A fair number didn't bother returning to the hotel for dinner, deciding instead to remain in the *kemeraltı* after work concluded at the agora. Saffron had not yet worked up the courage to do so herself, though her curiosity grew by the day. As did the sense that she was wasting time, somehow. That she was not getting all she could out of her first experience on an expedition.

She might have tempered her expectations while awaiting news of who would be going on the expedition, but once she'd learned she would be spending the autumn in the Mediterranean with her fiancé, she'd spent the summer in almost feverish anticipation. There would be work—new and important and fascinating—but there would also be a new culture, and an entirely new city laid out before her. Her romantic heart, more influential than ever with the promises of the marriage to come, dreamed of evening strolls through dusty streets, stolen kisses in the shadows, secret smiles across work tables, even a daring dip in the sea.

Not to mention a role reversal she'd rather looked forward to: as the one with experience in this area of the world, Alexander would be *her* guide in adventure. She'd seen hints of the daring young man he must have been before the war and the injury that occasionally still bothered him in mind and body. She was keen to draw him out. A man of discipline and routine Alexander may be, but his eyes lit up when he spoke of travel. After just a few days in this new place, she'd seen him come alive in ways she'd never seen in the staid halls of the university. It was magnetic, yet she never seemed to have the time to explore this new facet of attraction.

It made her quite tetchy, made worse by the fact she felt an idiot for expecting an expedition with a lot of scientists and historians to be a grand romantic adventure. She'd felt stupid often enough without her own brain's betrayal.

The rest of the week passed in a mixture of boredom and dust as Saffron waited for more to be revealed in the agora. She stepped in to help the other researchers when she could, usually by sketching, as she'd proven to be the most apt artist in the crew. She liked to draw, but it occasionally felt like secretarial work. Something assigned to her in the same manner she'd been told to make a tea tray, as if it were obviously her job. But it was better than falling prey to the afternoon slump that many of the crew—local and from the university—fell into soon after lunch. Autumn on the Aegean coast was a far cry from London in October. It was more like summer when the heat of midday hit, when the sun baked the earth and the sky became as blue as she'd ever seen. She'd squint down at her sketchpad, the white of the paper hurting her eyes, and draw out quick lines of carved stones or interesting layers of rock for whomever asked it while most of the workers and researchers retreated to the tent for tea and a sweet someone had purchased from the market, or a nap.

The rhythm of work was broken only by brief sparks of amazement. Coins were found in the dirt, uneven rounded metal pieces with faces pressed into them. They were passed around at lunch as the archaeologists and historians battled over whether they were minted in 655 BC or 675 BC. A vase was unearthed, then a piece of a statue that Clark theorized was a sign the rest might be soon uncovered. Even he was unable to pretend at ennui at the discoveries, even if he continued to be obnoxious.

Later in the week, the morning hum of the city and gentle tap-tapping of the excavation was broken by a cry from the pit. Alexander, who'd been sitting next to Saffron at a table in the tent to see her progress on the urn's contents, rocketed from his seat and toward the pit. Saffron followed.

Shouts in Turkish and English collided in the dusty air, and the site went from mellow to chaotic in a minute. A line was forming between the pit and the field. Locals and crew alike began passing wooden poles down the line toward the pit.

Dr. Henry came barreling across the field from the south gate. When he drew near, he tore out of his jacket and tossed aside his hat. He was shouting instructions before he'd even gotten to the edge of the pit. "Move aside! Let me through."

A moment later, Mr. Hayrettin came jogging over. "Dr. Henry, you must allow . . ." He, too, disappeared into the pit.

"Well, this is quite something," said a low, arch voice.

Mrs. Henry had meandered to her side, Mrs. Demirel following. Mrs. Henry wore a pristine white linen suit, smoked lenses, and a smirk, Mrs. Demirel wore a worried grimace and long-sleeved yellow frock that looked more appropriate for English spring than Turkish autumn. At her side, her husband spoke to one of the local guides, and Mrs. Demirel seemed to be doing all in her power to avoid looking at the man.

"Er, yes," Saffron said to Mrs. Henry, eyes drawn back to the men. The line had collapsed, and many of the men were edging toward the pit, looking unsure if they should, or could, go down to help or gawk at whatever had happened.

"We might as well get comfortable waiting," Mrs. Henry said. "We won't be allowed to miss anything truly important, I'm sure." She turned to Saffron. "How is your own research progressing?"

"It's going well, thank you," she answered, and furnished a few details about the herbs she'd been examining.

Mr. Demirel stumped closer to the pit. Mrs. Demirel hurried after him, looking as if she would protest, but was waved away by her husband.

"Join us, Mrs. Demirel," Mrs. Henry said. "Miss Everleigh, won't you show us some of your own work? I trust we don't have to descend into that madness to see it."

Saffron obliged, feeling rather silly to be showing bits of dried leaves to the ladies when there was clearly something much more exciting afoot. When Mrs. Henry noticed her sketches, she asked to see more, which led to her asking to see the spot from which Saffron had sketched a particularly good vista of the dig site.

"What exactly do you plan to do with the information you've discovered about the herbs?" Mrs. Henry asked as they trooped into the tall grass of the field.

"I believe learning about their preservation will tell us more about the ways they used the herbs. Different methods might reveal if a leaf was intended to be brewed into a tea or ground into a powder, for example."

"And that relates to your other work?" Mrs. Henry asked. "I understand you've made something of a name for yourself at the university as a poisons expert."

"Oh," Saffron began awkwardly, "well, I don't know about that. My other research does include poisonous plants . . . and this does relate, in a roundabout sort of way. I suppose it may seem unrelated, since the plants in the urns have been more gastronomical and medicinal."

Mrs. Henry paused, peering at Saffron from over her smoked lenses. "I read your application. Your study proposal mentioned something about searching for remnants of henbane, belladonna. Those are poisonous. Why not speak about those?"

Saffron was still taken aback to learn Mrs. Henry had read her application. "Well, I . . ."

"It could be that you believe I lack enough knowledge about your field of study, or indeed, this field"—she nodded to the literal field they stood in—"to have any interest or potential for real conversation about your work." She set off again through the grass. "Or you might think to be coy with your plans. That is fair, in this climate."

As she trotted to keep up, Mrs. Demirel looked between Saffron and Mrs. Henry as one might watch a tennis match if one was desperately concerned about the outcome.

Mrs. Henry smiled back at Saffron. "Academics, you know, are terribly competitive. Secrets kept are studies published, or so my dear husband has told me."

Unsure if she was being teased, shamed, or challenged, Saffron said nothing, and found herself naming the plants they walked over in the sooth, unconscious manner of a botanist. It was mostly species of grass she'd learned on arrival, but her eyes caught on a cottony tuft trapped in spiny bracts, and she smiled, comforted by the familiar plant.

She threw her arm out just in time to catch Mrs. Demirel before she trod on the milk thistle. "I wouldn't step on that," she cautioned, but Mrs. Demirel scrambled away, clawing at Saffron's arm.

"A snake!" she cried, her eyes wild as she looked about the now trampled grass. Then her scrambling abruptly stopped. "Oh, but it's just s—" She glanced at Saffron, then back down at the thistle. "I actually don't know what that's called."

Surely, Mrs. Demirel wasn't poking fun at her, too. Saffron exhaled, telling herself to stop hearing insult in every word. "It's *Silybum marianum,* milk thistle." And as Mrs. Henry was looking at her with an arched brow, added hesitantly, "The seeds have been used to ease stomach and liver troubles. But it would be quite unpleasant to step on."

Mrs. Demirel was staring down at the plant with an abstracted frown.

"Did it scratch you?" Saffron asked her, peering down at Mrs. Demirel's canvas Mary-Janes, not an ideal shoe to be walking a field or a dig site in.

She shook her head, flashing her a quick, strained smile. "No, not at all. Just, it's such a strange-looking thing, with all those spikes, isn't it? But there are more flowers here, aren't there? More pleasant ones? What about that one?" She pointed to a small flower peeking between two discarded, overgrown rocks.

Its thin petals were palest purple, the color of clouds at sunrise, and crested with long stamens of gold. "Oh!" Saffron hurried over to crouch by the plant. "This is meadow saffron!"

"Meadow . . . saffron?" Mrs. Henry repeated with a smile playing at her red lips.

Too pleased to wonder if mockery was forthcoming, she traced one delicate petal with a finger. How could she have missed it during her rambles around the site? "*Colchicum autumnale.* It's not the source of the spice, that is *Crocus sativus.*"

Mrs. Henry peered down at the little flower. "Is this one edible, like saffron?"

"Not at all. It's poisonous, too." She had the exact information about meadow saffron, along with dozens of other species she'd predicted finding in the agora's stores, stashed away in a notebook or one of the textbooks she'd brought with her. She vaguely recalled meadow saffron was used for joint pain. "Though, like many poisonous plants, it can be used medicinally. But I certainly wouldn't recommend taking a bite out of it."

"Cynthia!"

Dr. Henry's voice was so loud, it carried from the edge of the pit, which Saffron hadn't noticed they'd ventured so far from. They made their way back across the field, and found the flurry of movement had ebbed, but the excitement had not.

Dr. Henry stood at the center of it, hands braced on his hips, covered in dust and his clothing stained with sweat. He watched his wife's approach with a gleam in his eyes and a smirk on his hard face.

"Cynthia," he growled, "come here."

Mrs. Henry shot Saffron a quick grin. "Yes, darling."

He led his wife down the steps to the pit with all the care of a knight guiding his lady queen.

Wakefield walked by, hefting a large crate. "Had a nice stroll through the flowers, did you?" he sneered between huffs.

"Evaluating the local landscape is part of my research, yes," she said stiffly.

She'd have left it at that, but Mrs. Demirel decided to speak up. "Do you enjoy plants, too, Mr. Wakefield?"

He grinned. "I enjoy the ones I can eat and smoke, ma'am."

"Oh, you shouldn't eat the ones Miss Everleigh showed us," Mrs. Demirel said, deadly serious. "Even the charming little meadow saffron is dangerous. Isn't that right, Miss Everleigh?"

Wakefield's eyes glittered at her. "Meadow *saffron?*"

Saffron wouldn't have minded if Mrs. Demirel's timidity had been more pronounced just then. "Yes. It is a local species here," she said with as much unbothered dignity she could manage, knowing this was going to be used to mock her later.

Alexander had appeared over the edge of the pit, and waved her over. "Excuse me," she told Wakefield and Mrs. Demirel, and went to him.

The interior of the pit itself had been cleared away of most of the crew, save for a handful of people in the middle of the trench.

Mr. Hayrettin stood with a few of the Turkish guides and a few crew members. Alexander was grinning when she reached him at the bottom of the steps. His cheeks were ruddy and sweat streaked the dust clinging to his skin. Utterly distracted, she followed the progress of a droplet as it trickled from his temple to his jaw and down his neck to disappear into the parted collar of his rumpled shirt.

She swallowed hard, and forced her eyes back to his. His smile had faded, leaving behind a rather hungry expression.

"Ashton!"

Dr. Henry's bark drew their attention. He stood in a crooked arch of mismatched wood built into the wall. Saffron blinked. That doorway had not been there yesterday.

"Take a look," Henry said. His gruff tones couldn't hide his delight.

"What happened?" Saffron asked as she followed Alexander closer.

"The wall they were working on collapsed inward," he said over his shoulder. "It was partially hollow inside. Look."

With wonder, Saffron peered inside the arch. There was only a few feet of space immediately within the door, the rest blocked by loose dirt and rock. Her eyes caught on the edge of one of the piles of rubble and what it covered. Or rather, what had been uncovered.

"Oh," she gasped, and pressed her hands to her mouth.

There were three rows of urns, just like the ones she'd opened. She could see at least seven, and if the shelves on which they sat was any indication—

"This room might hold dozens of vessels," Alexander told her quietly.

She tore her gaze away from urns. "That's amazing," she whispered. It promised that the study she'd set out to do would actually be possible.

Alexander reached into a pocket and retrieved a clean handkerchief before carefully swiping it over her mouth. She could feel the grit she'd left behind from her dirty hands pressing against it a moment before, but she got the feeling this gesture was more tender than simply clearing away dirt.

He smiled at her. "It is amazing. I can't wait to see what you discover in here."

And for the first time since setting foot on the boat to Turkey, she felt the same.

Chapter 12

The thrill of the new room's discovery gave new life to the expedition team. Alexander hadn't realized how much the men were already flagging. He suspected it was because they felt like guests rather than having ownership of the site and its finds—which, of course, they did not. He struggled to remember that himself occasionally.

Protocols put into place by the Turks had to be followed. They wanted to preserve the agora as well as possible—a dictate most of the crew could appreciate—and that meant going slowly, carefully. Each bucket of dirt was sieved and washed. Every bit of carved rock and artifact was to be photographed, sketched, measured, and recorded into multiple places.

The new room was dubbed the storeroom, and it had soon been revealed there was an additional space off the back. The potential for what was in that room was thrilling, but they had already waited nearly a full week to have access to it. Alexander wanted to crack open the new vessels right away, for his own research and for Saffron's. She hadn't been flagging, not like some of the other fellows who complained of the lack of things to do while they awaited the storeroom. She kept herself busy, so busy it felt like days since they'd gotten the chance to say more than a few words to each other. When the rest of the crew was resting after lunch, she was on the site, sketching and exploring, usually with Martin Neill. The other fellows occasionally joked his fiancée paid more attention to the boy than him. It was easy to laugh off, which was enough to move conversation onto a different topic.

That topic, more often than not, was the latest artifact find. They were coming quickly now that dirt was being removed constantly to clear the storeroom. It was mostly broken bits of vessels and the occasional coin, but an assistant had found a fragment of a bracelet believed to be of the fourth century just yesterday, and had been smacked on the back in congratulations so many times that he must have been black and blue.

Dr. Henry, Alexander had noticed, tended to spend a good deal of time staring down at the artifacts smugly, clearly pleased the expedition was going according to plan.

Alexander found him there at the artifact table two days after the stall had been opened.

"You wanted to see me?" he prompted Dr. Henry as he approached.

Dr. Henry's face showed no trace of smugness now. His icy blue eyes flashed with anger instead. "Look," he growled, jabbing a finger at the artifacts.

Alexander did. But he didn't see what Henry clearly thought was obvious. "What is it?"

"Something is missing," Henry hissed.

Surprised, Alexander looked harder at the objects on the dusty table. Most had little labels, like "oil lamp shard, 3B, believed sixth century, Clark" and "candle holder, 5C, clay, Wakefield" to indicate where in the agora it had come from, who had pulled it out of the dirt, and any other details they had ascertained or guessed about it. A dozen pieces were laid out, and now he was carefully looking, Alexander didn't see the coins that had been unearthed the previous day.

"The coins?" Alexander asked. They had caused quite a stir among the crew; the second-century coins pressed with an image of Zeus battling Athena had thus far only been found near Athens.

Already, the historians were debating how they could have arrived in Smyrna.

Dr. Henry glared around the empty tent. "Keep your voice down. The moment the Turks hear something is missing, they'll put up a huge fuss. Our presence here depends upon all the artifacts remaining here." He wiped his brow with the back of his hand and shook his head. "They'll turn up soon, I know it."

From the uneasy way he drummed the table, Alexander doubted he truly thought that. Otherwise, he wouldn't have pointed out the coins were missing to begin with. But Dr. Henry had wanted him on this expedition to keep a cool head, so a cool head he would have. "I'll keep an eye out for them."

"What's the status of the storeroom?" Dr. Henry asked.

"Should be ready by tomorrow," he reported. "They're covering it up now in preparation for lunch."

Despite having people in and out of the storeroom for days, they still took the precaution of covering it with a large, heavy wooden door. They had the cellar left to excavate, and no one wanted to risk someone pillaging any goods still left inside, or be crushed by a cave-in when there was still structural work to do.

"Good, good," Dr. Henry muttered, eyes back on the artifacts. "Eyes open, Ashton."

Alexander took that to be his dismissal. He left the tent, immediately scanning the field for Saffron's tan duster. He wanted to see her. Perhaps they could go into the *kemeraltı* for lunch today. He'd been neglecting taking advantage of the opportunities here, like showing her around. It would do them both good to get off-site and have the chance to talk.

Hunger, heat, and a red-faced Martin Neill dogged Saffron all the way across the field and to the pit. None of them were urgent enough to prevent her searching out the man who'd been playing a game of hide-and-seek with her all day. Clark had promised to review their notes over the vessels from the first stall, but every time Saffron thought she knew where to find him, he'd apparently "just left," according to Templeton in the mess tent, an archaeology assistant working on organizing timber on the far side of the site, and Wakefield standing outside the supply tent. She and Martin had been back and forth across the field three times and had nothing to show for it but a stubbed toe and a bucket of sweat between the pair of them.

Martin nearly ran into her when she stopped abruptly at the top of the steps to the pit. "Have you seen Mr. Clark?" she asked Mr. Apak as he emerged.

The Turk mopped his brow with a handkerchief and looked at her with confusion. "Why, yes. He is below with his team."

"The biology team is working in that tent today," she said, pointing to where she'd spent half the morning waiting.

"Ah, yes," he said, nodding. "I apologize, but I mean the other team. The archaeologists. They just concluded stabilizing the cellar portion of the storeroom—"

Anger flared in her, just as hot as the sun beating down overhead. "So, he's been putting supports in all morning?" And not in any of the places the others had sent her in search of him.

"Yes," Mr. Apak said, his confusion clear.

"I see," she said, and forced a more pleasant tone. "Thank you very much, Mr. Apak."

She passed by him to descend into the pit.

With so much sunlight streaming down into the wide channel of the pit, she'd felt no trepidation about being down there. Especially with so many workers about, it didn't remind her at all of the dark, dank places she feared.

She squeezed past a dozen men wielding various tools until she reached the cluster at the far end of the pit. They were all sweating and dirty, and each one looked immensely pleased.

"Mr. Clark?" Saffron called.

He turned to her, and his eyes lit with unpleasant humor. "Tracked me down at last, I see."

"You said we would be going over the notes—"

"Naturally, you've come to see what real work looks like around here. You can be the first of the rest of the crew to see inside the new cellar." He stepped into the stall and looked back at her with a crooked grin. On another man, it would have been charming. On him, it looked like mockery. "Allow me to show you." He glanced behind her. "And your little puppy, too."

She refused to react. "I would be happy to view the cellar, but we are supposed to prepare to examine the first set—"

He clicked his tongue dismissively. "But, of course, if you're too—"

"If you wouldn't *mind* allowing me to finish speaking," she said over him. "We need to review our notes and prepare for the new vessels. If you cannot be bothered to prepare to examine artifacts, then I will find someone else to assist me. I'm sure there are many here who would like to make discoveries."

She glanced around at the others, clearly milling around to overhear their argument. They looked pointedly away from her. Heat scorched her already overheated cheeks.

Clark gave her a pitying smile. "I doubt any of my colleagues want to play with your little jars when there is an entire site to explore. Now, do you want to see inside, or not?"

Saffron swallowed. It was obvious she had to go inside. "Very well."

He smirked. "Don't allow me to convince you. If you're too uneasy to go inside . . ."

"Lead the way."

Clark retreated into the stall, shadow falling over his face. She stepped inside after him.

Dirt had been cleared from the floor and shelves, illuminated by a single lamp left burning on the floor in one corner. Three rows of vessels sat there, waiting to be opened in the coming days.

"Well, go on," Clark said to her before turning to Martin. He began questioning Martin about his knowledge of the agora and its history in the manner of a tutor quizzing a student. It soon gave way to something of a lecture.

It was a pity, Saffron thought as she carefully stepped across the uneven floor toward the cellar, that Clark was so rude. His speech was insightful, amusing, and had it not come from him, Saffron would have enjoyed it.

Despite this lively academic commentary in the background, the cool, humid air settled heavily on her, clinging to the damp patches on her back and collar. The gloom and smell of musty damp burrowed into her senses, leaving behind holes for fear to seep in.

"Steady on," she whispered impatiently to herself. She went to the corner to retrieve the lantern. The moment it was in her hands, she felt better, and willed herself deeper into the stall.

Though the back room was little more than a closet, there was just enough room to step inside. Memories of being encased by dirt washed over her, and, heedless of protocol, she planted a hand on the wall to ground herself while old fear rose up within her.

The past few months she'd struggled to keep herself from pushing away memories of her mother, Bill, and the ice cellar at Ellington. Burying them would only make them grow into fully fledged fears, and she had no desire to connect her idea of her mother to bloodshed and terror. It was the reason she'd ensured she regularly spoke to her mother, despite the strain on their relationship from all Saffron had learned of her mother and her secrets. It was the reason she and Alexander had returned to Ellington in June, to have lunch with her mother and grandparents—albeit an awkward lunch—and share their vague plans for their wedding. She was trying to mend things with them all, her mother especially, though she'd much rather retreat into her life in London. Just as she was trying now, standing in this tiny, underground room, to mend something inside her that felt broken.

A strange sound, a heavy scraping noise, reverberated in the space. She peered around warily. Dust from the ceiling drifted down, catching in the light of the lantern. The thin white glow of daylight was fading, and a massive *thunk* cut it off entirely. Panicked, she stumbled from the stall's back room. Distant thunder perturbed the still air.

By God, was it a cave-in?

Her breath caught in her throat. She hurtled forward before pain exploded in her toe and she fell to the ground. There was nothing but silence and still air. The smell of cool dirt filled her senses, tinged with the tang of iron.

"No," she gasped.

Images of darkened stone steps and fog intruded into her vision. She wrapped her arms around her legs, pulling them close and clutching the fabric of her trousers so she didn't have to touch the dirt, didn't have to remind herself of the press of it all around her.

Her breath came shallow and fast. A cool voice filled her head, soft and threatening. Alexander, covered in blood. The crack of a gun. Blood seeping into the stone floor. Her mother's eyes, blank.

Saffron was trapped there, in the memory, just as surely as she was trapped in ruins two thousand miles away. And it went on, a terrible newsreel destined to repeat again and again until it warped, spinning off into variations where she was the one lying on the ground, bleeding out, then buried, then forgotten.

A rumble drew her from her fugue. Then voices.

Throat tight and dry, she managed, "Hello?"

A faint outline of light traced darkness before her. It was there only a moment before light poured inside, blinding her.

She drew back and shielded her eyes.

A familiar voice swore, and then hands were gripping her arms and pulling her upward.

"What happened?" Alexander sounded horribly angry.

She started to speak, only to have another voice speak over her.

"I don't know, sir!" Martin Neill said plaintively.

She managed to blink several times, her eyes adjusting to the dim light. She was standing against Alexander, his arm pressing her into his side. He faced Martin, who stood at the door, eyes huge and hands worrying the edge of his hat.

"I thought she'd already left," he told Alexander. "Mr. Clark was telling me all about what he and Wakefield planned—"

"Clark led you off?" Alexander bit out.

"Yes, sir. He told the locals we were finished in the storeroom . . ." He gulped and looked at Saffron. "I'm so sorry, Miss Everleigh. This is all my fault."

Alexander jerked his chin at him. "You can go."

As disoriented as she still was, she wanted to chide Alexander for his curt dismissal. It wasn't Martin's fault, but she wasn't in any state to stand up for him, even against Alexander.

He was silent, his heart pounding hard enough she could feel it in her own chest. She pressed her forehead against his shoulder. Her lungs hadn't quite caught up to the fact she was no longer trapped in the storeroom.

"Come on," Alexander said, and gently pulled her from the room.

She walked unsteadily, using him as an anchor. Once outside in the sun-drenched pit, he paused, easing away from her. "I'm going to—you're hurt."

She looked down to where his eyes fixed on her. Her knee was bleeding. "Oh," she said stupidly. Tears flooded her eyes, blurring the red staining the knee of her trousers.

Alexander swore softly, gathering her to him again. A sob broke out of her.

He gripped her harder, and in a dark voice muttered, "I'm going to kill Clark."

Chapter 13

"I don't see what is to be done about it," Dr. Henry said, pausing in his pacing to fan his face with his hat. "Apart from telling the men to check before they block up any more doors."

"I doubt it was a local worker," Alexander said, his mouth barely moving. His anger was just barely in check. Saffron sat at one of the tables on the other side of the tent, wrapped tightly in her jacket and staring somewhat blankly at the drink in her hand. He'd never seen her in shock like this, not even after being kidnapped and concussed, finding him covered in blood, or discovering a dead body. "Neill said Clark told the locals they'd taken care of blocking it up for lunch."

Dr. Henry grunted. "Sounds like a bad bit of luck. But this . . . reaction, Ashton." He glanced over at Saffron.

Alexander silently cursed. To someone who'd never experienced shock or panic attacks, he knew exactly what her reaction would look like.

"I was assured that Everleigh could put up with danger, Ashton," Dr. Henry said. "We haven't the time to play nanny to anyone!" He glanced around them, then added in an undertone, "Another item has gone missing. That bit of chain Templeton and I dug out of the wall at 8C a few days ago. I don't know where the devil it's gone, and Hayrettin has started asking questions. That's got to take priority, not your team's hysterics! You need to get your woman in hand."

"Lawrence."

Dr. Henry grimaced. They both turned to the white-clad woman where she stood just outside the tent, her eyes as sharp and cold as her voice.

"Cynthia!" Henry said, striding into the sun and offering her his arm. "I didn't know you'd be coming for lunch."

Alexander took that as his excuse to leave. He went to Saffron.

Saffron eventually drank the tea in her glass and told him what happened, leaving unsaid why she was so shaken. Her voice was low, quiet enough the crew couldn't hear her. She didn't name Clark as the culprit, but Alexander was sure he was at the top of her suspect list. After the tea, she stood.

Alexander had opened his mouth to suggest she sit and rest, or at least eat something, but the set of her mouth told him he was going to be ignored. He followed her to where the Henrys stood. The expression of disdain on Mrs. Henry's face disappeared as she asked Saffron how the morning had gone.

"Well, thank you." Saffron gave Mrs. Henry a strained smile, nodded to Dr. Henry, and walked away.

Mrs. Henry rounded on Dr. Henry again. "Honestly, Lawrence, it wouldn't kill you to exercise an *iota* of empathy—"

"This is the field," he exclaimed. "This isn't the place for empathy. If the girl can't hack it—"

Alexander walked away, his head buzzing with frustration. If Dr. Henry wasn't going to do something about Clark's antics, which grew more and more dangerous by the moment, he would have to do something about it himself.

That night at the hotel, after bathing and dressing, Saffron sat staring into the vanity mirror in her room, the sounds of the growing party downstairs floating in through her window. The last thing she wanted to do was give Clark yet another reason to poke fun at her, but a close second was going down to dinner. She'd been too overcome with shock after Alexander helped her out of the storeroom to realize how she must have looked to the crew. Clark had been kind enough to ask her many times if she was well and what he could do to make her experience at the site less harrowing.

She'd finally snapped, and with tears burning her eyes, had told him, "Try leaving me alone. That might help."

To which he, of course, replied with false concern, "But you *were* left alone, Miss Everleigh, that's the problem."

Martin Neill had apologized to her a dozen times. Mrs. Henry had sought her out at the site, asking again about how her work was progressing, perhaps in an effort to distract her from the incident, though it only made her feel stupid yet again. And Alexander . . .

She'd only ever experienced one attack of panic before, and that had also ended with her in Alexander's arms. She was grateful he'd been there to find her again, but it didn't ease her stinging irritation with how curtly he treated Martin. Yes, he had said *she* was babysitting Martin, but it was clear Alexander held Martin partially responsible for her getting trapped in the storeroom, which he would not have had he not considered Martin to be her watcher.

She felt at odds with everyone. But it was time for dinner, and she had to make an appearance.

She rose and smoothed her dress, a dark green with black embroidery, smart and comfortable. Elizabeth would tell her to go out and give her colleagues something real to talk about. She was afraid she already had, and none of it flattering.

She frowned at her reflection before stepping into the hallway.

The quiet voice behind her made her jump. "How are you feeling?"

Saffron turned and glared at her fiancé, who clearly didn't know he was still on her wrong side. "Fine, thank you."

Alexander didn't reply, simply offered her his arm, and they made their way to the multicolored staircase. They stepped down, Saffron's ire ebbing away slightly at the sight of the twinkling lights through the mosaic globes above. She was just about to turn to Alexander and be pleasant when he put a hand over hers on his arm and said quietly, "I wanted you to know that I'm going to speak to Clark after dinner."

"No," Saffron said, "don't, Alexander."

He frowned. "I can't not say anything."

"Yes, you can. I don't have any proof he's done anything to me." Nothing she could make a real, formal complaint of, anyway. The snake incident had already been dismissed by Dr. Henry and everyone else as a harmless prank, and she couldn't prove Clark had intentionally left her in the storeroom or drugged her champagne. It was likely to only make matters worse for her if she did put up a fuss about Clark. "He won't listen, anyway."

Saffron was surprised to see Alexander's expression darken slightly, his mouth thinning to a line. "He will listen. I'm his supervisor for the next few weeks."

She withheld an impatient sigh. "He doesn't see you as his supervisor. He'll assume I sent you after him. It'll just make it worse."

"Saffron, he trapped you in a dark hole that might have collapsed on you. I have to say something."

They'd reached the bottom of the stairs. With a firm tone she hoped didn't give away her misgivings, she said, "I do not want you to speak to him about it. Please, don't say anything."

She walked toward the dining room without giving him a chance to reply. She knew his heart was in the right place, but he didn't understand. She couldn't rely on others to stand up for her. On the expedition, she had to be self-sufficient if she was ever going to win respect on her own.

Dinner was uncomfortable, but Saffron managed to get through it without sinking into her chair in the hopes of disappearing. As they had several evenings thus far, the Turkish officials had joined their party, and Saffron was invited, due to Alexander's position, to dine with them, the Henrys, and the Demirels. There was much talk of the potential discoveries in the new storeroom, and Saffron appreciated that neither of the Henrys gave her sideways glances when it came up. The only sticky point was when Hayrettin mentioned summoning historians from Istanbul University to examine the recent finds, and Dr. Henry was so abruptly negative in response that Mrs. Henry had to jump in to firmly steer the conversation into friendlier waters.

When the party broke up to join the rest of the crew, or those present at the hotel that evening, Saffron found Mrs. Henry in a chair outside in the dark garden, smoking a cigarette.

"I have been thinking about what you said, Mrs. Henry," Saffron said, sitting in the chair at Mrs. Henry's side. The other woman faced her, face softly illuminated by the light from the open windows, looking mildly interested. "Our conversation the other day has been bothering me. I certainly do not think of you as someone unable to converse about my work and science. Or any topic, really. In fact, I admire how you can speak so easily to anyone. A crew member, or the officials. I am . . ." She exhaled, feeling foolish, but determined. "I have often been considered boring."

"Boring?" Mrs. Henry repeated, looking genuinely surprised. "My dear, with your record of mischief, I doubt anyone could consider you boring. You've solved crimes and confronted criminals. Been poisoned yourself. From reading your expedition application alone, I could never consider you *boring*."

Heat crept into her face. "I have been involved with the solving of crimes," she said quietly. "But I do not tend to bring it up in conversation. And those experiences have all been rather recent. I mean, I have been told my interests are boring. Plants are well and good for most ladies, if they are blooming in a pot or vase, but it is rather unusual for another woman, one not studying at the U, to be genuinely interested in my work. I have been dismissed a good deal more than listened to, and I fear I've lost my nerve for trying."

The cynical smile Saffron remembered from her first introduction to Mrs. Henry formed on her perfectly made-up face. "Miss Everleigh, I fear you must recover it. Allow me to let you in on a secret." She did not lean forward, but she did drop her voice lower.

"Lawrence is a middling researcher, at best. I have read all his papers and I have never been particularly impressed with his discoveries. But do you know who has been published in the most journals, and lead the most expeditions in his department? It is Lawrence. He has been given opportunities—and taken them, I would never deny—because those who matter at the university and in the academic world do not care about the work." She tutted at Saffron's dismay. "They do not, and you are aware of it. They care about who puts on the best show. Yes, names on papers are important, but those who book conferences and are interviewed by newspapers and magazines or even on the radio are the people who will inspire the donors and convince them to pass over their funds. That is what they care about. *Personality*." She flicked ash from her ignored cigarette and slipped it between her lips. With smoke slithering from her mouth, she said, "And you need to think about how you present yourself. Constantly. I may not be a donor myself, but I know nearly all of them. If I were to go to lunch with Lord Cavendish or Lady Agatha Leister and they asked me where they might put their next donation, I would have nothing to say about the work of Saffron Everleigh." She took another drag from her cigarette. Her eyes glittered as she watched Saffron struggle to come up with a response. "If you want success, you must work for it. If you spend all your time crafting your papers and none on crafting yourself, you'll never truly have it."

Saffron swallowed, feeling every single one of Mrs. Henry's words. "You are right."

Mrs. Henry's brows arched sardonically, and she took another drag from her cigarette, letting Saffron sit in uncomfortable silence.

Unsure if she was answering the unspoken question, Saffron said, "I hope that by studying the preserved plants from the agora, I might get a sense of how the uses of certain plants changed over time and how their use might have influenced the evolution of the plants themselves through cultivation."

"Oh, yes?" Mrs. Henry sounded bored.

"Medicinal plants are often gathered under a single umbrella," Saffron ventured, "but the useful qualities of these species are often double-edged swords. Paracelsus said, *Dosis sola facit venenum*."

Mrs. Henry's brow puckered, then smoothed as she smiled. "Only the dose makes the poison."

Saffron nodded. "Nearly all the plants I've studied, the poisonous ones, are also used as medicines. I aspire to discovering when they shifted from solely dangerous to useful."

Mrs. Henry rose to her feet. "A good start, Miss Everleigh."

She wafted away, trailing smoke into the darkness in the direction of the hotel's lobby, leaving Saffron feeling at once vindicated and belittled. It was a curious feeling, but at least it was invigorating. Mrs. Henry made her feel as if she had something to prove, but also that she *could* prove it.

Chapter 14

The next morning, Saffron stood before the storeroom, lantern in one hand and notebook in the other.

"Are you—are you sure, Miss Everleigh?" Martin whispered at her side.

"Yes," she said firmly. "I will go inside. If I don't go now . . ." She perhaps never would. The bone-deep fear that had shackled her when she'd been trapped had not disappeared when she'd emerged. It lingered, threatening on the edges of her mind. She needed to banish it by walking back into that room.

And she wouldn't be doing it with an audience. She'd told Martin last night to be ready to go to the agora bright and early. She'd had trouble finding him until nearly eleven in the evening, when most of the party had drifted to their rooms to rest, but he agreed readily enough to be in the hotel lobby just before dawn.

This early, only three or four of the local men were on the site, as well as one of the Turkish guides who'd looked nonplussed when she and Martin showed up at the gate just as the call to prayer sounded from the mosque in the *kemeralti*. He agreed to accompany them into the pit, and now they stood, ready to go into the storeroom. With no one to tell them they couldn't go inside without an archaeologist, for that was generally the protocol, she was going to do just that.

She took three steps into the darkness, forcing air out through her nose so she wasn't immediately overtaken by the earthy smell. Her eyes traced the shelves, the vessels, the stone structures and wooden poles holding it all together.

It was fine. Really. She would just stay near the door for a minute.

Martin had already ventured deeper into the room, eager to explore on his own.

Saffron focused on her breathing, deep and slow, just as Alexander had demonstrated to her. His habit of meditation was not for her, she'd found, but the breathing method did help to settle her nerves.

"Ow!"

Opening her eyes, she saw Martin on the ground, rubbing his knees. "Are you all right?"

"Yes," Martin said breathlessly. "Just tripped on that rock there."

It was the same one she must have tripped on herself. A squarish stone set in the floor, one corner not quite level with the ground.

"They ought to fix that," Saffron said, peering around. "Someone else might trip and drop something important. Hello there?"

The Turkish guide appeared in the door, and Saffron asked him to call for a few of the workers to move the stone.

It wasn't until they had the rock nearly out of the floor that Martin asked, "Will we get into trouble for moving this without approval?"

"I hadn't thought of that," Saffron said, biting her lip. "I just figured we'd mark it and set it in the field, and the men could pack in some dirt."

They did so, managing to fill the hole and set the rock in the field just as the beginnings of the crew showed up to start work. The sky was now a cheerful blue, and sunlight streamed between the buildings of the *kemeraltı*.

Not wanting to be present when the archaeologists found they'd altered the storeroom, Saffron retreated to the field, where she looked over the relocated rock. If she was sure it was unimportant, just a fallen piece of wall or arch, it wouldn't be a problem. They'd marked it properly, after all, numbering it in the same manner that Clark had explained to their group.

She knelt to examine the pattern of the stone. Color caught her eye, surprisingly vibrant against the dirty gray rock. Had the locals already marked it? She didn't recognize the marking at all.

She looked up and caught sight of Banks striding toward the tent.

"Mr. Banks," she called to him, waving a hand.

He changed direction and approached her with a smile. "Good morning, Miss Everleigh."

"Good morning," she said quickly. "Would you mind looking at this?"

Banks crouched next to her, setting his satchel down on the ground. He removed his hat, pushed his overlong auburn hair from his eyes, and squinted at the markings. "What . . . what is this?"

He sounded rather strangled. She peered again at the markings. "You can't read it? I was hoping you could make it out. I fear I've made a mistake . . ." Her words faded as Banks sat straight up, pressing a hand to his mouth.

"This is—Miss Everleigh." He swallowed, blinking hard. Then he turned to her and gripped her arm tightly. "*Miss Everleigh.* Where is this stone from?"

"The storeroom," she said gently, easing her arm away. "It was buried in the floor and we kept tripping over it. You can read it, then?"

He shot to his feet, then sat down on the ground again, hard. "This is incredible. This is *incredible.* Yes, I can read it. I'm probably the only one here who can. This is—" Banks looked like he might start laughing or crying at any moment. "You've discovered graffiti. *Third century* graffiti."

It took some maneuvering, some bribery, and a lot of tamping down on smug smiles, but Saffron managed the revelation of the graffiti's discovery without a hitch.

Martin was the easiest to convince. Saffron explained to him that they would get into horrible trouble for ordering the removal of the graffitied stone from the storeroom, and he was ready to do anything to avoid that. The locals who had done the actual removal were also easy to convince; they didn't want to be sacked for breaking protocol. The Turkish guide, however, required a bribe. Saffron had never bribed anyone but her cousin John and Elizabeth on occasion as children, and so went about it in a clumsy way that left her several pounds poorer, but confident she wouldn't be sacked.

Banks, she decided, would be the one to take credit. He wasn't an archaeologist, but he had enough clout that she thought any trouble he might be in would be easily mitigated by the importance of the find. She certainly wasn't handing over such an incredible discovery to Clark. Banks agreed, hesitantly, both because of the lying and because it didn't give any credit to Saffron or Martin, but was too caught up in excitement to fret for long.

That evening, more secreted champagne flowed freely. Banks was toasted a dozen times, and nearly every time, he glanced guilty over at where Saffron stood with Alexander in the corner of the hotel's parlor. Perhaps Banks was regretting the lie now, but it was too late.

"Is there anything you want to tell me?" Alexander murmured.

"Hm?"

He leaned closer, lips almost on her ear. "Do you want to tell me the real story of how that stone was discovered?"

"What do you mean?" she asked in a very unconvincing tone.

"I rode in the motorcar with Banks this morning," he said quietly, "I know he did not get to the site early enough to have the stone dug out before anyone else showed up. I also know your handwriting very, very well."

That brought a blush to her cheeks, not from his words, but from how his hand had slipped around her back. A finger brushed over the thin silk of her gown at her hip. She swallowed. "If you're suggesting I was the one to mark up that stone with ancient Greek—"

"I know you were the one to mark it with the location."

"I was available to lend a hand."

"You were on the site with Banks at dawn with nobody else around?"

She couldn't help a smirk. "Are you jealous, Alexander?"

"It's not Banks I'm supposed to be worried about," he said dryly.

She turned to him, and they were so close she could count his eyelashes. "What is that supposed to mean?" He looked like he regretted his words, but Saffron certainly would not let it go. "Alexander?"

Resigned, he took her by the hand. She followed him through the open double doors leading to the lobby. There was a small alcove under the stairs, and that was where he came to a stop.

Saffron crossed her arms. "Well?"

"People are being stupid," he said.

"That isn't an explanation."

"The idiots among the crew—"

She scoffed, and he smiled slightly, softening his words. "They're making much out of Martin Neill's presence in our group."

"His presence with me, you mean."

"Yes."

"The presence *you* insisted on, in fact."

"Yes."

"And now they're saying, what? He's trailing me like a puppy because he has a—a romantic interest, or something?"

He hesitated before nodding. She narrowed her eyes. "Is that what they are saying?"

He shrugged. "I wouldn't put too much store in what they say."

"You obviously put enough store in it to bring it up."

"It was a poor attempt at a joke."

Saffron hummed in response. She found she didn't have anything to say. In fact, she was rather done with this conversation.

She had been having a good time, for once, and now the weight of her frustrations was back, squashing any bit of pleasure from the evening. She might as well go up to bed.

She pushed a smile on her lips. "Good joke. Good night." She started toward the stairs.

"Saffron . . ."

She allowed him to tug her back to him, and he took her in his arms. He pressed his lips to her neck, just below her ear. She tried not to melt against him.

"I'm sorry," he murmured. "Let me make it up to you."

That sounded promising. "How?"

"This Friday. Let me take you somewhere after we're finished at the agora," he whispered.

"Where?"

"I'll find somewhere."

"Somewhere private?"

He sighed against her neck and drew back enough to give her a sardonic look. "Probably not private enough for your liking."

She ran a hand through his hair affectionately. "Honestly, after the last few weeks, I'll take moderately private."

He looked alarmed. She grinned.

"I'm looking forward to it." She pressed one last kiss to his lips and sauntered away, suddenly feeling much more positive.

Chapter 15

Weekends were a tricky thing for the expedition crew. Muslim country that it was, Turkey observed Friday and Saturday as their version of the Sabbath. The crew had several staunch members of the church—one church or another, anyway—and took offense at the notion of working on Sunday as per the customs of the country. This left Dr. Henry in a conundrum, one he resolved by declaring the crew would decide individually which days would be their weekend, Friday and Saturday, or Saturday and Sunday. Whichever day other than Saturday would be considered a half day. The working part of the day would be devoted to writing up reports and attending to administrative duties, and the rest was left up to the crew member.

Saffron and Alexander had claimed Fridays and Saturdays as their weekend to maximize their time in the agora. Saffron's first weekend had been spent documenting her work, catching up on correspondence, and resting. This weekend, however, would be spent with Alexander, apparently, and she couldn't wait. After the uproar the graffitied stone had caused, and the subsequent mania to find more marked stones, she was glad to be finished at the agora for a few days.

He'd told her to dress comfortably for walking, which Saffron took to mean she ought to wear her low boots rather than her work boots or the heels she wore in the evenings. She donned a lightweight dress of cheerful blue cotton and a broad-brimmed hat, and she was ready to go.

Excitement bubbled inside her as she descended the stairs. They would explore the city, she guessed. It would be quiet, with many residents observing their holy day. The doors in the lobby were thrown open as usual to encourage a breeze, and Saffron spotted one of the government motorcars that ferried them up and down the mountain to the agora. A daydream overtook her, of her and Alexander venturing off along the coast, alone with the sun and fresh air and nature. More particularly, alone.

Her mind strayed to the things Elizabeth had stashed in her trunk, only to be brought back to the lobby, which was suddenly flooded with people.

Crew members emerged from the parlor, faces ranging from annoyed to buoyant.

She'd missed a meeting, it seemed.

Alexander emerged from the room alongside Templeton. Templeton looked fit to burst with excitement, while Alexander's expression was neutral. He caught sight of her and left Templeton mid-sentence.

"Change of plans," he told her, taking her by the elbow and guiding her back to the stairs.

"What's happened?"

Alexander glanced to either side and apparently satisfied none of the crew would hear him, muttered, "Henry is packing us all off to the castle ruins on Mount Pagos."

Saffron blinked. "What? Now?"

"Yes." He took her arm in his and walked her up the stairs, still speaking low. "There is concern over the location of certain items."

"Certain—? Ah, yes," Saffron said, catching on. Alexander had mentioned a coin had gone missing. "Certain items, plural?"

He nodded grimly. "The coin depicting Zeus battling Athena, and the fragment of the bracelet. Hayrettin seems to have noticed something is amiss. Henry wants our rooms cleared out so he can search them."

Saffron stumbled on a stair, and he caught her before she fell. "He's going to search our rooms?"

"Yes. So be sure to pack anything you don't want him or the Turkish officials to see. We'll be camping out at Kadifekale tonight, possibly tomorrow evening, too."

They came to a stop outside Saffron's room. On the upper levels, men opened and slammed doors and called to one another.

"What if he doesn't find anything?" she asked.

Alexander shrugged, looking pensive. "I almost hope he doesn't. I hate to think anyone on the crew would steal something from the site."

She didn't get along with many of the crew, but they were all scholars. Was it naïve to assume they had respect and enthusiasm for their expedition's goals, or respect for their hosts? Just then, Clark clambered down the stairs. He paused at the landing, taking in Saffron and Alexander standing close together just outside her bedroom door. With an unpleasant smile, he winked and disappeared down the stairs.

Yes, she decided, glaring after him, it was naïve to assume some people had any respect at all.

Saffron had never known a more perfect day. The bay was a glittering sapphire embraced by golden mountains patinaed with muted green. The city seemed so far below, though the castle ruins were only half a mile or so away from the agora. The fire-scorched buildings along the northern portion of the bay were harder to make out from here.

A breeze coasted over her heated skin, fluttering the silk scarf around her neck. It was like suspended bliss, standing atop the tower. She could almost imagine there was no dusty, tense camp waiting for her below.

She was in no hurry to return. Dr. Henry's announcement had launched the crew into a frenzy of preparations, complaints, and excitement. The process of moving the entire group from the hotel to the campsite atop Mount Pagos had been chaotic, but Dr. Henry brooked no argument. He was back to his domineering ways, ordering everyone to pack and load up the motorcars within the hour, then to erect the tents and construct camp in an equally unreasonable amount of time. Then, he sent them all off to "work," without any more instruction than that, despite the fact that the majority of the party had no relevant research to do at Kadifekale. Had Saffron not been aware of the need to search for the missing artifacts, she would have been quite put out.

Even with that knowledge and the incredible view spread out before her, she *was* rather put out. At the very least, if her plans with Alexander had been interrupted, she would have hoped he'd come and explore the ruins with her.

But no, it was Martin Neill who huffed after her as she'd climbed to the tallest point of the mountain and up the only remaining tower to look out over the city and the bay. It was Martin watching her warily from the ground, clearly biting his tongue on an admonition to be careful. The Turkish guides—or the ones who could be persuaded to join the crew at Kadifekale—had warned them the third century ruins were not well looked after, and they made no promises of the crew's safety on them. That wasn't going to stop Saffron from having a good look around.

"You ought to come take a look," Saffron called down to Martin.

He squinted up at her. "I'm not so sure—"

"It is perfectly stable." He'd watched her climb the weathered, makeshift steps someone had constructed to get to the tower, and not the one had slipped.

"Er—"

"Martin," she said sternly. "Are you truly going to spend the entire time at Kadifekale worried rocks are going to fall down around you? You'll miss everything if you don't—"

But he was climbing up to the tower now. She grinned.

"Oh my." His smile was tremulous, but his large, dark eyes sparkled as he took in the view. "It is quite something, isn't it?"

They stood atop the tower, looking out on the city and the bay. After being ignored on more than one occasion, it seemed Martin had at last learned there was no need to fill every silence with chatter.

"Thank you," he said quietly some minutes later.

"For bullying you to climb up here?"

The rosy flush on his cheeks intensified as Martin looked down at his feet. "For putting up with me. I know Mr. Ashton finds me a burden more than an asset. He only stuck me with you because you'd be nice to me."

Surprised, Saffron began to deny his unfortunately correct assumption, but they were hailed by a voice from below. They both peered over the edge of the tower—tricky, as there were only sporadic crenellations at knee-height to keep them toppling over.

"I do beg your pardon," Clark called. "I didn't mean to interrupt."

"Not at all, Mr. Clark," Martin replied, unaware of Clark's syrupy tone. "It's quite an extraordinary view up here. You ought to come up—" He put his hand on top of one of the crenellations, and the whole thing rocked to the side.

Saffron grabbed Martin by the arm, and they tumbled backward. Her hip hit the stone platform and she let out a grunt at the impact.

"Miss Everleigh!" Martin cried, and rolled to his knees, hands raised as if he'd examine her for injuries.

She rushed to her feet to show it was unnecessary. "I'm fine. We must report that to the guides immediately, it's terribly dangerous!"

They made their way down the steps—more carefully, now Saffron had been proven wrong about how sound the construction truly was—and found Clark and Wakefield lurking under the shade of one of the skinny-trunked pines in the vacant, rocky perimeter of the ruins.

"Watch out for loose bits up there," Martin told them earnestly. "We're going to tell the others now. You could fall to your death if you're not careful!"

"Thank you, Mr. Neill." Clark nodded to him solemnly and then ruined it by winking at Saffron. "You two be careful, now."

Chapter 16

After reporting to the guides that the tower was not safe to mount, Saffron intended to do as she ought and document the flora of the area. But she could see Alexander on the other side of camp, speaking with the other team leaders. She wanted to see if she could salvage at least a bit of time together.

She sidled up to the group and regretted it when she realized that tension was thick in the air.

"Just spit it out," growled Balthazar, archaeology's team lead, his craggy face darkening.

"Dr. Henry—" Alexander began, but the linguist, Hazelwood, cut him off with cleared throat and a frown. Alexander continued, "Several artifacts have gone missing."

Hazelwood paced away, shaking his head in obvious disapproval, while Balthazar's mouth fell open. "Why the devil wasn't I told?"

"Probably because it was likely someone on your team that nicked it," grumbled Templeton.

"What?" Balthazar rounded on him. "What did you say?"

The historian and the archaeologist began bickering. Hazelwood looked keen to simply walk away, and Alexander pinched the bridge of his nose.

This might be the ideal time for a rescue. Softly, she called, "Alexander?"

His expression was equal parts relief and consternation as he stepped away to where she stood at the edge of the tent. "What is it?"

"Would you like a break?" she asked with an empathetic smile.

"I would," he said, "but I need to sort this out. If I leave them to it, the whole camp will hear about the missing artifacts and we'll have a near mutiny, if Balthazar's reaction is anything to go by."

Saffron nodded, trying to cover her disappointment with very real understanding. With Dr. Henry off-site, it was up to the team leaders to keep everyone on track. "I'll see you later, then. At dinner?"

Alexander smiled tiredly. "We're cooking on the fire tonight. You'll get to have some true field experiences, after all."

She squeezed his arm and took her leave. Though the camp was bristling with people, she didn't see Martin. That was just as well; it would be nice to wander without her little shadow for once.

Notebook in hand, she made a slow circuit of the exterior of the castle ruins. The interior was open to the elements and therefore also full of plants, but it was currently being trampled by any number of men setting up camp or flitting about in search of something to do. A number of people were also outside the half-circle of the castle walls, but they paid her no mind as she bent and knelt to dash down names and descriptions of the plants she found along the perimeter.

Sweat trickled down her back as she straightened up after sketching a lovely little plant she could have sworn was a relative of sweet pea. She stretched her sore back, contemplating returning to camp for water. Looking around for the direction she needed to go, she found she was a dozen yards from the base of the tower she'd climbed earlier. The view of the sea would be lovely, now the sun was starting to ease toward the horizon.

She began in that direction, then turned when she heard a faint male voice. Martin walked toward her, red-faced and anxious-looking. She sighed. He'd likely been looking for her this whole time.

Not looking forward to consoling him, she paused—only for him to rush at her like a rugby player and tackle her to the ground.

Something hammered the ground, shaking it underneath her. Pain burned in her ankle.

"Miss Everleigh? Are you all right?"

Saffron blinked and tried to sit up but her head swam. Martin leaned over her, his eyes wide as dinner plates and his hair totally awry.

"I'm all right, I think," Saffron said, a bit dazed. "What happened?"

"A piece of the watchtower fell." She looked where he gestured. Just a few feet away now lay a pile of stone, dust still hovering around it.

"The crenellation," she said, craning her neck back to look at the tower. There was nothing but the side of the tower, blue sky, and tops of the pines.

"I'm sorry—I'm *so* sorry I pushed you out of the way like that, but it looked like it was going to fall right on top of you! Are you hurt?"

As much as she wanted to say she was fine, her ankle hurt. Badly. She sat up gingerly and tried to rotate it, but pain struck her like lightning. She bit her lip. Something was wrong.

She pushed up, maneuvering around her skirt to crouch on one foot before Martin helped her stand. Pain lashed her the moment she put her foot to the ground.

Martin winced at how she hissed in pain. "I can carry you—"

"That will not be necessary." Naturally, her leg nearly collapsed on her the moment she attempted forward movement.

Martin lowered her to the ground, and she followed, unable to balance alone. "Don't move, I'll run and find someone."

"No," Saffron said quickly. "I can manage—"

But Martin was already jogging away.

"Please, just Mr. Ashton," Saffron called. She huffed disconsolately. This was going to be a nightmare.

Martin didn't return with Alexander. It was Banks who accompanied Martin around the bend of the castle's wall.

"I'm sorry to interrupt your work, Mr. Banks," Saffron said, her facing burning.

"Not at all," he said, kneeling next to her. "Not much for me to do around here but translate the same phrases again and again. You'd think the fellows would learn them by now. Neill said there's something amiss with your leg, and I see you've managed to get your boot off. With your permission, I'll just take a look to see what the trouble is."

Saffron gave it, and soon Banks was examining her ankle while Martin looked anxiously on, rocking back and forth on his heels while his eyes flitted from Saffron's foot to anything else. There was nothing lewd about examining an injury—the ankle was already swollen to something less than attractive—but it seemed Banks was the only one not embarrassed by the situation.

"I'm afraid this will put you out of commission for a few days." Banks articulated her ankle, watching her face for signs of discomfort. She didn't hide any. "I don't think it's broken but it's certainly hurt. Let's get you to camp see if one of the drivers can take you back to the hotel to see a doctor before nightfall."

Despite protests against leaving camp and needing a doctor, then further protests when Banks swept her up into his very well-muscled arms, Saffron found her face burning as she was brought back to the campsite on the far side of the castle. Her bare foot and swollen ankle indicated she was injured, but plenty of their colleagues saw her being carried like a bride over the threshold and looked on with blatant curiosity.

"Ah, there's Ashton," Banks said, turning his steps toward the same tent she'd sought him out before.

When he caught sight of Saffron and Banks, with Martin trailing behind carrying her boot, his expression went from confused to concerned in a heartbeat and he moved toward them.

"What happened?" he asked her, his eyes moving from her face, which must have been a tomato by now, to her exposed foot.

"I hurt my ankle, but it's barely—"

Martin piped up. "A piece of the watchtower fell, sir, and I pushed her out of the way, but I'm afraid her ankle was hurt."

Alexander backed up to the nearest bench. "Set her here. Neill, get someone to bring one of the motorcars."

Banks set her down and Neill scampered off in the direction of where the motorcars were parked.

"Neill knocked you over?" Alexander asked Saffron.

"He knocked me out of the way of the falling bit of the tower. He didn't mean to hurt my ankle."

Banks gave a brief report of his examination of the injury, adding his experience taught him Saffron's ankle was definitely in need of several days' rest despite her looking imploringly at him.

"I need you to go give that tower a once-over," Alexander told him.

"Martin and I already reported it to the guides," Saffron said, and they both turned to her in surprise. "Earlier, we'd climbed to the top, and one of the crenellations was loose. Martin nearly knocked it over . . ."

Realization turned her blood to ice. A wave of dizziness blurred her vision momentarily.

Alexander dropped to his knees, his hands coming up to brace her shoulders.

"I'll get water," Banks said, rushing out of the tent.

"Clark saw that piece was loose," Saffron whispered to Alexander. His eyes flared, but he remained silent. "He saw Martin nearly knock it over."

He was quiet for a long moment before asking carefully, "You believe Clark tried to drop ruins on you?"

"No. No, of course I'm not saying—" She broke off. She didn't like to believe it, but it was all there. "He's hated being paired with me, and I'm sure he suspects I helped Banks with the graffiti. You know how he is, Alexander. Three times already he's done something to me that could have caused significant damage."

His dark brows winged up. "Three? There was the snake, then the storeroom. What else happened?"

She swallowed, but he wouldn't let her avert her gaze from his. His fingers found her chin, lifting it so she couldn't avoid his eyes. "What else?"

"He might have put something in my champagne the evening we arrived at the hotel."

His nostrils flared, and he dropped her chin. He got to his feet, and with hands propped on his hips, frowned down at her. "Why didn't you tell me?"

"The usual reasons. You're busy being responsible for the team. I refuse to let you fight my battles. I have no proof it was him. And it was quite enjoyable to see Clark shocked to see me awake and upright the next morning. I didn't want to ruin it by letting him know his plan nearly worked."

Alexander ran his hand through his hair in an agitated way. "What do you want me to do?"

"I . . . I don't know, truly. It's one thing to menace me with snakes and things, but if Martin hadn't knocked me out of the way, I might have been killed."

"I'll inform Dr. Henry, then."

That would be as if she was running off to tattle. "No—" Alexander lifted a brow. "I don't want anyone to think I'm letting you or Dr. Henry solve my problems."

"Clark sabotaging you and nearly flattening you with a ruin is not just your problem."

"It might not have been him," she said quickly. "I'm upset from the fright of it and the pain. It probably just fell over on its own after Martin loosened it."

Banks ducked into the tent and said the motorcar would be there in a moment. Alexander stepped over to him and they spoke quietly for a moment, Banks raising an eyebrow to whatever Alexander told him. He jogged off through the gate to the exterior of the castle.

"What did you tell him?" She didn't like the grim expression on Alexander's face.

"Nothing. I'll just go find our team to inform them they'll be on their own for the next day."

Saffron caught his hand before he got too far. "Alexander," she said, pulling him back and onto the bench beside her. "You don't need to come back with me. I can see a doctor alone. The Henrys and the Demirels are at the hotel, besides. I don't want you to miss anything because of me."

"I won't be missing anything." His eyes softened slightly. "Believe it or not, I'm fairly used to tending to your injuries."

"You don't need to this time. This is just a bruise and some swelling and it'll be taken care of in no time. Plus, imagine the nonsense Clark will say if you leave with me."

Outrage momentarily flared in his eyes. "I don't care what Clark might say."

They looked at each other, the air around them very warm and still.

Saffron took a deep breath. "I do care. I'm already going to be a laughingstock after Banks carried me into camp like that."

"He was a stretcher-bearer in the war. If anyone was going to help you apart from me, better it was him."

Martin cleared his throat from a few paces away. He carried Saffron and Alexander's bags. "The car is ready, Mr. Ashton. Miss Everleigh, I hope you recover quickly."

Alexander carefully untangled her arm from his, ensured she was steady, and took the bags to the boot of the motorcar.

"Miss Everleigh?"

Saffron looked at Martin, who was hovering in his usual nervous manner. "Yes?"

"I am dreadfully sorry about your ankle," he told her, doe-like eyes bouncing between hers. "And I'm sure it is horrible for me to ask a favor of you but—" He swallowed audibly. "This diversion here, to the castle, it means I can't—there was a young lady on the ship—"

"The one Mr. Clark put you off of introducing to me?"

"Yes, that's the one. She is in Smyrna, you see, and I was supposed to meet with her this evening." A bead of sweat tumbled down his temple, and there was an ashen quality to his skin. He looked painfully uncomfortable.

"I understand," she said quickly. "You didn't get a chance to send her a message that our plans changed."

He nodded, and his gaze darted to the left, where Alexander was making his way back up the hill to where they stood. He dropped his voice. "Would you be kind enough to send a note to her and tell her? I can't bear the thought of standing her up."

Saffron agreed, and he shared the girl's name and hotel. He was still thanking her when Alexander returned, and scuttled away moments before Alexander swung her up into his arms. He ignored her complaints, which were half-hearted as her ankle was now throbbing in time with her heartbeat. Once he helped her into the back seat, he slid in beside her, and they pulled away from the castle ruins.

CHAPTER 17

Nearly as soon as the motorcar pulled up to the drive, Dr. Henry was striding out of the lobby, a frown planted firmly across his brow.

"Ashton!" he barked the moment Alexander emerged from the motorcar. "What the hell are you doing back here?"

"Miss Everleigh was injured," he replied, offering Saffron his hands so she could straighten up out of the vehicle.

She gave Dr. Henry a forced smile. "It's nothing serious, Dr. Henry. Alexander is just being cautious."

Dr. Henry did not look pleased. "Get inside and have Koray summon a doctor, then," he said tersely. Then he paused, in a kinder tone, added, "Damned bad luck to be hurt."

Alexander helped Saffron inside and up the stairs—she refused to let him carry her even though the hotel was mostly empty—and when she was settled in her bedroom, he returned to the lobby to find the hotel's proprietor to summon a doctor. Then, he went in search for Dr. Henry.

Yes, Saffron had told him not to 'tattle' to Dr. Henry about Clark's behavior. And he wouldn't be complaining about Clark's behavior toward his fiancée, but another team member, interrupting their work and endangering the crew.

Dr. Henry was in his rooms, and he grudgingly led him to the suite's small sitting room, where it looked he'd been privately brooding over a glass of whiskey. Mrs. Henry sat with her own glass of whiskey resting at her elbow as she paged through a fashion magazine.

"Mrs. Henry," Alexander said with a polite nod, "would you mind if I had a word with Dr. Henry?"

"She knows all about it, Ashton," Dr. Henry said heavily. He'd clearly had more to drink than the mostly empty glass cradled in his hands suggested. "And she'll pry it out of me anyway. Lay it all out for us."

Mrs. Henry sent him a coy smile over the pages of her magazine before disappearing behind them. "Nonsense, Lawrence. Do go on, Mr. Ashton. I assure you, I've grown weary of crew business. It's nothing but dirty shoes and sunburns, and complaints about officials and missing artifacts. Especially now the room search has turned up nothing but some very interesting reading material."

From the smirk in her voice, Alexander guessed she didn't mean the fashion magazine she was all but hiding behind.

It didn't matter if Mrs. Henry did hear what he had to say; if anything, she would likely be helpful, given how warmly she'd treated Saffron.

And, indeed, by the time he'd concluded his story, Mrs. Henry's magazine had drifted back down to the table and her eyes were riveted on Alexander, lips pursed. She seemed far more interested in the tale than her husband, unfortunately.

"Look, Ashton," said Dr. Henry. "These things Clark has done, these pranks, they sound like the same sort of things the chaps always get up to with new members of the crew. Toads in cots and clothes mysteriously soaking wet in someone's trunk. What did the lads on your first expedition do?"

Alexander ran a hand through his hair impatiently. "They tossed me into a river."

"See? They do it to everyone. Miss Everleigh should be glad she's not being treated differently, even if she doesn't like the pranks they're pulling."

Alexander opened his mouth to point out wet clothing didn't put anyone's life at risk, but Mrs. Henry snapped, "Use your brain, Lawrence. Giving a woman a sleeping powder and pushing a ruin over where she stood—these are not harmless jokes. Anything might have happened."

"That is my concern," Alexander jumped in. "Clark could have seriously injured her. She's already going to miss at least a few days of work because of her ankle."

Dr. Henry hauled himself to his feet, face flushing. "Everleigh knew what she was getting into when she applied to join. You said"—he pointed to Alexander, and then his wife, a little unsteadily—"she'd be up for the task. Until she comes to me and says she's had enough, or until Clark does something actually worth a fuss, there's nothing to do. Clark is your man for the next few weeks, Ashton. Find a way to keep him *and* Everleigh in order."

Mrs. Henry glared at him. "Lawrence, really—"

He reared back, stumbling to the left before catching himself on a wall. "This is my expedition, Cynthia!" he shouted. "Mine, damn it, and I'm not letting you women muck it up for me!"

Mrs. Henry rose to her feet, set her magazine down on the table, and, not breaking eye contact with her husband, stalked out of the room.

The door slammed shut behind her, and Dr. Henry sagged into the nearest chair. "Oh, blazing hell," he muttered. "Stepped right in it, didn't I?"

Fingers pinching the bridge of his nose, Alexander sighed. "Yes, sir. You did."

A soft tap at the door announced the arrival of someone Saffron hoped was the doctor. Her ankle was now impossible to articulate without her whimpering in pain, and seemed to be somehow swelling further by the minute.

Mrs. Henry opened the door and peered inside. "Miss Everleigh, a Dr. Yenmeck and his assistant have arrived. May we come in?"

Saffron straightened up best she could and bade them enter. An older, gray-haired man with spectacles and a young, heavy man followed Mrs. Henry into the room. Mrs. Henry came to stand at Saffron's side, offering her a brief, commiserating smile as the doctor, facilitated by his interpreter, interviewed Saffron regarding her injury. He moved on to examining the ankle—Saffron hoped he wasn't offended at her lack of stockings—and soon declared it was not broken.

She sagged with relief. She didn't know what she would have done had it been broken. One couldn't hobble about a dig site in a cast, of course.

Dr. Yenmeck prescribed rest and pain medication, which Mrs. Henry assured him Saffron would receive in abundance. He promised to return in a day or two to check on her recovery.

Saffron was not left alone to rest as she'd expected—and, quite honestly, hoped. She was tired, in pain, and terribly dusty from the afternoon at the ruins. But Mrs. Henry came to sit with her after the doctor's departure, and not long after, they were joined by Mrs. Demirel.

After explaining to the two women what had happened at the site, she had to bite her lip to keep it from wobbling as she realized the truth of the matter: She simply wasn't wanted on the expedition team.

Maybe Clark was right. Maybe it was a mistake for her to be here.

She didn't believe that, not really. She knew she had a place at the metaphorical table, one she'd earned by crafting a relevant study and doing the legwork to ensure anything she discovered here would be properly reported on. But she also knew just because *she* was ready to be out in the field didn't mean the others were ready for a young, unmarried woman to be ankle-deep in dirt with them.

Her already low mood sunk still lower. She'd been at University College London nearly six years, employed there for two. She was one of many women employed there, many of whom were professors and researchers in their own right, though most had years of experience and stacks of publications to their names. They'd fought for their places at the U and in the academic world. Did she really want to spend years fighting for respect and acceptance?

She wasn't even sure she would be able to complete her work at the agora now, let alone write anything with Clark's cooperation. Could she bear to see their names together in print, knowing how he despised her? Why did he hate her so much? She wasn't holding him back, as he frequently complained, especially because she only wanted to do *more* work.

Mrs. Henry interpreted her silence as exhaustion and rose to leave, drawing Mrs. Demirel along out of her seat and to the door. "Good evening, Miss Everleigh. Do send for me, should you have need of anything."

Mrs. Demirel bobbled her head, wide-eyed. "Oh, yes. Please call for either of us, Miss Everleigh. I'm only too experienced with such things. I tend my boys' ailments and injuries all the time. My husband's, too," she added, laughing awkwardly.

"Thank you, both of you," Saffron said, forcing a smile. "Oh, actually, Martin Neill asked me to relay a message to someone. Would one of you be so kind as to telephone the Sağlık Hotel and tell a Miss Corsianna Moore that he was unexpectedly called away for a few days?"

Mrs. Henry asked, "Made a quick friend, our Mr. Neill, has he? How unexpected."

It was unexpected, Saffron agreed, but perhaps not so much as to warrant the look of shock on Mrs. Demirel's face.

"He met the girl on the ship," Saffron explained. "I believe he hoped to deepen the friendship while she and her family were still in town."

"I'll take care of it," Mrs. Demirel said. Saffron rather got the impression she was trying to make up for the rudeness of her shock that Martin might have caught the eye of a young lady. "Don't you worry, Miss Everleigh. I shall come to you in the morning, shall I? Perhaps we can all breakfast up here. Oh, yes, that will be lovely.

I'll arrange it all." She flashed Saffron and Mrs. Henry a smile and fluttered out of the room.

"Brace yourself, Miss Everleigh," Mrs. Henry said with dark humor, "for if you thought the menfolk were a challenge to conquer, the real trial by fire is about to begin."

CHAPTER 18

After a very long breakfast with Mrs. Henry and Mrs. Demirel that morning, Saffron was left to rest, but found herself unable to settle on anything. Surrounded by discarded books, papers, and sweating glasses of water and juice, she spent much of the day glaring at her swollen, purple ankle and wondering what Alexander and their team were doing at Kadifekale.

At her insistence, and Dr. Henry's, Alexander had departed after assuring himself that Saffron was well taken care of. She was, if only in body. Her spirit was quite low, and the solitude, occasionally interrupted by one of the ladies poking their head in through her door to check on her, did little to soothe her.

The sleepy heat of midafternoon did manage to send her into a doze, only to be interrupted by rumbling.

She jolted upright, heart hammering as she struggled to understand that it was not the thunder of rocks showering down around her, but motorcars coming up the drive. She managed to disentangle herself from the skirt she'd kicked round her legs and carefully crept to her door.

She needn't have bothered, as the moment the men stomped into the hotel, their voices and footsteps could have been heard down in the agora. Most of what she overheard was declaring their intention to bathe, or complaining they ought to have gone to the sea for a dip.

She lingered at her door for long enough that the hotel had gone quiet as the men filed into their rooms or down to the parlor for tea. It didn't take long for Saffron to conclude Alexander was among the number to go to the sea after leaving Kadifekale.

It was confirmed several hours later, when he arrived at her door with the bridge of his nose red and the smell of salt on him. She had decided not to begrudge him a jaunt to the sea; he'd told her many a tale of swimming in the Mediterranean when visiting family in Greece and the way it made his eyes light up made her glad that he had gone. Not to mention it did swooping things to her belly to see him standing in her doorway with salt-kissed curls falling over his forehead, a shadow of a dark beard tracing his jaw, and his shirt crumpled and open at the collar.

"You look better" were the first words out of his mouth as he took her in with apparent equal interest.

"I feel much better," she said, avoiding putting weight on her ankle without the appearance of doing so. "How was the rest of the time at the ruins? Did anyone find anything? Mrs. Henry mentioned—"

He took a step into her space, so close she could feel the heat coming off him. "Do you mind if I come inside?"

"No," she said automatically, pivoting so he could slip into the room. She glanced into the hall and smiled when she saw it was vacant.

The moment the door was shut, he kissed her. She wrapped an arm around his waist, the better to anchor herself so she wouldn't topple over and completely ruin the moment. He tasted like salt and smelled like sunshine and it felt rather wild to have his beard rasping against her skin and his hands mapping her body like she was the uncharted ruin to discover.

Things grew heady and hot, spiraling so quickly she barely had time to feel gleeful when Alexander bodily lifted her so she was fully pressed against him in such a delicious way that she completely forgot where they were.

It all came crashing down when a knock at the door broke them apart. They looked at each other with glazed, hungry eyes until a nervous voice called, "Miss Everleigh?"

"Blast," Saffron whispered, pressing her overheated face into Alexander's heaving chest. Why did Martin have to interrupt just when things were perfect?

"I just wanted—" Martin broke off, and through the door at Alexander's back, she could hear him muttering to himself, "Just shut up and go away, Martin, she doesn't want to speak to the fellow who knocked her to the ground like a great lummox . . ."

Sighing, she slipped from Alexander's arms, nudging him behind the door. His hand shot out when she reached for the doorknob, stilling her while he gently brushed her hair back from her flushed face. The look he gave her was so intent, so lovely, that she really didn't want to open the door. But there was a young man on the other side who she couldn't bear knowing felt so downcast when he'd done absolutely nothing wrong.

"Hello, Martin," she said when she opened the door.

"Miss Everleigh," he said, perking up a bit. He looked bedraggled, with his dark hair in greasy disarray and deep shadows under his eyes. "How are you? Is your ankle better? Mr. Banks told me that it wasn't broken, of course, but I've been so worried."

He sucked in a breath, and she took advantage of it to say, "It isn't broken. The doctor said I'll be fine to return to work in a few days, once the swelling goes down. Thank you again for rescuing me. If not for you, I might be much worse off."

His already flushed face flared rosy, but she didn't want for her, or Alexander, who was watching her with a faint smile behind the door, to be trapped by more of Martin's guilty rambling. "I'm really not supposed to be walking on the ankle much . . ."

"Of course, of course, how stupid of me," he said, backing away from the door with hands lifted as if in surrender. "I just wanted to say again how sorry I am that you're laid up for a few days. I'll see you later, when you're feeling better."

He scurried down the hall, his own door shutting a few moments later. She hadn't realized their rooms were in the same corridor.

Alexander closed the door with a soft click, his small smile still in place. "I think you're rather fond of Neill."

"How can I not be? He is a puppy." She eased back onto the bed, sighing in relief.

"Your ankle is not better," Alexander muttered in a lightly accusatory way. He pulled the desk chair to sit at her side, and gently lifted her leg so her calf rested on his thigh. He looked down at it, tracing a finger along the bruised skin. She hadn't bothered with stockings, not when it was so hot and she had no company but the ladies.

"This reminds me of something," he said quietly, his finger brushing the hem of her skirt at her knee.

Her breath came faster with every sweep of his fingertips. "Oh?"

He looked up at her from beneath his heavy brow. "Yes. I recall examining your legs just like this after you'd insisted on poisoning yourself."

"You are dreadful," she whispered.

"I am." He leaned forward so his words caressed her ear as he tipped her backward onto the mattress. "Let me show you just how dreadful I can be."

Chapter 19

As it turned out, Alexander was *quite* dreadful, though not as dreadful as he might have been, given how complete their privacy had seemed and how relaxed his swim at the beach had made him. Still, when he left Saffron for a real wash and to prepare for dinner, which Sir Randolph and the Turkish officials would be attending, Saffron was in as good a mood as possible, given she was still shut up in her bedroom with an aching ankle.

Sitting at the window was agreeable now the sun was set. The air was warm and fragrant, and she could imagine she could hear the wash of waves from the sea. She lingered over the memory of Alexander, smelling of the sun and sea. He would have taken her to the beach, he'd told her, had their afternoon not been interrupted on Friday. She would have seen him in the water, hair wet and untamed, body splashing in the waves . . .

A very pleasant daydream was interrupted by a raucous laughter from below. She peered down to see a handful of gentlemen had drifted into the back garden. Cigarette smoke drifted up to her, and wrinkling her nose, she pulled back from the windowsill.

The usual male banter proceeded below. Saffron rolled her eyes when she recognized Wakefield's stocky form among them. If he was there, Clark was sure to be down there, too. She'd just decided to close her window and perhaps put pen to paper to write

Elizabeth when she heard a comment that could have only been referencing her.

"Did you see the state of her trousers?" Wakefield guffawed. "Dirt all over her knees. You know why."

Rowdy laughter ensued, but only for a moment. Wakefield broke off, and the group around him fell quiet. Saffron dared to peer over the edge of the windowsill.

Alexander and Banks had come within earshot of Wakefield's comments. Banks's angry face was illuminated by the glow of the house, and Alexander, facing away from the group, stood absolutely still.

Saffron realized her fingernails were digging into the painted wood of the sill, anticipation thrumming through her. What was Alexander going to do? She wanted him to thrash Wakefield for the slanderous things he'd implied about her—really, she wanted to thrash him herself, but that hardly seemed an option—and yet she also couldn't stand the thought of anyone protecting her honor. It was hers to defend, wasn't it?

In a tangle, she watched as Alexander turned to face the group of men. Coolly, he asked, "Why?"

Wakefield shifted on his feet. Was he brave enough to say it right to Alexander's face?

He was, apparently. He lifted his chin defiantly and asked, "Why what?"

All Saffron could see of Alexander was the farthest quarter of his profile, but she could read the tension in his shoulders. "Why would someone's knees be covered in dirt at an archaeological dig site, Wakefield?"

Silence spiraled out between them for a beat before Wakefield forced a laugh. "You know, I think the only thing your Miss Everleigh has been discovering down in the storerooms is that assistant's unimpressive—"

"I've noticed your knees have dirt on them regularly," Alexander said quietly. "Maybe you and Miss Everleigh were engaged in the same sort of activities down in the agora."

"But wait," Banks put in, arms crossed over his chest. He put on an expression of mock confusion. "Miss Everleigh was involved in the find of the decade when she helped me identify the graffitied stone. That would explain why *her* knees were dirty."

Two of the fellows standing in Wakefield's circle smothered laughs.

"Well, this certainly explains some things," came Clark's voice. He stepped into the light, clad in work clothing and with a cigarette between his lips. He took it out and flicked ash before continuing. "Sharing Miss Everleigh with Linguistics, are you, Ashton? Let Banks teach her how to use her tongue. What a generous wedding gift."

Saffron gasped, then immediately slapped a hand over her mouth. How *dare* he—

There was a scuffle beyond the window, and Banks's low voice saying things she couldn't make out. When she dared peek over the sill again, he and Alexander had gone. Clark and his cronies remained, laughing.

Fuming, Saffron got to her feet, only to topple over onto her bed. She swore, glaring at her ankle, and rolled over to face her pillows, where she let out a petulant shriek, muffled by their pressure.

She was going to get Clark back for this. This and every other cruel word and horrible and dangerous prank.

It was late by the time Alexander returned to the hotel. Banks had been wise to take him away from Clark and Wakefield's taunting; after the events of the past week, he was bursting at the seams with frustration.

After Banks had pulled him away, Alexander had walked away from the hotel, willing the darkness of the peaceful, summer-like night to leech his fury away. He found himself at the bottom of the hill, looking up at the pinpricks of light that made up the hotel.

By the time he returned, most of the men had found their beds or other employments. He was tempted to trounce Clark or Wakefield or any of their pals at cards, but he didn't want to be further goaded, nor did he want his presence to encourage more badmouthing of Saffron.

He paused at the landing of her floor, staring absently down the hall at her door. Damn it all, why hadn't he realized just how bad things were? Why hadn't he anticipated this level of animosity toward her? He ran a hand through his hair, unsure if it was possible to have predicted this situation. Clark's apparent hatred of Saffron was so intense that he ought to have found her someone else to work with. He didn't want to admit to himself that he'd hoped this would be a learning experience for them both; give Saffron the chance to further shore up her armor and Clark a chance to see women could and did contribute to academia.

Now Saffron was cooped up in her room, injured and reviled by half the crew.

This was his fault. But he had no idea how to make it right.

Footsteps roused him, and a moment later, Martin Neill came down the steps in a haphazard way that told Alexander he'd been drinking.

"All right, Neill?" Alexander asked him, reaching for the young man's shoulder to steady him.

Neill blinked blearily up at him, then blanched. "Mr. Ashton—"

"It's all right," Alexander said. "Let me help you to your room."

"Oh no," Neill groaned, slapping a hand to his face. "Oh no. You're going to kill me."

"It'll be fine. You'll sleep it off and feel better in the morning," Alexander said, and he was struck by just how many times he'd said those same words, both to himself and his brother over the years.

"I swear, I've never touched her, sir," Neill babbled. "Never, not even when—"

"Christ," Alexander muttered. "Shut up, Neill. What room number?"

The young man struggled to walk straight, so Alexander took hold of his lapel and dragged him to his room, taking the key from his trembling hands and shoving the door open.

"There," he said when Neill had collapsed onto his bed. "Go to sleep. Be ready to work in the morning."

Neill nodded, eyes already closed, though his brow was pinched.

"And Neill?"

He blinked his eyes open.

Alexander sighed. "Stay away from Clark and the fellows in the card room. They'll take you for all you've got, even if you're too drunk to sign your name."

Neill groaned, rubbing his eyes. "I know. I know. Mr. Clark's got so many of my vowels . . ."

"Well, be sure he doesn't get any more of them. We're here to work, not sit at the card table."

He wasn't sure Neill had heard him; he was fumbling for something on his nightstand.

Alexander left him to it, wondering why he bothered to give advice at all. When he was Neill's age, he certainly wouldn't have followed it. In fact, he'd done just the opposite of the advice given him and headed straight into a war.

Neill was lucky. He had the chance to turn away from the path before him and try out another. Alexander could only hope he'd heed some of the signposts others had left along the way.

Chapter 20

Saffron woke with a start. The moon made a square on her bedclothes. Nothing moved in her room, but something was moving outside her door.

Alarm rose the little hairs on her neck. She got to her feet, and arming herself with one of her heavy textbooks, she crept to the door, and—

The arm hefting the weight fell to her side. No one was outside. She felt suddenly quite silly. She must have had another bad dream of sabotage at the ruins.

But a door opened down the hall, and Saffron opened her door just enough to see who was moving about at this hour.

Dr. Yenmeck's balding gray head was immediately recognizable as he emerged from the room. Concern was written into the deep lines of his face as he carefully shut the door Saffron knew to be Martin Neill's.

That was not good. The doctor being summoned in the middle of the night could only mean Martin was very ill.

She closed the door softly. Though she worried for Martin, she couldn't look in on him, not in the middle of the night. She was struck by the need to seek out Alexander, to share her sudden fear for Martin, but that was likely an equally poor idea.

She hobbled back to bed. A few more months, maybe a year, and Alexander would be in her bed, waiting for her to return and confide her worries. That was a comforting thought, and one that drew her back into sleep.

When Alexander found Saffron in the breakfast room, he shook his head. "No, Saffron. You cannot come to the agora yet."

"I can," she said, shooting him a withering glare he couldn't quite tell was serious or playful. "If I wanted to go, you couldn't stop me. But I'm not here to insist on going to the dig site, anyway."

He sat in the chair to her right. She'd clearly been there a while; her plate was empty but for crumbs and her cup of half-finished tea was no longer steaming. "Did you get tired of your room?"

"Yes," she said with feeling, and held up a finger. "But I'm here because you need to check on Martin before you go to the site this morning. He is very ill and I'm worried about him."

His brows rose. "A hangover doesn't warrant me busting into his bedroom—"

"Hangovers don't warrant doctors being summoned in the middle of the night." She explained Dr. Yenmeck's visit in the wee hours of the morning. "I want you to see how he is."

"If the doctor's been to see him—"

"I want you to go," she said firmly, lowering her voice, "because I want to know his symptoms."

He frowned. "Why?"

"A certain person on our team enjoys pulling pranks, Ashton. I want to be sure Martin's sudden illness wasn't caused by someone slipping him something they shouldn't have. He's more likely to tell you the truth of how he's feeling than me," she added, unnecessarily shifting her dishes about the table. "No one wants to detail the contents of their washbasin after a rough night, do they, least of all to a woman?"

Alexander couldn't argue with that. It would take but a moment to ask Neill about anything strange he'd eaten, and it would put Saffron's mind at ease. And possibly his own.

When he made it to Neill's room, it was very dark, just a candle lit next to the bed, and it reeked of sick.

"Are you all right, Neill?" Alexander asked, coming next to the bed. By the light of the candle, Alexander could see Neill blinking up at him. "Do you mind if I turn a light on, open a window?"

"My eyes are a bit off," Neill said weakly. "The light makes it worse. I think it's all the smoke. I'm never around so much smoke at home." He tried to laugh, but it ended on a groan. "I just ate something funny, that's all."

"What did you eat?"

"Just the same as everyone. But they all say sometimes when you go somewhere foreign, the water can—" He took a sharp intake of breath and clutched at his side.

"Easy," Alexander said, looking about for something that might help him. Several medicine bottles littered his nightstand and dresser, all in English but none Alexander recognized would help stomach pain. "Dr. Yenmeck came you see you? What did he say?"

A gagging sound had Alexander hurrying to the bedside. He held the basin while Neill retched, and ignored the pitiful whimpers that followed.

"He said—" Neill reached with trembling hands for a soiled handkerchief on the nightstand and patted his mouth with it. "He said I would be fine after a day or two, if I can just have to enough to drink."

"Have you been drinking?"

"I've tried." His voice broke. "It just keeps coming back up. I feel like I'm going to die."

Suddenly, Alexander had to wash his hands. He could cope with the acrid smell of vomit and the moans Neill made as he lay back on the pillow, but it was like he could *feel* the tiny organisms crawling on his skin.

He forced himself to move slowly toward the door. "I'll send a maid with tea and broth." He paused to crack the window open.

"Drink it all, even if it comes back up, Neill. I'll send for Dr. Yenmeck again." If the boy couldn't stay hydrated, he'd need to be admitted to the hospital for fluids. Dehydration was a killer in these circumstances.

He left the room, intent on his purpose, but Clark was descending the stairs just then.

"Clark," Alexander barked, striding to him.

Clark paused, darting a glance down the stairs.

It gave Alexander a little smug pleasure to think he might actually try to run away. But Clark's crude comments last night, though worth punishment, were not why he needed to speak to him now. "Did you give Martin Neill anything to eat or drink or smoke last night?"

Clark frowned. For once, he looked genuine. "Neill? No. Why?"

"He's very ill," Alexander said. "I wanted to make sure this wasn't another of your pranks gone wrong."

With a sneer, Clark replied, "I didn't give the boy anything. Why waste my time?"

Immediately, Alexander's temper flared hot. "Why waste your time sabotaging Miss Everleigh? What has she done to deserve it?"

A shrug was all the response Alexander got. And that was fine; Alexander had to move on. Between Neill being ill, Saffron being injured, and Clark clearly uncaring at the mayhem he'd caused, his team was a wreck. The expedition, which should have been an easy two months of work, was going off the rails, and it was up to him to course correct before it became a disaster.

Chapter 21

Alexander's reporting of Martin's symptoms was less than thorough, which meant Saffron's scouring of her notes an exercise in frustration. As extensive as her notes on local botanicals were, she found very little of direct use. Nearly all botanical poisons made someone nauseated to the point of vomiting. Most poisons would dehydrate someone through that avenue—and other similarly wretched means—and those sorts of deeply unpleasant reactions led to one being weak and sweating. Not one Saffron had ever heard of or could find mention of in her reference texts made someone's eyes sensitive to light.

Unwilling to admit defeat, she decided to brave going directly to the source of information in the hopes that she could ascertain whether or not Clark, or anyone else, had poisoned Martin.

She paused outside his door, one hand firmly planted on the wall to prevent herself aggravating her ankle. It was quite possible she was seeing a poisoning where there was nothing more at work than particularly malevolent bacteria. She could admit learning all she had about poisonous plants led to her noticing them more and more often. It wasn't an unknown phenomenon among her peers. One only had to watch Dunmore walk across a field to see that his passion for reptiles made him sensitive to any sign of them in the grasses, or observe her bacteriologist fiancé's reluctance to eat without thoroughly cleaning his hands in fresh water with proper soap, ignoring the ribbing he got from his less circumspect comrades on the dig. Knowledge was a wonderful thing, but it did have a way of influencing one's habits.

Still, having knowledge also meant one had the responsibility to use it for the good of others. And if the retching from the other side of the door was any indication, Martin Neill was in great need of some good.

She waited until the horrible sounds stopped, silently wishing that Mrs. Demirel's positive report on Martin's improving health at lunch had been true, then waited two minutes more for the poor boy to catch his breath before she knocked.

"Martin," she called, easing the door open, but she faltered upon seeing him. He was slumped in his bed in a sweat-soaked shirt, the curtains drawn and a lamp lit dimly next to him.

"Miss Everleigh," Martin said, blinking at her. "I'm sorry, I'm in no fit state—"

"Don't be ridiculous," she said quickly. "I was just coming to check in on you."

She poured a glass of water from the pitcher on the desk and passed it to him. He took minute sips with trembling hands, his jaw clenched in between. His eyes were sunken and his face ashen, and it was quite difficult to look at him without feeling immediate, deep concern. He certainly was not better.

"I think you ought to go to the hospital," she told him.

"No," he whispered, closing his eyes. "I'll be fine. And the doctor gave me some medicine, and Mrs. Henry and Mrs. Demirel brought me some, too . . ."

In an attempt to sound heartening, she said, "You'll have the strongest constitution out of all of us once this has passed. I think several members of the crew have already been trying to toughen you up."

This brought a wan smile to Martin's face. "I suppose so."

"Mr. Clark in particular seems interested in your progress. Mr. Ashton mentioned he's been sure you're never, er, thirsty when you all sit down to cards."

Martin's eyes grew wide. "Er, I—"

Saffron smiled slightly. "I only mention it out of concern. Whose liquor is it, at the card table?"

"J-Johnson," he mumbled, still looking chagrined. "Dunno how he managed it, with it being illegal here."

"Champagne? Wine?"

"Whiskey. Last time was whiskey." He gulped. "Didn't have any at the castle ruins. Stomach was—" He clamped his jaw shut and swallowed again.

To give him a moment to master himself, she moved to the window and pushed aside the curtain, causing a sharp intake of breath from the bed. She opened the window wider to allow for better air circulation before drawing the curtain back over it. The room was very warm and that couldn't be helpful. Not to mention the smell.

"Did you eat dinner there? Mr. Ashton mentioned cooking over a fire. It sounded quite rustic," she said. Depending on who was doing the cooking, it would have been the perfect opportunity to slip something in his food. With no one else ill, it was unlikely to be food poisoning.

"N-no. Wasn't long after you and Mr. Ashton left that I started feeling rotten. Pain in my side, headache. Eyes have been burning and burning, and nothing helps . . ." He fell silent, and Saffron turned back to him.

In the dim light of his solitary lamp, he looked so dreadfully ill and upset. His lip was trembling. "I didn't want it to go this way. Being ill. And all the t-talk . . ." His face screwed up, and he threw an arm over it to hide it from her. "I'm s-sorry."

"Oh, Martin," she said, but stopped herself going to his side. He clearly didn't want her as an audience to his pain, bodily or otherwise. "There's nothing to be sorry for. All you need focus on is recovering. It will all be well, I promise." She went to the door.

"Just . . . Miss . . ." Martin's voice came faintly.

"Yes?" Saffron turned back to the bed.

"The girl . . . from the ship," he said, hand falling away from his face. "Miss Moore. Did you . . . ?"

"Send your apologies?" Saffron asked, and he nodded. It was sweet he could think of the young woman when he was so unwell. "All taken care of. You rest now, Martin."

As was too common these days, Saffron heard a tumult from below stairs. Rather than the usual hubbub when the crew returned to the hotel, however, this was a house-shaking uproar that Saffron worried either meant the city was on fire again or the agora had collapsed.

Hand bracing the wall, she started toward the stairs, unwilling to be left out yet again. She paused at Martin's door but found all was quiet within. She was glad he was resting rather than retching. She hoped the noise didn't disturb him.

Rather than panic, the parlor was filled with smiling faces when she reached it.

She found Banks first, speaking animatedly to his team leader, Hazelwood. "Miss Everleigh! I'm afraid you've missed something quite exciting!"

Of course she had. "What am I toasting?" she asked, accepting a small glass from Hazelwood. She sniffed it and found it was some sort of juice.

"An incredible find," Hazelwood said, nodding over to a cluster of men still covered in dirt from the agora. "A necklace."

"Oh!" Saffron craned her neck to see who was in the center of the celebration. "Oh," she repeated, far less enthusiastically when she saw Dr. Henry clapping Clark on the back. He raised his own glass and called, "Gentlemen! Gentlemen! Let us raise a glass to the find of the dig!"

The room hushed slightly, only to break into cheers when Clark held aloft a ring of metal. Like a prizefighter, he walked a slow, tight circle with his treasure, showing it off. It must have been cleaned at least a little, for Saffron caught a flash of gold.

"Well done, Clark!" Dr. Henry shouted. "Let's celebrate!"

Saffron didn't feel like celebrating. Out of all the archaeologists to get credit for an amazing find, Clark was the least deserving. And unless he'd somehow unearthed the necklace in one of the vessels from the storeroom, he hadn't found it while doing the work he was meant to be doing for their project.

She found Alexander on the other side of the room and was just making her way there when the current of the party shifted, forcing her right into the path of Clark as he made another circuit to receive congratulations.

"Miss Everleigh!" he crowed, coming forward. The necklace was draped in his hand, a twisted piece of gold that, now she got a proper look at it, was admittedly quite extraordinary. About the circumference of her outstretched hand, one end was a narrowing switchback of a coil, and the other, a slender but unmistakably serpentine head. Twin green gems glimmered at her from its etched face.

"Well done, Mr. Clark," she told him, intending to brush past.

"It is you who I must thank for this rare and significant find," he told her, "for if you hadn't seen fit to lay up in bed for a few days, I would have never had the chance to discover it. To Miss Everleigh!"

A chorus of laughter and echoes of her name sounded around them. Her face burned.

"Next time," Clark said in a voice meant just for her, "you'll know better than to cut me out of a find. I'll always come out on top, you see."

Forgetting Alexander, she pushed away from Clark and toward the door through the crush of celebrating men. She'd follow the advice she'd been given and not move from her bedroom.

Just as she would have escaped, Mrs. Demirel rushed into the room. Tears streamed down her blotchy red face. She practically fell into Saffron's arms. "He's dead. Oh, no. He's dead."

Shock reeled through Saffron. The sounds of the party dimmed around her. There was only one person she could mean. "Mrs. Demirel, is—is Martin is dead?"

Now sobbing into her shoulder, Mrs. Demirel gasped, "That poor boy. Oh, Miss Everleigh. That poor boy."

Chapter 22

"Of course we have to go back to the agora tomorrow." Knuckles braced on the table, Dr. Henry stared around, daring the others to disagree. "It's not an option to let progress stagnate simply because—"

"One of your crew died?" Mrs. Henry asked dryly.

"This is the field," Dr. Henry said, rounding on her. "Bad things happen."

Alexander's head throbbed as the team leaders turned to each other to argue Henry's point. They'd been in the dining room for the last twenty minutes, sequestered together after the Henrys and the Demirels had spoken with the doctor who'd been called to examine Martin Neill. Or rather, his body.

Alexander glanced at Saffron, who'd been motionless at his side for the length of the conversation. She hadn't said a word as Mrs. Henry explained to everyone the circumstances of Martin's death, fending off questions she couldn't answer as to how his condition deteriorated when they'd thought he was on the mend. Mr. Demirel hadn't been able to add anything to the tale, nor had his wife, since she was currently in their room, unwell after the shock of finding Neill's corpse.

Saffron's eyes were vacant as she stared across the table at no one in particular. Her fingers were turning white in her lap where they clutched each other. He covered them with one of his own, and she jumped slightly.

I should have helped him, her sad eyes said when they found his. He hoped his gentle squeeze of her hands told her it hadn't been her responsibility. How could she have predicted he would perish just hours after they'd spoken?

"Ashton!"

Alexander knew what he was being asked. "I say we wait at least a day," he said, looking back at Dr. Henry and the rest of the waiting table. "We ought to wait to ensure no one else becomes ill, and for the doctor to determine how, exactly, Neill died." There were more mutterings from the others, but he ignored them and drew Saffron out of her seat as he rose. "Excuse us."

Alexander stepped into Saffron's room when they reached it. He wrapped her in a hug the moment the door was shut. She shook against him, her sobs muffled by his chest.

He had no words of comfort or encouragement. Neill's death was too unexpected for that. The feeling was the same as the shock of noticing one's brother-in-arms was suddenly missing from the line, only to discover them empty-eyed, slumped against the muddy wall. Such suddenness was violent in the way it tore at the mind as it tried to take hold of the new reality.

And work his mind did, shuffling and reshuffling the events of the last few days, his worries, his anger, trying to make sense of it even though he knew he wouldn't be able to for some time. He didn't try to stop it, though, and held Saffron all the tighter for it, for at least he knew she was safe and well even as her heart broke for Martin Neill.

Arrangements were made for Martin Neill's body and a perfunctory memorial was held. Saffron was still too much in shock to pay much attention to either, other than appreciating someone had saw fit to honor Martin's Catholic faith with a priest from a local Catholic order. In fact, it was not until two days had passed and her ankle was well enough she could join the others at the agora that she seemed to wake from a sort of grief-induced stupor. Once she realized it, it reminded her most uncomfortably of what had happened to her mother when her father had been killed in the war. Violet had been all but comatose for weeks, and Saffron didn't like to think she might harbor the same tendency to step back from reality when it became too painful.

She was determined to face the day, and that meant getting back to work. She went down to breakfast, slowly, so as not to aggravate her ankle, gathered her food, then went to the table where Alexander sat with Banks, Kent, and Dunmore.

"Good morning," she said as she sat.

The others returned her greeting, save for Dunmore, who gave her a tight-lipped nod but did not meet her eyes. In fact, he stood and excused himself practically the moment Saffron picked up her fork and knife. He went to another table rather than leaving the room, however.

Alexander frowned after him, but soon was speaking to Banks about his progress on the graffiti, and Saffron found their discussion quite comforting. She liked to think Martin would have been glad that the discovery they'd inadvertently made was being researched with such care and enthusiasm.

And just like that, tears clouded her vision. She bit her lip, hard, trying to clear them before anyone noticed she'd become a watering pot at the breakfast table.

The swatch of white that appeared in her vision, however, meant Alexander, at least, had noticed. She patted her eyes as surreptitiously as she could.

Dr. Henry came into the room with Mr. Hayrettin and another Turkish gentleman at his side, looking furious.

"Listen up," Dr. Henry said, and the room fell quiet. "This is Mr. Polat." He jerked a thumb at the Turk wearing something reminiscent of a military or police uniform. "He's going to be speaking to some of you today as you go about your work. Answer his questions, or you'll be answering to me."

Mr. Hayrettin scowled and looked like he wanted to speak, but Dr. Henry called, "Now, move out!"

People streamed into the entry and outside to the motorcars. Saffron picked up her hat and satchel, which Alexander commandeered without a word, and they loaded into one of the motorcars.

Fluffy white clouds brushed the blue of the early morning sky. The breeze from the open windows was almost sharp on her skin, bringing her to further wakefulness and soothing her swollen eyes. It was slightly cooler, a welcome change that she hoped meant it would be a little more bearable at the agora come midday. Being outside, in fresh air and among the crew, was pleasant.

Pleasant was perhaps too strong a word. She wouldn't be able to look at any corner of the agora without remembering Martin scurrying after her. At least in her mind, he'd joined the centuries' worth of ghosts of long ago, forever tied to that place. She'd do her best to remember him fondly, as an enthusiastic young scholar, and not the fear-riddled boy, pale and sweating in a dark room.

"Ashton, come over here," Dr. Henry called.

Alexander turned, swinging around the crate he'd been carrying, and squinted over at where Dr. Henry stood at the mouth of one of the smaller tents used for storage. He was with the two Turks he'd been with at the hotel earlier that morning, Mr. Hayrettin and the other fellow. None looked at ease, least of all Dr. Henry, whose hands were in fists at his side.

Alexander set the crate down where he was; it was just packing materials and would keep just fine in the sun. He ducked into the tent, brushing his hands on his trousers.

Dr. Henry nodded at the uniformed Turkish man. "This is Polat."

"Inspector Okan Polat," the man said, stepping forward to offer Alexander a very firm handshake. His uniform was dark, military green with a belted jacket and tall, polished boots. His skin was bronze, and his precisely trimmed mustache and short hair were sprinkled with gray. Sharp eyes of light green watched Alexander carefully.

"Inspector," he said politely. He glanced at Dr. Henry, who was stony-faced. Alexander suspected he was angry Hayrettin had called in the police to deal with the missing artifacts. They hadn't turned up, and now that more valuables had been discovered, it was essential they resolved the thefts before the new pieces went missing, too.

Polat gestured for Alexander to sit at the little table nestled among the stacks of crates, and the other two men left the tent.

"Mr. Ashton," the Turkish inspector began, lacing his fingers on the top of the table, "tell me your responsibilities. Why is it you are here?"

Finding his choice of words curious, Alexander answered, "I lead the team of biologists here at the dig."

"You are a leader?" Polat asked. "Carrying boxes is leading?"

Surprised, Alexander replied, "I carry boxes of equipment when necessary."

Polat's brows lifted as if doubtful. He moved on to a few more questions about his responsibilities, then inquired about Alexander's movements of the last week, down to the hour, in some cases. After twenty minutes, Alexander was getting impatient. Inspector Polat had yet to ask about the missing coins or the bracelet.

"Very good," Polat said at the end of Alexander's recollection of his time at the dig site the day Clark had discovered the necklace. "And now tell me about your team."

He described each one, and when he came to Martin Neill, he found it hard to continue. "And then there was our assistant, Martin Neill." He could see Neill's face, twisted with pain. "He died a few days ago."

"I have been told," Polat said without sympathy. "Tell me about him."

"He was twenty-one years old and was due to complete his degree in the spring. He was deciding on the specific field he wished to pursue a graduate degree in. I had him working mostly with Miss Everleigh."

"This is the woman you will marry," the inspector interrupted.

"Yes, my fiancée," Alexander said. "They worked on the samples taken from one of the storerooms."

"They worked closely?"

If he'd spoken to many of the crew, Alexander had no doubt they'd already seen fit to mention the rumor going around about Saffron and Neill. He'd been overhearing snippets of conversation about it all day, some intentionally spoken within his hearing, no doubt to provoke a reaction. With his emotions riding high, it was a task to keep himself composed. "I assigned Neill to help Miss Everleigh."

Polat hummed, writing something in the little notebook in which he'd recorded Alexander's recollections. "Tell me about his death."

Taken aback again by the direct phrasing, Alexander did, including visiting Neill in his room.

Polat wrote a few notes, and when Alexander fell silent, steepled his hands on the tabletop. Those green eyes bore into his for a long moment before he asked, "And what do you make of his sudden death, Mr. Ashton?"

"It's a tragedy," he answered. "Young men dying before their time always is, especially when it could have likely been prevented."

"What do you mean?"

"I'm a bacteriologist. I know how easily illness-causing bacteria can be managed. Martin Neill might have been alive today if he'd avoided whatever food or drink—"

"Martin Neill died of cardiovascular failure," Polat interrupted, pronouncing the words carefully. "His kidneys, liver, lungs, and heart were damaged." He leaned back, eyes riveted on Alexander's face like he was trying to see into his mind. "I am no doctor, but that does not sound like a man who ate something which made him ill."

Alexander stared at him. This police officer thought Neill had been poisoned.

And from the way the inspector was studying him, Alexander had the chilling suspicion that Inspector Polat thought he knew something about it.

Chapter 23

Alexander had no time to warn Saffron of Inspector Polat and his suspicions. At the conclusion of their interview, he told Alexander he wished to see her next, but before he could excuse himself to find her and tell her what had happened, she was there, walking arm in arm with Mrs. Demirel across the grass from the gate.

"I will speak to Miss Everleigh now," Polat announced, and he strode to where Hayrettin and Dr. Henry were ignoring each other a few yards away.

Alexander followed him. "Dr. Henry—"

He'd just lifted his arm to wave Saffron over. "What is it, Ashton?"

"I need—"

Saffron had seen them. "Yes, Dr. Henry?" Her eyes darted between Dr. Henry, Alexander, and the inspector, standing with hands clasped behind his back next to Mr. Hayrettin, who cleared his throat loudly.

Dr. Henry huffed. "Well, go on, then," he growled at Hayrettin.

"This is Inspector Polat, from the Smyrna police," Hayrettin said to Saffron, clearly trying to maintain some dignity in the face of Henry's touchy temper. "If you please, he would like to ask you questions."

Saffron was already nodding. "Of course."

"Saffron," Alexander said quietly, "let's speak a moment—"

"Good," Polat said, "this way."

Alexander put a hand on her arm. "One moment—"

Polat rounded on him, drawing himself up to his full height. "Sir! You will not impede my investigation."

Everyone froze, perhaps as baffled as Alexander was at the strident way Polat had spoken.

Alexander spoke calmly. "Miss Everleigh is my fiancée, Inspector Polat. She is my responsibility." At his side, Saffron made a noise of annoyance.

"This means nothing," Polat said, and he waved a hand like he was shooing away a fly. "Miss, this way."

Still looking at Alexander with annoyed curiosity, Saffron followed Polat in the direction of the tent.

"I will accompany the lady," Hayrettin said, and Henry stepped forward, saying louder, "*I* will accompany the lady. She's under my charge as long as she's a member of my crew!" He stormed after Polat and Saffron before Hayrettin or Alexander could argue.

It was tense in the tent, and not just because it was quite stuffy among the crates. Dr. Henry attempted to pace but was stymied by the close quarters. The Turkish inspector said nothing as she sat in the wooden chair across from him. "What can I help you with, Inspector Polat?"

She was all too aware Alexander had been uneasy with her speaking to the inspector. That signaled either he was uncomfortable with the man himself, in which case Dr. Henry's apt act of a caged animal would do plenty to assist her, or Alexander was hesitant about her answering the inspector's questions. What, exactly, was all this about?

"Martin Neill's death was not due to illness," Inspector Polat said.

Saffron blinked. "What happened, then?" she asked automatically.

"I hope you will tell me."

Her mouth opened and then closed. Behind the inspector, Dr. Henry gaped, first at her, then at Polat.

"I have heard much about your reputation, Miss Everleigh," the inspector said evenly. His eyes, eerily bright in his tanned face, did not leave hers.

"I . . ." Her head spun, trying to wrangle her thoughts. "If Martin did not die from food poisoning, what do you believe he died of?"

Polat's eyes narrowed minutely, but Saffron didn't get to hear his response.

Dr. Henry exploded. "You devil!"

Polat was out of his seat and backing away from Dr. Henry in a moment, looking both frightened and furious as Dr. Henry towered over him, shoving a finger into his chest. "You are a damned liar, Polit!"

The inspector batted his hand away. "I am Inspector *Polat*—"

"You told me you were looking into the missing artifacts. What are you doing, suggesting one of my men was murdered!"

The word crashed into Saffron. "Murdered?"

Polat jabbed his own finger right back into Dr. Henry's chest, though he had to raise his arm to do it. "I said nothing of the kind. Now leave before I arrest you."

"For what?" spat Dr. Henry.

"Interrupting questioning the suspect!"

Hayrettin rushed into the tent, hands raised placatingly. "Inspector Polat, Dr. Henry, please . . ."

Polat broke into rapid Turkish.

"Don't you go saying things I don't understand!" Dr. Henry roared. "Hazelwood! Banks! Get in here!"

In the chaos, Saffron edged to the open flap of the tent. Alexander wasn't far, and Dr. Henry's shout must have alerted him that things weren't going well, for he was already coming over.

"He thinks Martin was murdered," she said the moment he was near enough. "How can that be true? What did he say to you?"

Hazelwood came trotting over, eyebrows nearly risen into his hairline. He ducked into the tent.

Alexander took Saffron by the arm a few steps away. "He actually said he thought Neill had been murdered?" he asked in a low voice.

"Dr. Henry inferred it from the inspector's questions. That's what's causing all this fuss." She nodded to the tent, from which angry voices were drifting. "Do you think it's true? Who on earth would have killed Martin?"

"I don't know," he replied. "He said Neill died of cardiovascular failure, and his liver and kidney had been damaged."

Dr. Henry roared something from behind them. A dozen or so crew and locals paused in their activities and turned to the tent. Alexander drew her away a few steps further.

"That . . . that does sound like it might not have been food poisoning," Saffron said, biting her lip. Could someone really have slipped Martin something? A prank was one thing, and actually killing someone was quite another. Her mind rebelled at any of their party intentionally killing Martin. "Many diseases cause liver and kidney damage. And he'd been drinking recently, hadn't he? The night before Dr. Henry banished the crew to Kadifekale, you said he was quite drunk. Perhaps he had a condition we didn't know about, and the drinking exacerbated it."

"I'm sure they would have discovered that in the autopsy."

Voices rose within the tent again, then quickly fell.

"They didn't discover the disease that killed Demian Petrov during his autopsy," Saffron countered. "How could we find out?"

"*We* don't need to find out anything," Alexander said, and before she could disagree, he added, "I was his team leader. It's my responsibility to answer Inspector Polat's questions and make sure he has all the relevant data. Everyone had to have a doctor sign off on their health status as a part of their application. I'll make sure Polat gets Neill's paperwork. Templeton should have it somewhere."

Her teeth worried her lip. It didn't seem like enough. "I should go back and answer his questions."

Alexander's hesitation was momentary, but she noted it before he nodded. She could sense he was trying not to revert back to his old ways of discouraging her from helping the police. She might have information that could help, especially since she'd spent a good deal of time with Martin the last few weeks. She couldn't imagine anyone would want to kill him; he'd been so eager to please. But maybe she'd observed something Polat could use to decipher a motive, or at least inform him of the history of pranks among the crew, particularly orchestrated by Clark.

She wasn't convinced Martin had been killed intentionally, but if he had been, she wanted justice for him. She squeezed Alexander's arm before returning to the tent, intent on answering any questions Polat might have for her.

CHAPTER 24

Saffron's day had begun with a to-do list consisting of sketching vessels and tracking down the perpetually absent Clark. By noon, her list of tasks had quite transformed.

Identify suspects
Discover motives
~~Establish opportunities~~
Discover Martin's movements
Learn cause of death, specific toxin if possible

She'd struck "Establish opportunities" from the list as soon as she wrote it because, with so much coming and going during mealtimes at the hotel and on-site, she figured more than fifty people would have had the chance to slip Martin something in his food or drink. But that was if Martin had, in fact, been poisoned. And from the seemingly endless questions the Turkish inspector had asked her about herself, Martin, the dig, and the other crew members, it certainly was plain that was the official conclusion. If only she knew why.

Considering Martin had been dead three days and Inspector Polat came today to interview the crew, she surmised the suspicion of murder was a recent development, and therefore the order for an autopsy had been, as well. The information it would provide would be essential in discovering what was the cause of death and whether or not a toxin had caused it, but she had little hope she'd get lucky as she had in the past and see the autopsy report. It was likely to be written in Turkish, anyway.

So, Saffron determined as she shut her notebook on her list and got to her feet, she would have to discover the truth of what had happened to Martin using her wits, rather than relying on science. There was no way she'd be leaving it to Inspector Polat; he'd all but told her and Dr. Henry that she was a suspect.

She huffed at the idea as she carefully rose from the sunbaked pile of rocks she'd perched on to write down her thoughts. As if she'd be so stupid as to use poison to kill someone!

She made her slow way the far end of the pit, where the majority of the assistants had been assigned to examine dirt.

There were three assistants there at present, with their necks red and white shirts clinging to bent backs over the large, wood-framed sieves. Other than herself, the assistants were the people Martin had spent the most time with. If they had any insights into Martin's death, being friendly was her best chance of hearing them.

"Any luck?" Saffron asked as she approached.

All three looked up. The spotty-faced young man who'd asked after Alexander's potential assistant position rubbed an arm over his face to blot the sweat before saying, "Hello there, Miss Everleigh."

"No luck at all," grumbled the taller of his companions, a portly fellow she'd seen Clark bossing around.

"Not every bucketful of dirt can be full of treasures," she said with a smile.

"Not everyone can have Callahan's luck," grumbled the third man, whose arms were dusty with fawn-colored earth.

The spotty man sighed wistfully. "Or Wakefield's."

"Or Giltrap's."

The quickness with which the young men spat out names made Saffron bite back a smile. They certainly held a bit of resentment that they were stuck sieving dirt while their superiors were discovering artifacts.

The dirt-covered assistant counted off on his equally caked fingers. "Or Clark's, or Guy-Dawkins, or Neill, or—"

"Neill?" Saffron repeated. "You mean Martin Neill found something?"

She narrowed her eyes on the three men, who suddenly looked anywhere but at her. They didn't look chagrined, but almost . . . guilty.

"Come now," she said gently, "I know it's a dreadful thing to have happened. But I haven't heard anything about him finding an artifact." At least, not any that were not hulking stones with ancient graffiti. "You know Martin Neill was the good sort. If he found something, he ought to get credit for it. Especially now . . ." She let out a hot, hollow breath full of entirely real emotion. "It would be a comfort, I think, for his family to know he'd left a bit of a legacy behind. I know Mr. Ashton would like to carry such a message back to them." She resolved to tell Alexander he would be doing exactly that the next time she saw him. "What did Mr. Neill find? When?"

The dusty assistant mashed his lips together and went back to his sieving, looking at once upset by her words and disinclined to respond. But the other two straightened all the way up and brushed off their hands.

"When Ashton gave him a break from Biology, er, when you were injured, Neill was assigned to the sieves. He found a bit of pottery," the larger assistant said, voice low. "Not anything so exciting as the coins, or the necklace—"

"But it was interesting," the spotty one interrupted. "Ceramic, with intact patterns. Mr. Clark knew right away it came from Italy."

"Neill showed it to Mr. Clark?" Saffron asked.

"Yes, he did. Neill worried he'd be laughed at if he made a big to-do about something that might have been a contemporary piece mixed in with the dirt, you know."

"It did look rather modern," put in the larger one. "White with a red pattern."

The spotty one was nodding right along. "So, he asked Mr. Clark to look at it, and, well—"

"Mr. Clark said he didn't want the fellows ribbing Neill if it turned out to be nothing special," finished the larger one. "He suggested he could get it checked out first."

The fellow still sieving muttered, "Not much of a suggestion."

"I see," Saffron said, and she truly did, for she could perfectly imagine the conversation between Martin Neill and Clark. Martin, naïve and hopeful, and Clark, impressive and intimidating with his knowledge and experience. How had Martin felt when he saw his find listed under Clark's name on the artifact table?

She cleared her throat. "As I said, Mr. Ashton planned to send a letter to Neill's family, so I'm hunting up some stories he might share, to let them know that his last few weeks of life were at least enjoyable before he fell ill. I won't make trouble for Mr. Clark about the ceramic fragment, but what else do you know Mr. Neill got up to?" She sent them a smile she hoped came off as knowing, and perhaps inviting. "Did you lot get up to any trouble in the city?"

"Oh, plenty," the spotty one said, laughing nervously. The other assistant elbowed him. He cleared his throat. "That is to say, we did, not Neill. He stayed behind to play at Johnson's table. Didn't want to offend anyone by not attending."

That meant she'd need to talk to the poker-playing fellows, and she did not look forward to it. "Thank you all so much for your thoughts. I'll be sure to ask Mr. Ashton to pass on to Martin Neill's family that he was well thought of among the crew."

The spotty one snatched his hat off his head, exposing blond hair matted with sweat. "He was, Miss Everleigh. I think it's just awful what's happened to Neill. And the crew. Your team, particularly. It's got to be hard, going without Neill's help. I just hope you know that if Mr. Ashton needs another hand, I'm here and ready."

The warmth his candor had kindled in her heart sputtered out. "Right," she said, withholding a sigh. "I'll be sure to let him know."

She walked slowly back to the tent in which she ought to be working, eyes wandering over the pit as she went. She was, admittedly, looking for Clark. Ought she go down into the pit and see if she could force him into work? She had a feeling that if she did find him now, she might not be able to restrain herself from giving him a piece of her mind. Hearing the assistants' account of Clark claiming Martin's find and summarizing for Inspector Polat all that Clark had done to her—and through her, Martin—only served to remind her just how dreadful Clark had been.

One of the workers she was more familiar with—if one could claim familiarity with a man one had subtly threatened by suggesting he'd be sacked if he revealed one's questionable actions—was just climbing up out of the pit as she passed, and he shot her a sideways glance that suggested the subtle threats were at the top of his mind, too.

Guilt prickled at her, and on its heels came an idea. She spun on her heel and spotted Banks leaving the mess tent.

"Mr. Banks," Saffron called out, walking toward him.

He gave her a gallant nod that put to mind a courtly bow. "Miss Everleigh."

"I wonder if you could answer a question for me."

"Certainly, if I can." He dug into his pocket, pulled out a handkerchief, and wiped sweat from his face.

"About your discovery," she said carefully. "I wondered if you recalled the names of the local workers who assisted you with the stone's excavation."

"I do." His equally cautious tone suggested he was aware this was more than a question of passing interest asked in hearing range of the crew walking all around. "Do you need those names?"

"I might," she said slowly. "It occurred to me there might be some ill feeling between one or all of those men and Martin Neill, considering the, er, unusual way the stone was discovered."

Banks looked taken aback. "Good Lord." He darted a glance over his shoulder before confiding, "Considering one of those men was recently dismissed from the dig, I think you may be right, Miss Everleigh."

Chapter 25

Of all the ways Saffron had contemplated exploring Turkey, she hadn't once thought she might do so for the first time in such a rushed manner, and alongside not her fiancé, but Christopher Banks.

But, as Alexander himself had said just a few days previously, if Saffron couldn't be out with him, better it was Banks. Who was better suited to navigating the backstreets of Smyrna than a man not only fluent in any language commonly spoken in the city, but a large man with whom no one was likely to make trouble?

They'd left the agora only a few minutes after Banks had explained Yusef Çağrı had been dismissed by the Turkish foreman of the site just one day after the graffitied stone was removed from the market stall at Saffron's behest, which in turn was a mere handful of days before Martin had fallen ill.

Her stomach churned as she considered the impact of her decision to ask the locals to dig that rock out. Yes, it had been an incredible discovery for not only Banks, who would get the credit, but for the whole dig. But it had also cost Mr. Çağrı his position. She knew next to nothing about any of the local diggers, but she had to imagine the job was a good one, what with the extra money Dr. Henry insisted the Turks pay them to safeguard the site. Her and Martin forcing the locals who'd helped them into secrecy had put their jobs at risk, and if Mr. Çağrı had taken his dismissal hard, he might have taken it out on Martin.

Banks had gotten Mr. Çağrı's address from the dig site's foreman, and they'd taken a carriage to a neighborhood Banks called *Tenekeciler.*

"Tinsmith," he said over the clatter of hooves on the uneven street as they climbed slightly higher in the city. "This area is known for it."

The neighborhood certainly had the smell of metalworking; the tang of it grew heavier in the air with every roll of the carriage wheels. But perhaps it was the lingering smell of the fire of 1922, for the street they traveled looked to be parallel to the line of destruction. Viewing the damage, even years removed, gave Saffron the same uneasy feeling she'd had in the still war-torn French countryside a year ago. A weighty stone of grief and guilt gathered in her stomach. Their mission was a grim one, which only made the feeling worse as the carriage came to a stop outside a humble building of wood and stone.

"Wait here, if you don't mind," Banks told her with the sort of politeness men often paired with orders they were confident would be followed.

"I do mind, actually," Saffron said, and stood.

"Miss Everleigh . . ." Banks grimaced. "I don't mean to be indelicate, but it is, frankly, not appropriate for you to come to the house of a man—"

"I have heard quite a bit about what is appropriate or not for myself and various men lately," she said acidly. "The fact of the matter is that Martin Neill is dead, and I doubt adhering to cultural mores will help me find justice for him."

Rather than bristle at her sharp words, Banks smiled sadly. "I agree. But as is oft quoted, 'Patience is bitter, but its fruit is sweet.' We will not get answers if we offend those from whom we need them. Not to mention your concern Mr. Çağrı might be responsible for Neill's death. Surely if he took issue with Neill, he would feel the same way about you . . . ?" He left off delicately, and Saffron found herself chagrined that he was right, and right in such a diplomatic way.

"Very well," she grumbled, and was left sitting in the carriage.

It lasted only a moment, for Banks came out of the dwelling nearly immediately with a look of discontent to match Saffron's mood.

"He's not here," he said, hopping into the carriage. "His daughter-in-law gave me directions." He rattled off instructions to the driver, and they set off back the way they came.

An hour later, they had traveled much farther than Saffron would have contemplated without a plan, passing out of Smyrna and down a sparsely populated road along the southern coast. Alexander would have noted her absence a while ago, and with Clark's record of mischief-making, Alexander probably thought he'd trapped her in another ruin.

As the town came into view, Saffron's mind turned to the task at hand. They'd nearly arrived, and they were going to ask questions of a suspect. She had to make the most of it.

Banks held another brief consultation with the driver, and he settled back into his seat to tell Saffron, "The driver says we're not far now, but it turns out that the place Çağrı's daughter sent us is a thermal spring."

Saffron blinked. "Oh."

"I thought it was the name of the town," he said, pinching the space between his brows. "Do you think I could bribe you into never mentioning my pitiful misunderstanding of basic Turkish to anyone?"

"Considering I know about four words of the language, I'm in no position to complain."

The town had a worn look to it, with streets of hard-packed dirt, sporadic buildings of various sizes and materials, and the sort of scrubby vegetation that, though she knew it was endemic to the area, looked weather-beaten to her eyes. There were a number of people who gave the impression of going about their usual business with no care for the foreigners that'd just arrived, rather like country folk back home unimpressed by new arrivals. The driver stopped their carriage outside one of the low buildings with a red tile roof, set into the side of a low mountain covered in dark green brush.

"This is it." Banks's boots raised a little cloud of dust about his feet as he hopped out of the carriage.

"This is a traditional bathhouse, then?" It looked nothing like the many domed bathhouses she'd seen illustrations of in her travel books, but just like all the other nondescript buildings.

"Er, yes."

She strove to keep the petulance from her voice. "I suppose I have to just stay here and wait for you."

Banks eyed her uncertainly. "Well, you certainly can't come into the men's section of the *hammam* and search out Çağrı, can you?"

Saffron didn't bother hiding the resignation in her voice this time. "No, I suppose I can't."

He gave her a brief, apologetic smile, said, "Back in a tick," and hurried into the bathhouse.

She knew she ought to just sit back down in the carriage, but she was unwilling to return to its hard bench after such a long, bumpy ride. She could manage a brief stretch of her legs without finding too much trouble.

A brief stretch of her legs turned into a painful hobble when the path she'd elected to follow proved too treacherous. She'd intended only to follow the road long enough to observe a cluster of late-blooming oleander just before the bend, but the rattle of a cart coming around the corner startled her, and she'd turned too quickly on her weak ankle. Each step back toward the bathhouse felt like whatever parts had recently been repaired were being painfully plucked and strained, and she could still only make out what she thought was the distant red roof of the bathhouse.

She swiped at the sweat gathering under her hat along her brow. A fine pickle she'd put herself into. "Let's wander away from my companion and translator, and my ride back to Smyrna on an injured ankle. Yes, a marvelous idea."

A female voice called out from behind her, making her jump again. She hurriedly hobbled to the side of the path to get out of the way of the approaching party.

The voice grew closer, speaking in rapid Turkish that cut off when the woman caught up with Saffron. She was a short woman maybe ten years Saffron's senior, her burgeoning belly announcing her before she herself came into Saffron's view. The woman frowned at her, looking between her face and the foot Saffron kept off the ground.

She spoke again, and this time Saffron caught a word she understood, the word for help.

Grimacing, Saffron shook her head and pointed to her ankle. If only Banks could materialize to help her explain! "It's only my ankle," she said slowly, hoping the woman had some English. "I'm just going back to my carriage at the *hammam*."

The pregnant woman's expression cleared immediately. "*Hammam, evet, evet!*" She took Saffron's arm in hers and began walking down the path toward the bathhouse.

She felt quite awkward, being hauled along by a much shorter stranger, but she couldn't risk upsetting their balance, with her ankle twinging and her new companion's advanced stage of pregnancy, so Saffron walked along with the woman. She wore a loose kaftan, belted over her belly, and a colorful scarf draped casually around her shoulders. Her skin was tanned olive, rather like Alexander's, and her eyes were green, sparkling with amusement when she caught Saffron looking down at her. She said something, rubbed her belly with her free hand, and then gestured toward the bathhouse.

The woman guided her to the side of the building facing the mountain, rather than the door facing the street that Banks had entered. An elderly woman sat in the foyer within, smoking a pipe.

The two women greeted each other with obvious pleasure. There were exclamations and kisses on cheeks. After the warm exchange, the pregnant woman explained that she'd come across

Saffron on the path, plain from the way she gestured at Saffron and then down to her ankle. The older woman tutted, looked Saffron up and down, tutted again, then swept her arm toward a door. Saffron was taken by the arm again by the pregnant woman, and Saffron faced only a brief battle between practicality and curiosity. Would she really deny herself the opportunity to explore a Turkish bathhouse—and furthermore, would she really turn down these women's hospitality?

The answer was an easy no. In the next room, a line of baskets sat along a long wooden bench that spanned the wall. Even if Saffron hadn't seen the clothing within the baskets, the fact her guide started stripping the moment the door closed would have informed Saffron that this was a changing room. Her guidebooks had explained this was a traditional practice, and indeed, it was expected for bathers at the *hammam* to go about completely naked.

Reading information and experiencing its reality were two different things, however. The notion of going about starkers in front of strangers, even female ones, was bizarre.

The pregnant woman had shed her kaftan, scarf, belt, and a plain tunic before she noticed Saffron was sitting on the wooden bench with only her boots off—a relief, with her ankle aching again.

She smiled placatingly at Saffron and motioned down her body, then pointed to the basket. She gave instruction in Turkish, slowly. Then she mimed something about Saffron's trousers.

It was unfortunate that today, of all days, she wore the jodhpurs she usually donned when visiting the dig site, for out of all her wardrobe, it was certainly the least convenient for dealing with her ankle. If she'd been in a dress or skirt, she might have just hiked it up and let her ankle soak in the hot water, the mineral scent of which permeated the whole building. As it was, she truly didn't have a choice but to strip down to her camiknicks.

"May I keep my lingerie on?" Saffron asked when the rest of her clothes were folded neatly in a basket.

The woman brightened. "*Lingerie,*" she repeated, giving the word its native French pronunciation. "*Vous parlez français, madame?*"

Saffron did speak French, poorly, but it made the next hour go much more smoothly, for none of the women they found within the baths spoke English, but many had a few words or more of French. The pregnant woman, Bahar, was nearly fluent, and so she became Saffron's guide through the process of a proper Turkish bath. She was scrubbed and massaged as Bahar led her through three rooms, each warmer than the last, until they emerged into the largest, hottest room.

The bathhouse was constructed of plain stone and dark wood, humble compared to the stunning illustrations of the most famous bathhouses in Turkey from her guidebook, but this room was quite striking. The ceiling was pierced by white dots of light set into a geometrical pattern. A massive stone surface was set about knee-height in the center of the round room, on which sat a number of women atop thin, wet cloths. A few more women were massaging those who sat on the bench. This was where Bahar led Saffron, and as soon as she was settled on the stone top—it was shockingly, delightfully warm—Bahar gave instructions to an attendant to massage her ankle.

"Oh, I don't know—" Saffron broke off as her foot was yanked into the lap of the attendant. Her protestations fell away as some sort of magic was massaged into her ankle, and the pain, already lessened by her soak in the hot mineral waters, was rubbed away.

Bahar nodded with satisfaction from her seat at Saffron's side. "*Bien, n'est-ce pas?*"

"*Oui*," she said weakly, unable to stay worried when the attendant knew just how to soothe the ache of her ankle. In the humid dimness, scented by chalky water and the rose soap with which the attendants scrubbed their patrons, and filled with the soft susurrations of feminine conversation and water, she could almost imagine there was no mysterious poison, no inspector full of suspicion. No dead friend for whom she sought justice.

That thought took the savor from the experience. Ten minutes later, most of which was spent thanking Bahar for the rescue and attempting to pay the modest fee for her bath but being gently but firmly rebuffed by no less than four different people, Saffron was pink-faced and dressed outside of the bathhouse in air that felt bone-dry and chilled by comparison.

She'd just climbed into the carriage, eager to rest her ankle—it was significantly better, but she had no wish to aggravate it again—when Banks emerged from the building.

His face was flushed, his auburn hair damp, and he walked with a languor she likely would have shared had her ankle not hurt.

"Did you find Mr. Çağrı?" she asked as he climbed into the carriage alongside her.

After a brief direction to the driver, who'd looked to be napping when Saffron had come back, Banks turned to her with a half-smile. "Do you want the good news, or the bad news?"

"The bad news," she said without consideration.

"The good and bad news are one and the same," Banks said. Their driver prodded his animals, and the carriage leaped into motion. "Our quarry was there, and willing to talk. He was dismissed from the dig, but it was because he was injured. He strained some previous injury pulling the stone from the stall's floor and came here for a soak in the waters to ease it."

"So, he wasn't dismissed as a result of our subterfuge," Saffron said, "and therefore it is unlikely he held anything against Martin Neill, at least so much that he might have wanted to poison him."

"He had no particular memory of poor Mr. Neill other than he was there when you requested the stone be moved, and, to be honest, I don't think he minded leaving the dig. I don't think he's responsible for Neill's death."

They fell into silence. Saffron was unsure if she should be relieved or disappointed her theory had been proven incorrect; it would have been a neat solution to offer up to Inspector Polat, and, as poor a person as it made her for thinking so, one that would not have implicated any of the expedition crew. Now the only suspects she had were the ones she worked alongside daily and those with whom she shared lodgings.

Chapter 26

The sun had nearly disappeared behind the rolling hills by the time they returned to Smyrna. Rather than go to the agora, Saffron and Banks returned to the hotel. There, Saffron lurked in the foyer for Templeton. She planned to request Martin's papers in the hopes of discovering if he had a previous health condition.

It was Alexander who walked in first, and he made a beeline for her. He was red-cheeked and dirty, a sure sign he'd been doing some heavy lifting on behalf of the other teams at the agora.

"Where've you been?" he asked without preamble.

"I am happy to tell you," she said, peering around him toward the door. "But did Templeton come back with you?"

"Templeton was talking to Dr. Henry when I left the site. Where were you this afternoon?" He took a half step closer, his head tucking in closer to hers. "And why do you smell like you've been rolling around in a garden?"

A laugh bubbled out of her at the image. "*That's* the first guess you have as to why I smell like lovely roses?"

"You forget, Everleigh, I've witnessed your garden-lolling tendencies."

"Lolling?" she sputtered. His lips twitched, and she pushed softly at his arm. "Honestly, Alexander." She sighed. "Do you know when Templeton will be back? I wanted to speak to him, just a quick inquiry."

Alexander's brow twitched upward. "A quick inquiry. Why do I get the feeling this quick inquiry is into Martin Neill's papers? Indeed, why do I get the feeling your absence was also related to Neill?"

"Because you are uncommonly insightful. Or perhaps a better word is suspicious."

"If I were to interpret the Turkish inspector's tone while questioning me this morning, I would agree I am suspicious," he said dryly.

"You're not alone in that, I'm afraid," Saffron said, frowning. "I've been wondering all day who could have harmed Martin, and why. He was so . . . well, harmless. No one has a bad thing to say about him."

Alexander looked pained. "You've been asking around for opinions?"

"Well, no, but I have been asking some questions. I won't have access to the autopsy report—" She poked his chest. "There is no need to make that face, Alexander. My friend died. He was possibly murdered, if the inspector's conjecture is to be believed. You can't expect I'll do *nothing* about it."

He seemed to think this over for a long time, his eyes distant, jaw clenched. Finally, he gave a short nod. "What have you found out?"

"Nothing of consequence," she said, relieved there wasn't to be an argument they'd both rather not repeat. "Martin found a minor artifact Clark took credit for. He was liked well enough among his peers. The lads say he never went out with them in the evenings, but I think he did go out with them the first night we were here. I looked for him, the night you were sent into the city to retrieve them, and couldn't find him. But I suppose that's too long ago to make a difference. I've a list of places I know he's visited, and I've made a plan for who I need to ask about what." She dug into her satchel for her notebook, and showed Alexander the notes she'd written. "Then it occurred to me"—she screwed up her face in anticipation of her fiancé's inevitable displeasure—"one of the men we bribed to keep quiet about the graffitied stone's discovery might have held a grudge against Martin because he was recently sacked, but it turns out he wasn't sacked but injured and didn't show signs of animosity toward Martin and therefore unlikely to have tried to hurt him."

"You . . ." Alexander stared at her, then slowly shook his head. "You unraveled all this in the space of, what, six hours?"

She frowned down at the page of messy ideas and questions, made messier by her scribbling during the bumpy carriage ride back to the city. "Well, I could have accomplished a lot more had Mrs. Henry or Mrs. Demirel been on-site. They doubtless know more about Martin's illness as they tended him themselves and spoke with Dr. Yenmeck. Or to his interpreter, rather. Determining Martin's movements, the suspects, and possible motives is all well and good, but if he was poisoned by some rare toxin, then the question of who did it will be much more easily answered."

He smiled at her chagrin. "I understand your point. May I make a suggestion?"

"You may *make* a suggestion."

"Let me speak to Templeton. I'll get the papers, and you can have as much time as you'd like with them. I have a good reason to look at them. Dr. Henry has been putting off writing to the U to inform them of Neill's death, so I ought to tend to it."

Saffron's mouth fell open. "Why on earth hasn't he done it?"

"I believe he's putting it off because he doesn't want to report that something on his all-important expedition has gone wrong."

"That," she declared, "is horribly selfish of him."

They fell silent as the foyer filled with another round of newly returned crew. Templeton straggled in last, walking slowly and looking rather like he'd walked the whole way back to the hotel rather than being driven.

Alexander murmured, "I'll meet you on the patio with the papers. Give me a few minutes." He hailed Templeton, then Saffron had nothing to do but slip outside and wait.

Chapter 27

Inspector Polat returned to the dig site the next morning, arriving at dawn alongside the crew.

Word of his presence had spread quickly the previous day, though it seemed there was no consensus about what, exactly, he was investigating. There were two popular theories: the artifacts that had gone missing, and foul play with Martin Neill's death.

Alexander overheard both ideas being discussed while the men went about their work. Rumors flew that anything from simple stones from the agora's arches to Clark's gold necklace had been stolen.

"Already been sold," he heard, as well as, "They want to nail the burglar before we heave ho and it's gone forever."

Alexander was curious what Polat had been asking the crew members to inspire such ideas. It was plain from the questions he'd asked Alexander and Saffron that the reason for his presence was Martin Neill's death.

A number of people asked Alexander directly about Neill's death. The same people who'd shrugged it off as unfortunate suddenly wanted to know all the details of his illness, and the same people who'd taunted him with the rumors of his fiancée dallying with the dead man were now looking at him sideways.

"They'll be watching what they say to you now," Banks muttered to him as they entered the stone structure where the crew kept the more valuable tools at the end of the day. "Don't want to provoke you now they think you might have bumped off Neill."

"No one thinks I killed Neill."

Banks sighed, setting delicate brushes into their box. "No, no one thinks *you* killed Neill."

Alexander's hands tightened around a chisel. Closing the lid with a snap, Banks shot him a meaningful look.

"They seriously believe Saffron killed him?" Alexander asked him.

"I don't know how serious they are, but they're certainly saying it. Even the assistants think she had a *particular* interest in Martin Neill. And I doubt you need to look far to discover the origin of that particular idea."

"Polat has barely been on-site for twenty-four hours." He pushed a hand through his hair, wrinkling his nose at the grit he found clinging to it. "I'd hoped the work would be interesting enough to keep people too busy to talk this much."

"'See how great a forest a little fire kindles! And the tongue is a fire, a world of iniquity,'" Banks said blandly. "I hate to say it, but the kindling is even drier and more plentiful here, my friend."

A maid woke Saffron early the next morning asking if she would receive Inspector Polat in the dining room.

Saffron agreed, of course, and dressed swiftly, nerves making her hands tremble as she recalled the way the Turkish inspector had snapped during their first meeting. One minute, he'd been intent but reasonable, and the next, threatening to arrest Dr. Henry after the slightest provocation. He was a touchy man, and experience told her she must tread carefully. Very few men liked being handed information and being told what it meant, and she had to do just that. The inspector had not approached her the previous day as he continued his questioning of the crew, and she had to ensure he was aware of all the facts about Martin's death.

The maid led her to the smaller dining room where Saffron and Alexander had dined with the team leaders and the officials. She knocked softly and Saffron entered when Polat called out.

"Ah, Miss Everleigh," he said with a tilt of his lips that caused his mustache to quirk to the left. "Please, be seated. I have called for refreshments."

Saffron sat at the table, unsure if she should trust this gracious attitude.

They sat in awkward silence, Polat watching her with a polite little smile, and Saffron, in turn, trying to make out why he didn't speak. It reminded her of Detective Inspector Green and his strategic silences when he'd questioned her about Mrs. Henry's poisoning.

"Oh," she murmured as realization flicked on like a light bulb.

Polat raised an eyebrow. "Yes?"

Heat flushed her face. "I beg your pardon," she mumbled, feeling foolish. He *was* intentionally making her uncomfortable.

The maid entered with a cart of tea. It was a very proper tea cart, though the tea pots were stacked atop one another in the fashion the Turks called *çaydanlık* and the cups were the tulip-shaped glass variety with facets around the base.

Polat waited until the young woman left before standing and walking to the tea cart. He raised a tea glass to inspect in the morning light pouring across over the polished tabletop. Rainbows scattered before him with every turn of the glass. "It must be odd, being in a new country. Many new traditions." He set the glass down and poured dark tea from the top pot of the *çaydanlık*. He lifted it to his nose and smelled it, his mustache twitching, then poured hot water from the larger base pot to dilute the brew to a rich shade of honey.

Saffron accepted the cup, as well as a lump of sugar which he deposited onto the little disk of a saucer. The sunlight caught in the steam wafting from the cup, so thick it looked as if a candle had just been snuffed out.

Polat poured another glass of tea. "Our nation is very new. We have many old ways that are put aside. You have heard of *alafranga*, perhaps?"

"No, I haven't," she replied, sipping the tea. It was scalding hot and bitter.

"It is the ways of your people." Polat sat across from her. "Europeans. Many think we should do away with the *alaturca* and take up your ways, instead." He blew steam from the top of his tea, green eyes somber on her as if awaiting her response. She kept her face politely neutral.

"Me?" He set his glass down without drinking it. "I am proud of my people, where we come from. The wisdom of *Allah* is in our rules of behavior. Respect for our elders, our betters. Caring for the stranger, the poor, the weak. These laws are protection.

"For example, women are not permitted to be in the company of a man not of their family," he said easily. "This is not permitted. *Haram*, we call it." He nodded at the closed door. "It is understood that as a police officer, it is sometimes necessary, but we see there are evils when a man and woman are together unaccompanied."

This was said in a suggestive manner, not as though Polat meant something inappropriate, but that he was coming around to bringing up something *he* thought was.

"A man was seen leaving your room on Sunday," Polat said, confirming her guess. "A man with dark hair."

Heat stung her face. "My fiancé has dark hair, Inspector."

He didn't reply. She had to explain it, then. "Mr. Ashton came to my room when he returned with the crew from Kadifekale. He wanted to learn if my injury had improved. I'm sure you have heard from others that my ankle was injured when a piece of the castle fell near me during our visit to Kadifekale."

Polat grunted.

She didn't want to say it, but it had to be said because it might be important to Polat's investigation. "Mr. Neill did come to my door that evening to inquire as to the condition of my ankle. We spoke only a few words before he went away again. He didn't come inside. He was merely being polite."

Her throat tightened at the words. Martin *had* been polite, and sweet, and kind. How dreadful was it that he was dead. Murdered.

She opened her mouth to begin sharing what she had learned, as she ought to have done before he lectured her on his culture's correct behavior.

"The others in your group think you and the dead man were having a love affair," Polat said.

"We were not," she said firmly. "I am engaged to Mr. Ashton."

"Yet there are several who said they have seen you and the dead man be . . ." He looked back down at his notes. "Cozy. This word can mean many things but I believe it means close together. Private, maybe."

More heat burned in her, humiliation and anger. "It means Martin Neill and I worked closely together at the dig site," she said sharply. "*My fiancé* assigned us to work together. He would hardly have done so if he had a concern over my loyalty."

Satisfaction gleamed in Polat's green eyes. "This disturbs you. Why?"

Exasperated, Saffron shot back, "Because it is ridiculous. I was not having an affair with Martin Neill."

"Why is it ridiculous?"

It was ridiculous for him to ask why the notion was ridiculous, but she saw how her temper had been roused. She'd intended to be useful, not fall into the trap of being considered a hysterical woman. With a tight leash on her temper, she explained, "I was not having an affair with Martin Neill. That is a nasty rumor, and this line of thinking will not help find out what really happened to Martin. I have information for you, some observations from his peers and some insights that you might be not yet be aware of." She explained the discovery Clark had claimed for himself and the night Martin had left the hotel. Alexander had confirmed Martin had not been among the assistants smoking the water pipe at the *han* in the marketplace. She decided leave out her adventure to the *hammam* to clear Yusef Çağrı of suspicion.

Polat did not respond, leaving her unsure if she ought to continue.

He looked at her for a long, uncomfortable moment before nodding. "I see. I have been told by your superiors that you were to engage in some . . ." He paused, and flipped back through his notebook. "Chemistry, yes? You have chemicals for what purpose?"

Alarm trilled down her spine. He had ignored her information and jumped straight to a question which could only suggest an accusation. "Yes," she replied stiffly. "I have a set of chemicals for the analysis of plants found in the agora's storerooms."

"Where is it?"

"It is in my hotel room."

His green eyes sharpened. "Oh?"

"Yes," Saffron said, dreading his impending assumption. "When I was injured, I asked Mr. Ashton to bring it to me so I could do my work from the hotel, since I was to rest my ankle."

"I see. I would like to see this set," he said, standing.

Saffron led the inspector out of the room and up the stairs. Clark and his friends were milling around just inside the open doors of the dining room, and his eyes glittered when their eyes met.

Just as they reached the first floor's landing, Mrs. Demirel emerged from her room. A thought leapt into Saffron's mind, and she called to her.

"Mrs. Demirel," she said, "would you be kind enough to accompany Inspector Polat and myself to my bedroom? The inspector informs me that it is not appropriate for us to be alone in each other's company."

Mrs. Demirel's eyes flicked nervously between them. "Er, why, yes, Miss Everleigh. It is, er, wise, to have a chaperone, is it not?" In a voice that was meant to be a whisper but clearly was not, she added, "It might have saved you from a good deal of trouble, had Mr. Ashton thought to provide you one, don't you think?"

Any feelings of relief at having a witness to her room's search soured at that comment. "Indeed," she muttered.

She unlocked her room and let the inspector and Mrs. Demirel inside.

He surveyed the room for a moment, taking in the curtains stirring in the breeze, the neatly made bed and tidy desk. "The chemicals?"

Saffron withdrew the case from the desk drawer and stepped back for Polat to examine it. He undid the leather strap securing the case from the loop and flipped the lid up. "There are some glasses broken."

"What?"

She took a step forward to look inside, but he held up a hand. "Do not touch."

She did manage to look, however, and saw there were at least two cracked vials. Polat held one up, exposing how the chemicals had leaked, darkening the leather base. Her stomach turned. "I don't know how that happened. I checked it all over just a few days ago, and everything was intact."

"I see." Polat looked around the room with new interest and nodded. "I will search the rest of the room now."

Saffron flinched. Mrs. Demirel reached a hand out to her with a noise of distress. "Is that quite necessary, Inspector? Surely . . ." She bit her lip, then visibly stiffened her spine. "My husband is the liaison between the expedition team and the government. I believe he will have some things to say about this, as I'm sure will Hayrettin *efendi*. And there are . . ." She wavered. "I am sure there must be some laws about property searches. One must have a warrant in England. I think it must be the same here."

Polat glared at her. "Where is your husband, then?"

"I will take you to him," Mrs. Demirel said firmly.

The inspector stomped to the door, and swung around to point a finger at Saffron. "You give your key to me. No one will enter this room until I allow."

He marched from the room. Mrs. Demirel gave Saffron's arm a brief, reassuring squeeze. "It will be all right, dear. Mr. Demirel will sort it all out, I'm sure."

Saffron followed them out and watched as Inspector Polat locked the door and pocketed the key, willing that to be true, though she couldn't quite make herself believe it.

Chapter 28

Saffron followed Mrs. Demirel and Inspector Polat as if in a dream, uncertain how things had spiraled so quickly out of control. Polat had ignored her information and instead listened to the crew's malicious gossip. He wanted to search her room. He clearly thought she was responsible for Martin's death.

Alexander stood at the bottom of the stairs, and he looked to be arguing with Dr. Henry.

"—find someone at the embassy—" he was saying, voice low.

Dr. Henry shook his head, frowning. "Getting the embassy involved will ruin everything! Lot of stuffed-shirt diplomats will descend on us and fuss like a bunch of old hens, picking at everything we do."

Alexander halted his rebuttal when he saw Saffron trailing Inspector Polat and Mrs. Demirel down the stairs.

Dr. Henry clapped Alexander on the back with a ringing *smack*. "This will be cleared up in no time, Ashton. Now, get your lads together. This has already eaten into our schedule!" He strode away.

"This way, Inspector," Mrs. Demirel said, and they went down the hall in search of Mr. Demirel.

Saffron arrived at the bottom of the stairs just as Alexander had turned to speak to her. "I think you're right."

His shoulders slumped. "You heard that?"

"I've been hearing all sorts of things," she said bitterly. "Including that Inspector Polat wants to search my room. Mrs. Demirel managed to head him off for now. But it's not looking good, Alexander. I think he has serious suspicions about me."

His hand found hers, rough from the work in the agora, and he squeezed. "We'll work it out."

"When the inspector opened my chemistry kit, some of the vials were damaged. It looked exactly like I'd tried to hide that I'd used some of the materials."

"That no doubt looked bad," Alexander said slowly. "But it's nothing an analysis of the case can't prove is innocent." His gaze strayed to where the motorcars sat before the hotel, visible through the hotel's perpetually open front doors. "We've got to get moving. You haven't eaten, have you?"

They entered the dining room. Naturally, Clark and his friends were arrayed at one of the tables. He smirked at her as she passed.

She went to the *çaydanlık* and poured herself a cup of tea into which she put a good deal of sugar. She wanted to wash the taste of Polat's bitter offering from her mouth. She poured Alexander a glass and offered it to him.

"I wouldn't touch that, if I were you, Ashton," Clark called. "Dunmore, weren't you recently telling me of a certain kind of spider found in these parts? *Latrodectus tredecimguttatus.* The black widow." He paused to allow his friends to snicker. "Kills its lovers, doesn't it?"

Dunmore sat at the table next to Clark's, and when Alexander turned to stare at him, he flushed.

Clark grinned. "Don't worry, we've plenty of witnesses here, Dunmore. She has to lure you away into a dark corner before she bites."

Looking Clark dead in the eye, Saffron said, "I did not lure Martin anywhere, and I did not kill him."

With a face of mocking shock, he laughed. "I didn't say anything about poor Mr. Neill. Interesting that's where your mind jumped so easily."

"You are the one spreading the rumors that I was involved with his death, which have reached the inspector—"

Clark looked positively gleeful. "Oh, dear."

"—and now he believes I had something to do with it," Saffron finished.

He dropped his voice to a hiss. "You had an awful lot to say to the inspector. Maybe if you'd kept your mouth shut, you wouldn't be so interesting to him."

She might have hoped Clark all but admitting he started the rumor of her infidelity out of some sort of revenge for her telling the inspector about his actions against her would have swayed the opinions of those present, but no one else seemed perturbed by the admission. She saw only amusement and discomfort in the faces around her.

"I am trying to help the inspector find out what happened to Martin." She hardened her voice, forcing the spectators to meet her eyes. "And if he truly was murdered and the inspector is focused on me, that means he will not find whoever actually did it. That means everyone here is in danger."

"We have no interest in your fearmongering, Miss Everleigh," Clark said, turning away with a dismissive wave. "Someone might take it as a threat, you know."

Alexander stirred at her side, and fury glinted in his eyes. She grasped his arm. It was clear that Clark had the support of these people, and any move made against him would only be a further black mark against her. No matter how badly she wanted to throttle him herself.

"Who knows," Clark added, eying the hand she'd laid on Alexander, "poor Ashton might be the next. Then we'd know for sure, wouldn't we?"

Something inside her cracked at the way the others tittered around them. As if it was all a joke: Martin's death, her suddenly perilous future, the idea that Alexander might get hurt, too. "Why?" The word burst out of that cracked place, no longer strong or accusatory, but plaintive. "Why do you hate me so much?"

Clark's gaze was lazy and indifferent. A cruel little smile cut his lips. "Because you're in my way." He flicked his wrist at her. "Go away, then."

Though she felt uneasy leaving the hotel with Polat's threat of searching her things hanging over her, Saffron went to the dig site. She thought being among the bustle of the site might alleviate some of her worry or grief, but nothing could fix her attention. Everywhere she looked held a shadow of Martin. Not long after arriving, she took herself on a walk around the site under the pretext of sketching some of the discarded stones strewn over the field and the plants tangled around them.

She passed an hour in that way, and then another, and soon rocks and weeds could no longer distract her from the sense of impending doom. She sat down in the shade of a neighboring building and watched the men around the pit. Good progress had been made in digging out more of the arcade of the agora. Clark's discovery of the necklace had only inspired more enthusiastic effort. Everyone wanted to be the next to find something of interest.

She opened her notebook to her page of conjectures about Martin's death, and reviewed the words already spinning in her mind once again.

Suspects: Joseph Clark, Yusef Çağrı, and, unfortunately, *Saffron Everleigh.*

Motives: Clark's desire to keep quiet about taking credit for Martin's artifact (unlikely, since according to the other assistants, Martin had no plans to claim it), and . . . What was her motivation supposed to be for killing Martin? They were supposedly having an affair. Why would she kill him, then? To keep it quiet, most likely. That certainly would make her a vicious creature, to kill her lover so casually. Black widow, indeed.

In her section about Martin's movements, she returned to the question of where Martin had gone the first night in Smyrna. Alexander had confirmed that he had not been among the assistants at the *han*. Where had he gone? Had he consumed something there that took two weeks to make its effects known? Or had he made an enemy that night, one that found him later?

She tapped her pen against the page, eyes trained on the locals slowly climbing up from the pit, arms straining to carry buckets loaded with dirt. They crossed to where the assistants were clustered around the sieves. As she watched the assistants scoop the new dirt into wooden frames, Clark swaggered over. He leaned an arm on the tripod used to suspend the largest sieve, and she imagined his oily voice asking what things the assistants had found that day. "Pass it over here," he'd say, "let an expert have a look. And while we're at it, I'll just take this over and show Dr. Balthazar. Don't mind me if I mention I discovered it while hard at work . . ."

"What rot," she muttered to herself, and without quite deciding on it, stowed her notebook in her satchel and got to her feet. She didn't care if it made her an outcast, she would not let Clark get away with intimidating any more of the crew into handing over what they'd rightly found.

By the time she'd marched across the field and around the pit, the group had abandoned the sieves and were retreating into the mess tent. She made for them, but Clark broke off and rounded the tent, disappearing from view. Torn between wanting to confront him and wanting to warn the assistants, she stood there, staring at the gap in the tents with consternation.

Finally, she decided chasing after Clark would do her no good. She'd only waste her breath, whereas the assistants might be convinced to band together to stand up to him.

She passed by the prize table—what the crew called the artifact table when out of earshot of the Turks—and paused to search out the fragment Clark had stolen from Martin. Ceramic, they'd said, white with red patterns.

Her eyes skated over dusty bits of clay pottery, twisted pieces of rusted metal, and a number of informative but ultimately average items. There was a piece of a ceramic dish, creamy white, no longer than her finger, and marked "Balthazar, 5D, Italian, likely fifteenth century," but that didn't match the description.

She stared hard at the table, her intention to warn the assistants fading from her mind as she realized that Clark hadn't turned in the fragment Martin had found.

As if the universe were conspiring to kick her when she was down, heavy pain gathered low in Saffron's abdomen throughout the afternoon. By the time she'd climbed into the motorcar to return to the hotel, she'd have liked nothing better than to retreat into a scalding hot bath and then into bed to wait out the first few days of her courses. A working woman didn't wait it out, of course, but with how many suspicious or outright hostile looks she was getting around the dig site now, she could admit to herself that she would like to hide right about now. The voice of Elizabeth in her head didn't even harass her for wanting to avoid the attention and the consequences of her biology; Elizabeth always treated menstruation as a dire illness that required tending. She would have been the one to tuck Saffron into her bed with a hot water bottle and a book of poetry written by one of her angry poetess friends.

Of course, there was no Elizabeth here, and as she stepped into the hotel foyer and queued for her room key, she remembered that there was to be no bath or bed, either. Polat had barred her entry to her bedroom.

"A thousand apologies, Miss Everleigh," Mr. Koray said in a hushed voice when she reached the counter, "but Inspector Polat was so insistent—"

"I understand, Mr. Koray. Did the inspector give any indication how long it would take to settle whether or not he would carry out his search today?"

Mr. Koray glanced at the clock on the desk. It was nearly six in the evening. "I do apologize, miss, but he did not. I believe his intention was to search as soon as possible, but . . ." He shrugged helplessly, and Saffron believed it truly did give him distress to have to tell her she could not access her room.

Ordinarily, she would not have pushed, but given how it felt her organs were being wrung out like a dishtowel, it was only a matter of time before she was in true, urgent need of the supplies in her room. "Are Mrs. Henry or Mrs. Demirel here?"

"No, miss," he said regretfully. "They dine with the consul general this evening."

"Is there—" She shifted on her feet, and at the sensation of a warm rush of pure disaster, she froze. "Is there a maid, or cook, or—" She bit her lip, utterly mortified.

Mr. Koray was looking at her with wide, uncertain eyes. "Miss Everleigh? What is the matter?"

"I am in need of some of the things in my room," she whispered. "I would not ask, Mr. Koray, but it is quite urgent. You could stand at the door, and ensure I don't take anything other than—than what I need. You could search what I take yourself."

He studied her face, and his obvious anxiety fell away. "You are in great need, I think." He straightened up, tugging down the bottom of his waistcoat, and nodded once. "I will accompany you."

As she had all day, she wondered what would be the harm in Polat searching her room. She hadn't had a problem when Dr. Henry had searched her room and everyone else's for the missing artifacts. Despite Elizabeth's best efforts to convince her otherwise, Saffron's camiknickers were nicely boring white art silk, nothing that a reformed Lothario like Dr. Henry wouldn't have seen a hundred times over, nor would the products Elizabeth had stashed in her cases have given him pause; Saffron had to think that Dr. Henry was familiar with Mrs. Stopes's contraceptive wares.

Mr. Koray unlocked the door to her room and stood back for her to slip inside. She went to the dressing table, opened the drawer containing her box of Kotex, and hesitated before turning to Mr. Koray. She held up the prewrapped, rectangular gauze and slim belt it would be pinned to. "This is for, er, lady's business."

It took only one look to confirm what Saffron had guessed; from the cursory glance and the color heating his cheeks, the man must have a wife.

With a look of pained politeness, he nodded and turned slightly toward the hall. Perhaps he understood she would need underthings as well, bless him. Since she was in the room, she might as well gather a few more harmless things as she had no idea when Inspector Polat would allow her back inside. She opened another drawer for a rack of pins, and her finger pricked on something sharp.

She drew her hand back with a swallowed hiss. She pulled the drawer back to find a shard of glass. Several, in fact, sitting just inside, as if a vial had been sitting there and been shattered by the drawer catching on it.

The telltale lip on one of the smooth curves told her it was just that, a vial. She lifted it and a faint chemical smell drifted from it.

How on earth had one of her chemical vials slipped into this drawer for her to break?

Her heartbeat sped up as a horrible understanding began to simmer in her mind. *She* hadn't broken a vial. She hadn't removed the vials of chemicals from their case when she'd looked it over when Alexander had delivered it to her, and she was sure this drawer had been shut when Inspector Polat had examined the chemical case that morning.

Someone had put this here. Someone who knew her room would be searched.

She stared down at the shards in horror. What if the person who'd actually harmed Martin—if they existed—had planted this here? What if she'd just pricked her finger on the vial that had held the poison that killed him?

She stepped back, heart now thudding painfully against her chest. She was afraid, that was why her heart was beating like that. She was alarmed, that was why her head was spinning. She was not poisoned. She was not.

"Miss?"

She flinched at Mr. Koray's gentle voice. "I beg your pardon," she said quickly, "just a moment more."

With as much care as she could manage with hands shaking and watchful eyes on her back, she used tweezers to pick the shards into a handkerchief, then used another to wipe the drawer of the tiniest pieces. She bundled both into her pocket, then hurried to the wardrobe to retrieve the clothing she needed. These she shook out in front of Mr. Koray, guilt eating at her as she took full advantage of his kindness to do the very thing Polat feared she would do, hide evidence.

She managed her hygiene problem in the lavatory downstairs. When she was dressed, with the handkerchief containing the broken glass carefully tucked in her soiled clothing, she stood in the center of the small room and forced her lungs to fill and empty several times. Then she went to find Alexander.

Chapter 29

Alexander slipped on a shirt over damp skin before answering the quiet knock on the door. When he saw it was Saffron standing outside with a bundle of fabric that look suspiciously like the clothing she'd worn that day, he hurried her inside, unwilling for her to be seen standing outside in a hall lined with the rooms of their colleagues. Her face was pale, her lips pursed, and her eyes were haunted.

"What is it?" he asked the moment the door was shut.

She pressed her back against it, her head falling back and eyes closing. With her jaw clenched, the lines of her pale throat were strong, tempting even. Any sensual curiosity was banished when sob tore from her.

He stepped into her, pressing her to him while she shook. "What is it?" he repeated softly.

Face red and streaked with tears, she looked up at him. "I think I'm in real trouble."

She showed him the broken glass and explained her suspicions about why it was planted.

"Surely no one truly believes me capable of murder, even if I do study poisons," she said, her damp eyes searching his. "Clark just said those things to be horrible. Right?"

Alexander wanted desperately to be able to agree with her, but he wasn't sure he could. "For once, you're not underestimated," he said with a sorry attempt at a smile.

She didn't return it. In fact, that set her off crying again.

"I shouldn't have come," she choked out. He helped her to the bed, where he drew her onto his lap. "I should have just stayed behind."

He allowed her to cry uninterrupted as more doubts and regrets and fear poured out of her. It weighed him down, realizing the extent of her tortured feelings, especially when guilt began to taint her words.

"I should have helped him," she whispered brokenly. "Martin was *poisoned*. I should have realized it and helped him."

She was silent after that. Alexander's brain, meanwhile, kicked into high gear. Dr. Henry had dismissed his concerns that morning. If he'd just acted, he could have already found legal help. He needed to find a way to protect Saffron, and the evidence planted in her room—for that had to be what the broken vial was—made it plain that the rules he'd thought this investigation would follow had been changed by Martin Neill's killer. It was only a matter of time before they found a way to put more evidence in Inspector Polat's path and Saffron would be officially charged with murder.

Gently, he shifted her onto the mattress and stood. Then he went onto his knees before her, and took her cold hands in his.

"Saffron." Her eyes lifted to his. "Marry me."

Her face broke into a sad smile. "I already said I would."

A feeling of rightness settled over him, chased by urgency. "Marry me now. Right now."

Saffron stared at him. "Polat is probably going to arrest me!"

Alexander tucked a hair behind her ear absently. "I know."

"I can't bring any more trouble on you. It's better if—"

Surprising even himself, he smiled. "Saffron, you've brought me trouble since I met you. Trouble, adventure, excitement . . . I can't imagine my life without you." He kissed her briefly, fiercely. "I won't consider it. If we marry now, I can act for you and arrange everything for a lawyer. As your fiancé I can't do much. As . . . as your husband I would have more rights to protect you and act for you."

He could see the internal battle she faced. The image of her surrounded by flowers and smiles, the one he'd imagined countless times since setting his ring on her finger, faded into the cold reality they faced. "It's not what either of us want, but I can't let you deal with being wrongly arrested for murder in a foreign country alone. Let me protect you."

"But . . . we should get married because we love each other. Not because I'm being charged with *murder*!" Saffron said, her voice thick with tears.

His own throat grew tight. "It's because I love you that I can't let you face this alone."

As an answer, Saffron kissed him.

Then they went to find the Henrys.

The Henrys agreed immediately to be their witnesses, and a brief conversation with the hotel's proprietor informed them that the nearest church was just down the hill. Mr. Koray mentioned apologetically that it was unlikely to be led by someone with any English.

"Miss Everleigh," Mrs. Henry murmured as Alexander hurried away to find Banks to translate, "I know time is of the essence, but perhaps you would care to take the time to change into something a little more celebratory." She glanced meaningfully down at Saffron. "Or perhaps even just don some stockings?"

Saffron was still a little dazed to find it was her wedding day, or night, rather, since the sun was setting. "That would be a good idea."

Mrs. Henry bundled her off to her own rooms, a suite she shared with Dr. Henry. She pressed a snifter of liquor of some kind into Saffron's hands, then went to work primping her. She helped Saffron change into a dress of her own, light-colored powder blue silk trimmed with lace that tickled Saffron's arms and calves, and offered her a pair of earrings of silver figured into flowers, all the while recounting her own wedding day with soothing blandness and the occasional quiet laugh.

Fifteen minutes later, the party met in the lobby. They set out in a pair of taxis ordered by Mr. Koray down the quiet, dusty road. They sat in silence, hands clasped tightly in darkness, for only a few minutes before the motorcar wrenched to a stop.

"My grandparents will never speak to me again," Saffron said, voice wavering.

Alexander's eyes gleamed in the darkness. "Neither will my mother. Let's go."

The church was a matchbox of a place in a stand of cypress trees. Saffron was reminded of a jewelry box when they walked inside. The ceiling was set with octagonal insets, their centers stamped with flowers. The light of dozens of candles softly flickered off unlit stained glass in the apse and glimmered on the brass incense braziers and candle holders. The scents of old books, frankincense, and something herbal lingered in the air, familiar and exotic all at once.

Banks and the Henrys were already inside, and Banks was in conversation with an elderly man in black who could only be the priest. Banks waved them forward.

"He'll do it," he said breathlessly.

The priest was shorter than she was and wore a long robe that hung from a rounded belly, and when he met her eyes, he spoke softly.

"He wants to know you want this," Banks translated for her. "He says you look afraid."

"I am," she said, an anxious laugh bubbling up out of her, followed by a rush of tears. She blinked them back to look at Alexander. "And I do. I do want this."

The ceremony was brief. Saffron's heart was pounding too loudly in her ears to make out the measured words of the priest, or Banks's murmured translation. Hysteria lingered in her periphery, held back only by the steady pressure of Alexander's warm hands on hers.

And then Alexander was speaking to her, and she focused on his lips as they spoke the words binding them together. Then it was her turn to stumble over them. Then they were married.

Emotion rose up and crashed into her, tender and sweet and stinging. She searched Alexander's eyes, unsure what she was looking for in their dark depths, but she found it there all the same.

Their witnesses offered congratulations, and Saffron was surprised to see a twinkle of tears in Dr. Henry's eyes as he gruffly offered his best wishes. They signed the church's registry, and Alexander led her back outside, leaving Banks and the Henrys to talk to the priest.

In the shadow of the cypresses, Alexander took her in his arms. His kiss was one to blot out thought of anything but what they had just become to one another.

Breathless, they went to the waiting taxi.

A giddy laugh burst out of Saffron as she asked, "How are you, husband?"

Smiling, he kissed her hand. "Quite well, wife."

"I suppose we shouldn't tell people, should we?" she asked, her smile fading.

"I don't expect it'll come up with anyone except the police."

"But if anyone sees you . . ." She pressed her lips together, too embarrassed to continue. Perhaps he meant this marriage to be for the benefit of the investigation only, at least until things settled down. Perhaps he didn't mean to make it *officially* official tonight.

Alexander's brow dipped before a rather boyish grin spread over his face. "Don't worry about that, Mrs. Ashton." He kissed her.

She wanted to enjoy the moment of giddy pleasure it brought her, but the closer they got to the hotel, the harder reality pressed in on them.

When they arrived, another motorcar was parked outside.

Fear flared in Saffron's chest. It was possible it was not Polat, returned to with the warrant he needed to search her things, but she knew that it was.

Alexander tucked her close to him and they stepped into the warmly lit lobby.

Mr. Koray hurried around the reception desk when he saw them enter.

"Mr. Ashton, Miss Everleigh," he said, "a moment, if you please—"

Polat interrupted him from the landing of the stairs. "There is no need, *efendi*. I have finished." He came down the rest of the stairs to stand before Saffron and Alexander. He looked only at her, satisfaction in his cold green eyes. "You will come with me to the police station now, Miss Everleigh."

"Why?" Saffron was glad her voice didn't shake. "I'm sure I can answer any additional questions here."

"There are no more questions to ask. I am arresting you for the murder of Martin Neill."

Although they were all expecting it, the impact of the words felt like an enormous gong that rang and reverberated around the room. Voices quieted beyond the open parlor doors.

Her voice did shake this time. "I did not kill Martin Neill."

Polat's mustache tipped up to one side as he gave her a curt smile. "Come."

She looked to Alexander, unable to hide the panic welling up in her. He glared at Polat. "You are making a mistake, Inspector."

"Now, Miss Everleigh," Polat snapped, reaching out a hand for her.

She released Alexander's arm and moved to the door, unwilling to let Polat touch her, much less drag her to his motorcar. She gave Alexander a nervous twitch of a smile. "Will you come to the police station?"

He nodded gravely.

"Good," she said. "Don't worry about me. I'll be all right."

And then Polat stepped past her and led her down the stairs, into the motorcar, and away from her husband.

CHAPTER 30

The Henrys and Banks arrived just as the dust from Polat's vehicle was settling. After Alexander had explained Saffron had just been taken away, the two other men burst into a cacophony of outrage and ideas.

"We are not doing this here," Mrs. Henry hissed, cutting off Dr. Henry's demands that they go down to the police station to protest immediately. "Come to our suite, Mr. Ashton, Mr. Banks."

Alexander allowed himself to be whisked upstairs. He didn't bother to correct Dr. Henry when he pushed a drink into his hand, nor prevent him from raging around the room as he complained about the unreasonable treatment of his crew. Banks stood at Alexander's side, silent and worried, while Mrs. Henry sat at the writing desk and began writing something.

"Get Demirel in here," Dr. Henry growled at them, and Banks slipped from the room. "He was supposed to fix this, wasn't he?"

Alexander stared down into the amber depths of the liquid in his glass, and for a moment wished he could numb himself in its burn. But that wouldn't do anyone any good, least of all Saffron.

"Excuse me," he said to no one in particular, and left the room.

He went to his own room, shucking his suit jacket and loosening his tie before opening the window to air out the over-warm room. He allowed himself ten minutes to wallow in fear and self-pity, then he went to the desk.

The letter to Saffron's cousin, John, was awkward. He was her closest male relation other than her grandfather, and an attorney besides. It required several drafts before he was satisfied it conveyed the appropriate urgency without being alarming. There was a good chance he'd decide to send him a telegraph tomorrow rather than wait for the mail, but it helped to put all the facts and theories in writing.

Writing to Violet Everleigh, his now mother-in-law, was another story. He made several attempts, but they all sounded wrong. How was he to explain that her only child was under arrest for murder in a foreign country? That he, whom she'd met exactly twice, was now married to her daughter?

After staring at yet another discarded paper, he realized that he was in the same situation. Saffron had never met his parents. His mother was a whirlwind of emotion and affection, and she'd raged from wild excitement that her son was getting married to deep hurt that she hadn't met the girl he'd asked to join their family. His father was her foil, hard and unperturbed, the rocky shore against which his mother crashed. As to the rest of his family, individually they were manageable, but all together they were overwhelming, even to him. Saffron had had a hard time after all that had happened with her own family earlier that year, and there'd never seemed to be a good time to reveal the extent of his own familial drama to her.

They hadn't even started properly planning their wedding, yet here they were, married. His father would be disappointed. His mother would be heartbroken. And that would only be their reaction to their quick marriage, not that his wife was being accused of poisoning and killing a man.

He leaned back in his chair, gazing out through the window onto the black night. What was he going to do? He'd no doubt at the time that marrying Saffron now was the best option. He didn't regret it. But the whole situation seemed suddenly eight times more complicated.

Putting aside the letter to Mrs. Everleigh for the moment, Alexander instead wrote to Adrian. It was comforting to think that his older brother would be cackling with laughter that his brother had managed to get married and his new sister-in-law was wrapped up in more trouble. He, at least, would appreciate the absurdity of it all.

He felt better after writing it all out for Adrian. He addressed the envelopes and put them into a stack on his desk, rearranging the items on the small desk as precisely as he could. A thought had occurred to him as he wrote out Adrian's address. Two, actually. He opened the envelope addressed to Adrian and added a postscript which made him smile slightly, despite everything. He put it aside, then took out another paper to write to Elizabeth Hale. The letter came easily enough. He knew she'd be furious to miss their wedding, but glad he'd be able to better help Saffron.

He stood. There was a possibility that he wouldn't even need to send the letters. This could be all resolved in a matter of hours.

That optimistic thought flickered and died as he recalled the broken glass now hidden in an envelope between the pages of his thickest book in his trunk.

He paced around the room for a minute. The police had searched Saffron's room. What had they found? Was there more hidden there?

He wished he could search it himself. He wanted to see her things, soak up whatever of her presence he could.

He rubbed a hand over his face. He was being pathetic, he knew, but he couldn't help it. Saffron had been his wife for all of half an hour, and already, she'd been torn away.

Searching her room wouldn't help. Dr. Henry was too upset to be of use, and he didn't know what Demirel could do so late in the evening. The Turks weren't likely to take kindly to diplomats—

Alexander froze, hand still covering his mouth. Then he went to the desk and began another letter, this one addressed to the British embassy.

Saffron stared at the cracked wall of her room. Now that the police station was quiet, she had a lot of time to herself to think.

Though it was quite late, her mind buzzed. Polat had questioned her for more than an hour upon reaching the police station, and he did, indeed, formally arrest her at the end of it. Alexander had been there; she could hear him arguing with the other officer on duty, but he'd apparently been sent away before Polat was finished with her.

Her arrest paperwork, all in the languid Arabic script the Turks used, was completely incomprehensible to her. She'd had to interrupt them to correct her name. She was no longer Saffron Everleigh, at least for legal purposes.

"What?" Polat had spat at her.

"Mr. Ashton and I were married earlier this evening."

"Why? And why did you say nothing of this before?"

"You may check the registry at St. Mary Magdalene in Bornova to confirm it."

She was photographed by the second police officer, a mostly silent middle-aged man, and then shown to the little room in which she would spend the night. For all she knew, she'd spend the foreseeable future there.

Inspector Polat had, as promised, searched her room, and taken a number of her research materials as evidence. She saw them being processed by the second officer when she'd arrived: a stack of her books and notebooks, as well as her chemistry set. He did not, of course, find the broken vial someone had planted in her bedroom, but what else might the person have stashed among her things?

It was Polat's questioning that revealed to her the majority of his evidence: the testimony of the crew members that not only had she been seen going in and out of Martin's room before his death, but she had been morally wounded by the rumor of her infidelity, and that *Martin* had been the one to tell others of their affair. Polat therefore viewed her motive as revenge for her damaged honor, something that seemed to be very serious to him.

When she demanded to know who told him that Martin had started the rumor of their affair, he would not answer.

"If it was Mr. Clark, you should know that he has it out for me," Saffron had told him. "I told you he's been sabotaging my participation in the expedition for weeks. He admitted he circulated the rumor about the affair—he did so in front of half a dozen witnesses. Ask them."

But Polat had ignored that, and the explanations of her purpose in Martin's room, the reason she'd spent so much time with him, and the other possible suspects and their motives.

She asked why she was arrested and not Mrs. Henry or Mrs. Demirel, who were also in and out of Martin's room. Polat just sneered that they both appeared to have some sense of loyalty to their husbands. She bit her tongue on what she thought about that.

It was beyond irritating that this was how she was to be cast: a faithless seducer foolish enough to let people see her leaving the room of her poisoned lover. If she ever did contemplate murder, she certainly wouldn't be stupid enough to be seen near the scene of the crime or choose poison. Everyone knew it was her special area of study. Still more maddening was that Polat gave her no indication of what the toxin was. If she knew, she could prove she had no access to it, or better still, perhaps tell him who did have access and point him in the direction of Martin's real killer.

The police station was now quiet. A clock ticking loudly somewhere beyond her stuffy little room was the only sound within the walls. Her chest began to feel tight and heavy, the lump in her throat painful.

She couldn't believe she was spending her wedding night in a Turkish jail cell. She and Elizabeth had joked about wedding nights being scary, but this was a little on the nose.

Good Lord, what would Eliza say? She tried to imagine her best friend ribbing her about the ridiculous circumstances, but could only imagine her disappointment that she'd missed Saffron's wedding.

Her fingers idly traced the pattern of the lace on her dress. She looked down at it, realizing that this was her wedding dress. Her pang of sadness recollecting Elizabeth's excited ideas for her wedding outfit were replaced by a surge of gratitude for Mrs. Henry for giving her something pretty to wear. The dress was rather lovely. It was a pity she'd ruin it by sleeping in it.

And Alexander . . .

She couldn't think of him now, how she ached for him, how he must be feeling. She would tuck those thoughts away; they'd do her no good, stuck in here.

Perhaps when morning came, he would bring some solution. She would walk out of the police station with him, and they could forget any of this ever happened.

Chapter 31

The taxi driver looked suspiciously at Alexander when he asked to be taken to the police station. He was sure his appearance didn't help; he knew he looked ghoulish after getting no sleep. His night had been spent in restless despair and fruitless plotting, but now he was going to see Saffron, and that meant things could only improve.

The police station was a rather small building not far from the train station they'd passed by two weeks before to reach the hotel in Bornova. In daylight, the first thing Alexander noticed about it, apart from its commonplace exterior, were the thick bars on the windows.

He was used to the police station in London that Inspector Green inhabited, constantly teeming with bobbies in uniforms and crooks being led here and there, and stuffed with desks, benches, chairs, and file cabinets. Inside the Bornova police station, there were only a handful of desks where solemn-looking people sat, some in uniform and some in plain Western suits. They all looked at him when he entered. A young man came forward and began in Turkish. Alexander asked for someone who spoke English or French and an older man with a long scar along his left cheek rose heavily from his desk and came forward.

"How can I help you?" he asked in a husky voice.

"I'm here to see Saffron Everleigh, she was arrested yesterday," Alexander said.

The man narrowed his eyes at him. "Why do you wish to see her?"

"She's my wife." He'd imagined saying those very words what felt like years ago, when they'd first got engaged. It was strange to hear them coming out of his mouth in this setting.

"One moment." The officer walked into the back of the building and Alexander was left standing awkwardly in the midst of the desks. He could feel the eyes of the other police officers on him.

The man with the scar returned a moment later, followed by Inspector Polat.

He looked even more irate than before; the color in his cheeks was high and his eyes were bright. "Why are you here, Mr. Ashton?"

"As I told your colleague, Saffron is my wife. I have the right to see her."

"So she says," Polat said. "Why did you marry so suddenly? You planned to be married in Turkey?"

"I'm sure you can understand why we decided to get married when we did."

"I do not. Explain it."

"From a legal standpoint, it's better I'm able to act for her."

"Why would you need to act for her if she's innocent?"

"The innocent also require lawyers, Inspector."

This didn't seem like a satisfactory answer to Polat. "I think it is strange that you have decided to marry a murderer. Perhaps you were both plotting against Mr. Neill. Mrs. Ashton"—he enunciated the name with disdain—"might be the poisoner, but I would not want my woman to be the subject of the rumors Martin Neill spread. Maybe before long you will also be found guilty."

"I believe that's the responsibility of the courts, not you."

"It will happen no matter whose responsibility it is."

A throat cleared, and Inspector Polat shot a glare at the scarred officer sitting a few feet away. Polat smoothed his uniform jacket. When he spoke again, his voice was calmer. "Why poison, Mr. Ashton?"

Alexander's fists clenched at his sides. "Am I being questioned? I came to see my wife."

Polat went on. "You are not a small, weak man. If you wanted to punish Martin Neil for ruining your wife's reputation, why did you not push him down the stairs of the agora? Or beat him? Why allow your wife to poison him?"

Martin Neill might have entertained an infatuation for Saffron, but he'd been too skittish to even talk to the other men properly. He couldn't imagine the boy suggesting he was having an affair with her to any of them. By all accounts, Neill wanted desperately to make a good impression on all the leaders of the expedition, including Alexander. He would have been an idiot to invent an affair with his superior's fiancée.

He forced his voice to be calm. "Neither of us plotted against Mr. Neill. Mrs. Ashton didn't poison him. Neither of us bore any ill will toward him, even when the rumor was circulated. As I've told you, Mr. Clark had been targeting her for weeks; it was he who started the rumor."

Polat actually laughed at this. "You and your wife have made a tight story. I have heard from several people that she was seen going into Mr. Neill's room, which tells me that their affair was real and she had many chances to poison him. She admits she went to Mr. Neill when he was ill. That is the perfect opportunity."

"Rather than listening to stories, you should be investigating the other members of the expedition team. Some depart soon for field work."

Polat held his gaze, his eyes bulging with indignation. "And you should stay out of it, Mr. Ashton, unless you want to be arrested, too."

Alexander gritted his teeth. "I would like to see my wife now."

Their staring contest was broken by the scarred officer saying, "I will show you to her."

CHAPTER 32

The scarred officer led Alexander to a hall at the back of the building where the air was stagnant and chalky. With a jangle of the keys, the door swung inward to reveal a room just big enough for Alexander to stand with his arms spread, and his wife sitting on a cot.

She got to her feet, a tremulous smile on her face. "Thank you, Inspector Adem," Saffron said to the scarred man, then to Alexander, "Good morning."

He couldn't help but soften a little. "Good morning. Thank you, Inspector."

Inspector Adem locked them in together, and though their time was short, Alexander was sure to make good use of it by kissing his wife within an inch of her life.

"How are you?" he asked when he at last forced himself away from her.

"Much better now," she whispered against his neck.

"Me, too."

They sat on the cot, hands entwined. "Have you eaten? How does your ankle feel?"

"I'd quite forgotten about my ankle, you know," she said, looking down at it. "It's nearly back to normal. And I've eaten. Inspector Adem brought me something from a bakery this morning. It was delicious," she added sheepishly.

"I'm glad. I've written to John, but not your mother and grandparents."

"Oh, good," she said, suddenly anxious. "Don't. I don't want to shock them. I'll write when this is all sorted out. No need to worry them over nothing."

"Right." This was certainly not nothing, but he wasn't going to remind her when she seemed determined to be positive. "I'm going to see Sir Randolph this morning, and see if I can find a telephone to connect to the embassy in Istanbul."

"Shouldn't Mr. Demirel do that?"

"I'm not leaving it to chance. And I had an idea—"

"So have I!" She leaned closer, lowering her voice. "Martin became truly ill when he returned from Kadifekale. We must discover what he got up to there. Can you find out? Perhaps he was drinking with Dr. Johnson's crowd again and was slipped something."

"If that's the case, it'll be long gone by now," Alexander said heavily. "If the poisoner hadn't washed out his flask immediately after poisoning Neill, he would have by now with the police asking questions."

"But someone else might have taken a sip by accident and felt unwell. I also had a thought about Dunmore." She nodded when his brow lifted in confusion. "Yes, Dunmore. Do you remember what Clark said at breakfast, about me being a black widow spider? It occurred to me that it could be venom rather than poison!"

"And you think Dunmore might have given it to Neill?"

"No, Martin was far too helpful to him to want him dead, but Dunmore has venomous specimens, doesn't he?"

Despite himself, Alexander smiled, marveling at his wife's mind. "A brilliant idea, but Dunmore keeps his specimens only as long as it takes to document them, and since his study has nothing to do with venom, I don't believe he has the equipment on hand to extract it."

"He wouldn't have to extract it—"

"The doctor would have noted if Neill had been bitten. The bite would have been irritated and easily spotted on Neill's body, and Dr. Yenmeck is probably familiar with the symptoms of local snakes' venom, anyway."

Saffron attempted a weak smile. "I suppose that counts out Clark slipping one of those spiders into Martin's bedding at Kadifekale, too. Blast."

Footsteps, then the jingle of keys, signaled the end of their conversation. Alexander swiftly kissed her, and they both got to their feet as the door opened.

"I'll be back soon," he told her, squeezing her hand. "Later today, if I have any news." Despite the fact Inspector Adem was at the door, he pressed one more gentle kiss to her lips and murmured, "I love you."

"I love you, too," she whispered back.

Once he was back in the main room with Inspector Adem, Alexander said, loudly enough that Polat, who sat at a desk in the corner, could hear him clearly, "I'm concerned about the conditions under which my wife is being kept. That room is not properly ventilated"—he went on to list several other things he didn't care for about the room—"and I'm afraid my wife's grandfather, Lord Easting, will be most displeased about the conditions in addition to the fact she has not yet had access to legal counsel."

Adem blinked at him. "I understand," he said slowly. Then he turned to Polat and said some things in Turkish that sounded displeased.

Polat got to his feet and stalked over to them. "Who is Lord Easting?"

Of course, Saffron hadn't thought to mention her grandfather was a viscount. "My wife's grandfather is a lord and a very active man in politics. He would not think kindly on your government to learn what has happened here."

Lord Easting was a powerful man in the realm of agriculture and business, but had little to do with politics. A small lie to give Saffron a better place to be locked up in didn't trouble him at all.

Polat's eyes narrowed on him, but Adem looked a little alarmed. He hoped the scarred inspector, at least, took his words to heart. "I will be back later today, and I expect to find improvements."

Polat merely glared at him, and Alexander left the police station to carry out his next task of the morning.

The British Consulate of Smyrna had not been rebuilt after the fires, and so the home of the man in charge of British interests in the city acted as the temporary institution. It was up in the hills of Bornova, a place of medium grandeur similar to that of the hotel. There was no hushed efficiency typical of a government office. The absence of clattering typewriters and hum of familiar accents in conversation told him this place saw few staff or visitors.

A brief, unsatisfying conversation with Sir Randolph Waverly, the consul general, left Alexander at loose ends. Sir Randolph's disinterestedness bothered him, not the least because they'd shared a dinner table with the man several times now, and he was personally acquainted with Saffron. Not even mention of Lord Easting had moved him very much. Mr. Feldman, his secretary, was the one to assure Alexander of Sir Randolph's cooperation and assistance, and he provided no details other than promising to assign someone to look into the case, and no timeline as to when that would happen.

Alexander left the house itching to do something but was at a loss as to what.

He went to the agora, where the rest of the crew was at work, if only to avoid pacing his hotel room. Dr. Henry gave him an approving nod when he walked through the gate.

"My wife wants to talk to you," Dr. Henry told him.

"Now?"

He waved to the mess tent. "Over there."

Alexander found Mrs. Henry and the Demirels inside, sitting around tea and sweets.

"Mr. Ashton," Mrs. Henry said with an inviting smile. "You look like you could do with a cup of tea."

Mrs. Demirel took this as a cue to prepare one for him, and he accepted it gladly. He could certainly do with a dose of caffeine.

"How is Mrs.—Miss Everleigh?" Mrs. Henry asked him, covering her near slip easily. Alexander had asked the Henrys and Banks to keep the marriage a secret for the time being.

"As well as can be expected," he answered honestly. To Mr. Demirel he asked, "Have you learned anything?"

The older man sipped from his glass of tea thoughtfully. "She's lucky the new constitution did away with Sharia law, and that things haven't quite formed up yet in terms of the new judicial system. It's a strange conglomeration of past law and the little prescribed in the new constitution, which is scant on specifics. But the crime she is accused of, murder, is still a capital offense. It's the death penalty."

Everyone went still, staring at Demirel. He sent Alexander an apologetic look. "Miss Everleigh is a British citizen, and a young woman of good character, and from nobility at that. I cannot imagine it will come to pass."

That didn't keep Alexander's heart from pounding near out of his chest. "What can be done?"

"An attorney will be selected from among Sir Randolph's connections, most likely in Istanbul. I've put a call in to the embassy, and I hope to hear from them before Friday."

Mrs. Henry set down her glass of tea with a *clink*. "But then she will stay in jail for days. That's unacceptable."

Demirel raised his hands placatingly. "I'll see what Sir Randolph can do. He might be able to convince them to move her to the consulate for the time being. It's not unheard of, especially for a young woman. Can't imagine what might occur if she stays in the jail."

Alexander's hand fisted around the tea glass so tightly he wouldn't have been surprised if it cracked.

Mrs. Demirel shivered visibly. "Oh, dear."

Demirel seemed to realize his comment had distressed everyone. "I'll go to Sir Randolph this afternoon. Not a worry."

Not long after this, Dr. Henry called for Mr. Demirel to play translator for him, and Alexander found himself left with the ladies.

"I take it that you were not reassured by Mr. Demirel's commentary," Mrs. Henry said without preamble. She reached into her handbag for a cigarette case, flicked it in Alexander's direction in offering, then removed a cigarette and placed it between her lips. Mrs. Demirel flinched at the scratch of her lighter flaring to life. "I beg your pardon, Agatha," Mrs. Henry said flatly. "Did you want one?"

"Oh no." Mrs. Demirel shook her head so vigorously that her hat went askew. "No, no, certainly not."

"What of your own progress, Mr. Ashton?" Mrs. Henry asked. "I don't imagine you've been placated by the police's efforts, nor those of the English diplomacy thus far."

Feeling curiously reassured, he told Mrs. Henry about his attempts to connect with a solicitor and his letter to Saffron's cousin, and mentioned his visit to the jail.

She nodded approvingly when he mentioned bringing up Lord Easting. "I hope that's enough to keep them on their toes, at least until Mr. Demirel's own efforts come to fruition."

Alexander hoped so, too, though he wasn't sure what he could do if he returned to the jail and found Saffron's quarters had not been improved. He would write to Lord Easting and explain it all, even if it meant more trouble in the long run. "Did Dr. Henry ever run into this sort of situation before? Not murder, but foreign police investigating a member of the crew?"

Mrs. Henry's carefully penciled eyebrows lifted. "You assume much if you think Lawrence has told me anything whatsoever of his travels." She lent him a sly smile. "But yes, he has had a number of interactions with foreign authorities. One usually does, when one works in the artifact business. My husband learned early in his career that one is invited to dig up more artifacts if one does not break local laws, nor steal what one digs up. One wouldn't expect such prudence from the man, I know, but on this, he has a surprisingly firmly set moral compass." She tapped ash into the tarnished metal bowl sitting on the coarse surface of the table. "It's one reason why the missing coins and such bother him so much. He's never had something go missing from a dig before. Rather wounds his pride. Not to mention any funny business will upset his ambitions for that new department at the university."

"Artifacts have gone missing?" Mrs. Demirel asked timidly.

Mrs. Henry nodded. "And I think it's a terrible shame Lawrence told Mr. Demirel only after poor Mr. Neill's death. I've reminded him that keeping secrets will make him look complicit, but also garnering the support of the government and the local workers might be essential in discovering what's become of the missing items.

"Having been aware of his peers and their—frankly—amateur methods of getting items out of the countries to which they rightly belong, Lawrence thought he'd devised a rather sound scheme for making sure nothing accidentally leaves the country. Your team's materials are not hundreds of years old, save for Miss Everleigh's, and those are already being co-managed by that professor from the University of Istanbul. I suppose Lawrence felt he had little reason explain to you and your team that all the crew packs up for home will be thoroughly scrutinized."

"You believe the artifacts will be disposed of before we leave," Alexander said, guessing what Mrs. Henry had left unsaid.

Mrs. Demirel looked between them, a frown forming. "But why wait until Mr. Neill's death to tell the locals? Does Dr. Henry think his death is related to the missing objects?"

Smoke snaked out of Mrs. Henry's lips on a sigh. "I couldn't say. But I would hazard a guess he realized that when Dr. Yenmeck reported to the police Martin Neill's death was not natural, any investigating would likely uncover that artifacts had gone missing. He didn't want to be seen as deceiving our hosts."

Alexander had been wondering why the police got involved with Martin Neill's death, but having seen all Neill's paperwork, including his medical report that indicated he was perfectly healthy before they set sail, he supposed he ought to have concluded the doctor had reported it as a suspicious death. Neill being a part of a government-sponsored expedition from a friendly foreign land would certainly make the locals want everything to be squared neatly away. And Dr. Henry admitting things had gone missing certainly upped the stakes further. No wonder Inspector Polat had asked questions about both mysteries.

It made sense, but it inspired new questions: Was Martin Neill killed because he knew something about the artifacts? And if so, did that mean Alexander had to discover what had happened to them in order to prove Saffron's innocence?

Some hours later, Alexander was pacing his room. He'd returned to the hotel to check for messages—he'd had none—and lingered there waiting for Demirel. The older man hadn't returned until after dinner, much to Alexander's frustration. He'd missed his chance to see Saffron that afternoon, for he'd wanted to return to her with news. But Demirel came back without anything more promising than an assurance he'd done all he could with Sir Randolph, and all they could do was wait for legal counsel to arrive from Istanbul.

Alexander paused when a knock sounded at his door. A breathless hotel footman stood outside, a slip of paper in his hand.

"Message for you, sir," the man said, eyes round. "From the British embassy."

He accepted the paper and closed the door. Holding his breath, he held up the message. It read:

Message received. Midnight, blue Molfiada.

Alexander stared down at the telegram in his shaking right hand. It was an odd message, as if someone had misheard every other word of a telephone caller. The note was dated that day, the tenth of October, 1924.

It was ten in the evening now. He had no idea if the message meant midnight tonight, but he had no option but to try to decipher what "Molfiada" meant. His Turkish-English dictionary held no answers, so he dressed in his working clothes, laced his dusty boots, and left his room.

CHAPTER 33

The port was not the kind of place a foreigner should be after dark, Alexander decided as he walked down a grimy dockside street. The docks were shadowy and quiet, it being both too late and too early for much work to be going on there. A few people moved about in and out of view; they had the look of tired sailors, uninterested in anything but rest, drink, or company.

At least he had a vague idea of where he needed to go. Against his better judgement, he'd mentioned "Molfiada" to the man at the hotel's reception desk. The man had frowned for a long moment before asking, "The importers, *efendi*?"

Alexander had shaken his head and said no, he must be mistaken, but that was clear enough. Now he just needed to locate the ship belonging to the Molfiada importers and find whatever was blue.

The scent of salt and fish and the musty undercurrent of persistently wet things greeted him as he turned the corner to the dark glitter of the bay. The moon was bright and high in the sky, casting gently undulating shadows from the ships swaying in the water.

He walked slowly along the dock, hoping to appear more wandering than intentional. He scanned each vessel for its name and squinted at cargo labels on crates as he passed. There were a fair number of both at the moment; freighters, tug boats, large passenger ships bobbed next to the dock stacked four or five crates high in places. At the end of the dock, however, he'd seen nothing referencing Molfiada.

Alexander eased himself against the wall of the building at the end of the dock, thinking furiously as he stared at the dark water. It was possible the message had not meant tonight, but tomorrow. He would return, of course, but it was irritating he'd wasted time on this venture.

He let out a harsh breath, almost a laugh. He'd only wasted time he would have had no idea how to fill.

Through a line of warehouses he walked, lost in thought about how to locate the ship, or building, or cargo, when the sound of footsteps caught his attention. Resisting the temptation to look over his shoulder, Alexander slid against the wall of the warehouse as he turned the corner and waited for whoever had been walking behind him to pass. But they didn't.

He continued down the twisting, cobbled alleyways back toward the main road, but again heard footsteps. Slowing his pace, Alexander pretended to look for a street sign, and spotted someone out of the corner of his eye. They were behind him, half concealed behind a wall.

His first thought was of thieves; the second was that Polat had sent a man to tail him. He wasn't doing anything wrong, but it certainly would look suspicious, wandering around the docks late at night.

Then another idea wriggled its way into his mind: Bey. He hadn't gone back to the old man's tea house, as he'd requested. Could it be him? They weren't far at all from his *han* at the edge of the *kemeraltı*.

His unease only grew as Alexander made his way deeper into the city. The *kemeraltı* would be more populated, even this late at night. He had no desire to be caught on a vacant street, no matter who was following him.

He sharply turned a corner and ducked into a doorway, waiting to see if he could get behind his follower. The doorway was plenty deep, and he knelt with an eye to the street. A portly figure continued past him, dressed in trousers and a white shirt. He wore a plain, dark cap over dark hair, but in the darkness, Alexander could see no more. The man walked with purpose onward. After a long moment, Alexander stepped from his doorway and followed, for the man was going in the direction of the *kemeraltı*, and that was where Alexander was likely to find a taxi back to Bornova.

The man from the docks stopped to speak with some men outside a tea house, greeting them and joining their table. Alexander walked past, and the man seemed to pay him no attention.

He felt quite stupid, then. He'd allowed the drama of the past few days to turn a man meeting some friends into something dangerous.

He paused at the end of the street to get his bearings, and that was when he noticed a young man come to an abrupt stop a dozen feet away. He flung himself against the nearest wall, clearly trying to look like a casual pedestrian. It was not the same man as before; Alexander could still see that man with his companions a few storefronts down. This fellow had the gangly look of someone young enough to still be in school. If it was Bey's man following him, perhaps it was young Behlul.

With a sigh, Alexander turned and slowly started back the way he came, toward the young man.

The tail stayed leaned against the wall, fiddling with a cigarette and a match for a moment too long. When he'd successfully lit his cigarette, Alexander was nearly upon him. He looked up, and his eyes widened with surprise before he launched the cigarette at Alexander and tore off down the street.

Had it been Behlul, Alexander might have let him go. But Alexander did chase after him, past houses and buildings with people staring, because he'd gotten a good look at that young man's face, and he looked every bit as pale and European as the lads back at the hotel. He'd bet all the IOUs he held that this boy was no mere pickpocket.

Several sharp turns into alleys nearly lost Alexander the young man's trail, but fortunately the sound of his feet pounding the dusty stone streets echoed loudly. Deeper and deeper into the city they ran, past unlit windows and under awnings and clotheslines laden with wash, farther from the colorful storefronts and into the darker, dirtier areas, the places still skeletal after the fire.

Alexander's heart pounded against his throat and his chest burned, but the tail must have been losing steam, too; he was slowing down ahead of him. The buildings around them were fire-gnawed and stained. More places to hide.

Just as he realized that following a stranger into dark, unsavory places was an incredibly stupid thing to do, the echo of footsteps signaled another change in his direction. Alexander jogged along, catching sight of the boy just as he turned down another street. One Alexander recognized.

Somehow, the boy had led him to the edge of the *kemeraltı*, to Bey's tea house.

Though he was sweating from the exertion, Alexander went cold. This *did* lead back to Bey.

He backed away, eyes sweeping over the surrounding buildings. He might have walked into some sort of trap, though he couldn't fathom why Bey would do such a thing.

A stone building abutted the street opposite the one he'd just come down. In the weak light emanating from the lanterns outside Bey's *han*, he could make out a sign painted on its side. On a faded background of blue, in peeling letters, was painted "Molfiada—Importers 1877."

"Took you long enough," said a voice behind him.

Nick Hale grinned at him from the shattered window of a vacant house.

Chapter 34

"If you intended on me coming here, you could have just put it in your message," Alexander said as he settled into the proffered chair across the table from Nick.

The table was covered in papers. Receipts and ship logs and schedules in several languages. A pair of lanterns on either side of the long table illuminated the papers and their faces, and not much else. That was a good thing; the house was filthy, full of dust and debris shoved along the dirt-streaked walls Alexander had avoided touching as Nick had led him inside the vacant building.

"First of all, I didn't know if the police would have someone following you. Second, I liked the idea of giving my trainee something to do," Nick said, still grinning. He stretched his arms behind his head. He looked different than Alexander had last seen him in London in the midst of a disastrous investigation, and not just because he was clothed in the casual manner of a market vendor, with a loose shirt under an unbuttoned vest. It wouldn't be much of a disguise considering Nick was an inch or two taller than Alexander's height and probably weighed a stone more, putting him far above the heads of most Turks. His sandy blond hair was overlong, and hazel eyes gleamed from a tan face. If anything, Nick looked . . . happier.

Alexander shook his head. "You could have told me you were in the city. I wouldn't have wasted time—"

A tap at the door made them both freeze before it opened and the young man Alexander had been chasing rushed inside, looking terrified.

He came to an abrupt halt when he noticed Alexander at the table. "But—but, you—!" he stammered, red-faced and sweating and looking as if he'd faint. "What the bloody hell are you doing here?"

If Alexander hadn't known the fellow was a fellow Brit from his coloring, his rhotic accent would have placed him in the west of England immediately.

"Bagshott, this is Mr. Ashton, my associate." Nick lit a cigarette and offered one to Alexander.

Bagshott gaped at him. "But, sir—"

"I told you, if you were spotted, to go anywhere *but* here. As penance, you'll go back to your position. Tell me if there's movement the usual way," Nick said sharply. The young man snapped his mouth shut and left.

"Young Bagshott was stationed here with the last fellow running this operation. I've only been here a short time, so he's not quite used to the way I run things. I think he finds me difficult. So," Nick said, with a smile that showed Alexander he'd slipped back out of his working mode. "Here we are on this side of the world again. What are you doing here? I hope not attempting to mend Turkish-Greek relations."

They'd met when Alexander had been briefly employed by the British government as a translator during the end of the Great War, and Nick . . . Well, this was not the first time Nick had engaged in covert activities. "You know why I'm here, and you know why I contacted you."

Nick released a plume of smoke. "I find people don't like it when I already know things. They're more comfortable when they feel they're in control of how much information I'm privy to." He puffed thoughtfully on his cigarette. "Well. Saffron has managed to be arrested for poisoning someone on the expedition team. Did she do it?" Alexander looked coolly at him. Nick shrugged. "It's a fair enough question."

"She's being framed. I can imagine a few people who might have done it, though I don't know why. The man who died—"

"Martin Neill," Nick supplied. "O'Neill, legally. He changed it when he entered university. Not a good time to be Irish, is it? No trouble with the law, no debts, no nasty habits, no familial drama or psychosis. Altogether decent young chap."

He was loath to admit, but Nick was right; it was disconcerting that he already knew so much. "You've read the police report?"

"It doesn't look good for her, Alexander. Seen going into Neill's room, the rumor about their affair . . ." He snorted. "I find it all rather cliché. A woman scorned is very played out, but her being a poisons expert doesn't help."

He straightened up suddenly, his eyes on the window beyond Alexander. It was covered up save for a few slivers of the street visible through crookedly hung boards. He snatched up a dark jacket and a cap and gestured to Alexander to follow him. Alexander didn't bother asking what they were doing or where they were going; the look of sudden and absolute concentration on Nick's face told him whatever signal he was waiting for from Bagshott had been received. Whatever it was, the sooner it was dealt with, the sooner Nick might offer help or advice.

They returned to the stairs, and at the top, Nick opened a door that led to the roof of the building. The roof had been marked with chalk. Nick bent down and followed the chalk lines, and at the edge of the roof, he lay flat on his belly. Alexander followed suit.

From his vantage, he could see the street below, the alley, and the street beyond, the middle of which was the *han*.

There was a motorcar parked in front, reminiscent of the government cars that carted them to and from the agora. Nick's eyes were locked on the motorcar.

"What are we looking at?" Alexander muttered.

"The house of Ali Fethi Bey. That's his tea house and his base of operation."

"Operation of what?"

"Many things, some of which are illegal." Nick reached into his pocket for a pair of tiny binoculars, which looked wrong in his large hands. He propped himself on his elbows and brought them to his eye. "If they just went in, it'll still be a while before they come out."

They lay on the ground in silence for a moment before Nick asked, "What are you going to do about Saffron?"

"The inspector in charge is convinced she killed Martin Neill, even though the evidence is scarce. It's as if he wants her to be guilty."

"From what my sources tell me," Nick said, "Inspector Polat likely thinks this case will do a lot for his reputation. The fires drove him out of the city, but the war sent him right back here. His arrest and conviction records aren't good. Catching a British citizen murdering people and stealing priceless artifacts would be a boon."

Alexander's head snapped toward Nick. "He thinks she's the one stealing artifacts? What do you know about that?"

He didn't look away from his binoculars. "Wouldn't it be convenient if Saffron had been stealing things and killed the innocent boy who'd discovered her in the act? Two birds with one stone and all." He glanced at Alexander, his grin flashing in the dark. "You seriously hadn't pieced that together yet?"

Alexander ground his teeth together.

Nick returned to his spying. "It will be too easy for Polat—or the person who is actually stealing the artifacts—to plant the evidence. Saffron's hotel room will be fertile ground to sprinkle in a few seeds. I doubt the staff are keeping too close an eye on the key. I'd nip in there, if I were you, to make sure nobody has left anything suggestive behind. Though that won't help if Polat is the one to plant something."

"How helpful. Thanks." Alexander let out a breath. "She did find something in her room just before she was arrested. A broken vial. She worried the real killer planted it."

Nick glanced at him, interest on his face. "Where is it now?"

"I have it in my room."

"Better get it out of there. It's only a matter of time before Polat drags you into it and gets permission to search your things, too."

"Why do you say that?"

Nick rolled onto his side and set the binoculars down. "He lost everything when the Greeks supposedly burned the city down. Several members of his family, his home, his career. He'll find out before long who your people are. When he learns you're Greek, he'll do all he can to make sure you go down right along with Saffron."

Alexander sat in silence for a long time, contemplating all Nick had revealed as Nick watched Bey's tea house. The city was quiet around them, the sky bright with stars and moon.

"You said you saw the police report," he said at last. "What was the toxin that killed Neill?"

"Didn't say," Nick said, not moving from his vigil. "Their laboratories aren't quite up to the standard you're used to, I'm afraid. It'll take ages for them to process all the tests. Half of the possible toxins will have metabolized before they can be identified."

Alexander hadn't thought of that. Another challenge. If the police didn't identify the poison, it would be that much easier to pin it on the poison researcher. Lost in thought, he turned away from the sky to watch the house. A door opening cast a long rectangle of golden lighten the ground before few people walked out.

He took up the binoculars Nick had set down and focused them on the pair walking out of the tea house. "Damn it, those idiots came back," Alexander hissed as two young men staggered down the street and around a corner. The assistants would be all but useless tomorrow morning.

"Friends of yours?"

"I had to dig them out of trouble at that *han* before."

"You know this place?" Nick asked sharply.

"I met the old man, Bey, when I retrieved our assistants."

"What do you know about him? What did he say?"

Alexander lowered himself from his elbows and turned on his back. "He tried to teach me a lesson on manners. Spoke to me in Greek. He told me to come back and see him."

Nick was quiet for a long time as he watched the house. "Will you? Go see him?"

Despite his light tone, Alexander knew better than to take this for an innocent question. "Is this a real question, or am I expected to go in repayment of your assistance?"

Nick turned to him, frowning. "Believe it or not, I'm not going to let Saffron hang. We may have had some disagreements in the past, but she is a good woman."

Saying they'd had disagreements was a two-dimensional way to describe the strange connection between Saffron, Nick, and Nick's sister, Elizabeth. The mystery Nick had pulled them into when he'd convinced Saffron to help solve a pair of murders at a government laboratory last year had been as troublesome as Alexander had feared. It had left Saffron with a bad taste in her mouth for government work, and Nick. He could practically hear her announcing she never wanted to see him again, a sentiment Elizabeth had echoed. He hadn't wanted to see Nick Hale again, either, yet here he was, so damned glad to find that Nick was not only in the city, but willing to help.

He had to swallow twice for his dry throat to work. "We got married. The day she was arrested, we went to a church and got married."

The ache in his chest he had pushed to the side for the majority of the day throbbed powerfully. He passed a hand over his face, pressing his palms on his eyes until he saw spots. He felt Nick's eyes on him. "I shouldn't have done it."

"Why?"

"I married her when she didn't have a choice. I said we should, so I could act for her and protect her. How could she have said no?" Alexander's voice fought to be steady and failed.

Nick chuckled, drawing Alexander's incredulous glare. He shook his head, picking up the binoculars again. "You were already engaged. It's not like you forced her to agree to marry you in the first place. When have you ever known her to do anything she didn't want to do?"

This reminder was, surprisingly, helpful.

Alexander waited with Nick for an hour on the roof, all told. After a trio of figures conversed on the doorstep of the *han* before disappearing into the fine motorcar, they slunk back downstairs to the dilapidated room with the paper-covered table. Bagshott was there, looking like he'd collapsed the moment his body had hit the cushion of the crooked armchair he'd fallen asleep in.

"I'll see what I can do about the autopsy tests," Nick said, walking Alexander to the door.

Alexander was weary, in body and in mind, but that promise heartened him. He offered Nick his hand. "Thank you."

Chapter 35

Saffron woke to pain twisting her insides. In the hazy place between dreaming and full wakefulness, awareness of it crept into her mind like a twining *Pueraria montana* vine, and she woke with a start.

She pressed a hand to her aching belly, the other pressed to her mouth. Fear rose up within her like bile. Was she going to be sick?

When she stood, intending to go for the door to ask for help, a distinct warm rush informed her that she was not poisoned, but in a deeply uncomfortable conundrum. Her courses. She'd forgotten. Perfectly normal and perfectly inconvenient, considering she'd already used the supplies she'd tucked in her handbag before she'd left to get married. Now she was stuck in a Turkish jail, for heaven's sake!

Depending on who was on duty, she'd have to figure out a way to explain she needed supplies. That would be humiliating beyond belief.

The jingle of keys and footsteps indicated she would get her chance without having to call for anyone. She just prayed it was someone who spoke English.

She ought to have added another caveat, she thought as Polat appeared in the doorway. Anyone who spoke English but him.

"Come," he said gruffly, not looking at her.

"I must use the necessary," she told him.

He shot her a disgusted look. "Later. Come, they are waiting for you."

She didn't move. "Inspector, this is a matter of urgency." He looked as if he would argue, so she told him what the matter was.

He visibly recoiled, muttering under his breath, but led her to the police station's lavatory. She was incredibly lucky they had one; she'd had to run across the street from the agora's site to an old, shuttered bathhouse when she'd needed to relieve herself, and she could only imagine the sort of commotion that would cause when she was under arrest.

In the privacy of the lavatory, Saffron did her best to manage the situation. She would still have to further address it with Polat if she was to get the needed supplies, but it could wait until she discovered who was waiting for her. She hoped it was Alexander. He hadn't returned yesterday, which she hoped indicated he'd been pursuing some way of helping her. She didn't relish the thought of asking him to go out in search of menstrual supplies, but he *was* her husband. It would have been nice for them to actually get to the married bit before she sent him on embarrassing errands, though.

Her heart fell when she saw it was not Alexander waiting for her in the little room Polat used as an interrogation room, but an older man she'd never seen before. He was quite tall and lean, with a heavily lined face that spoke to Western origin and iron-gray hair. A lawyer, perhaps?

He nodded solemnly to her and sat when she did at the little table. "Mrs. Ashton," he began.

Her stomach fluttered unexpectedly at being addressed by her married name. It was the first time she'd heard someone who wasn't a police officer say it. "Yes?"

"I am Harold Feldman, the secretary to Sir Randolph Waverly, the consul general in Smyrna," he said.

Saffron soon learned that not only had Alexander been to see Sir Randolph, but so had Mr. Demirel and the Henrys. His secretary wanted to know the details of the case to communicate to Sir Randolph before he would make a decision about whether or not

Saffron could be moved to the consulate while the case was being sorted out.

Hope rose within her as she related everything with as much care and detail as she could, especially in regards to Clark and his behavior toward her. She was sure Polat wouldn't include anything about his attempts to discredit and sabotage her, and she wanted to give Mr. Feldman and the consul general every opportunity to see that the rumors upon which her arrest had been predicated were all lies made up by Clark.

Mr. Feldman left her to telephone Sir Randolph, and Saffron was left in the interrogation room, almost queasy with anticipation. Her pains had worsened, and she was growing desperate for a meal, her supplies, and a hot bath. She didn't know if she'd get any of those at the consulate, but she had to imagine they were more likely to be helpful than Polat.

She glanced at the door, which Feldman had left open, and flinched when she saw Polat standing there, watching her.

He said nothing, only looked at her with those piercing green eyes like he expected her to do something. She stared back at him, caught between wanting to confront him as to how he could think she was guilty of murder based on so little evidence, and the desire to appear non-threatening, so that he might change his mind.

Mr. Feldman returned a minute later, a small smile on his lips as he told Polat that Sir Randolph had decided Saffron would be moved to the British consulate. He invited her, most graciously, to follow him out of the interrogation room and into the motorcar he had parked outside.

Polat said nothing, but his face steadily reddened, and by the time Saffron stepped into the back seat of the posh black motorcar, he looked ready to explode. He watched them drive away, and Saffron couldn't help but wonder if she'd made a mistake in leaving the police station. If she'd learned anything about Polat the last few days, it was that he valued control and respect. Both had been violated by the consul general sweeping Saffron away from him. The inspector didn't seem like the sort of man to take that lightly, and she dreaded what he might do in response.

Saffron had taken not two steps into her new "jail cell" before she'd decided it was worth Inspector Polat's potential revenge to spend the rest of her imprisonment in the British consulate. Her cell was a bedroom, and the only sign it was anything other than that was the fact that she was to be locked inside of it at all times. Her windows had bars on them, which, from her experience at the hotel, was not unusual. It meant she could open the windows, anyway. After two days and nights in the airless back room of the police station, it was a privilege she would have traded away quite a lot of freedoms for.

Her request for some of her things was denied by Sir Randolph through Mr. Feldman when she asked, citing that her room and belongings were still being investigated, and neither man was married, so there were no other women living at the consulate apart from a few servants. When she explained with painstaking vagueness that she required certain hygienic items, Mr. Feldman's solemn expression didn't waver.

"It will be seen to," he told her, and then left her alone in her locked bedroom.

Hot water for a cat wash and breakfast was delivered a short while later, both deeply appreciated. The maid who delivered them, supervised by none other than Mr. Feldman, also passed her a bundle which turned out to be undyed cotton rags. Saffron thanked her sincerely; she hadn't used plain rags since she was newly initiated into womanhood, but anything was better than her utter lack.

A few hours later, a knock came at the door—it was Mr. Feldman, announcing she had guests.

"I'm allowed to have guests?" she asked him with a smile she couldn't help.

"Visitors, then, and only within reason," he answered in his unruffled manner. "And with supervision. I will remain with you during any visits you might have."

Saffron wondered at this; surely the secretary of the consul general had better things to do than accompany a would-be murderer. Things must be slow for them.

He returned a moment later with two people, and Saffron did her best to not appear disappointed. "Mrs. Henry, Mrs. Demirel, thank you for coming."

"It seemed most expedient," Mrs. Henry said, and she took only a few steps into the room before she shot Mr. Feldman a wry look. "May I greet Mrs. Ashton, or . . . ?"

He inclined his head with the faintest hint of a smile.

Mrs. Henry grinned at him, then planted a kiss on Saffron's cheeks. "How are you, my dear? Holding up? No, don't answer. Clearly, this is a miserable business."

"Oh, most certainly," added Mrs. Demirel, coming forward. She looked as tired as Saffron, with bags under her eyes. "We've been doing just everything we can do resolve this."

"Thank you," Saffron said. Her eyes fell to the satchel Mrs. Henry carried. "Will I appear totally ungrateful if I . . . ?"

"Not at all," Mrs. Henry said. "It's all been searched already. We'll just pop outside, then when you're settled we can have a little chat."

Everyone shuffled out of the room, and Saffron quickly changed into the clean frock Mrs. Henry had brought for her. And, bless her, she had included a hairbrush and several other comforts. They were not hers, but she appreciated Mrs. Henry's sacrifice in giving her some of her things.

"We were so concerned when the telephone call came that you were being moved here," Mrs. Demirel said when they came back into the room. "For Mr. Ashton had already left for the dig site, and we didn't want to rummage through your things—"

"I doubt that inspector would have allowed us to take anything from your room, anyway," Mrs. Henry said darkly.

Mrs. Demirel blinked rapidly, then nodded. "Of course, of course. Here I was, worrying about Mr. Ashton going through your things, when I'd forgotten your room isn't to be bothered at all!

They've taken away your things and locked up the rest, haven't they?" She went on without waiting for Saffron's response. "It's so dreadful everything must be searched. I suppose you haven't heard the police are searching the rest of the expedition crew's hotel rooms." With a too-loud whisper, she added, "You know, for the artifacts."

Mrs. Henry equipped herself with a cigarette. "Your arrest has pushed dear Mr. Hayrettin over the edge, I'm afraid. There were questions about the team being permitted to continue after they learned of Mr. Neill's death and the initial missing items, of course"—she let out a slow stream of smoke—"and now, with a member of the crew under arrest, Mr. Hayrettin has tried to put his foot down. Lawrence has done well to pick that foot back up, but it's only a matter of time before Mr. Hayrettin's concerns sway Mr. Assam."

Mrs. Demirel made a strange noise, like she might have wanted to speak but turned it into a cough.

Mrs. Henry gave her a sardonic look. "Agatha, I know that we don't speak the language, but the conversations between Mr. Hayrettin and Mr. Assam could not be more clear. He is obviously angling to shut the dig down, and he needs Mr. Assam's agreement to do it."

Mrs. Demirel colored when Saffron sent her a questioning look, she nodded in a defeated manner. "Mr. Demirel might have mentioned . . ."

The conversation soon devolved into the same sort of chatter that, a week ago, had driven Saffron rather mad, but she now found immensely comforting. Their visit was a short one and ended with Mrs. Henry declaring they would return on the morrow after confirming with Mr. Feldman that it would be allowed.

"We will send Mr. Ashton over when he returns this evening," she told Saffron, pressing a brief kiss to her cheek. "Never fear, my dear. I've never seen a man so determined to get his wife back." Her eyes glittered, and she let out a little laugh. "Actually, I have."

Saffron couldn't help but smile at the memory of Dr. Henry's drunken wallowing when he thought Mrs. Henry was truly going to leave him.

The women left, along with Mr. Feldman, and Saffron found herself exhausted. She took to the bed gratefully, and went to sleep.

Alexander blinked against the harsh light. Nick had snapped it on without warning, and after they'd spent the last hour lurking outside in the dark, waiting for the last of the staff to disappear and to get inside themselves, his eyes hadn't been prepared for the glare of the bare light bulb.

"When you said you would do something about the lab results, I didn't think you meant we would be doing the tests," Alexander muttered. He'd agreed readily enough when Nick telephoned the hotel that afternoon to tell him they would be visiting the laboratory doing the tests on Martin Neill's body, but now he was inside and it was clear this was not just the laboratory but the morgue, as well, he was regretting not getting clarification.

The room was cooler than any Alexander had experienced in Smyrna, due to it being underground. It was the basement level of the laboratory, without any windows cut into its unadorned plaster walls. There was a smell of damp mixed with stringent chemicals, the scents combining to fill Alexander with unease nearly as much as the line of white-sheet-covered bodies lying on tables about the small room.

"We're not performing the tests," Nick said easily, "we're just getting samples for those who will. The lab here isn't getting through them quickly enough, so we'll just send them off to Istanbul. Bagshott can be there and back in Smyrna in two days, and the results will likely beat him back, anyway."

"For the record, I don't feel comfortable with this," Alexander said as Nick moved to the shrouded body on a table a few feet away. Alexander's insides twisted as Nick gently lifted the cloth and pulled it back to reveal Martin Neill's body.

"In truth," Nick said, frowning down at the lifeless boy, "neither do I. But needs must."

He picked up a file on the table next to Neill's feet and his lips moved as he read. Alexander moved next to him, waiting for Nick to sort through the Arabic characters and tell him what it said. He felt some measure of relief that Saffron was no longer housed at the jail—she'd certainly seemed more comfortable when he'd seen her that afternoon—but now the consulate was involved and representation was on the way from Istanbul, it felt too real that his wife was close to standing trial for murder. Nick was right, needs must.

Alexander had done his best to sort through the evidence Polat had that was not based on rumors and hearsay, and he'd found nothing to point to who the real culprit was. He needed to find the truth about what had happened to Martin Neill, and the sooner, the better.

As if his eyes couldn't stop themselves, they fell on the uncovered face of Neill. He looked like a boy, without much beard and not a wrinkle on his gray face.

His throat grew tight. This was too familiar, a dead man barely old enough to be called a man. He'd seen far too many just like Martin Neill. A youth caught up in his first adventure.

He'd been a decent person. He didn't deserve such a miserable end. He'd been afraid, so terribly ill that he couldn't keep anything down, terrible cramps, burning eyes . . .

"Does the report say anything about his eyes?" he asked. He'd complained several times, including just when he'd become really ill.

"No . . ." Nick murmured, flipping back a few pages in the report. "Here it just says they were clouded." He looked up. "Did he have a condition?"

Alexander shook his head. "His paperwork said his vision was fine. He'd mentioned irritation a few times, said his sight had been a bit blurry. But he wasn't used to being around so much smoke. It's thick in the evenings when the crew gets together for cards."

Nick frowned and set down the file. With a look of resignation, he gently lifted the lids on Neill's eye. Alexander leaned over him and looked. The eye was brown, but slightly opaque.

"I suppose he could have had a condition he never brought to a doctor's attention. But . . . young men aren't likely to complain about something like that. He'd more likely try to hide it, especially with this lot. They look for things to harp on," Alexander said. "And it would have put Dr. Henry off approving him for future expeditions. He must have been bothered by it quite a lot to have brought it up." He looked hard at the still body laid out before him. He didn't want to interrupt the peace of the dead, but if he really had been murdered and there was no other way of discovering how it was done, this would be necessary. "You said some of the possible toxins would metabolize out of his system . . ."

The next thirty minutes were some of the most disturbing of Alexander's life. Yes, he was a biologist, and yes, he'd seen his fair share of dead bodies, but treating the body of a former colleague like it was a lab sample was nothing short of agonizing. At the end of it, they had samples of blood, tissue, and a number of fluids Alexander didn't want to know how Nick knew how to extract, including a sample taken from the fluid of Martin Neill's eye.

Alexander watched Nick package it all up in the laboratory's materials. "They'll notice you stabbed his eye with a syringe."

"They might," Nick said, unbothered. "But it seems they're done with the corpse until burial."

"What is the policy for that?" Alexander asked.

Nick sighed, closed the file he'd been pursuing, and squinted at the wall for a long moment. "I don't know what it is now. They used to send anyone who died over here home."

A pang went through Alexander, the same regretful, achingly guilty one he'd felt looking down at Martin Neill's boyish face. He nodded, unable to think of anything else to say.

He helped Nick put everything back into place, and they stole out into the night, leaving behind nothing but the young man under the sheet.

Chapter 36

Without anything else to do but look out of the window at the dusty street and flip idly through the books on the little bookshelf in the corner of her room, Saffron took every opportunity to speak to anyone who came to her door.

Mr. Feldman did not furnish much conversation, and he continued to supervise her visits, whether it was Mrs. Henry and Mrs. Demirel or Alexander. He also inspected her food trays before and after her meals. She was allowed a knife, and she was sure to put it in plain sight when he and the maid came back to collect the tray each time. She didn't want him to think she was preparing an escape attempt or planning to harm someone.

The maid was a small woman who couldn't be older than Saffron's age. She was a local girl with a persistent bright smile and black hair usually covered in a white handkerchief, and she always made some attempt at conversation with Saffron when she came to the room. Her English was not quite fluent, but it was far better than Saffron's Turkish, and they always managed a pleasant exchange. The first day, she had asked Saffron bluntly, "You kill that man?"

Nonplussed, Saffron had responded with an adamant "*No*," and the girl had nodded once, like that was all she needed to be at ease serving her.

"Eggs and toast and tea," Kadriye announced as she entered with the breakfast tray on the third day of Saffron's captivity. "I hope you like."

Saffron replied with a phrase the pregnant woman from the *hammam* taught her, which meant something like "God bless your hands," and Kadriye beamed at her.

"We cook good English food," she said, stepping away from the table. "You eat, please."

"Truth be told," Saffron said a little shyly, taking her seat, "I wouldn't mind Turkish fare. I haven't had much chance to have a truly local meal."

Kadriye's brow puckered. "That is very sad, *hanım*." Her eyes brightened. "I bring you the *dolmas* of Feldman *efendi*."

Saffron glanced at the door, where Feldman was clearly not paying attention to them. He never did, usually drifting to stand near the door while she spoke with her visitors. "Mr. Feldman makes *dolmas*?" Alexander had taken her for *dolmades*, a Greek dish of grape leaves stuffed with savory fillings, in London and she guessed it was something similar. She couldn't imagine the very upright Mr. Feldman cooking anything, let alone wrapping meat and rice into leaves.

Kadriye laughed, putting a hand to her belly. "No, no! I get for him at *Büyük Balık Han*."

A *han* was the only place she was likely to get the sort of food she was hoping to try. "I would like that very much."

Kadriye was as good as her word; that afternoon Saffron received a lunch tray with not only *dolmas*, but a number of other divine-looking Turkish dishes. The maid set out rice, fish, and vegetables on the little table in her bedroom like a banquet for a king. If this was what she had been missing by taking all her meals at the hotel or in the mess tent, it was an additional reason to despise whoever had killed Martin and framed her.

"This is extraordinary," Saffron told the maid gratefully.

"*Büyük Balık Han* is very good. Far away, but . . ." She shrugged as if to say it was worth the effort, and Saffron was inclined to believe it. "I go there for Feldman *efendi*. Every week, like a clock. I bring *dolmas* on *pazar*." She paused in perfecting the alignment of the plates on the table and cast her brown eyes toward Saffron. "That is Sunday, yes?"

Saffron nodded. "I think so."

She beamed. "I practice, you know. Sir Randolph wants that we speak English."

At the front of the house, the bell rang. Kadriye glanced at Mr. Feldman, who stood at Saffron's open door, and he jerked his head as if to command her to answer the door bell. Kadriye dipped a curtsy to Saffron and left with Feldman.

Saffron's disappointment at being left alone lasted only as long as it took Kadriye to walk to the door and back, and she returned escorting someone.

"Mrs. Demirel," Saffron said in surprise, getting to her feet.

"Hello, Miss Everleigh, how do you do?" The older woman scurried into the room, extending her gloved hands to squeeze Saffron's. Her eyes swept over Saffron and over the table ladened with food. "Oh my, you do have quite a feast here. What delicious-looking fare! I see why Mr. Ashton was so keen to have you stay here rather than the jail, if this is what you are served at meal times!" She tittered.

"Kadriye was so kind to bring me some of the local foods, so I might not miss out on the chance to try them," Saffron explained. "Won't you join me? I surely cannot eat this all myself."

"Oh." Mrs. Demirel bit her lip. She didn't look disturbed by the idea, not like when Mrs. Henry offered her a cigarette, but rather fascinated. "I would . . . I would like that, yes, thank you. Thank you very much indeed." She fussed for a moment getting settled with a napkin draped over her lap.

Kadriye served them in smiling silence, including when she took a small plate of *dolmas* to Mr. Feldman at the door, but spoke when it came time for Saffron to take her first bite of what looked to be a dumpling.

"You must eat *mantı* this way," Kadriye said, and demonstrated how to arrange a bite so the dumpling, glistening with butter, was covered in equal parts rich tomato sauce and a white sauce she explained was yogurt.

"Yogurt?" Saffron repeated, eying the thick sauce with suspicion.

"It is ours, Turkish," Kadriye said proudly, dolloping a generous helping onto Saffron's plate. "With *sarımsak*, very good."

She offered the carefully constructed bite to Saffron. She ate it, chewed experimentally, and sighed with delight. The flavors of moist lamb tangy with tomato and rich with garlic filled her mouth. "Oh my," she murmured, and accepted another bite from Kadriye.

Spice exploded over her tongue, shocking but delicious. "What did you add to it?" she wheezed.

Kadriye shrugged with a smile. "Hot oil."

"Goodness," she said, patting her mouth with her napkin. "Mrs. Demirel, do you eat like this every day?"

Mrs. Demirel paused in her own chewing, looked down at the spoon already containing her next bite of perfectly sauced dumplings topped with silky red oil, and smiled sheepishly. She, too, patted her mouth delicately before saying, "If you can believe it, I've never cooked Turkish food for my husband. I ask that our cook stick to good, plain English cooking. It's so healthful for the children, you know." She looked longingly at the dishes still gently steaming on the table. "But for the adult palate . . ."

Kadriye took that as her cue to pile more food on Mrs. Demirel's plate with plenty of the hot oil, since Mrs. Demirel could tolerate it, until the older woman was begging to be excused from another bite. When she could no longer keep up with Kadriye's generosity, Saffron, too, admitted defeat.

As they sipped tea and ate sweet, tawny-colored orbs of *helva*, Mrs. Demirel gave Saffron the usual report of who'd announced what interesting find or theory from the dig site, then soon departed. Saffron couldn't help but feel the meal had done Mrs. Demirel some good; her cheeks were flushed with color, and her eyes still drifted to the food even after Kadriye finally acquiesced and took away her plate. Perhaps this trip to Turkey was exactly what Mrs. Demirel needed to come out of her shell. Maybe she had a hint of a gourmand in her that needed only a little nudge to indulge.

When Saffron's door was locked once again, she sighed. The hearty food had lifted her spirits, but she would have very much liked to experience such a meal at the *han* itself. She would go there with Alexander when she got out, she resolved. Even as the days passed, she refused to doubt that she would be released. Alexander was doing all he could.

That thought usually buoyed her, but with seemingly endless hours of lonely boredom stretching out before her, it did not. She felt useless, stuck in this little room with no information but the tidbits given to her.

Alexander had told her that the lab results would be back soon. With all luck, they would know what killed Martin. That, at least, she might have some insight into.

When Alexander happened by the mess tent and found it occupied by Dr. Henry, Clark, and Wakefield, alarm bells went off in his mind. Dr. Henry was frowning, and Clark was speaking to him in a singularly adamant way suggesting something serious.

Alexander stepped into the tent without a second thought and caught the tail end of Clark saying, ". . . see this as the opportunity that it is, Henry. Keep the dig—" He broke off when he noticed Alexander, his earnest expression darkening with annoyance. "Ashton."

"Clark," Alexander said stiffly. "What's going on?"

Clark's jaw ticked, but he said nothing. Henry and Wakefield exchanged a look so laden with guilt that Alexander had no doubt they'd been discussing something unsavory. He'd already heard Wakefield's enthusiastic commentary on prostitution being legal in this country. He hated to think of newly reformed Dr. Henry being caught up in Wakefield's ideas of "opportunities."

"You need something, Ashton?" Dr. Henry finally asked.

"No, sir," he replied, not bothering to hide his disapproval before he left the tent.

Mr. Apak hailed him from across the pit, and Alexander went to meet him.

"A man is at the gate for you, Mr. Ashton," he said. "The guard just informed me."

Alexander turned to look across the field in that direction. A large man in a light-colored suit stood just beyond the gate, and as Alexander squinted at him, he raised a hand in greeting. That had to be Nick.

He thanked Mr. Apak and followed him back to the gate. It was Nick, with an easy smile on his freshly shaven face that only emphasized the shadows under his eyes. He offered his hand. They shook. "Let's be on our way to the consulate, then," Nick said.

Alexander took it in stride; they had no plans to visit Saffron today, especially together, but he didn't know how much the guards might gossip about later.

Alexander retrieved his jacket and they set off in the motorcar Nick had waiting. They zipped through the streets in silence. As much as he wanted to ask Nick why they were going to the consulate right now, he didn't want the driver to hear anything.

That was, until the driver leaned over to check if the street was clear before a turn, and he realized the driver was Bagshott.

"What are we doing?" Alexander asked Nick.

"Seeing your wife. I have it on good authority that Tuesdays at noon is when Sir Randolph dines with a friend of his a few streets over in Bornova. It's the only time I know he will not be at the consulate."

"Why do you care if he's there?"

"I don't want him to know I'm here," Nick said bluntly. "We met during the war, and I'd prefer he remain unaware I'm in the city."

"You didn't catch him doing something treasonous, did you?"

This was no flippant comment; Alexander had watched at a distance as Nick had ruined the lives of men and women working against the Allies in the war.

Nick rolled his eyes. "If I had, he'd hardly have his own consulate to run. No, I just don't want him thinking he has any oversight on our operations here. The things Bey is up to are likely to touch his realm of connections, and I don't want Sir Randolph to do anything that might spook Bey before we're ready to move."

The consulate was quiet when they arrived, with only a Turkish maid to greet them.

"Mr. Feldman," the maid said, poking her head into the nearest open door. "Mr. Ashton and Mr. Carmichael for Mrs. Ashton."

Feldman emerged, nodding to Alexander and offering a hand to Nick, who was apparently styling himself as Mr. Carmichael for this meeting. "How do you do?"

"Gregory Carmichael, esquire," Nick said confidently, pumping Feldman's arm.

Feldman frowned at them. "I was given to understand the embassy would be providing Mrs. Ashton with legal assistance."

"Oh, indeed," Nick said, "but Ashton here is a mate of mine from the army, and I thought to offer any advice I might. I settled in Bursa, you see. Heard about it from a friend in Istanbul, wanted to see if I could help."

It was startling just how easily Nick could spin out a perfectly reasonable but uninteresting story that Feldman, or anyone else, just glossed right over.

"I see," Feldman said. "If you'll follow me?"

Outside Saffron's room, Feldman gave Nick the same instructions he'd given Alexander and any of Saffron's other visitors: Do not bring weapons of any kind into the room, and do not make any attempt to help Saffron vacate the room or the consulate. Should they have any wish to do those things, a stern warning from Feldman wouldn't stop them, but Alexander supposed it was part of his duty to rattle off the warnings anyway.

He knocked, announced them, and opened the door when Saffron called out her permission.

Seeing her was like a punch to the gut every time. He didn't know if it was because it was the circumstances, the fact they were now married, or simply because it was *her*, but he ached to close the distance between them, Nick and Feldman be damned.

But her eyes weren't on Alexander—they were locked on Nick. Her mouth opened in surprise, and Nick smoothly cut in front of her to take her hand and kiss in the air over the back of it. "Mrs. Ashton, I am so very glad to see you holding up so well. We haven't had the pleasure; I am Gregory Carmichael. Your husband and I served together."

Her blue eyes bounced between Nick and Alexander, and he shook his head the barest degree. Her eyes darted to Feldman before she added uncertainly, "How do you do?"

"Carmichael is here to offer legal advice," Alexander said by way of explanation, though it was no explanation at all, from the questioning look Saffron gave him.

"Let us sit," Nick said briskly, helping Saffron onto the couch she'd clearly just been sitting on. Alexander went to sit at her side, and Nick nudged the nearest chair so it was impolitely close to Saffron's other side. His purpose was clear: He didn't want them to be overheard.

Feldman took up his usual position, sitting on the chair near the door, looking more likely to fall asleep than eavesdrop.

Still, when Nick revealed a file tucked into his jacket pocket, Alexander was glad for his precaution.

"The lab results from Martin Neill's autopsy," Nick said quietly. "Poor fellow was riddled with damage, from his liver to his lungs to even his eyes."

"What did it?" Saffron breathed. Her hand found Alexander's in his lap.

"There were moderate amounts of a toxin called colchicine in his body," Nick said in an undertone, reading from the report. "It was found in his blood, his kidneys, his feces and urine, even in the sample taken from his eyes. The only place they didn't find it was his stomach contents. Considering he was otherwise healthy when you set sail, it had to be the colchicine. Do you know anything about it?"

Saffron had gone very still, and now Alexander looked from Nick to her, he saw she'd gone white. Her eyes were squeezed shut, but a tear escaped and dropped onto Alexander's wrist. "Saffron?"

"Colchicine is the toxin found in the family of plants called *Colchicum*," she said in a rasping voice. She looked at Nick, not at him. "The most well-known of that species is *Colchicum autumnale*, or autumn crocus." She took a shuddering breath, and her eyes slid to his. The despair in their blue depths crushed his lungs. "Another name for that flower is meadow saffron."

Chapter 37

Alexander stared at her. His voice came out harsh. "The poison came from a plant called meadow *saffron*?"

Saffron could see in his eyes the same violent panic that had her in a vice. "Yes. It's not the same flower I'm named for. That's *Crocus sativus.* But it's also called autumn crocus. It's a common enough mistake. It grows here. I found some in the field at the dig site." She shook her head. "Inspector Polat already thinks I'm a hysterical woman hellbent on revenge. This will only confirm it. What better way for a mad botanist to exact her revenge than with a poison made from a flower with her own name?"

Saying it out loud did make her feel a little hysterical. It rose up in her throat, choking her.

Alexander took her chin between his fingers, forcing her eyes to his. They were nearly black, and so fierce it took her remaining breath away. "It will be all right. We will figure this out."

Nick cleared his throat pointedly, reminding them he was still there. She didn't need the reminder; Nick Hale was impossible to ignore, even when she wanted to. Last time she'd seen him, she'd promised herself she'd never be bothered by him again. How she was eating her words now. He was mercenary, yes, but if he bent his considerable skills and focus to her case, she would gladly have his help. She needed it.

"It looks rather black at this point, but we're just in the middle," he said in the sort of hearty voice people used when telling children to buck up after taking a tumble. "We don't know if the police know what the toxin is yet, nor if they'll ever make the connection to your name. They'll likely have a different name for it, at least. Whoever killed Mr. Neill has to be among the expedition team and someone he trusted enough to eat or drink something they gave him. From what I've heard about this poison"—Alexander looked at him sharply—"it seems that the toxic dosage is relatively small. It could have been one drink and he was dead."

Saffron exhaled slowly, counting her heartbeats as they slowed. "We need more information about how the toxin works to narrow down when he could have consumed it to become so ill. For multiple organs to fail, it took some time or a large dose, I would wager. I wrote down information about fifty-some plants I was likely to find on this trip, including meadow saffron. If the murderer knew it grew at the dig site, I suppose they could have pulled the plant and snuck it into Martin's food, or distilled it to slip into a drink, but I don't know the specifics, like how much of the plant would be needed or if the taste would be obvious. I'm not the only person with a chemistry kit, but everyone else is rooming with someone. No one could hide it if they'd been stewing flower bits in their room." She stood, intending to pace to help her think, but at her movement, Mr. Feldman's eyes opened. She hastily sat back down. "I pointed the plant out to Mrs. Henry and Mrs. Demirel, who then mentioned it to Wakefield." She blew out a breath, recalling how he'd laughed at her and the plant's name. "That doesn't narrow it down, though. With how much gossip gets passed around, anyone on the crew might know it's poisonous and nearby."

"Including Clark," Alexander said darkly. "I'll check to see if the flower is still in the field at the agora."

Nick leaned forward. "You might not need to. Colchicine is used as a medication for a few things, but mostly it's used to treat gout."

Saffron sucked in a breath.

He raised his eyebrow. "You know someone on the crew who has gout?"

"Yes," she said quickly, "Mr. Demirel, our liaison. But why on earth would he kill Martin?" She bit her lip, thinking of Mrs. Demirel's revelation that the crew's rooms were being searched for the missing artifacts. "Is it possible Mr. Demirel has something to do with the missing artifacts?"

Alexander squeezed her hand. "Mrs. Henry suggested whoever took the artifacts would want to sell them off here to circumvent the policies to prevent us taking artifacts out of the country. Demirel might have the connections and the knowledge to move artifacts here in the city."

"If Mr. Demirel used his medication—but *Mrs.* Demirel gave Martin medicines." Saffron's mind raced ahead. "He could have known that and mixed his gout medication into something his wife planned to give to Martin. How dastardly."

Alexander nodded. "We need to find out if any of the medications from Martin's bedside contained the toxin. That could determine if Demirel is a suspect."

"What can I do?" She didn't like the plaintive note in her voice, but now she knew what had killed Martin, she felt she'd crawl out of her skin unless she could piece together why.

"I'll see if I can find any texts about the toxin," Alexander offered.

"Or how to make it," she added. "My materials were confiscated, unfortunately."

Her eyes lingered on his. She had so many questions, and as glad as she was Nick was helping, he didn't need to hear the rest. She glanced at him.

His lips twitched upward, and his hazel eyes took her in with that arch humor that made her ache for Elizabeth. Nick was her brother, after all; as much as Saffron resented the way he'd treated them, he reminded her so much of her dearest friend.

Nick stood, gave her a ridiculous little bow, and murmured, "I'll be outside, Ashton." He winked at her. "Mrs. Ashton."

"Have you heard from anyone?" Saffron asked when Nick left the room.

Alexander shook his head. "I don't expect the letters will arrive for a few days yet. I considered sending John a telegram, but I worried it would alarm him more than help."

"That is likely true. Not much he can do from France." She glanced at the door and saw Mr. Feldman was gazing into the hall, perhaps where Nick waited. "While I appreciate the additional help, I know what him being here might mean. Is it . . . related?"

"I have some suspicions, but nothing concrete. I sent him a message when you were arrested asking if he had any contacts nearby who might be able to help, since he served in this part of the world. The next day he sent me a message, and here he is." She suppressed a smile at his bland recitation. She imagined he'd been far more surprised than he let on. "He has an interest in a certain Turk I visited on our first night here."

He paused to give her time to remember his adventure with Banks to the *han* in the market to find the assistants. Alexander had said that he felt the fellow who ran the place was involved in shady business, she recalled. It must be quite disreputable to have attracted the attention of the British government. She wondered what it was, but knew better than to ask with Mr. Feldman present. She didn't think he could hear them, they were practically whispering, but there was a reason Nick had come here under a false name. She didn't want to ruin his subterfuge.

"Now we know what the toxin was, I want to have that broken vial tested for it."

"How did you hide it so it wasn't found when they searched the rest of the crew's rooms?"

He tapped his jacket pocket. "I've been carrying it with me. They haven't decided to search us yet, though if they don't start turning up the artifacts soon, they might. I'll find somewhere out of the way to have it tested for colchicine. Then I'll find out about Mr. Demirel's gout medication and who might have known about it."

"If Mrs. Demirel speaks to others in the crew about her family's ailments half so much as she does to me, then most of them probably know he suffers gout. But why do you want to have the vial tested? It's almost certainly the vial that was used, or at least one contaminated in order to frame me."

"It is possible," Alexander said, and he said it almost reluctantly, "that the vial does not have colchicine. If that is the case, I have a nasty suspicion Clark was responsible. He knew you had the chemical set; you discussed it with him at least once when planning your paper. He knew you were under suspicion for poisoning Neill. He easily could have done it to provide Polat more evidence."

Saffron sucked in a breath. "Do you think he would really do that? He hates me, but . . . but do you believe he would go that far?"

"He targeted you for weeks and could have seriously harmed you in the process. He all but started the rumor that led to you being arrested," he said heavily. "I do believe he would do it."

"This is assuming you don't believe Clark is involved in Martin's death. He is among my suspects." She let out a breath. "What a mess. I hate that all I can do is talk about this. I should be poking around in Clark's room and questioning Mr. Demirel. Interviewing the crew." She waved off the reassurances she was sure were forthcoming. "You are doing more than any woman could hope. I appreciate it." She squeezed his hand, savoring the warmth of his returning pressure. "Please, Alexander, do take care of yourself. Get some rest. And . . . If you're with Nick, please take care. Even if he's just watching the *han*, you've got to be careful."

"I have a feeling I'll be doing far more than just watching the tea house with him," he said darkly, and before she could ask what he meant, he got to his feet.

He pressed a chaste kiss to her cheek and, with a murmured endearment, departed.

Chapter 38

Alexander received the results for the broken vial the next morning. The nearby city of Manisa had a hospital, and the little man in charge of its laboratory was readily bribed to analyze the broken vial Saffron had found in her room. Alexander barely batted an eye when he saw the word colchicine.

The two villains—the one to poison Martin Neill and the person who placed the tainted vial in Saffron's room—were likely the same person. That suggested they had something against both Martin Neill and Saffron, though it was equally possible they simply found Saffron to be the ideal candidate for framing.

He'd suspected Clark had planted the vial, but had it been another way to sabotage Saffron, or specifically to implicate her in Neill's murder? If it was the latter, did that mean Clark had a reason to give the police a strong suspect?

Clark could be the murderer.

Alexander stared unseeing out at the hills surrounding Smyrna rolling by beyond the taxi's windows as he re-examined his conclusions about Joseph Clark.

The man had been very quiet following Saffron's arrest. In the evenings, he kept to his friends and the card table, and when he was at the site, he was productive and friendly, even helpful to the others on their team. Alexander had only had occasion to talk directly to him twice, and both times Clark responded with civility, as if he'd never thoroughly insulted Alexander or his now wife. As if he no longer had a grudge to sour his mood.

He'd teased Martin Neill in the way of the crew hazing new members of their ranks, and any additional attention seemed to be used to further antagonize Saffron, like the incident with the snake. He'd taken Neill's vowels during many rounds of cards. If anything, he'd have a motive to keep Neill alive if he hoped to make good on Neill's debts to him.

Perhaps it was the fact he'd been sleeping so poorly it could hardly be called that, but Alexander's brain simply couldn't stop looping around the possibility of Clark's involvement. But with no data to support it or refute it, he was getting nowhere.

Damn, but he wished he could speak to Saffron freely. Or get enough sleep for his brain to function properly.

The taxi rolled up to the police station, but Alexander did not immediately step onto the quiet street. Never one to shy from an uncomfortable conversation, he did dread getting out of the taxi and walking into the police station yet again. He needed to be strategic in this next interaction with Inspector Polat. Suggesting the inspector immediately test all the containers found in Martin Neill's room would elicit only more of the suspicion and indignant anger he'd come to expect from Polat.

Another vehicle pulled up alongside the police station, and a hulking figure emerged from within. Rather than entering the station, the man took off down the street, only to turn on his heel and march back toward the station.

Alexander stared in befuddlement as Dr. Henry turned and strode away from the police station yet again. What the devil was he doing?

He slid out of his own vehicle and took off after Dr. Henry. The man turned sharply and came up short when he saw Alexander was only a few feet behind him.

"Oh," he said, blinking at Alexander. "Oh, Ashton. Hello."

"Hello." He waited for Dr. Henry to say something else. He held himself stiffly with his shoulders nearly at his ears. He looked almost . . . guilty. Shock flared within him for the half second it took for his reason to rise up and douse it; Dr. Henry surely wasn't there to confess to Neill's murder. But he was acting damnably strange.

"Is everything all right?" Alexander asked him.

"Er, yes. Yes, of course. Just popping in to see the status of the case," Dr. Henry said. His wince told Alexander he heard how strained his voice was. His massive shoulders fell. "Ah, hell. I need a drink."

"It's seven in the morning, sir."

"I know that," Henry barked. "I need it anyway. Might not have agreed to this stupid plan if I'd taken a minute to mull things over with a glass of something." He squinted up and down the street like he expected a pub to materialize. "Damn. Damn it all, Ashton. What are you doing here at this hour?"

"I'm here to speak to Inspector Polat," Alexander said, resisting the urge to turn the question back on him.

Dr. Henry grunted, propping his hands on his hips, only to wince down at something in his hand.

Alexander managed to get a look at what it was before Dr. Henry shoved his hands into his trouser pockets, the guilty look back on his face.

"Sir," Alexander asked slowly, "why do you have the piece of pottery Martin Neill discovered at the agora?"

The walk from the police station to the hotel was a long one, leaving Alexander parched and sweating. It was a good thing, for by the time he'd made it up the hill and through the open doors of the foyer, he'd worked off most of his fury.

The idea that Clark and Wakefield would even conceive of using a dead boy as the expedition crew's scapegoat was enough to infuriate Alexander, but it was the astonishment of Dr. Henry actually agreeing to it that had sent Alexander on his long trek through the city to prevent him throwing fists. Even now, panting in the silent foyer, he thought he'd rather like to break some things. Clark's nose, for a start, for giving Dr. Henry the "evidence" that would convince Inspector Polat Martin Neill had been the one to steal the missing artifacts: the shard of pottery Saffron had described Martin having found. Blaming Martin for the thefts would clear the remaining crew of suspicions, therefore preventing the Turks from shutting down the dig, and provide a perfectly feasible explanation of Neill's death. The murder in this convenient story was doubtless related to his dealings with the nefarious characters in Smyrna to whom Neill had sold the lost artifacts. It was perfect, except for one thing.

"All of that is completely and utterly false," Alexander spat upon the conclusion of Dr. Henry's optimistic explanation. "And you know it."

"But it would have helped your wife!" Dr. Henry had cried, brandishing a hand at the police station. "It would have cleared her—"

"Saffron would *never*," he had shot back, "accept her freedom at the cost of blackening an innocent man's name."

This he said with absolute certainty, and even after cooling his head—figuratively—he stood by that conviction. Saffron would have never compromised her integrity, or Martin Neill's reputation, to get out of jail, even if it meant she would stay behind bars.

Alexander had only just held back from telling Dr. Henry what he thought of *his* integrity before walking away. He couldn't stand to look at him a minute longer, a compulsion he'd teased out during his long walk. Alexander had worked with Dr. Henry too long to respect him much as an academic or an individual—he'd seen too many flaws in his methods and character for that—but he'd thought Dr. Henry at least had basic human decency.

There was one thing he hadn't had long enough to mull over: what to do with the truth, should Dr. Henry decide to move forward with the plan to frame Martin Neill for the thefts. He'd surely be in the minority in objecting. And if it worked, and Polat accepted Neill's death was related to the thefts and *not* Saffron, she would be free. They could work together, unhampered, to find out the truth. But at what cost to Martin Neill's reputation, and at what cost to their honor?

These were the questions haunting him as he sat a chair in the empty parlor, and the questions that were chased from his mind when a disturbance arose in the hotel's entry. Anticipating Polat, he went to the parlor's door, but saw a young woman in a pink dress and matching wide-brimmed hat standing before the reception desk, speaking to Mr. Koray.

The proprietor, upon seeing Alexander at the door, beckoned him and spoke in Turkish to the woman. As Alexander approached, he added in English, "Perhaps he can answer your questions."

The woman turned to him, and Alexander saw immediately she was not a local and she was agitated. Her round face was pink, not just from sun but around the nose and eyes, as if she'd been crying. He went to the desk, looking between the young woman and Mr. Koray. "How can I be of assistance?"

The young woman sniffed. "The proprietor said you might be able to answer my questions," she said in a husky, elegant voice that didn't match her youthful face. She couldn't have been more than twenty. "You're a part of the expedition from the university, aren't you? The proprietor said—h-he said that—" A sob overtook her. Alexander automatically reached for and offered his handkerchief.

She accepted it, patting her eyes dry. On a choked breath, she said, "He said that Martin Neill is dead. Is it true?"

Chapter 39

Alexander put to work the single greatest antidote to any ailment he knew: tea. He and the girl sat down in the parlor with glasses of strong tea as he explained Martin's sudden illness.

"I see," she said, doing her best not to cry again. "I don't mean to be such a watering pot, it's only . . . I knew Martin for such a short time, but he was such a lovely person. I can't believe he's dead."

"I'm sorry to be the bearer of bad news. I understood you'd received word he was ill." Saffron had mentioned Martin's request to send word to a girl he'd met, and this had to be her. Corsianna Moore, she'd mumbled when Alexander had offered her his own name.

Miss Moore shook her head. "I didn't know. When he didn't come to meet me . . ." Her cheeks colored. "Well, I got tired of wondering why he didn't come back. We'd had so many wonderful conversations. My mother said I was foolish to chase after a young man off on an adventure, but . . ." She shrugged helplessly. "I liked him."

"I'm glad you did come," Alexander said gently. "The circumstances surrounding Mr. Neill's illness and death are being investigated as murder. You said you'd seen him here, in Smyrna?"

Miss Moore blanched. "M-Martin was murdered?"

Alexander nodded. "The police believe he was poisoned."

She shot to her feet, looking around in a panic. She began to say something, but stopped, blinking. She sank slowly back into her chair. "I beg your pardon, I . . . It's just a shock, you know. Poisoned?"

He nodded solemnly.

"Martin and I met for tea the other night. He . . ." She bit her lip. "He wanted to see me after we left the ship, while my parents and I were still in the city. We met at a tea house after dinner one evening. I snuck away, you see. My stepfather doesn't approve of me going out into the city on my own, even though I lived here when I was a child." She was still trembling but smiled slightly at her admission. "But that was the day after the ship arrived in Smyrna. Martin told me he would meet me at the *han* again a few days later, but he didn't come. I knew what hotel he was staying in, and this was my first chance to get away again. I expected to leave him an angry note." Her tight voice shrank with the effort to keep from tears.

That was where Martin Neill had disappeared to their first night in Smyrna; he must have gone to see Miss Moore. It was therefore unlikely his location that evening would be useful in discovering how he'd been poisoned; if she was tearful over his death after seeking him out, it was unlikely Miss Moore had poisoned Neill herself.

Alexander gave her a moment to dab at her eyes and take a sip of tea before he ventured, "Did Mr. Neill tell you anything about the expedition? Any troubles he was having with anyone?"

She shook her head. "He was so terribly excited to be working at the agora, Mr. Ashton." She pronounced 'agora' the same way the Turks did.

"I'm afraid the police might want to ask you a few questions about Mr. Neill—"

Miss Moore shook her head, sending her red-blond hair flying, and gasped, "No, no, Mr. Ashton. They can't! My mother would be furious!"

Alexander didn't know how to reply to that. He certainly couldn't make the girl talk to the police, but it wasn't as if her information would be very helpful.

She rose to leave, and when he asked if he might call on her to ask her further questions, she bit her lip again, looking deeply unsettled at the notion. "I do want to help, Mr. Ashton, I do. If *you* came, that would be all right. But the police . . . My mother had poor experiences with the police here in the past. My father . . . Well, I couldn't put her through that all again. You might send a note, and we could arrange to meet somewhere. I'm staying at the Sağlık Hotel for another week before we leave for Antalya." She gave him a wan smile. "We're going to all my mother's favorite places. She was just remarried, and this is a bit of a honeymoon. How mortifying, to bring along her grown daughter. But I couldn't resist. I wanted to see this place again."

Alexander thanked her, and she left. Alexander returned to his room for a fresh handkerchief before he left for the agora, but was waylaid by Mrs. Demirel on the stairs.

"Oh, I beg your pardon, Mr. Ashton! Whatever are you doing here? I ought to have invited you to take tea with Mr. Demirel and myself. How terribly thoughtless of me. My husband hasn't been well enough to leave the room yesterday or today, I'm afraid. His allergies are playing havoc with his sinuses. Though I doubt he has anything meaningful to contribute to dear Miss Everleigh's defense, which I imagine is at the forefront of your mind," she added in a loud whisper. "Are you going to see her now?"

"Not now, but perhaps before dinner, on the way back from the agora."

"I'll go to see her at lunch," she said brightly. "Take her a few more clothes, I think, and sit with her. It must be terribly lonely, being held in a room all by herself."

"Thank you," Alexander said, meaning it. "I know she appreciated your company the other day, when the maid brought the food. It drives Saffron wild, being cooped up with no way of helping with the investigation."

Mrs. Demirel gave him a strained smile, as if the idea of helping an investigation was mortifying. "Oh, indeed."

Alexander took his leave soon after. With the question of Martin Neill's disappearance answered, he turned his thoughts back to the other questions left unanswered. And at the moment, they all centered on one man.

Alexander was in a taxi to the agora when he spotted the red-banded straw hat Clark wore among the crowd of pedestrians on the street just a quarter mile from the dig site.

Instinct had him shoving coins into the driver's hand and jumping out of the taxi.

The hot weight of the sun settled on his shoulders, the smells of the *kemeraltı* closing around him like curtains. Alexander hastened to spot Clark, and that distinctive hat caught his eye quickly.

His quarry moved with the crowd deeper into the market. It was just before noon, and on a Friday, it was just before the locals quit work for their Sabbath and the crew members returned to the hotel for their administrative work. He couldn't imagine why Clark felt like going for a walk just then, but he was going to find out.

It turned out it was not a long walk. Soon they were immersed in the *kemeraltı*, with all its bustle and brightly colored awnings, the call to prayer growing louder with every step. The streets were so heavily draped that when Clark disappeared behind an open wrought iron gate and Alexander made to follow, he was shocked to find himself confronted by a steep set of stone stairs bright with sunlight rather than a passageway or market stall.

When Alexander climbed the stairs, he was in a courtyard filled with the throaty song of the call to prayer. He squinted up at a tall tower eclipsing the sun, and yes, sure enough, he was in front of a mosque. Four simple, ruddy stone columns supported white arches of a portico sheltering a steady stream of Turks as they deposited their shoes and stepped under the elaborate script engraved over the open double doors.

It was a sign of how overtired Alexander was that he simply stood there, gaping at the mosque while the sun heated his head like a pot on a stove, for a full thirty seconds before he realized Clark must have gone inside, for he was certainly the only Englishman in the courtyard.

Should he go inside to see if Clark had suddenly found faith in the Muslim religion—doubtful—or simply leave him to whatever cultural exploration he might be pursuing? Something told him the reason Clark was here had nothing to do with faith or culture.

More faithful were climbing the stairs to the mosque; many were damp about the neck and arms, perhaps having washed before they entered the courtyard. More shoes were deposited on either side of the doors. A pair of boys darted here and there to straighten them.

The crowd thinned. The last plaintive note of the caller's voice drifted away on a hot wind. The two boys scurried into the double doors, out of which rolled a loud, deep voice.

He'd go inside, Alexander decided, and see if Clark was inside. It'd put his relentless suspicions to rest, at least for a little while.

Just as he reached one of the portico's columns, one of the shoe boys slipped back out through the double doors. The youth moved quickly, efficiently stepping across dozens of shoes to the far corner of the portico. Peering around the column, Alexander watched the boy kneel next to a pair of tall, dusty boots, the only ones among the shoes lining the floor. They had to be Clark's. The boy's back blocked what exactly was so interesting about Clark's footwear, but he was there for just a moment before standing and retreating inside.

There was no thought in what Alexander did next; he was hopping over a dozen worn leather slippers and dusty oxfords the moment the boy had disappeared into the mosque's dim interior. The smell was fantastically unpleasant, made slightly more bearable by the smoky, woody scent of incense drifting from the open doors.

Clark's boots were no exception, but Alexander could ignore their odor to see what the young man had been doing. It was disappointing to find there was absolutely nothing worthy of attention about the boots. The deep brown leather was dusty from the agora, but clearly well-maintained. The soles had recently been replaced and were exceptionally thick, even for a pair of work boots.

He set the boot back down on the ground, glaring at it. Couldn't it have been as simple as looking inside and discovering a note or something obvious?

He picked up the other boot, and when the dark, dank interior revealed nothing, tossed it to the ground in disgust.

It smacked the ground with an odd, hollow *thunk*. He stared at the shoe in disbelief before he picked it back up, reached inside, and peeled the leather insole up.

A long breath left Alexander.

In the hollow place between the insole and the heel was a tiny piece of folded paper.

Hand trembling, he opened it. It was written in a long looping scrawl that had to be Turkish or Arabic.

His heartbeat thrummed in his ears. A shoe with a hollow space ideal for concealing small objects like coins, jewelry, a shard of pottery, or a message. A message he could not read.

He pocketed the note, replaced the insole, set the boot down, and strode back to the stairs. He didn't know how long he had before the prayers came to an end and Clark would leave, but he had to learn what this message said. He had to know if it had anything to do with Saffron, the missing artifacts, or both.

A plume of dust coming up the drive announced Saffron's next visitor long before their motorcar arrived. It was an unusual time for a visit; the ladies usually came in the morning around ten, and Alexander came by the consulate after work at the agora was concluded, five or six in the evening. It was noon, nearing the time Kadriye, the maid, brought her lunch. Then again, Sir Randolph had to meet with people on occasion, she supposed. It was likely someone to see him.

She did not see who it was, as the drive curved away from her window, but she quickly realized the new arrival had come for her when rapid, hard footsteps approached her door.

She rose to her feet and faced the door, arranging her face to be polite when the door opened.

"Mrs. Ashton," Mr. Feldman said, but his voice was a little harder than usual and his nostrils were flared, "Inspector Polat of the Smyrna police is here to see you. Are you available?"

Mr. Feldman would have been a very good butler, Saffron decided. Polat was standing behind him, clearly fuming, and Feldman was giving her the choice to not speak with him. She smiled at Feldman. "Of course I will see the inspector. I want to help as much as I can to find Mr. Neill's killer."

Those last words were for Polat's benefit, of course. She wasn't sure if she wanted to rankle him or pacify him, but it was clear as he strode into the room and glared around at the comforts she'd been given that she had no hope for the latter.

"You are dismissed," he told Mr. Feldman when he sat in the chair he usually occupied.

"I have been instructed not to leave Mrs. Ashton alone with any visitors," Feldman returned without emotion.

"I am not a *visitor*," spat Polat.

Mr. Feldman only gazed at him.

Polat rolled his shoulders as he turned his back on the secretary and focused on Saffron. "You will tell me what you did with the poison bottle."

Saffron's lips parted in surprise at the blunt question, but she quickly rallied. "As I did not poison anyone, I don't know where the container might be that held the poison responsible for harming Martin Neill." There, that was quite clear.

Polat seemed to struggle not to gnash his teeth at her as he stalked over to where she stood before the couch. His voice came out low but vicious. "You know what it is that killed your lover, and you know where the bottle is."

"I do not," she replied stoutly.

"You do," he hissed.

It was tempting to continue on in this childish way, but Saffron refrained, if only because Mr. Feldman was watching them.

"You may say it as often as you like, Inspector, but I had nothing to do with Martin's death, I was not having an affair with him, and I do not know where the poison went after it killed him."

"But you say it went somewhere," Polat shot back with a victorious gleam in his pale eyes.

"*You* implied it went somewhere when you asked me where it was."

Polat's demand to know where the poison bottle was could mean so many things. Had he received the chemical analysis and realized none of the medicines from Martin's room contained the fatal toxin? Did that mean Mr. Demirel's gout medication was not the cause of his death?

Her hands came together before her, squeezing tight. "Have you learned what toxin killed Martin?" she dared to ask.

"When I do, you will know. When I have that information, I will push the judge to move forward with the trial. You will not delay this case any longer." He looked her up and down with a sneer, then stormed from the room.

Stunned, Saffron automatically turned to Mr. Feldman, who got to his feet with a sort of weary displeasure. "What did he mean, Mr. Feldman?"

"He takes issue with the judge permitting the proceedings to be delayed as we await the arrival of your legal counsel," he said, and lumbered down the hall after Polat.

Saffron was left wondering not only where her lawyer was, but, if Polat didn't have it in his possession as evidence, where the poison could be.

"I need you to tell me what this says, right now," Alexander said the moment he reached the tent pitched over the graffitied stone.

Banks squinted up at him from where he sat on a short camp chair, still holding a magnifying glass over the stone's ancient writing. "Beg pardon?"

Alexander held out the small square of paper, now damp with sweat. In fact, all of him was damp with sweat; the dash from the mosque back to the agora had been short but brutally hot with the sun at full power overhead. "This. What does it say?"

Banks took it and rattled off a sentence in Turkish, then translated. "'Many thanks, friend. Gratitude at sunset.'"

"Gratitude . . ." Alexander stared down at the paper in Banks's hand. If this note meant what he thought it meant . . .

"*Minnettarlık* means gratitude," Banks said, studying Alexander with concern. "I say, are you all right?"

"Gratitude, as in, pure, out of the goodness of their heart gratitude, or—"

"It has undertones of appreciation, or indebtedness. Otherwise, they might have used *şükür*, which has religious connotations—"

"And sunset? The word means sunset, specifically, or sunset as in the prayer time?"

Banks's ruddy brows shot up. "The prayer time. Ashton, mate, what is this about? Is this about your—well, Saffron?"

Sunset. Clark would return to the mosque at sunset for payment for the artifacts he'd stolen—and apparently sold. Alexander blew out a breath, thinking furiously. He took up the notebook Banks had on the ground next to his camp chair, tore out a page, and handed it to Banks. "Yes, this might very well be about Saffron. I need you to write something for me."

Chapter 40

The sun had passed beyond the roofs of the houses, casting the streets into blue shadow. Merchants threw blankets and tarps over their wares, hitched animals to their carts, or dragged displays back into the shallow stalls built into the first levels of the market's buildings. The street was crowded with families, most of which walked in the same direction, toward the mosque.

Joseph Clark strode down the street among them like he had a business appointment to keep.

Alexander trailed him, not bothering to keep much distance between them.

At the corner stall overhung with a faded white-and-yellow striped cloth, Clark went to the right.

This was the fourth time Alexander had gone past this stall today: when he'd followed Clark to the mosque, then ran back to the agora, and when he returned to slip the note Banks had written for him back into Clark's boot. It being Friday, the sermon had kept Clark inside just long enough for Alexander to replace the paper and get away before the mosque had emptied. Navigating the *kemeralti* to the mosque that many times in quick succession had carved the route into his mind, and he knew the narrow street Clark walked now didn't lead to the mosque.

Sweat snaked down Alexander's back as he followed Clark deeper into the disjointed streets of the *kemeraltı*. His quarry's pace didn't slow as the light faded further from the sky.

When Clark turned west, Alexander was so surprised he knew exactly where they were that he stopped in the middle of the road, causing a veiled woman to bump into him with an undignified grunt. She rushed away from his murmured apology, and he turned to stare after Clark as he approached the *han* of Ali Fethi Bey.

As he had hoped, his forged note demanding Clark meet with his buyer immediately had brought Alexander directly to who had been paying for the stolen artifacts.

It became perfectly clear in a flash of understanding: Clark was working with Bey. Bey was buying the stolen artifacts from Clark. And if Clark was working for a man like Bey, interesting enough to the British government that Nick Hale was surveilling him, that meant Clark might be in deep.

The money. The *money.* Clark needed money; that was why he played cutthroat cards, why he would risk his career *and* the preservation of history to steal and sell what they discovered in the agora.

And if Clark was willing to risk so much, what might he have done to keep his actions secret? Would he have killed a young man who'd discovered it? Frame an innocent woman?

Fury ignited in Alexander, rage like he'd never felt before. It coursed through him, sudden and hot, galvanizing his body into action.

He was a step behind Clark before he knew what he was doing. The rapid tattoo of his boots on the ground must have alarmed Clark, for he swung around like Alexander had called his name.

Clark was clumsy when panicked. He scrambled away from him and immediately tripped, which was how Alexander caught him before he'd even had the chance to flee. He lifted Clark to his feet, only to hit Clark square in the jaw and knock him down again.

Clark's dusty face registered shock for only a second before it twisted into fury. "Ashton, what the—"

Alexander dragged Clark to his feet, ready to beat the man to a bloody pulp right there in the street for acting as if he had *no idea* of the damage he'd—

"Ashton," said a taut, low voice.

A pair of hands interposed themselves atop his own, pushing down.

It was Nick, his cap pulled low over his face. "Not here," he murmured, and grabbed Clark by the back of the neck.

He forced Clark ahead of him, and from the way Clark went rigid, Alexander guessed there was a barrel of a pistol pressed to his ribs. "Let's go somewhere a little more private for this chat, shall we?"

After checking to ensure no one had followed them from Bey's house, Nick shoved Clark into the back seat of a beat-up motorcar one street down.

Alexander got into the back seat with him, and Nick started driving.

"Joseph Clark," Nick said over the noise of the motorcar, "thirty-seven years of age, residence in London. Corporal in His Majesty's army stationed mostly in Belgium, discharged 1918. Eight years as a researcher at University College London, specializing in the field of archaeology of the Roman era, which has sent you to numerous countries, and in each one, you've had a rather close relationship with the nearest broker of antiquities." He took a sharp turn, sending Clark tumbling into Alexander. He shoved Clark back into place.

"What is this?" the man spat, returning Alexander's glare. It seemed his shock had worn off. "You hired some thug to kidnap me?"

"A *thug.*" Nick laughed. "I don't know whether to be flattered or offended."

Another sharp turn and Nick cutting the engine brought Alexander back to awareness of their location. They were no longer in the *kemeraltı*, though they hadn't gone far. The surrounding buildings were skeletons. Nick had pulled the motorcar into a structure composed of two walls and a lintel draped with cloth that Nick whipped down and tossed over the car when they got out of it.

Nick hustled them into the ruin across the debris-strewn street. One could see the darkening sky through the half-collapsed roof, but the walls were more or less intact, and its windows were boarded up, providing a sense of security.

Clark looked around uneasily, his sneer fading. He seemed to realize what sort of trouble he was in, being taken to a defunct building of blackened walls and fire-gnawed furniture.

Unable to wait any longer, Alexander asked, "Did you kill Martin Neill?"

A laugh burst out of Clark. "*What?*"

In two strides, Alexander had Clark by the collar. "You heard me. Did you kill Martin Neill?"

Clark shoved at his chest. "Get off me, you—"

Lifting the man nearly off his feet, Alexander swung Clark around and slammed him into the wall. The structure around them wobbled and creaked ominously, but Alexander didn't care. He might finally have the person responsible for not only a murder, but the imprisonment of his wife. "You'll answer me, Clark. Now."

"No," Clark snarled. "No, I didn't kill anyone, damn you. Now get off me!" He shoved away from Alexander again, and this time, Alexander let him go. Clark took a hasty step away, then made a show of brushing down the front of his jacket. "I don't have to say anything. To either of you. Where do you get off, pinching me off the damn street?"

"You've been—"

Nick cut Alexander off, his voice easy. "You're quite right, Mr. Clark. You don't have to answer any of our questions. But considering you've set my friend's wife up for murder—"

Clark shot a look at Alexander. "Your wife?"

Alexander glared in reply.

Nick leaned against a blackened wardrobe with an arch expression. "Yes, his wife. You set her up for murder. Actually, you've been harassing her for weeks, according to what I've heard." Clark didn't reply. He stood with arms crossed, looking bored. "What was it, Ashton? Set a snake on her, then trapped her in the ruins. My favorite—apart from the accusation of having an affair with the murdered man, of course—was trying to topple a ruin on her head."

"My favorite," Alexander said quietly, "was drugging her when he knew I was out of the way."

Nick let out a low whistle. "You know what they say, Ashton, sour grapes—"

"I didn't want her for myself," spat Clark, a sneer on his face. "What would I want with that pushy cow?"

Alexander knocked Clark into a broken chair with a punch to the jaw.

Nick sounded bored. "Mr. Clark, unless you want to be pummeled to a pulp, I suggest you keep your opinions to yourself."

Clark drew himself up and glowered at Alexander, pushing his stringy blond hair out of his face. "It doesn't make a difference what I say about her."

"It does to him," said Nick. "And it does to the crew, and that police inspector. Your 'evidence' is what got her arrested, according to my sources. But the question remains, *why?* Why have you been harassing her? Even an annoying woman could be dealt with without so much, er, enthusiasm."

Alexander had crossed his arms closely against his chest, hoping to suppress his inclination to continue beating Clark. He wanted answers. But even outnumbered in a ruined house far from his friends, Clark's arrogance was tireless. It made his blood boil.

Clark smiled unpleasantly. "Just passing the time."

Nick hummed and reached into his pocket. As he drew out cigarettes and a lighter, Alexander didn't miss Clark's twitch. Nick didn't either. With a wry smile, he passed a cigarette to Clark and lit it for him before his own. He blew out his smoke lazily. "You can rest assured, with the exception of Ashton here losing his temper, you have nothing to fear from us."

Clark blew smoke and glanced at Alexander with annoyance. "As I said, I found her irritating. Why bother dogging after her for a month before I could get to my real work? The sooner she realized her mistake and turned tail, the sooner I'd be rid of her."

"I see," said Nick evenly.

"And what concern is it of yours?" Clark asked, his eyes narrowed. "Who are you? Why do you know me?"

"I'm a friend of the accused. I don't like my friends to be locked up in foreign jails because someone decided to play a little joke on them."

Clark let out a noise of derision. "Well, if that's all—"

"You still haven't gotten to the point, Mr. Clark," said Nick, his voice ringing.

"And you still haven't told me why I should answer any of your questions."

Alexander grabbed his shirtfront and slammed him against the wall. "Because I'll be damned if Saffron hangs because of a worm like you."

He stared into Clark's pale eyes for a long moment before throwing him to the ground again.

Clark took a moment to get to his feet, more warily this time. "She's not going to hang. Clearly, the boy died of a stomach flux. Happens all the time to people in foreign parts."

"He was poisoned," Alexander said. "And the poison came from someone staying at the hotel."

"Then"—Clark wet his lips—"when they find the actual poisoner—"

"Saffron Everleigh is a poisons expert, Mr. Clark," Nick said, bored again. "And according to what the rumor *you* crafted, she had an affair to hide. Who else would have killed Martin Neill but the woman who knew exactly how to do it and had the motive you supplied?"

Clark looked for a long moment at Nick, his face draining of contempt as realization dawned.

Nick cocked his head and took another drag from his cigarette. "Ah. You didn't expect that your evidence would send her to the gallows."

He didn't reply. Alexander ground his teeth together. Selfish bastard.

"Very well," said Nick, now business-like. "This is easily remedied, Mr. Clark. You'll tell us what really happened. It'll all get sorted out at the police station."

Clark shook his head. "I'm not going to the police station."

Alexander took a step toward him. "Why not?"

The answering sneer had Alexander's fists curling at his sides, itching to hit it off Clark's face. "I've wasted enough time on talking to the police about your *wife*." He spat the last word.

"Ashton," Nick said quietly, "I don't think Mr. Clark quite understands the severity of his actions."

"I think you're right." Alexander discarded his jacket. Nick took it from him and folded it over an arm.

Clark looked between them with increasing alarm. "What, are you really going to act like—"

"Like you've doomed the woman he loves?" Nick asked. "Like your actions put her life at risk? No, we *are* certainly going to act like that."

"As if I was the only one incriminating her! You said it yourself, she is a so-called poisons expert. Besides, all I did was say out loud what everyone else was already thinking. I did see her going into Neill's room. And those two were together all the time, probably rutting in the ruins—"

The rage that curtailed the rest of Clark's words overcame any notion of self-control Alexander had planned on maintaining. His fists slammed into Clark's body indiscriminately. Blood pounded in his temples and began to show on Clark's face, his mouth and nose shining red. The sight of it did nothing to temper him.

But before his rage was spent, Nick pulled him off Clark, saying roughly, "Enough! Enough, he has to be able to talk when we're done with him."

Alexander jerked himself away. He got unsteadily to his feet, unable to take his eyes from Clark's battered and bloody face.

Sickly unease churned violently in his stomach, and he fled the ruin.

The haunting chant of a male voice reverberated through the empty street and hollowed out buildings.

Alexander forced himself to focus on the smooth invocation rather than the shame burning in his gut. He lost track of how many times he paced the short walk from the ruined house to the street.

His fists were beginning to throb. He looked at them; they were red and bloodied. They'd no doubt be purple in the morning.

He'd agreed Saffron should come on this expedition when he knew it would expose her to ridicule. He'd insisted Martin Neill stay close to her and thus gave Clark fuel for his stupid rumor. He hadn't done anything meaningful when he knew Clark was bothering her beyond normal expedition hijinks. He should have beat Clark senseless the moment he trapped her in the stall in the agora.

A memory floated up from the turbulence of his mind. A dark room and the sharp scent of arnica, nearly a year ago. He and Saffron had taken turns dabbing it on each other's wounds. They'd exchanged the words just hours before, the words he'd held close to his chest like a winning hand of cards for months, only to realize keeping his love for her a secret would make him lose *her.* But she'd felt the same, or so she'd said.

The arnica had been an affectionate gesture at first, something to show his love for her when he couldn't fully express it, because the simple words "I love you" hadn't been enough. But his guilt had been at least partially allayed when he treated her wounds, guilt for not removing her from harm's way, for not being there to protect her when the villains had come for her.

It was the same guilt he felt now, momentarily relieved by thrashing Clark. And he *was* guilty.

He'd only barely received the blessing of her family, on her grandfather's condition that he'd keep her safe. And he hadn't done that. He hadn't even done most of the work of this investigation. He was reliant on Nick, whose motives he still didn't understand.

Shame and anger were a mire he couldn't get caught in. Control, logic, and skill were what would save Saffron.

After a long moment of staring up at indigo sky, the call to prayer still wavering in the warm air, he stepped back through the gap in the wall.

Nick had lit a tiny lamp and stood smoking over a groaning Clark, who was sprawled against one of the more stable walls. When Alexander caught his eye, Nick understood his unspoken question.

"He'll hold up long enough to answer a few more questions," he said, and flicked his cigarette to the ground to light another. "I find it strange, Mr. Clark, that you're willing to insult a man's wife to his face—after grievously wronging her—but a little trip to the police station seems to frighten you. Why is that?"

Clark spat blood on the floor beside him before looking warily up at them. "Can't I just be a cad?"

"It's the antiquities," Alexander said flatly. "Clark has been smuggling them out of the dig site and selling them to Bey."

"Ah," Nick said, a little smile forming at the corners of his mouth. "Answers at last."

Alexander got the feeling he wasn't referring to Clark's motives. "He doesn't want to be in contact with the police any more than necessary. That's why he sent Dr. Henry with the pottery Martin Neill discovered at the agora to convince the inspector that it was Neill doing the smuggling." He stared hard at Clark, realizing the contradiction. "Why did you try to convince Dr. Henry to blame Martin Neill for the smuggling after spreading those rumors about him and Saffron? You'd already pushed the blame onto her. Why try to change the story a week later?"

"Turks were still asking questions, weren't they?" Clark grumbled, shifting uncomfortably against the wall. "Stupid Hayrettin still wants to shut down the dig. We need to tie it all up for them."

Alexander smiled thinly. "Considering I've seen you at Bey's *han* after receiving a message insisting on a meeting with the person buying your stolen goods, I'd say that'd tie things up neatly for *you*."

"Now, that's interesting." Nick's hazel eyes gleamed from behind a twisting cloud of smoke. "I wonder if all this might be the inspiration for his campaign against your wife, Ashton. She is rather known for solving mysteries."

Alexander stared at Nick, then at Clark, who now refused to meet his eye. "You targeted Saffron because you thought she would catch you." A harsh laugh worked its way out of his throat. "You bastard—you tortured her for weeks, trying to get her to cry off the expedition because you were worried she would figure out it was you when things started going missing." He went to where Clark slumped. He kneeled so they were face to bloody face. "I will relish telling her how highly you esteem her skills. But I hope you see the flaw in your plan now, Clark. When Saffron figured it out, as I have no doubt she would have, she would have at least left you with your dignity. Unfortunately for you, *I* figured it out first. And I have every intention of ruining you in every way possible."

Chapter 41

Alexander left Clark in Nick's care soon after, unable to look at the man without wanting to finish what he'd started with his fists. On foot, he made his way toward the *kemeraltı*, where he paused at the fountain outside a mosque to scrub the crust of blood and dirt from his hands. He got more than a few sidelong glances from another man performing his ablutions in the cool, mineral-scented water, but he said nothing. After ensuring he didn't look as wild as he felt, he went to the British consulate.

Saffron was shocked by Clark's subterfuge with the boots and Dr. Henry's willingness to frame Neill, but didn't appear surprised it connected to Nick's investigation of Bey, and though she did smile when he explained why Clark had been targeting her, it was only a shadow of her true one.

"And you've hurt yourself," she murmured, stroking a finger over his purpling knuckles.

He drew them gently away, unaccountably unnerved by her noticing them. "I'll be better tomorrow, when Clark confesses all to Polat. I think it'll be enough to force him to rescind your arrest."

"Then we can discover who actually killed Martin," she said, brightening only for a moment before worry clouded her eyes again. "It wasn't Clark, was it?"

"I don't think it was Clark. He was too shocked by the knowledge that Martin was actually murdered, and that you could have hanged for it. He's just a thief."

"A very rude one," she added, lips pursing. "Is that what Nick's business is all about? He was interested in Bey because of the artifacts?"

"It must be. I've seen only one other man involved in his surveillance, and it was a trainee. A small operation suggests a less dangerous crime, perhaps."

She worried her lip. "But why wait to do something about it? It seems he knew Bey was getting artifacts illegally. What's he been waiting for?" She shook her head before he could answer. "Nick wanted to know who he was working with. And now he has Clark." With a sigh, she rushed on. "But why is *Nick* the one to discover who is responsible for smuggling Turkish artifacts? Surely Mr. Hayrettin or Mr. Assam's departments would be responsible for that." She threw her hands in the air. "And if it wasn't Clark who killed Martin, who was it? Does it have anything to do with this business with Nick and Bey, or is it just coincidence?"

"Knowledge of the smuggling is a good motive. Clark is involved, but it's possible some of the other crew are, too. Hell, even the assistants that went to Bey's *han*. Any of Clark's friends, or anyone with access to the artifacts."

"But that's dozens of people. It could be Wakefield, or even Mr. Hayrettin or Mr. Assam! Anyone could have slipped the colchicine into Martin's drink at the dig site or during a meal at the hotel." She blew out a breath. "It looks like we're back to where we started."

"We're not," he said firmly, putting his hand over hers. He glanced at the consul general's secretary, who sat in his habitual seat. He wasn't sure the man was awake, but he lowered his voice further. "Nick's people have pulled some strings to slow down the release of the police lab's full findings in the interest of giving us more time before you are taken to trial. As soon as you're released, the report should be, too. We'll be able to find out more about which container held the toxin and trace it from there."

Fragile hope whispered to him that her release would mean a good many things, including taking their marriage out of this nightmare and bringing it into full reality. He smiled at her. "Get some rest, Mrs. Ashton. Tomorrow will be a big day."

Her returning smile was a little shy, and it did things to his heart. "I look forward to it."

It was nearly the dinner hour when Alexander finally returned to the hotel. He had walked from the consulate to the hotel after speaking to Saffron to give himself the chance to process all that had happened, and sort through all the things he needed to do for the next day. He admittedly got a little lost in a daydream about welcoming Saffron back to the hotel. He wondered if it would cause a scandal to request a suite of rooms. They certainly couldn't stay in Alexander's room; it was on a floor entirely occupied by the crew. Alexander didn't relish the idea of spending his delayed wedding night on the same floor as a dozen nosy bachelors.

But would Saffron want to cohabitate right away? He wasn't sure how she would feel once she was released. She had been through so much. She would want to find Martin Neill's killer, not explore new dimensions of their relationship. If the killer was as perceptive as Clark, they would be right to be wary of her once she was released. They'd want her out of the way. He wouldn't repeat his mistakes and ignore his instincts. He would be at hand to protect her.

He'd just decided he would insist on sharing a room, even if he had to strong-arm Saffron into it and sleep on the floor, when he stepped up into the warm glow of the hotel's entry and found Inspector Polat was waiting for him.

"Mr. Ashton," he said coolly. "I want to speak with you. Now."

They exchanged no niceties once they were ensconced in the small dining room down the hall from the reception desk.

"You had much interesting business today," Polat began, standing on the opposite side of the small polished table from Alexander. "You came to the police station but did not enter. Then you spent time in the *kemeraltı*. You visited a mosque, then a tea house." Polat's weighted pause invited Alexander to confront him about being under surveillance, but Alexander held his tongue. "The tea house is owned by a known criminal, Ali Fethi Bey. How do you know him?"

"He introduced himself when I visited the *han* some weeks ago."

Some of Polat's cool demeanor slipped away. "You admit to meeting this man many times?"

"Twice is hardly many. I did not see him today. In fact, you will need to school your spies better, for I did not actually enter the *han*, nor did I speak with Mr. Bey."

"This is true. You were seen on the street with Mr. Clark." His eyes gleamed, looking for all purposes like he relished each word. "The same man you blame for your wife's troubles. You were beating him."

Alexander didn't reply, but shifted his hands to be sure his bruised knuckles were out of view.

"And now that man is not here, at the hotel. No one of your party has seen him."

That wasn't entirely unexpected. It was possible Clark had needed medical attention and Nick took him to a physician. Or it was possible Nick had decided to detain Clark until he agreed to meet with the police.

Polat was looking at him expectantly. "I don't know where Clark is now," he told him. "I suspect he is spending the evening in the city, as many of our party do."

"I have an idea of where Mr. Clark is," Polat said, advancing around the table. "You are working with Ali Fethi Bey to sell the artifacts from the agora. Mr. Clark discovered it. You have done something to him to hide your crimes, as you did with Mr. Neill."

Despite the inspector now being only inches from him, Alexander held his ground. "I had nothing to do with Mr. Neill's death, nor have I done anything to put Mr. Clark in danger."

"Your people are all the same. I have seen your papers, Alexander *Theodoros* Ashton." He spat the Greek name like it was bitter on his tongue. "And then I knew the sort of man you are. Greedy. You came to my city to rob it, just like your people. But this time, there will be punishment." He rapped on the table suddenly, trying to make Alexander flinch. "I will find out! I will learn all you have done and when I do, the judge will move this case forward, without your wife's counsel." His lips curled into a cutting smile. "No special treatment when they learn you conspired with that—" He said a Turkish word with such guttural distaste that Alexander took as a nasty insult to Bey. "You and your wife can sit in my jail."

He swept out of the room, leaving Alexander with his swiftly crystalizing thoughts. He couldn't telephone or send a message of some kind to Nick. He had to go to the ramshackle headquarters in the *kemeraltı* to tell him to get Clark in front of Polat to confess what they knew about his dealings with Bey *now.* Polat had arrested Saffron based on nothing more than a rumor; Alexander feared Polat would do precisely the same to him. If Clark admitting his involvement in the smuggling wasn't enough to save Alexander from going behind bars where he'd be of no help to Saffron, he'd tell Neck to reveal his involvement and give them the full support of the British government. He would beg Nick if he had to.

CHAPTER 42

The spread laid out before Saffron was like something out of Elizabeth's wildest dream. Her gastronomically inclined best friend would have devolved into drooling giddiness upon seeing the cart Kadriye rolled into the room just as the sun went down.

"What's all this!" Saffron exclaimed, taking in the dishes laden with all manner of foods sweet and savory. The smells wafting off it were incredible.

Kadriye beamed at her. "A gift. Sir Randolph and Feldman *efendi* are not here. It must not go to waste." She wrinkled her nose. "I learn these words very quick: not go to waste."

Saffron laughed. "Sir Randolph is an economical employer?" When the maid quirked her brow in apparent confusion, she added, "He likes to save money?"

"Oh, yes. I think to work here will bring me good money, hard to find because I am Christian." She brought out a chain from her collar to show a tiny cross. "My family stay here after fire and war, but it is hard to find work. To be a maid here?" She shrugged. "An easy job but not good money." She gestured to the food again. "They bring this for Feldman *efendi*, but he is away with Sir Randolph."

"All this food was for Mr. Feldman?" She looked down at the tray, and nodded with understanding when she noticed the *dolmas*, which were identical to the ones she'd tried before. "This is from the same *han*, isn't it? How kind to send him a special meal. But he had to leave?"

"He did not look sad to work more," Kadriye said, looking dubious. "He is *makine*."

Saffron puzzled over the word for only a moment before laughing. "A machine?"

Kadriya nodded. "He works very hard, very much. More than Sir Randolph." Her smile was conspiring. "Feldman *efendi* reads all the papers, not Sir Randolph."

"Ah." Saffron took stock of the house, which was still and quiet about them. "I wish you would join me, Kadriye. As you said, it cannot go to waste, and I certainly can't eat all this food."

The young woman sent her another mischievous smile before darting to the door and closing it.

They ate companionably for some minutes, with Kadriye occasionally instructing Saffron in the correct method of eating certain foods and keeping one eye on Saffron's plate and heaping more scoops of food upon it the moment any space was available, while eating bird-like bites of her own much more modest portions.

"Which *han* did you say this is this from?" Saffron asked. "I must go there."

Kadriye grinned. "My mother says I must learn from the cook. She is the sister of my . . ." She paused, squinting up to the ceiling as if trying to work out the relationship, or perhaps how to explain it in English. Eventually, she said, "My mother wants a marriage for me. If I make food like Bey *efendi* serves—"

The food turned to ashes in Saffron's mouth. "This food comes from the *han* belonging to Bey *efendi*? Ali Fethi Bey?"

"You know the *efendi*?"

"No," she said slowly, thinking. "But my husband . . ." Her mind whirled. "This is a very generous meal. Does the *han* often send Mr. Feldman meals like this?"

Kadriye jerked her chin up with a tutting sound. "I get the *dolmas* on Sunday. This is different." She added with a sly smile, "Nice different."

"Very nice different," Saffron murmured, thinking. Was the food a bribe, perhaps? A very conveniently timed bribe, given what was happening with the dig and its missing artifacts. "Did they say why they wanted to give this food to Mr. Feldman?"

"I do not know. They brought it to the kitchen to give to him."

"Just the food?"

Kadriye frowned. "There is a paper of . . ." She muttered under her breath in Turkish. "A paper for the money for the food."

"A receipt." It would be rare for a servant to be able to read, especially a female one, so Kadriye likely wouldn't know what the receipt said, if it was, indeed, a receipt. But why would a gift come with a receipt? "May I see it? The receipt?"

With a frown, Kadriye hummed. "Why?"

"I'd like to know the English names for these foods." She smiled. "I'd like to order them, should I go to the *han*."

Kadriye hummed again, this time with understanding. "I get it." She stood, tipped a curtsy, and hurried from the room, leaving the door ajar.

Those three inches of darkened hallway were a temptation Saffron found almost too powerful to deny. It was a little too convenient, the timing of the food deliveries and Alexander's reporting on Clark's involvement in the smuggling operation with Bey. In fact, Mr. Feldman had been present for every single conversation she'd had since entering this house. If he'd been paying attention, as Saffron had been confident he had *not* been, that meant Mr. Feldman knew a good deal about Clark, the artifacts, Martin Neill's murder, and the threat to the expedition's continuation.

She could go to Mr. Feldman's office and poke around. She could look for evidence of his own involvement, if he was working in cahoots with Clark and Bey. It was possible—

Kadriye slipped back into the room, paper in hand. She came up short and asked, "Is all well, *hanım*?"

"I'm not sure," Saffron admitted, reaching for the paper with hands trembling with anticipation.

It drained away as swiftly as it came; the paper was not written in English. It wasn't Turkish, either, however, but a series of numbers.

"A receipt," she murmured, eyes dancing over the rows. It could mean anything. It could be an actual receipt—for what?—or it could be a code.

"Banks!" she exclaimed as the idea occurred to her. He'd spent a good part of their drive to the *hammam* describing to her his process of decoding ancient texts. Perhaps he could take a crack at these numbers. Or Nick, of course, who was a literal spy and must have had worked codes.

Hope made her a little giddy, even as the creeping realization of danger grew in her stomach. If Feldman was involved in the artifact smuggling . . .

A door closed somewhere within the house. Saffron flinched at the sound.

"It is only Feldman *efendi*," Kadriye said soothingly. She stood and started clearing the mostly full dishes onto the tray. "I go now."

The door flew open, banging against the wall. The tall form of Mr. Feldman stood in the door, looking a little wild. His appearance was in its usual tidy order, but his eyes were wide, his usually ruddy color pale.

"Mr. Feldman," Saffron began cautiously, "whatever is the—"

There was a silver glint at his waist. A gun, pointed at Saffron.

Kadriye must have noticed it also, for she gasped and took a step away from the food tray.

He didn't move but for his eyes, which darted from Saffron to Kadriye. Panic and frustration warred on his face. "Curse it," he muttered. To Kadriye, he barked a string of words in Turkish that sounded at once punitive and pleading.

Color drained from Kadriye's face. "*Hayır.* Feldman *efendi*, *hayır.* Please."

"What's happening?" Saffron asked, slowing rising to her feet.

Feldman looked back at her, raising the gun. "Stop there, Mrs. Ashton. Don't make this harder than it must be."

Saffron stopped moving but to raise her palms to him in clear surrender. "I don't know what *this* is. What's the matter? What do you want?"

"Eleven years," Feldman said, almost exasperated. "Eleven years, I've sat in this building, doing all the work of the consulate through wars and fires and a new bloody government and getting looked over for every opportunity to move up and out of this little hole. Ten years, I've worked with Bey to move things out of the city. We'd just gotten our system back together after all the damn wars, devil take it! And there you and your damned husband are, mucking it all up again. Ashton nabbed our man off the street in front of the *han*, right in front of the police officers tailing him, curse it!"

And he had returned to the consulate when he'd thought it was empty to remove Saffron? That could only be his motive in coming here with a weapon. And if he was here to deal with Saffron, Alexander was also in danger. Even now, Bey could be sending someone to find him and silence him, too. Her fear was drowned out by a hot, irrational anger at the man before her.

"*We* haven't mucked up anything," Saffron snapped at Feldman. "You're the one stealing artifacts and breaking the law! I'd barely had any idea of your involvement before you came in here waving a pistol around!" The hot wave of anger crested and faded, leaving her regretting deeply shouting at the man with said pistol.

Feldman's face hardened. "It's only a matter of time. And I've no intention of being imprisoned in this country or my own."

"So, you're just going to kill two innocent women?" She couldn't stop the incredulity in her voice.

Kadriye looked desperately between them, clearly struggling to keep up with what they were saying.

Saffron looked at her and said very clearly, "He wants to kill us. He works for Bey to steal things."

Her lips rounded in surprise. Then, shocking Saffron and Feldman, her hands flew to her hips and she began to—Saffron could only guess—scold him. Her tone was harsh, her frown disappointed and angry all in one.

Feldman gaped at them both, and tried to get a word in. "Don't be preposterous, *I'm* not going to—"

The louder Kadriye's voice grew, the more agitated Feldman became. His pallid face pinkened, and his mouth mashed into a frown. But he wasn't pointing the gun directly at either of them anymore, and Saffron needed to get it out of his hands. Then she needed to find help, but who? If Mr. Feldman was involved with Bey, then Sir Randolph might be, too. The police thought she was a murderer, and she had no means of getting in touch with Nick. She had to get to Alexander.

But the gun first.

Feldman had apparently had enough of Kadriye berating him. He argued with her, and Saffron momentarily wondered what, exactly, they were saying. Was Kadriye really berating him, or demanding she be let go?

Another possibility chilled her. The maid was the one who brought Feldman the food from the *han*. She could be in the employ of the smugglers just as easily and be just as dangerous. She shuddered to remember the last the time she'd underestimated such a woman.

Equally, Kadriye could be innocent and be purposefully distracting Feldman to allow Saffron to escape or knock the gun from his hands.

She would have to put her faith in the young woman who'd shown her kindness, and hope she could keep Feldman busy long enough to save them both.

Chapter 43

The maths of a woman weighing nine stone confronting a man a foot taller and nearly twice her weight was not promising. Luckily, maths was not Saffron's strong suit.

Kadriye's voice rose as her invectives increased in pace and fervor. Feldman growled back. Saffron inched closer.

A particularly shrill statement from Kadriye had Feldman stepping forward, raising his voice and the gun to point more directly at the girl.

Heat spilled over Saffron in a panicked wave, and she lunged for the weapon.

Time took on that strange, stretched-out quality that only happened in moments of dire straits. Her feet left the ground, her hands made contact with Feldman's arm. It recoiled slightly as she fell onto it and Feldman's reflexes responded. The pistol barked.

There was a crash, voices cried out—maybe her own—and then she was on the floor, and something struck her square in the back so hard the breath left her lungs.

Instinct told her to roll, and she did until she found herself nearly wrapped around something hard and stout—the foot of the couch, she saw when she opened her eyes.

Her lungs heaved fruitlessly, wrenching in an uneven pattern that burned against the blow to her back, but she scrambled away, too aware of the echo of the gun's report in her ears and the shot's acrid scent in the air.

She spun in time to see Kadriye dive for the food scattered all over the floor. Feldman was also on the ground, hands skittering over the carpet like he was searching for something.

The *gun*.

Saffron rolled to her belly, stretching her arms so her hands could feel for it. Her back screamed with pain at the movement.

Her arm struck something under the couch, and it skidded heavily over the wooden floor. Feldman froze just as Saffron did. He crawled forward, lurching and desperate, and she scrambled for the pistol, stretching hopelessly against the bulk of the couch.

With a furious grunt, Feldman shoved the couch. One of the legs smashed into her chin, leaving a burning, stinging throb. A sound she'd never heard before tore from her throat, somewhere between a sob and a frustrated growl. She rolled out from under the couch and climbed over it, ready to pounce on Feldman and—

He rose before her from behind the couch like a cliffside materializing from fog before a hapless ship.

She wheeled back, wobbling on the couch cushions, and just as he raised the pistol to point at her, something thrummed through the room. Feldman's face went slack, and he crashed down to his knees.

Kadriye stood behind him, teeth bared. She smacked him on the back of the head with the tray with another resounding thrum, and he collapsed forward, hitting the ground hard enough to shake the room.

A male voice swore.

Saffron bit back a scream when she caught sight of a man's silhouette in the doorway.

He propped his hands on his hips, and with childlike petulance, grumbled, "I was gonna do that."

All of Alexander's swirling, panicked thoughts congealed upon taking in the empty room.

Nick's dilapidated headquarters in the *kemeraltı* was vacant. No papers, no furniture or creature comforts, no Nick.

And no Joseph Clark.

If the place had shown signs of continued occupation or a quick escape, cold dread might not have trickled into Alexander's gut. If he'd received word that their security had been compromised, that they were moving Clark elsewhere—

But no. This was absolute, purposeful. The place looked like no one had touched it in years.

He knew what this was. Nick had disappeared the moment a valuable witness had appeared. Not a witness on behalf of Saffron, but of the smuggling operation he'd been tracking. Clark was valuable to Nick, and Alexander had been too stupid to realize Nick wouldn't hesitate to use him to the greatest advantage for himself. He'd left Alexander and Saffron at the most critical moment. He wouldn't let Saffron hang? *Liar.*

A moment of pure, blackest rage overtook him, and it cleared from his vision only when he came back to himself, chest heaving and shaking hands filthy.

The room no longer looked undisturbed. Broken furniture littered the floor. Before the reality of his actions could sink in, a bit of white in the debris caught Alexander's eye. He lunged for it and discovered it was a sheave of papers, apparently overlooked in the cleanup. He could barely make them out in the weak yellow glow from the gaps in the boarded windows, but they looked like official documents.

Fierce, vindictive pleasure struck him. Nick would be back for these. And then Alexander would nail him to the wall. All he had to do was wait.

A noise stirred from below stairs, and Alexander couldn't help but smile. No wait was needed, apparently.

He melted into the shadow behind the door and lifted his hands before him, ready to strike.

The stairs creaked, and a moment later, the door swung open, accompanied by a shaft of light that swung around the room before freezing. An oval of light illuminated the destruction Alexander had wrought.

Voice low, Alexander asked, "Looking for these?"

The oval of light jerked, a footstep sounded, and then the light found the papers in Alexander's hand.

"You again?"

That adolescent, West Country voice belonged to Bagshott, not Nick. Very well. Alexander wouldn't be picky about who told him where the hell Clark was.

Alexander didn't flinch when the light flashed in his face. "Yes. Me. The man whose witness your boss absconded with. Where is Joseph Clark?"

Bagshott dropped the light to the floor. "Give me those papers."

"A trade?"

Through the barely-there light reflecting off the dusty floor, he could make out Bagshott's scowl. "I need those papers, mister."

"And I need Clark."

Bagshott took a slow step away. "If you'll just—"

"The only way you're getting these papers is if you give me Joseph Clark's location. He is the witness that can save my wife from being convicted of murder."

"The woman—she's your wife?"

"Saffron Everleigh," Alexander said, squinting into the flare of the light. "He's told you about her?"

Silence stretched between them, straining Alexander's already paper-thin patience.

Then the light of Bagshott's torch went out, and the thundering sound of feet on the stairs disoriented Alexander for a split second before he realized Bagshott was running away.

A vicious curse preceded Alexander diving down the stairs after him.

Chapter 44

Bagshott was just as infuriating to chase the second time as the first, but this time he made no effort to conceal himself or dodge behind buildings. He made a straight dash down the street, boots brazenly pounding against the uneven surface.

Alexander followed the young man as he sprinted into the darkness, down street after street. Occasional pedestrians followed them with curious eyes. Soon closed tea houses and covered carts gave way to shuttered shop fronts and darkened windows as his path shifted south.

Sweat poured from Alexander's face, stinging his eyes. His chest ached, his breath sawing in and out of him. Bagshott fleeing across the city could easily be a diversionary tactic. He could be leading Alexander farther away from Nick, Clark, and his and Saffron's only chance for safety.

His quarry turned a corner and when Alexander reached it, his feet skidded to a stop on the dusty stones before a trio of dark shops. Bagshott had disappeared.

Cursing under his labored breath, Alexander scanned their dusty glass fronts. The door to the closed chemist was indeed locked, as was the bookshop. The door to the final building was unlocked. Alexander pushed it open warily.

It was a tea house. Similar to Bey's establishment, it looked like a house that only occasionally operated as a business. It was quite late now, and a few patrons sat within, all older. Knowing how wild he must look, Alexander nodded respectfully at them, swallowing down his panting. A large but slow-moving older man, with his heavy face deeply lined and his mouth turned down, lumbered to his feet and came forward with the look of being about to toss him onto the street.

"My friend," Alexander attempted in Turkish, "is here. Like me." He waved down at his clothing to indicate his casual Western dress. It was dusty and clinging, but he hoped to make his point without wasting more time. He could practically feel Bagshott—and his chances of helping Saffron—disappearing with every second that ticked by.

The old man's frown deepened, and he glanced over Alexander's shoulder to the door before he shook his head.

"Please," Alexander said, then in desperation, added in English, "I need to find him."

Then a clear, very English voice spoke. "Alexander?"

His knees went weak, but he managed to stay upright long enough to move past the old man to the opening to the next room. But when he saw a pair of familiar, precious blue eyes peering up at him just around the corner, he allowed himself to sink to the ground in relief.

"Saffron," he breathed, "what are you doing here?"

Nick scowled at the young man across the table from him. "I told you we couldn't tell Ashton anything yet."

Bagshott shrugged and wiped at his sweating brow, unable to completely hide the smugness from his face. "I didn't tell him anything. He followed me."

Saffron smiled at Bagshott. The young man was rather rough around the edges, but he was her new hero, not the least because he'd circumvented Nick's order and brought Alexander to her.

Nick looked like he'd like to argue but instead turned to where she was bringing Alexander back to his feet. "You've discovered us, then. But the plan won't change. I need Clark."

Alexander opened his mouth to argue, but Saffron cut him off. "And I don't," she told him, placing a hand on his chest, where his heart was still thundering. The cut on her chin throbbed a little when she spoke, but at least it had stopped bleeding. "At least, not for a day or two. Polat can't move forward with the judge if I'm not there—"

"You don't need to worry about Polat," Nick said with a smile for her. "The lab results will be on his desk in the morning."

"What good will it do to let him discover the toxin comes from meadow saffron?" she asked. "I can't stay hidden, hoping Polat will be clever enough to sort out my innocence, especially with all that's happened with Mr. Feldman and—"

Alexander tensed all over again. "What's happened?" he asked sharply. His dark eyes found the cut on her chin and flared with anger.

Saffron sighed. She was very tired, and now she'd finally had the chance to sit down after the whirlwind of escaping the consulate with Mr. Bagshott and Kadriye, her injuries were starting to ache. Kadriye had volunteered the house of her uncle as a place they might hide for the night, and she'd been in the kitchen arguing for the last hour. Nick had spoken with the family, reporting back to Saffron that Kadriye's family was in favor of her leaving the city that very night. He'd reassured them his people would protect Kadriye from any fallout from Feldman or Bey, but from how she had not yet reappeared, Saffron wasn't confident they had accepted his word.

If Nick and Kadriye had told them the truth of how they'd fled the British consul general's house after being threatened by one of his personnel who was involved with the business of Ali Fethi Bey, she wouldn't blame them for being unconvinced by another officer of that same government.

And now Alexander was here, and while she was so desperately glad to see him, she didn't know if she could bear explaining it all again to him, especially not when she knew telling him what Feldman had almost done would infuriate him. "I'll tell you later. We need to decide what to do next."

Nick reached into his jacket pocket for a piece of paper and set it on the table. Saffron dragged Alexander to sit next to her at the low table. Kadriye's uncle's home, the first floor of which was a tea shop that stayed open Friday evenings for other Christians, was an unpolished, spacious place. They had nearly complete privacy in this back room, which was good considering the document Nick had produced looked quite official-looking.

Nick translated as he pointed to each section of what turned out to be a police report from the laboratory. When he reached the bottom, he paused before continuing, "Results of items marked as evidence: All items marked were free of the toxin colchicine save for the bottle of muriate of berberine."

"Which is?" Saffron asked eagerly.

"Eye drops."

Saffron's eyes went round. "Eye drops?"

"Prescribed by a Dr. Elliott Higgins-Scott of Silchester, Hampshire."

There was only one person who would have been prescribed something from Silchester. "But that means—"

"Demirel." Alexander shook his head slowly. "Demirel killed Martin Neill."

Saffron pressed a hand to her mouth. "He contaminated his medications before allowing his wife to give them to Martin. How dreadful, to think that . . ." She swallowed. "That Martin essentially poisoned himself, thinking the eyedrops would ease his eyes."

Alexander took her hand in his and squeezed. "Demirel must be mixed up in the smuggling."

A hundred thoughts barreled through her mind as she stared down at the document. One very displeasing one settled down at the forefront. She squinted down at the stamped seal at the top right corner of the paper. "This was officialized four days ago."

Nick watched her with a neutrality she found suddenly infuriating. "You've had this for four days. You've known everything about this case, including who gave Martin Neill the eye drops. You've known for *four days* who killed him. Why did you wait to tell us?"

Alexander finally spoke in a voice promising violence if he didn't receive the right answer. "And what are you going to do about it now?"

Kadriye won the argument with her family about staying in Smyrna. She returned to the main room, pink-cheeked and pinch-mouthed, and bundled Saffron away to a bedroom above stairs. Kadriye was conveniently deaf to her insistence she wanted to return to Alexander below stairs as she tucked her up in a bed, but after a few moments of quiet comfort, Saffron allowed herself to drift off to sleep. She would return to her problems soon enough, and maybe when she did, Nick and Alexander would have devised some scheme that would keep her and Alexander out of Feldman and Bey's grasp and capture Martin's killer.

When she did wake, Nick was gone, along with Bagshott. Alexander was not. He looked precisely like he'd stayed awake all night, with deep violet shadows beneath hooded eyes and the beginnings of a beard on his jaw. He sat at the same table in the back room of the silent tea house and had several sheets of paper and a pencil laid out before him. A cup of tea sat at his elbow, its billowing steam stirring in the bright sun coming in through the front windows.

Kadriye nudged her over to the table with a smile, then disappeared into the kitchen.

"Good morning," she said, coming to sit across from him.

"Good morning." His voice was tired but warm, like his eyes as they drifted over her. The clothing she'd escaped the consulate in was wrinkled, but Saffron didn't think he cared much. His gaze lingered on her chin, and she winced to think of the bruise haloing the gash from Feldman shoving the couch at her. "Are you all right?"

Her lip trembled at his gentle question. She didn't feel all right. She was hurt and afraid, and not at all confident that things would work out. She'd run from the consulate, for heaven's sake! She half expected Polat to come storming in, ready to haul her back to her little prison cell. But things could be worse. Feldman could have seriously hurt her or Kadriye. Bagshott could have come too late to spirit them away, or not at all.

She frowned at the question as it came to her and spoke it aloud. "Why did Bagshott go to the consulate last night?"

"Nick sent him to tell you he'd be releasing the lab report to Polat today," Alexander said. "He didn't want you to be unprepared for when Polat inevitably came to interrogate you again."

"He told you that?" she asked a little doubtfully.

"Bagshott did," he replied with a little smile. "We've got a plan."

Her eyes fell to the papers on the table. "Do tell."

He did, over a lovely breakfast and many cups of hot, strong tea.

"I don't like it," Saffron told him when he'd finished. "Clark could ruin it at any moment, should he choose to."

"Considering he'd face even more serious consequences for doing so—"

"He might try to escape."

"Nick said he'll have a force of about ten agents, with two assigned specifically to Clark," Alexander said smoothly.

"Who is to say any of them are to be trusted? The consul general's own secretary was involved in smuggling. There's no reason to assume anyone from the embassy is trustworthy."

"Saffron," he said gently.

"And why must it be done at the dig site?" she demanded, ignoring him. "And then in the middle of the countryside! Anything could happen." He placed his hand on hers, and she shook it loose. "And I don't understand why you have to be involved at all!" She looked away, fighting for her fear to stay out of her voice. "Why do you have to be there?"

Alexander murmured her name again, but it wasn't until he tilted her face toward his with gentle fingers that she looked him in the eye.

"So much has gone wrong already," she whispered. "I don't want you to get hurt."

"I'll be fine."

"You can't know that."

"I will be fine," he said with just as much calm certainty as before, "because my wife will be waiting for me. And I'll do everything in my power to return to her."

She nodded, mashing her lips together to prevent them trembling.

"I'd better get going," he said after a long moment of stroking her cheek in silence.

"All right." She stood with him, and after glancing around to ensure none of Kadriye's family were about, captured Alexander's mouth in a long kiss. She broke away only when satisfied she'd communicated every nuance of her feelings.

His smile was a little wicked. "I didn't need any more motivation to return in one piece."

Her returning smile was shy. "Oops."

"I'll see you tonight," he said, pressing a kiss to the top of her hand, "Mrs. Ashton."

Chapter 45

If Alexander hadn't met the agent driving the truck and assured himself of his allegiance to Nick and the government, he'd have assumed the fellow was trying to kill them. He took another turn that felt far too sharp, causing the crate in which Alexander sat to slide ominously to the left. There was only the metal railing of the truck's shallow bed to prevent Alexander from toppling off the truck and likely down a rocky hill in the middle of the Turkish countryside. His crate wasn't tied down properly, otherwise he wouldn't be able to push aside the lid when the time came. Nick's crate, on the other side of the one containing the third-century graffitied stone, wasn't secured either.

This was perhaps why Saffron had said she didn't like the plan to trap more of the network of smugglers, though she couldn't have known he'd end up crouching in a wooden crate, packed in with wood shavings like he, too, was an antiquity that might tempt Bey into unwise action.

The expedition crew was unhappy with Nick's plan as well, though they only knew that the spectacular find of the graffitied stone was going to be transported to Istanbul that very afternoon, ostensibly to be put into place at a museum immediately. Many grumbles and protests had been sounded, not the least of which from Dr. Henry, who'd railed against Mr. Assam and Mr. Hayrettin's orders that the rock be loaded up and sent away. Alexander had considered advocating for informing Dr. Henry of the ploy, but only for the moment it took him to realize if Dr. Henry didn't put up an enormous fuss about it, it would be suspicious.

He'd heard Dr. Henry complaining the entire time the rock was loaded into the crate, and the crate into the truck between his crate and Nick's. They'd already been inside for nearly thirty minutes at that point to ensure no one who might have been watching the dig site would suspect there were two armed men loaded up to confront whoever tried to intercept the artifact.

Clark didn't know, for example. He'd been instructed to pass word to Bey of an incredibly valuable artifact being moved that very day, and to convince him it would be an excellent opportunity to steal it on the road from Smyrna. Nick had assured Alexander that the moment his agents confirmed the truck had left the city, Clark would be placed under arrest and handed over to the Turks to be prosecuted for theft of their antiquities, and to confess to starting the rumors about Saffron's affair with Martin Neill.

Just like Clark, Christopher Banks did not know that while the real artifact was being taken away, it was only temporary.

"Absolutely not," he'd told the driver, Mr. Assam, Mr. Hayrettin, and anyone else within earshot. "*Absolutely* not! This is *invaluable.* It is not going to be put into a *crate* where it'll be bumped around until the markings are so damaged we cannot read them!"

It had taken over an hour for him to be shunted out of the way long enough to get the stone into the crate, and only after he'd imposed himself as the one to wrap it in layers of cotton first.

"And I'm going," Banks then declared. "I want to meet the people taking charge of it."

No matter how many times he was deterred, Banks stubbornly insisted, to the point where Mr. Hayrettin lost his patience and exclaimed, "Very well! Very well! If it will make you get out of the way so the artifact may leave!"

Alexander was quite glad, after sweating within the wood shavings for nearly an hour and a half by then, that no one thought it odd that cool-headed Mr. Hayrettin was so agitated as to shout at one of his country's esteemed guests.

They'd been bumping along in relative peace—save for the hair-raising turns—up the road leading north through the plains between craggy hills. In the stuffy heat of the crate, it was tempting to tilt the lid to get a bit of a breeze, but if they were being followed, he couldn't reveal himself.

Over the noise of the engine, Alexander thought he heard shouting. It grew louder until he was certain it was not his imagination, and at that moment the truck jerked to the side, which sent the crates slamming against each other. Then the truck began to slow.

Alexander shifted, getting his feet under himself again and planting one hand on the lid. This had to be it, Bey's men come to steal the artifact.

Voices grew louder, and a moment later, the engine died down, leaving them in silence. But only for a moment. The voices were growing nearer, speaking in rapid Turkish.

He exhaled slowly as his grip on his pistol tightened.

When the creak and crack of the crate at his side sounded, he shoved aside the lid, pushed himself to his feet and out into the blindingly bright light of midday.

"There must be some mistake," Saffron said quietly, her face burning. "I know I was detained for several days, but—"

Mr. Koray's expression looked agonized, plainly unsure what to do with his guest who, last he'd heard, had been under arrest for the murder of another guest.

"Can't you put me back in the room I was in before?" she asked, and she could hear the edge of hysteria creeping into her voice. Nick had instructed Kadriye's uncle to deliver Saffron to the hotel well after the crew left for the dig site. With Mr. Demirel drawn away by the operation at the dig site, he'd deemed it the safest place for her until the operation was concluded, hopefully with several people in handcuffs. She could hole up in her room until everything was settled; no one would expect her to be at the hotel, of all places, after fleeing the consulate. Saffron needed to get her head on straight for the impending conversations with Inspector Polat and Nick's agents, and getting a moment of peace to rest and possibly bathe beforehand would help. If she only had a room to do those things in—any room.

"Saffron?" Mrs. Henry's voice came from behind her.

Saffron turned, face still hot with embarrassment. "Mrs. Henry, hello, I've just been released and it seems they no longer have my room—"

Mrs. Henry embraced her gently but firmly and offered her a reassuring smile before speaking to Mr. Koray in the haughty voice Saffron was more accustomed to. "Miss Everleigh was recently made Mrs. Ashton when she married her fiancé just a few days ago. I believe Mr. Ashton has already requested new accommodation."

Abashed, Mr. Koray offered Saffron a new room key as he apologized profusely, not quite meeting her eye.

Saffron didn't know whether to laugh or cry at this, so she merely accepted the key and followed Mrs. Henry upstairs. It was surreal to be walking through the quiet hotel; she could hardly believe that murder, smuggling, and violence had been her world for the last week.

"Does this mean they've caught whoever killed Mr. Neill?" Mrs. Henry asked.

She was hopeful they would catch Mr. Demirel in short order, but nothing was certain yet. Nick's instructions had included Demirel being present to send off the graffitied stone, but she had no way of knowing if he'd actually gone to the agora. "I'm afraid I can't say. I'm sorry, Mrs. Henry, I think I need to lay down. I'm feeling rather overwhelmed."

"I quite understand. But where is Mr. Ashton? Did they not inform him you were to be let go?"

"I thought I would surprise him," Saffron lied with a weak smile.

Mrs. Henry cast her a mischievous look as Saffron unlocked her door. "Best of luck then, my dear. Shall I request supper be sent up for the two of you this evening?"

Surely her face could not grow any more red. "That would be lovely."

Mrs. Henry departed with a knowing smile, and Saffron closed the door.

She was in Alexander's room. Her room. Their room.

Giddy laughter burbled out of her, swiftly transforming into a choked sob. She sank into the chair just next to the door and tried to rally. There was no cause for tears, not anymore. She was nearly in the clear. She needed to buck up, prepare to finish all this dreadful business. And then she could laugh and cry all she liked from the safety of Alexander's arms.

Her stomach did an odd sort of flip. She'd waited a very long time to share everything, including a bed, with Alexander, and now it was time, she was overwhelmed by the suddenness of it.

Anxiety weighted by something like sadness, or possibly regret, wrapped around her at the lack of fanfare their marriage had thus far incurred. She was surprised by the feeling considering she'd more or less put off the wedding planning. But that was the wedding, and this was the marriage. She'd wanted the marriage. Hadn't she?

She was all twisted up inside, and she decided to blame it on the extraordinary circumstances. No one could have anticipated an accusation of murder precipitating a hasty wedding, and she refused to let Clark or Polat or anyone else ruin anything else.

She looked about for her luggage, since Alexander had apparently had her things moved here, and spotted two notes left on the dressing table. One looked to be a telegraph—perhaps one of her family members responding to Alexander's report of her arrest—and the other was a note in a woman's hand. Intrigued, she picked it up. It had no address or stamp, merely Alexander's name in a slanting, feminine handwriting. Not feeling the least guilty about it, she opened it and read.

Dear Mr. Ashton,

I am sorry but I am leaving Smyrna this morning. I don't know what you told the police or anyone else about my involvement with Martin Neill, but I have received threatening notes and can no longer remain in the city. I will not give you the address of my next accommodation, in case someone truly means me harm, but please communicate to the police I know absolutely nothing more about poor Martin or his unfortunate death. I wish you the best and pray justice may find whoever is responsible.

Sincerely,
Corsianna Moore

Saffron stared at the note so long her eyes burned.

Corsianna Moore was the young lady Martin had met on the ship. Alexander had spoken with her about Martin, but he'd learned nothing useful. Why had someone threatened her into leaving the city? Even now they knew everything about Clark, Bey, and Demirel's smuggling, she'd found no indication that Martin had known anything about it. What could Miss Moore possibly know?

And furthermore, what did she say to Alexander that suggested she *did* know something important? And who had overheard her? Nobody knew Miss Moore had been at the hotel to see Alexander—

Except Mrs. Demirel. He'd run into her in the hall. She could have seen Corsianna Moore speaking with Alexander.

Saffron teetered on the edge of what felt like understanding, but couldn't quite take the leap into it. Mrs. Demirel . . . Well, Saffron simply couldn't believe she was involved in her husband's misdeeds. She was obsessed with her children. She wouldn't risk their futures for a piece of profit that carried the risk of being imprisoned so far away. And what would Mrs. Demirel even do to assist her husband in smuggling artifacts? She was an insubstantial little woman who was rarely at the dig site, did not speak more than pleasantries to the officials, and she wasn't familiar with the antiquities or the language or . . .

But that wasn't right. Mrs. Demirel had told her what Dr. Yenmeck had said about Martin's condition, but Saffron had seen the doctor leaving Martin's room without a translator. She'd acted so strangely when Mrs. Henry suggested she knew what the Turkish officials had been saying. She'd known Kadriye's secret to the perfect bite of Turkish dumplings, and eaten the more adventurous local foods with relish though she claimed to never eat them. Indeed, she'd acted just like Kadriye had acted with Nick, Bagshott, and Alexander when she'd served them their meal last night; she'd been demure and hadn't looked any of them in the eye, though Saffron had watched the girl shout at a man threatening her with a gun. Saffron had thought Mrs. Demirel too meek to look at any of the local men in the eye, but was that merely the *alaturca* way of doing things, as Inspector Polat had tried to explain to her?

It was logical Mrs. Demirel would have learned some of these things in the course of a marriage to a Turk, but it was strange, then, that she made so much of feeling out of place and overwhelmed here.

Saffron blinked several times when she realized she'd been staring at Miss Moore's note again. Mrs. Demirel might be hiding familiarity with the language and customs. And she'd known Miss Moore had been to see Alexander, possibly overheard them.

Mrs. Demirel given Martin the eye drops laced with colchicine, a happenstance Saffron had explained away by assigning blame to Mr. Demirel. But what if it had been purposeful? What if Mrs. Demirel had intentionally poisoned Martin?

Chapter 46

Saffron folded up the letter to place in her handbag. She'd have no time to change clothes before going to the dig site to intercept Nick and Alexander. If Mrs. Demirel had been the one to kill Martin, they needed to retool their theories about the murder. Something else was afoot, and she wouldn't have Alexander risking his life for a plan that might not work.

She'd taken only a step toward the door when a knock came. She opened it to find Mrs. Demirel standing just inches from herself. Her breath caught on Mrs. Demirel's old-fashioned scent of powdery rose, and she struggled not to show her alarm as the older woman smiled at her.

"Miss Everleigh," she said with a little nervous laugh. "Cynthia mentioned you'd just returned. How fortunate the police have realized their mistake in arresting you!"

Saffron forced a smile. "It is. I'm sorry, Mrs. Demirel, I'm just going—"

"But they must have discovered who did kill poor Mr. Neill, then," she continued. Her fingers were twisting around her handbag at her shoulder.

"No," Saffron said quickly. "I don't believe they have. They simply didn't have the evidence to keep me, so I was let go."

Mrs. Demirel's eyes darted between hers as if searching for the lie. Saffron hoped it wasn't visible.

"What will the police do now?" Mrs. Demirel asked.

"I have to believe they will keep looking for the killer," Saffron said, but she said it in the most gentle, non-accusatory way she could manage. She inched forward, hoping to chivy Mrs. Demirel away from the door.

"But—" Mrs. Demirel's wide eyes danced over her face, then out into the hallway, then back to her.

"If you'll just excuse me," Saffron said, a little more loudly than necessary.

Wetting her lips, Mrs. Demirel shook her head. "I—If I could just—" She closed her eyes and let out a breath, as if bracing herself. "You can't leave."

"What do you mean?" Saffron asked.

"You can't leave," she said, blinking several times as she looked to her hands, then back to Saffron. "You'll have to stay."

"What are you talking about?" Saffron said again, slowly. "Of course I can leave, the police let me go. They know I'm innocent."

"It's not a matter of innocence," the other woman said, her voice revealing an edge of panic. "It never was. Martin Neill . . . He was innocent, wasn't he?"

Saffron froze as tears welled in Mrs. Demirel's eyes. "You . . . you did kill Martin, didn't you?"

Mrs. Demirel reached into her handbag, and before Saffron could rationalize that the woman wasn't reaching for a handkerchief, she raised a knife, pointing it tremulously at Saffron.

Without conscious thought, Saffron took two swift steps backward, raising her hands as she went. Mrs. Demirel shuffled into the room and closed the door, pressing her back against it as if she needed its support. The blade was the length of Saffron's palm and gleamed as if freshly sharpened.

"But why?" Saffron breathed. "Why would you kill him?"

"Because he knew!" Mrs. Demirel whispered. Her whole body shook. "He found out. He could have ruined my life in an instant."

Saffron's mind worked to make sense of this. "What did he know? About your husband?"

Mrs. Demirel started. "What about my husband?"

Saffron couldn't tell if this was a real question. "Your husband's smuggling operation. He's working with a local, the consul general's secretary, and one of the members of the crew to steal and sell artifacts from the agora."

"He's—he's doing what?" The last of the color drained from her face. "No . . . No, he can't," she moaned. "How could he—how—"

"Martin didn't know about that?" Saffron took a step forward, hopeful Mrs. Demirel was too distressed to recall she was threatening her. "What did Martin find out?"

It was a long, fraught moment before Mrs. Demirel spoke again. She'd regained some composure, but it was an odd, trancelike calm that seemed thin as the first touch of frost on a windowpane.

"The truth about me," Mrs. Demirel said faintly. "That I'm just a nanny who married well. Too well, for most."

Saffron was taken aback. "But why would Martin have cared who or what you were before you married?"

"The girl would have told him. She saw me, and I saw her . . . She was my charge, but even grown I could recognize her. I saw her looking at me, and I knew what a terrible mistake I had made." She shuddered.

Saffron's mind worked to make sense of this. "Corsianna Moore? The girl from the ship?" Mrs. Demirel nodded. "And you killed Martin because you worried he'd gossip about you being a nanny?" Her question was sharp, reflecting the sudden anger she felt at such an irrational motive.

"Gossip," echoed Mrs. Demirel, and she shook her head slowly, like the word woke her from her trance. "That would be just the beginning. It's the words spoken behind hands that slip into the ears of the wrong people, and suddenly people remember. The diplomatic world is small, so small . . ." Tears shimmered in her pale eyes, and she blinked at them until they fell onto her soft, papery cheeks. "I ought to have remembered. I thought I would be safe, in this little corner of Turkey. So many people left after the wars . . . With a new name, I thought I would be safe. My husband insisted I come. He wished to show me his homeland, and he didn't accept no as an answer . . . And I *stayed away*, whenever Sir Randolph came to dine . . ." She was crying in earnest now. "I did what I was supposed to do, and kept away, but it didn't matter, did it? I still . . ."

"You lived here before," Saffron guessed. "You were nanny to a family here. A British family." Mrs. Demirel nodded, face screwed up against her tears. "And something happened. Something bad."

She nodded again. "It's been years and years, but sometimes he's still right there, in the corner of my eye. No matter where I go, or how many pills or tonics I take"—she gasped for breath, clutching the knife tightly—"I see him. And Corsianna was his child. I cared for her, loved her like a daughter, while he tormented me, night after night." She slumped, her shoulders caving and the knife's blade drooping.

Saffron took another step forward, eyes back on the knife. With a soothing voice, she murmured, "You had to protect yourself."

Mrs. Demirel didn't appear to hear her. "She was just a child, but she was old enough. She was always a bright girl. She could have worked out what I'd done, especially if she learned how Martin died. If she learned too many details . . . she was the one who found her father, after all."

A chill racked Saffron. She'd killed Martin in the same way she'd killed Miss Moore's father, by slipping him a toxin, then.

Saffron swallowed hard, still inching forward. In another foot or so, she might be able to bat the knife from her hands.

"I was so stupid. So stupid to come back here. So stupid to think I could be happy after what he did to me." Mrs. Demirel took in a great, gulping breath and looked at Saffron sadly. "Gossip is just the beginning, my dear. One word of the truth gets out, and what I did will be discovered. It is only a matter of time. But I will not allow it to happen. I won't allow my life to be ruined a second time. I won't let my boys' lives be ruined."

Mrs. Demirel lifted the knife, the point glinting. "You came back to the hotel after you were released, or escaped, or whatever you did to get out, and you were overcome with what you did. You found this knife and took your life. I will discover you. That'll explain the—the blood." Her voice shook, but she remained steady. "I've read your notebooks. I can copy your handwriting to write a note. You will take the blame so my boys can live a happy life with their mother."

Their eyes met, and what Saffron saw in Agatha Demirel's eyes shook her to her core. She'd seen the same calm certainty in her mother's gaze moments after she'd shot Bill Wyatt. Mrs. Demirel was going to protect her children, and this was how she meant to do it.

She should have tackled her like a rugby player before Mrs. Demirel had the chance to find her backbone.

Time. She needed time. "Why me? Why frame me? I've done nothing to you."

"It was because of the flowers. The meadow saffron."

"You made the connection between the Latin name for meadow saffron and the gout medication you administer to your husband." Things started to make more sense. "You were in and out of my room several times when I was injured. You took one of my books or notebooks. You found information about the plant's chemical compounds and their effects. You could have brought the book back the next time you visited my room and I'd be none the wiser." She blew out a slow breath. She would have to use her time very wisely. "But anyone could have had access to the flowers. All they had to do was pick them. Or steal into your rooms and take Mr. Demirel's gout tonic. You could have framed anyone."

"The men don't like you very much. I saw how they teased and harassed you. I heard them muttering about you and Mr. Neill. Even Mr. Banks." Mrs. Demirel did look apologetic now. "I knew they would think the worst of you, should accusations be made. And Mr. Clark had done a very good job of stirring up trouble for you. I didn't even have to start the rumor of your relationship with Mr. Neill. He did it for me." She shook her head, looking troubled.

"But that was more than a week after Martin met Miss Moore. Why did you wait to poison him? He had all that time to spread word of what he might know."

"I didn't wait," Mrs. Demirel replied with a faint, confused frown. "I gave him the eyedrops the evening we arrived in the city, when I overheard the other young men ribbing him for chasing after the young lady he met on the ship rather than go out carousing with them." She redoubled her grip on the knife, holding it out straight with both hands. "Colchicine is a mysterious, dangerous substance. The dosage must be precise, else you risk poisoning the patient. I watched him very closely and waited. Martin finally became ill when he went to the castle. When he came here, I checked on him. I offered to help him apply more eye drops. He was so weak, you see. The poor boy. And by then, everyone was talking about how you'd been cavorting with him."

Saffron felt sick at her words. "How can you have done it? When you yourself were a victim—how could you do that to someone else? Martin was innocent. Just like your boys. Did Martin not deserve a chance to live a happy life, just as they do? Or me? What of Alexander? He married me." And she might never see him again if she didn't get out of this. "Just an hour before I was arrested. He married me when he knew I might hang as a murderer." She took a step forward. "Doesn't he deserve a happy life, too? With his wife, who he was willing to risk his reputation, his career, and his family for?"

Mrs. Demirel stared at her. Saffron held her breath.

"I killed an innocent man. I put poison into his eyes with my own hand." She looked confused, as if realizing the truth of what she said as she voiced it aloud. "I killed Martin Neill with barely a thought except that he had the chance to reveal my identity and my guilt and ruin the life I created out of the ashes of my past." She raised the knife, and when their eyes met over the blade, there was no wavering, no uncertainty. "You know everything. I certainly won't hesitate to do what I have to do."

Chapter 47

"Sit on the bed," Mrs. Demirel said, taking a step forward. Her voice was high and tense as always, but her hands were steady. "It'll be quick, I promise. A better death than the others I've caused."

Saffron took a small step toward the bed. "Alexander will never believe I killed myself. He'll know it was you." Especially because of the note hidden in her handbag from Corsianna Moore. She angled herself so if Mrs. Demirel did manage to forced her to sit, she would do so on top of the bag to conceal it.

Mrs. Demirel's mouth pinched. "That may be true. But I've learned men often see what they wish to see when they look at us. My own husband has always seen me as an attentive, devoted wife. He has no idea I spent many years in his homeland. He's never once questioned that I knew how to arrange our household, prepare tea to his liking, or make him feel respected. Your husband has worked so very hard to save you. He considers you his damsel, and himself the knight. I believe he'll take your death very hard and blame himself." Her head tilted to one side, thoughtful. "Perhaps it will affect his heart. Mr. Demirel has several medications I could employ for that purpose."

That was the last straw.

Saffron lunged for Mrs. Demirel, heedless of the knife. Her arms crashed into the middle of the older woman, and they hit the floor. The rush of adrenaline pushed everything from Saffron's mind save her mission to get the knife away from Mrs. Demirel. Her hands scrambled for cold metal even as fingernails scratched at her face, her neck, her arms. Mrs. Demirel was shrieking and she wasn't sure if she was, too.

The rush of color and sound around her was meaningless until she heard her name being shouted over and over. She stopped moving as two pairs of hands took her by the arms and brought her up and off Mrs. Demirel.

She blinked hard, struggling to understand what was happening. Mrs. Demirel was sobbing as she was helped to her feet by Inspector Polat, who glared around the room. A swarm of Turkish police officers suddenly crowded the space.

Inspector Adem knelt to pick up Mrs. Demirel's knife from under the bed with a handkerchief. He showed it to Polat and said something, nodding to Mrs. Demirel.

Saffron was suddenly aware she was still being held by the arms. She pulled against them, but they held her firmly.

"Inspector Polat," she said quickly, looking desperately at him. "Please, Mrs. Demirel just told me everything, you must listen to me—"

Polat glared at her, his hand still on Mrs. Demirel's arm. "I must do nothing. I understand the situation perfectly. You escaped the consulate, returned to the hotel, and Mrs. Demirel found you—"

"Please, Inspector, you must understand—"

"Quiet!" he shouted, his eyes bulging.

Saffron struggled against the hands on her arms. "No! Mrs. Demirel confessed, she killed Martin Neill and—"

"We know," Inspector Adem said. "We heard her through the door." He nodded to whoever held Saffron, and they released her. She stumbled forward and nearly fell over.

"What?" Saffron stared between the inspectors. "You were behind the door the whole time? She could have stabbed me at any moment!"

With an indifferent shrug, Polat looked away. "We didn't know she had a knife."

After a long few minutes of continued confusion of Turkish police officers all about the room, hall, and lobby, Saffron was driven back to the police station to give her statement.

Polat was not the one to handle that, thankfully. Inspector Adem spoke with her. They sat in the little room Polat had interrogated her in, but without his ire bearing down on her, Saffron found the story came out easily. He also answered her questions rather than throwing them back in her face as Polat had. When she asked how they came to be at Hotel Bornova that morning, he told her they had received information direct from the British embassy in Istanbul that they were to remove her from the care of Sir Randolph as soon as possible. They had been alarmed to find chaos at the consulate, for Saffron had evidently disappeared from a locked room.

"My colleague believed you had escaped," Inspector Adem told her dryly. "He gathered those officers and brought them to the hotel in hopes that you would be present to re-arrest you."

It was on the tip of her tongue to ask if Polat's beliefs had been fueled by the recently delivered analysis from their laboratory, but she decided it would be a bad idea to reveal she'd known that information. She had no idea what Adem or Polat knew of Nick's operation, if anything. It might be a long time before the local police heard of Bey's arrest, or Feldman's—Lord, but what had happened to him? Had Nick or Bagshott gone back for him, or had he escaped?

Instead, she asked him, "Do you know where Mrs. Demirel lived when she cared for the girl, Corsianna Moore? She said it was a mistake to come back here, but I don't think she meant Smyrna."

Inspector Adem shrugged. "We will do our best to find that information. There is likely to be disruption in communication with the British consulate," he said, giving her a sidelong glance inviting her to explain her disappearance. When she did not, he added, "We will try to find the girl and her mother. It might take some time. But if we can find them and there is still evidence for it, it is possible Mrs. Demirel will be prosecuted for the murder of the girl's father."

He stood and opened the door for her. They walked out of the room and he gestured for another officer. "He will drive you to the hotel." He escorted her to the front door of the police station.

Polat sat at his desk on the far side of the room, looking rather like he was attempting to punch holes through his typewriter as he jabbed at the keys. He ignored her completely, though it was obvious he knew exactly where she was in the room.

Inspector Adem shot him a long-suffering glance. "Polat will not say it, but on behalf of the city of Smyrna, I offer you my apologies, Mrs. Ashton." He gave her a little bow. "May the rest of your stay in Smyrna be blessed."

CHAPTER 48

Had Cynthia Henry not had a will of iron, Alexander would have returned to find his bride in two-day old clothing, itching with dried sweat and stinging with scratches.

As it was, Mrs. Henry had taken charge of Saffron the moment she'd been deposited back at the hotel that afternoon. She'd swept Saffron up to her suite, where she discarded Saffron's clothing and plopped her in a cool bath.

"Good for the nerves, and those ghastly scratches," she informed Saffron, firmly placing a cake of soap into her hands. "Now wash."

After the bath—which was bracing, Saffron had to admit when she'd been wrapped in a bathing towel and stopped shivering—she'd been plied with food and drink until she'd grown sleepy.

It wasn't until Saffron was in bed that she realized that she was in what must have been Mrs. Henry's bed.

When she tried to address this, Mrs. Henry waved a hand. "Dr. Henry and I are vacating this chamber. You can't very well return to the place where that dreadful confrontation happened." She said it all as if it were obvious. "And besides, yours and Mr. Ashton's belongings have already been brought in here. Do try to rest, my dear. I've given you a reprieve for now, but come tomorrow, I and every other member of our party will want to hear all about what has happened, and how you managed to catch yet another killer."

That prospect kept her from sleep, though her body craved it.

Gossip is just the beginning, my dear.

Mrs. Demirel was not as easy to dismiss as the other killers—she cringed at Mrs. Henry's word—that she'd helped to apprehend. Mrs. Demirel had been murderous—but in the end, she'd believed she'd killed for the sake of safety for herself and her family. She was wrong, so *very* wrong, for it, but . . .

Saffron didn't think she was wrong about everything.

Even when one is innocent, it poisons the water just as surely as true guilt does.

The door to the room opened.

Her heart stuttered and then leaped when she heard her name being spoken by the only person in the world she wanted to see.

She bolted from the bed and froze in the open door to the sitting room.

Alexander stood there, hand still on the doorknob.

She drew in a ragged breath. And then she went to him.

He caught her in his arms, lifting her and crushing her to him. "They told me what happened—"

"You're *safe*—"

Their voices overlapped until only their mouths did. Then, there was silence, a kiss, and a desperate need for less space between them.

Saffron didn't realize she was crying until he'd pulled away and was brushing his fingers delicately over her cheeks.

"My God, Saffron, what did she . . ." His words broke off, his fingers tightening around the nape of her neck. His dark eyes flashed over the long scratches from Mrs. Demirel's nails marring her cheeks and forehead. "I should have pieced it together, damn it."

She swallowed thickly. "There was no way you could have known. Either of us."

They were both shaking.

"You made it back to me," she said with a tremulous smile. "It worked? You caught more of the smugglers?"

He nodded, and it appeared he was as unable to stop touching her as she was him. He took her hands in his, wincing at the red tracing her forearms. "The truck was stopped just short of Manisa. Bey sent three men, one in his direct employment. They were armed—"

She bit her lip, hands tightening on his. Alexander smiled wryly. "We were also armed, of course, but it turned out the firearms were unnecessary. Banks was the one to hold them off, if you can believe it."

"What on earth was Banks doing there!"

"He insisted on accompanying that rock," Alexander said with a touch of exasperation. "And when we were stopped, he came charging out of the cab, yelling at Bey's men. And, of course, he speaks Turkish like a local, and he distracted them swearing the air blue long enough for Nick and the agent driving the motorcar to take the men into custody."

As amusing as that was to imagine, she didn't think was the whole story. That was fine. She could be patient until he was ready to tell her all that had occurred. Just then, she didn't feel like she wanted to share all that had happened, either. She wanted to be there, with Alexander, not back in bad memories.

But some things needed to be discussed first, and it seemed Alexander had noticed one of them.

"You are . . ." He peered down at her, a question in his gaze. "You are wearing pajamas."

She was, and the sort one wore when the weather was warm: a nightgown of thin white cotton trimmed with a bit of lace. Thank heavens she wasn't wearing a nightcap, or curlers, for that matter. She touched her damp hair, shy.

"Mrs. Henry said we were to take this suite. She didn't want me to have to return to the other room after . . ." She trailed off with a sigh. "It was terribly nice of her. But it means we're both to stay here."

"Is that not what you want?"

She bit her lip. "We haven't had the chance to discuss . . . well, anything. We are legally married. A few people in the crew know, which means by the time we drop anchor in England again, everyone will know not only we're married, but that we've been . . ." Her hand fluttered toward the walls of the room. "In private. Together."

His lips quirked up. "In private together?"

Heat touched her cheeks. "Yes. The talk will be dreadful."

"Forget about the talk," he said calmly, taking her still-fluttering hand in his. "What do *you* want? Do you want to forget all this—murder and smuggling and everything that happened here—and do it all again, properly? Or do you want to start this now as it is?"

"I feel silly," she admitted, "worrying over this when you've been out pointing guns at smugglers and I've been clawed half to death by a murderer."

"This is important."

She nodded firmly. "It is. And I . . ." She searched his face, wishing she could read his own thoughts. "I don't think I can forget. I don't want to."

"So, you'll be my wife?"

A laugh that was half a sob burst out from her. "I will. I am."

His answering grin was hot and fierce, much like the kiss he dragged her into.

Giddy anticipation flooded her in a hot rush. She was dimly aware she was being lifted, her legs wrapping around Alexander's waist. Her fingers twined into his hair, pulling him impossibly closer and—

"Is this straw?" she laughed.

His hazy eyes focused on the broken strand of straw in her fingers between them. He set her down regretfully. "I probably smell like a barnyard."

"You're perfect," she said with a tender touch of his cheek. "But perhaps a bath and dinner, er, first."

He pressed a kiss to her forehead. "A bath might not go awry. Will you be all right for a few minutes?"

She nodded, suddenly too shy to look at him. She retreated to the other side of the room as he sorted through his belongings for his shaving kit and fresh clothing.

"What's this?" he asked, lifting a folded paper from his luggage.

"Oh, the telegram. It was here when I came in earlier, along with the message from Miss Moore. Whoever packed your things must have just packed it up along with everything else."

"You didn't open it?" he asked. "You'll only open notes from other women, then?"

She nodded unabashedly. "Yes."

He shook his head, unfolding the paper. His smile faded as he read it, and when he looked up at her, her stomach dropped. "What is it?"

"Saffron, your grandfather died six days ago."

"Oh." Nothing else came out of her mouth. Every other word seemed to have been shocked out of her mind.

Alexander came across the room and handed her the message. She looked down at the telegram blankly.

His hand felt impossibly heavy on her shoulder. "I'm sorry. I . . . We don't have the details. John's message is short but he said he would be at Ellington and to contact him as soon as possible."

Her cousin, John, suddenly the new viscount, a burden none of them expected he'd be handed so soon. He was at Ellington, with their grandmother, who was suddenly without her husband. Her mother, now bereft of the man Saffron had finally understood to be almost a father to her. They would all be shocked, grieving—

"I have to go," she said slowly. She looked up at Alexander. "I have to go now."

"Of course." He pulled her close so her ear pressed just where the steady beat of his heart thrummed in his chest. "I'll check when the next passenger ship out of here sails. Are you all right to pack?

I can send a maid up to see to our things. And I'll need to speak to Dr. Henry, of course."

She pulled away, frowning at him. It sounded like he was saying—

Alexander pulled her back to him and kissed away her confusion. "I'm coming with you."

Chapter 49

The swaying darkness was disconcerting for the minute it took for Saffron to remember where exactly she was. She reached out, hoping her hand would find a lamp and not knock it over.

When the warm glow of the lamp flicked on, Saffron recalled the lamp was bolted in place, the same as most of the rest of the furniture. She was on a ship, after all.

The past day churned in her mind. It had been such a blur, a terrifying, heartbreaking, yet somehow wonderful blur.

Saffron glanced next to her, hardly daring to expect to see Alexander stretched out next to her, still fast asleep. They were both still fully dressed, having barely the energy to kick off their shoes before falling onto the bed. The itinerary they'd pieced together would take them through three different countries in a little less than five days, and the first leg had taken them from Smyrna to Athens just two hours after Alexander had opened the telegram from John. They were aboard the ship that would take them from Athens to Gibraltar, where in two days they would part ways.

Dr. Henry had been near apoplectic to learn about their subterfuge with the graffitied stone, even after Alexander explained it was necessary to catch the smugglers and reclaim the missing artifacts. They'd nearly come to blows when he learned Alexander planned to "abandon his men in the field." Apparently, the loss of another member of the expedition was too much for Dr. Henry. With Martin's death, Clark's arrest, Saffron's impending departure, and the plans of Mr. Demirel—who'd proven innocent of collusion with Clark or his wife—to wait out Mrs. Demirel's trial in Istanbul, Alexander leaving, too, was a bridge too far. Alexander had managed to restore calm only when he agreed to return to Turkey for the last few weeks of the expedition.

Saffron had been unaware of this, of course, and only heard about it when Mrs. Henry had alluded to it when they departed the hotel.

"Cool as a cucumber, your new husband," Mrs. Henry had murmured, pressing a kiss to her cheek just before they dashed into the motorcar. "But he's got an explosive side, doesn't he? Enjoy it, my dear."

Saffron shook her head with a rueful smile as she recalled the cheeky comment and rose from the bed. She padded across the room, a lavish suite courtesy of Nick and the grateful British government, he'd said. He'd somehow been there at the dock when they boarded their first ship, offering nothing more than a murmur of condolences—how infuriating he already knew of her grandfather's death!—and a brief thanks in the form of first-class accommodations all the way back to England.

The suite's gold gilding and lush fabrics were dull in the dim light. Saffron opened the window and was immediately caught in a cold rush of salted night air. It served to push the lingering cobwebs of sleep from her head.

She sighed and leaned on the windowsill. The ship glided through the darkness with a gentle roll. There'd been moments of calm and quiet since she'd learned her grandfather had died, but she'd been numb to it, sheltered behind a barrier that prevented feeling from crowding in too close around her. Now that sturdy wall of logistics and practicality had thinned to a mere veil, she was left feeling rather like a little boat, pressing forward into darkness in choppy, uncharted waters. Which rock of emotion would she crash into first? The grief of losing one of her few family members, for whom she'd had hopes to repair their relationship? The anger for what Mrs. Demirel had done to Martin and tried to do to her, that Clark had targeted her, that the crew would no doubt spread more rumors about all that had occurred the moment they set foot on English soil, if not before? Or worst, lingering fear that even now threatened to drown her. She could still see Kadriye's panic, feel Mrs. Demirel's nails gouging her face. So many moments, had they gone just slightly different . . .

"You're either awake very late, or very early," Alexander's voice said from behind her.

He'd sat up on the bed and swung his legs over the side. With a sleepy smile, he crossed the room and took her in his arms.

"How are you feeling?" he murmured into her ear.

"As if I need to sleep for a decade to settle all the jumbles of emotions I'm experiencing." She put her face into his chest, her throat suddenly burning. "I can't believe all that's happened. Martin was murdered, I could have been convicted for killing him . . . My grandfather . . . It's been too fast."

He looked down at her, his eyes earnestly looking into her own as he eased her a few inches back. "I need to tell you something."

"What is it?"

"When you were arrested, I contacted John and explained the situation. I don't think the message reached him since he was likely already in England when it reached France. I wrote to Elizabeth and my brother, too."

She frowned. "So, they know what happened. The murder, the arrest. Our marriage."

He nodded, and his silence stretched until she realized what he hadn't said.

"But not my mother. Or your parents." Her lips pursed as she thought. "So, it will be a surprise to them. A shock, really. My mother . . ." Her mother had been so excited to plan their nuptials. And with Lord Easting's unexpected passing, there would likely be a period of mourning before they could be married in England. "Do we tell them, Alexander?"

"I don't know."

"What about your parents? Will they be very disappointed?"

"My mother certainly will be."

The last of her veil of numbness fell away. "This is going to be a disaster. A death in the family, a secret marriage, and rumors of murder and poison and guilt flying across the sea. And you have to go back to Smyrna for three more weeks."

"By the time I return with the crew, I'll have it all cleared up. And besides," he said, mischief creeping into his voice, "they know what happens to those who spread rumors about you."

"You are dreadful," Saffron said, poking his ribs even as she snuggled closer.

"I could be, if you wanted me to be."

His words were not playful, but so serious that she leaned back to search his shadowed face. "I do." Her throat grew tight. "I will."

Perhaps Alexander's recollection of their rushed vows was as vague as her own. He slid his hands down her back to her waist, then, with painful gentleness, took her hands in his. "I will. I will take you as my wife, for better, worse, richer, poorer, in jail or out."

She burst into a tearful laugh. "I love you."

"Wait a moment," he murmured, and strode to his trunk on the far side of the room.

"I have waited," she muttered under her breath.

He was back in a moment, a small box in hand.

Her jaw dropped when she saw it was a ring box. "Don't tell me you somehow thought to plan for the *infinitesimal* chance that we would get married—"

Then he opened the box.

The sapphire gleamed in the golden light, a dark drop the size of her fingernail and set in a swirl of silver filigree. But it wasn't the gem itself that conjured the sob Saffron choked back. "How—how do you have this?"

Alexander looked uncertain. "Your grandfather gave it to me before we left Ellington in February. I thought you would want to have it now . . ."

He broke off when she covered her mouth with her hands.

"What?" he asked, clearly sure he'd done something wrong.

"This was the ring my mother wore," she managed to say. "It's a family piece, a gift for after the next heir is born. My father gave it to my mother, anyway, when I was born. He used to say he didn't care—" She couldn't continue, couldn't say aloud the words that, even as a little girl, had made her tear up in gratitude that her father didn't care if she was a girl or a boy, just that she was herself.

"Oh." Alexander blinked, looking down at the ring in the ring box with apprehension. "I didn't—I'm sorry."

Saffron shook her head, reaching out for him. She fisted his shirt in her hand, anchoring herself to him in the midst of yet another wave of emotion. "If he gave this to you . . . If my grandfather gave this to you, Alexander, it means he approved. He approved of you, and that—" She tried in take in a whole breath. "That means the world to me. Especially now."

They only stared at each other for a long moment, their breathing too fast for a silent room on a quiet ship in the sea.

Then Alexander took the ring from the box and slipped it onto her finger, next to the simple ring she already wore. As Saffron examined how they sat together on her finger, unevenly, perfectly, she decided that no matter the path that had led them there, whether through crime and dusty streets or a beautiful ceremony surrounded by their family and friends, it was the right one.

Acknowledgments

Thank you to my husband, Erfawn, who makes it possible for me to write these books by providing me time, space, and a shoulder to cry on (or rage at) when things to awry. Thank you for inspiring what I hope is a realistic depiction of how strength shows up in different ways. Thank you to my children, who never cease to provoke me into growing as a mother and author, and who delight me with their enthusiasm for hawking my books to unsuspecting passersby.

Thank you to my parents and my parents-in-law, who support me in all ways. I am the luckiest daughter and daughter-in-law.

Thank you to Melissa Rechter, my original editor of the Saffron Everleigh mysteries, who took a chance on that very first mystery and hung on to finish out this book. Thank you for your guidance and friendship; Saffron would not have been the same without you, nor would I.

Thank you to the entire team at Crooked Lane and their contractors for making sure that, despite all my efforts, this book got out to the world in the best shape possible. A thank you is also owed to the team at Kaye Publicity for their work getting eyes on this book!

A special thank you to Begüm, my Turkish sensitivity reader and personal hero, for making sure that I didn't completely fumble the words and culture, and for making sure Saffron got to enjoy some really delicious food!

Thank you to my fellow Lady Sleuths: Jess Armstrong, Jenny Adams, and Katharine Schellman; you all made editing this book way less obnoxious than it would have been otherwise. I've been given a gift in your friendships! And to my fellow overly ambitious author, Jillian Forsberg, thank you for being the hand-holding, kick-in-the-pants friend I've always needed.

And finally, thanks to all the readers of this book and others who continue to make the world a better place by embracing new points of view, literacy, and community.

Author's Note

Maybe it'll be a shock to read that I find History terribly boring. That's History, as in what I was taught in school, things like the names of battles and treaties and changing lines on maps. Yet I always loved historical fiction.

This book was an opportunity for me to revisit the History I learned concerning World War I, its consequences, and the Ottoman Empire, because to tell Saffron's story in Turkey in 1924, I had to remember—or really, relearn—what those shifting lines on the map meant for the people who lived there, and what effect those treaties had on their lives.

Smyrna, modern day Izmir, boasts centuries of rich history as a bastion of trade and civilization on the Aegean, having belonged to the Romans, Byzantines, Greeks, and the Ottoman Empire, with several other briefly lived empires in between. That was clear enough from my historical sources, but what I uncovered as I began asking myself who Saffron would have actually interacted with in Smyrna in 1924, I found it wasn't so simple. Ottomans who were now called Turks under their 1922 Constitution represented a vast swath of cultures. One consequence of fires of 1922, called by Western media the 'Smyrna Catastrophe,' was that families who'd lived in Smyrna for generations were exiled for being Greek in origin. Nick Hale's brief comment about the Greeks supposedly burning the city down is how many Turks viewed what happened:

in the course of the Turkish-Greco War (1919–1922), the city was partially destroyed in a fire that, according to the Turks, was started by Greeks. According to the Greeks, the fire was started by the Turks to incriminate them. It led to Turkey banishing its Greek citizens, and Greece retaliating by doing the same to their Turks. It was a messy tragedy that influenced the relationship between Turkey and Greece for decades and set Saffron and Alexander up with an undercurrent of tension simply stepping off the ship.

The ancient history of Smyrna is equally as messy. A settlement first excavated in the district of Bornova in 2010 is one of the oldest settlements in the region, dating back to prehistoric times. The beginnings of Old Smyrna emerged in the Bronze Age, fully developed by around 1000 BC. Homer was supposedly born in Smyrna (Banks would have loved that, had it been known in 1924!) in the 7th or 8th century BC—though that is contested by Chios, which also claims him. Smyrna blossomed into a city-state, a center of trade and culture, but it was short lived. Old Smyrna was destroyed in 545 BC.

It was brought back to life, as Clark so kindly explained, on the orders of Alexander the Great some two-hundred years later. They chose another mountain to occupy, Mount Pagos. Soon Smyrna was in the hands of the Romans, and was mentioned in the Bible as one of the seven churches of Asia. It was around this time that Banks's graffitied stone came to be; this find was based on the real-life graffiti found in the Smyrna agora, including a crossword puzzle written in Greek. Sometimes fact is stranger than fiction!

Soon the Turkic peoples claimed Smyrna, then came the crusades, then various short-lived empires, then more crusades. The Ottomans finally captured it in the 1400's, and it stayed in their (embattled) control. The tides of fortune rose and fell over the centuries. This is all the stuff buried under the dirt—and I struggled to care much about it until I realized what all this push and pull between civilizations actually meant for the people of Smyrna.

By the end of World War I, even after the Ottoman Empire dissolved and Turkey became its own nation, it would have been impossible to call Smyrna merely Turkish. One report stated the population was only forty-two percent Turkish, while Greeks numbered about thirty-nine percent. One can see why the name 'Smyrna Catastrophe' was apt, if almost half the population of the city was forced out following the fires. No wonder the city was still half destroyed and a person like Bey found every opportunity to enrich himself. And no wonder a man like Inspector Polat took issue with half-Greek Alexander, and was concerned with the nascent culture of his city and his nation; Turkey was not starting from scratch, but trying to decide who and what it would be. Would their country be more *alafranga*—a fascinating term I found in Fatma Tunç Yaşar's papers on manner and etiquette—or *alaturka*? Turkey is often called the gateway between the East and West, and Saffron was standing on that threshold before it had quite been built.

Ever since I learned that Saffron's name had a connection to a poisonous plant, I've been plotting a way to get it into a book. The substance, colchicine, is derived from meadow saffron, *Colchicum autumnale,* and is also found in *Gloriosa superba*, glory lily. As are many poisons, colchicine has medicinal value: it is used to treat inflammation, such as the kind caused by gout. It is highly toxic and tricky to establish safe dosage. Like the city of Smyrna, it is ancient, having been used as a remedy for joint pain since at least 1500 BC.